The characters and events portrayed in this book are fictitious. Any similarity to real persons, living or dead, is coincidental and not intended by the author.

ISBN: 9798581512081

Printed in the United States of America

COSMOPOLIS

Jeffery K Strumski

For my wife. I couldn't have done this without you.

PROLOGUE

Eleven year-old Matthew Menounos was nervous. His forehead was sweating, but he took a breath and tried to calm down. "I can do this.", he told himself silently. He then got to his feet and walked to the front of the class. Reaching the podium, he steadied himself and read the first line of his notes out loud.

"A Short History of Ross 128 b." he said. The assignment was to give a three minute presentation. In practice before class, he had timed his speech at one minute and 31 seconds. He'd have to try to talk slowly.

"Our planet is Ross 128 b, or 'Ross b' as it is commonly called. It was discovered in 2017 by Xavier Bonfils." He knew he'd butchered the man's name, but he'd never heard anyone say it out loud, so had nothing to go by. "Ross b is located about 11 light years from Earth. It is the only planet in our system where humans can live."

"In 2089 the Higgs-Condensate Transmitter was invented by China and the United States, and humans could finally go to the stars. China chose to go to Luyten's Star, while the United States chose to visit Ross 128. On Ross b the scientists found life, including our trees which absorb special elements in the ground. We send the trees back to Earth where they are processed into superconductors. Our trees are our largest export. The scientists tried to explore the whole planet, but it was too big a job."

"Back on Earth, the United States had a problem with people coming into the country from South America. They wanted to stay, but it was illegal. The people still came, so the government said that their kids couldn't be Citizens. Eventually, there were just too many people. So, the government said that if they went to Ross b and worked there for 20 years to help make it a place to live, they would get to be U.S. Citizens. So they did. They tried hard to become Americans. Many of them didn't even teach Spanish to their kids so that they would fit in better."

"After they worked to make the cities and towns, Citizens moved in and Ross b was made into a United States Territory. A vote was held back on Earth to try to make the Hispanic people Citizens, but it didn't pass. Some people fought, but today they still aren't Citizens. People are still working today to try and make that happen."

Matthew glanced up at the clock. Three minutes and two seconds! More than he needed. He sighed and sat down. The teacher said, "Thank you Matthew." and glanced at the next name on the list. "Penelope?" A girl with dark hair rose from her seat and walked to the front of the class. Matthew had a crush on her, but so far he hadn't had the nerve to tell her. He watched her get ready to speak and marvelled at how calm she looked.

"Where We Live" she began, giving the title of her presentation. "Our star is called Ross 128. It is a red dwarf star, which is why the light from it looks red. We live on Ross 128 b, the closest planet to our star. There are two other planets in this system but they are too far away from the star, and are so cold that humans can't live there."

"One side of our planet is always facing the sun, so it is always day here. The night side can get very cold, while the day side can get very hot. People try to live on the day side, but near the edge so that it won't get too hot. The line between day and night is called the terminator."

"Our town is named Aberdeen. It was founded shortly after everyone came to Ross b. It is located about 30 miles from Cosmopolis, the capital of Ross b and the largest city. Our largest industry is logging. We cut down trees and ship them to Cosmopolis to be sent into orbit and then back to the United States on Earth. The trees absorb elements from the soil like yttrium, sulfur and others. On Earth they process the trees to separate the elements and use them to make superconductors."

"Cosmopolis is located almost exactly on the terminator line. Aberdeen is about 30 miles from Cosmopolis, but we are only 12 miles further into the daylight. Both Cosmopolis and Aberdeen were both named after cities on Earth in the United States. Cosmopolis has a spaceport which sends all the exports from our planet up to the transmitters. The transmitters change everything into energy and then send it back to Earth at light speed."

"We are very proud of where we live. Our great-grandparents settled this planet and made it a good place to live. It is our home."

Penelope stepped away from the podium and hurried back to her seat. Matthew thought she looked beautiful.

"Thank you, Penelope." said the teacher, looking down at the screen in front of her. "Has anyone not gone?" she asked. No one raised their hand. "Alright then, that is it for today. As I said earlier, the results from the DNA tests you all took as part of our unit 'Where did we come from?' have been uploaded to your micros. This is a reminder that the test results are meant to be private. Please do not share them with your friends or classmates. Not even I know what they say; you are to discuss them with your parents only. When you get home, I want you to use them to help complete the family trees we started last week. When you come in on Monday, we'll start looking at how your family histories fit in with the history of humanity as a whole. Thank you."

The students gathered their belongings and filed toward the door. As they left, the teacher sighed to herself; they weren't going to remember any of that, were they?

PART I:

MOLOTHRUS ATER

CHAPTER 1

The small town of Aberdeen had seen better days, figuratively speaking. The town was run down from years of neglect, and the lumber mill at the edge of town was no different. The perpetual red-orange light of the sun filtered down through clouds, giving the yard of the lumber mill a faint rose colored hue. It was as if there were a forest fire in the distance, though 40 year-old Jason Menounos knew this wasn't likely to be true; the trees on Ross b didn't burn very well.

Aberdeen was a logging town of about 1,500 people and had been founded during the intial rush to settle Ross b. At first the town had consisted only of a logging camp, but it eventually grew to include a lumber mill, some stores, a city hall, a school and even a library. People had come and taken root here, drawn by the steady work. Now, years later, the work remained steady but the pay was less than great. Still though, people stayed. Most of them simply had nowhere else to go, and were grateful for the work.

Jason found it darkly amusing that the first thing humans did after inventing interstellar space travel was to start logging the first planet they came to. He sighed and wiped his brow, sweating in the humidity that this world provided in abundance. He had spent his whole shift stacking logs to be cut and piling the cut logs to be shipped out again. His back ached and he was glad to hear the horn blast that signaled the end of his shift. Relieved, he began gathering his things.

It was odd that on a world with no night, people still measured time with a 24 hour day/night cycle. In reality, it was more out of habit and convenience than anything else.

Humanity had developed on a planet which took 24 hours to rotate, and so when they went to the stars, they carried that rhythm with them. They didn't have to; on Ross b they could have just as easily used 22 hour cycles, or 28. But people are stubborn, and when they came to Ross b, they brought that stubbornness with them in full measure. Further, as if to prove the point, most people continued using 12 hour clocks as well. Just like on Earth, people here counted the hours from 1 AM to 12 noon, then 1 PM to 12 AM. It was pointless in a world of continual daylight, but it continued as an intractable relic of home. People are creatures of habit, and the invention of space travel wasn't going to change that.

After having worked a nine hour shift in the lumber yard, Jason was finally getting off work. He headed for the gate following Mateo and Pablo, co-workers and friends who spent their days stacking, moving and cutting lumber just like him. They were both shorter than Jason, and stockier, with Mateo sporting a short goatee. Other than that, Mateo and Pablo could have almost been twins. They were joking together and turned to include Jason as he came up behind.

"Hey Jason, Pablo says that Luis and the rest of the shipping crew from Cosmopolis are back in town down at The Rooster. Wanna go try to win some of our money back?", Mateo asked. The shipping crew was based in Cosmopolis, but made the trek from the port to Aberdeen to pick up their logs three times a week. Often they would stop off at the local tavern to unwind before going back home. Last time they'd come through, Mateo and Pablo had lost half a shift's pay playing darts against them.

"I'll come for a while, but I can't stay all night." Jason replied. "Let me call Anne to let her and Matthew know I'll be a little late." Jason's son Matthew had given an oral presentation in school today and Jason wanted to know how it went. The subject had been history, and Jason had always liked it. He took out his beat up micro and placed the call while Pablo used his own device to summon a car for them. Requesting a self-driving car instead of walking seemed silly for such a short distance, but it had been a long day.

Nearly everyone at the lumber yard was changing shifts, and a large crowd had formed at the gate as people came and went. Nearly all of Jason's co-workers were Latino, yet every conversation he heard was in English. This wasn't surprising; when Hispanics came to Ross b, they had come with the expectation of becoming U.S. Citizens. To help their children assimilate, they had taught them English instead of Spanish. Now, over a hundred years later, Spanish was largely forgotten. It was a cultural loss that few people even noticed anymore.

It took several minutes for an empty car to arrive for them. When it did, they all climbed into the passenger cabin and Pablo made sure their destination was entered into the navigation. As Jason settled into the seat he saw that the video screen was playing a news summary for the day. Quantum transmission meant that news and other information could travel back and forth between Earth and Ross b without light delay. Or maybe it was sent trans-dimensionally? Jason didn't really know how it worked, but in practice what it meant was that the U.S. was able to keep a close watch on their colony. It felt claustrophobic at times.

On the screen, the news anchor was saying, "...vote failed in the House today by a count of 230 to 262, with 8 abstentions. Supporters vowed to bring the Citizenship bill up again in the next session, saying that it was past time for the government to make good on its promises." The reporter glanced down at an electronic pad in front of him. "In local news, Cosmopolis police are still searching for the suspect or suspects in last week's shooting at..."

Mateo reached over and killed the video. "Goddamn right they should make good on their promises! This planet was founded by us!" he said. He was mostly right; after the survey teams had approved the planet for development, the next group to arrive had been the unwanted migrant Latinos from the United States. In exchange for working on the planet, they were supposed to have been granted U.S. Citizenship when it was done. Predictably, that had never come to pass. They kept talking about it though, and that was almost worse; it kept the frustration on everyone's mind. Despite the fact they had been on the planet longer than almost anyone else, Hispanics on Ross b were discriminated against in a myriad of official and unofficial ways, from police harassment, to higher taxes, to lower wages. The effect was insidious and seemed to poison everything.

The subject made Jason uncomfortable. Nearly everyone who worked with Jason at the lumber yard was Latino, but Jason wasn't. At least, not officially. His family story was that Jason's great-grandmother had been Hispanic and had run off, leaving his Caucasian great-grandfather to raise their child alone. It wasn't a story that was talked about much. His great-grandfather had quickly married a White woman, and they had raised the child without telling anyone who his true mother had been. Jason's family retained the Citizenship passed down by his great-grandfather, and the only remnants of the story now were whispers within his family and Jason's vaguely tanned complexion.

Despite his hidden heritage, or maybe because of it, Jason identified more with the Hispanics and other poor people he worked with than with the rich Caucasians who ran things on Ross b. It seemed to Jason that the rich seemed to enjoy keeping people like Mateo and Pablo "in their place". Lost in thought, Jason was quiet as the car rumbled toward their destination.

****

The Rooster was an old tavern on 4th street, in the oldest part of Aberdeen. It had been built of timber from the surrounding forest, and if it had ever been painted, that paint had faded and flaked off long ago. Now, the gray-black of the bare wood was the primary color. Jason knew that back on Earth, using Ross b's timber as a mere construction material would have been an unbelievable waste. The wood's primary value was after it had been processed and the minerals it contained were extracted. Logging the wood and sending it off-world was the entire basis of Ross b's economy. Still, no matter it's value, on Ross b it was plentiful and its inherent strength made it a good choice for building.

As Mateo, Pablo and Jason got out of the car, the smell of stale beer washed out into the street as someone opened the door to the Rooster and stood leaning against the wall outside. The place didn't seem inviting at all and if it hadn't been familiar, Jason would never have gone inside. The three of them walked through the narrow door, and the orange light from outside didn't seem to penetrate the dirty windows. As his eyes adjusted to the dim interior, Jason could see a band beginning to set up on stage and faintly regretted that he wasn't going to be able to stay for more than a couple songs.

Mateo saw Luis standing with his friends near the bar and motioned to Pablo and Jason to follow him. They made their way past the other patrons and took up spots near Luis and the others. When Luis saw Mateo, he greeted him warmly.

"Hey, glad you guys showed up! I was beginning to think we might have to pay for our own drinks!" he said, smiling. Mateo laughed. There was definitely a sense of competition between them, but it was friendly.

"I thought I'd see if I could get you to pay for ours instead!" Mateo answered. "Want a rematch?" he asked, gesturing toward the dartboard hung crookedly on a nearby wall. Light flared briefly in the direction of the entrance as the door was flung open and a group of five or six men entered. Someone yelled "Beer!", and a few voices answered in already inebriated agreement.

Luis smiled as if he had been waiting for Mateo to make the offer. "You bet; I'll be glad to take your money! Your friends going to play?" he asked, looking at Pablo and Jason.

Jason shook his head. “No, I’ll sit this game out."

“I’ll just watch for a game or two first.” Pablo said.

Luis and Mateo agreed on a 20 dollar bet and each took up positions near the toe line about eight feet from the wall. A few patrons who were in the way took notice and hurried to move.

Luis went first and landed an expert series of shots. Pablo moved to keep score, with Luis’ two friends looking on. Then it was Mateo’s turn. He took up the darts and threw them in quick succession, matching Luis shot for shot.

Jason’s attention soon wandered from the game, as the band was now starting their set. A sign said the band was called ‘Lightning Strike’. A good name, but it didn’t tell him much about the music. He watched as the drummer clicked her sticks rapidly to count-off. “One! Two! Three! Four!" The band attacked the song, loud and fast. Punk music, then. Not a style he heard much here in Aberdeen; they definitely must have come over from Cosmopolis. A crowd began to gather in front of the stage. One of Luis’ friends raised his head as the band started, shouting “Alright! I love these guys!" Jason watched them for a while, enjoying the rhythm and being swept up along with it. Near the stage, a group of guys he didn’t recognize were getting rowdy, and starting to shove.

When Jason turned his attention back to the dart game, Mateo was losing. It was his turn to throw, and concentration furrowed his brow. One dart flew, burying itself in the double-20 space. The next one landed lower and to the right, scoring a single point. Mateo swore under his breath. His last toss stuck in the single-20 space, just below the double and brought his turn to a combined 61 points. Mateo’s total score now stood at 183 and Jason could see that unless Luis made a really large mistake, Mateo was not going to be able to win. Luis took his place only needing eight points to win. He threw the first dart, landing it near the four but out of bounds so that it didn’t count. The second dart followed and again was scoreless. He took careful aim with the last dart, holding his breath.

It landed with a soft 'thwip' sound, right in the double-four and earning him the eight points. Luis smiled and breathed out as Mateo swore. Nodding and conceding the loss, Mateo patted Luis on the shoulder and made a quick transfer on his micro to settle the bet. On stage, the band's first song ended and the sudden quiet felt like a physical thing.

"Rematch?" Luis asked.

"Not today." Mateo demurred. "I need to keep some money to feed my family."

Luis looked around. "Anyone else want to try?" The band counted in and the music's roar suddenly returned, flattening every other sound in the bar. Jason took this as his cue.

"Sorry, I've got to be getting home!" he said, shouting to be heard over the music. He grabbed Mateo and Pablo to get their attention. "I'm heading out!" he yelled. They nodded and Jason turned to make his way toward the door. As he began to push his way past the people gathered at the stage, a large Caucasian man with a shaved head stumbled backward out of the crowd and slammed into him, knocking Jason back and down. As the two disentangled, the big man turned with rage on his face.

"Fucking spic!" he shouted as he punched Jason in the face. Pain bloomed, and Jason covered his bleeding nose with one hand, using the other to shove his attacker back. "What the fuck?!", Jason swore at him. Mateo, Pablo and Luis were suddenly at Jason's side, and the crowd parted to reveal the big man's friends; a group of five White men with uniformly shaved heads. Jason thought, 'Oh shit. Anne's gonna be pissed.' The first attacker swung again, this time aiming for Jason's stomach. Jason dodged to the side and brought his knee up hard into the man's groin, knocking him to the ground.

As if this had been a signal, Jason's friends waded in, grabbing and punching the skinheads. The crowd in front of the stage pushed back, and Jason found himself pinned between the two groups. He didn't actually want to fight; he was merely trying to keep from getting hurt further. Distantly, he heard a bottle break and people yelling. Someone grabbed his shirt and pulled, but Jason shoved the man away. By now the band had stopped playing, and the singer seemed to be yelling at everyone to stop. No one paid any attention, and the struggling crowd washed over Jason for a moment.

Suddenly he heard two popping sounds in quick succession, followed by a high-pitched whine as the capacitors of the bar owner's tazeprod recharged. The bar owner stabbed forward again, discharging the prod for a second time into one of the skinheads.

"Knock it off, you sonsabitches! I already called the cops!" he shouted. Members of the crowd slowly picked themselves up and began to disperse. The band had given up, and was walking off stage. The bar owner turned on the group of skinheads. "You assholes are going to wait here for the cops. I don't want this shit in my place!", he snarled.

Jason's nose was still bleeding as he pulled himself to his feet. He began to move toward the door, but the bar owner blocked his exit. "I mean you *Josés* too!" he said, glaring at Jason, Luis and Mateo, and making it clear that *'José'* was an insult. "You are gonna wait here too. I'm tired of this shit!" He pointed with the tazeprod for emphasis and there was a warning look in his eye. Jason spared a glance toward Pablo. It seemed that the bar owner hadn't seen him, and he now was doing his best to melt back into the crowd.

A moment later the sound of a siren came from outside and the door opened, revealing a wash of alternating red and blue lights. Four officers in padded uniforms entered, looking around expectantly. Seeing the group of people being held near the back, they moved to take control of the situation. The owner looked relieved that this bunch of thugs would no longer be his problem. The officers began to efficiently handcuff them, starting with Luis.

"Come with us." one of the officers said, and indicated that they were to go outside to the waiting police transport van. Jason, Luis and Mateo knew better than to resist and began to walk toward the door but the biggest skinhead raised his head indignantly.

"What? Those fucking spics started it." he protested sullenly.

"I said come on." repeated the officer. He sounded annoyed and shoved the man in the back, forcing him to start walking or fall on his face.

They stepped outside into a light rain and one by one they were put into the back of the police transport van. The interior dimmed as the officer slammed the door, and Jason overheard him mutter, "Goddamn spics..."

The ride to the station house was in silence.

CHAPTER 2

Jason, Mateo and Luis sat in the holding cell, their only company a sleeping Hispanic man who smelled of alcohol. The skinheads had gotten out earlier, their Citizenship allowing them the option of posting bail. They only had to pay, then promise to show up at their hearing. The booking officer was still confirming Jason's Citizenship status but once that was done, he too would be allowed to post bail and go. Without Citizenship, Mateo and Luis would be stuck in the cell until their hearing, no bail allowed.

Jason heard a few raised voices and the officers standing near the cells moved into the next room to listen to their lieutenant. A video screen was partially visible in the next room, and the volume was turned up loud enough that Jason was able to hear it. It appeared that the program had been interrupted by a report on another shooting.

"We are reporting this hour that there has been a shooting in Rose Park, near the Cosmopolis marina. Five people are reported dead, with at least 15 more injured. The suspect has fled the scene and police are in pursuit."

"Cosmopolis police captain Joseph Clinton has asked that people avoid the downtown area at this time." The camera switched to a shot of Captain Clinton, a middle-aged Black man in a dark blue uniform as he stood in front of the crime scene. He was saying, "We now believe that this incident is tied to the three previous shootings earlier this month. This cannot be allowed to continue, and our department will take all actions necessary to bring this violence to an end. I vow to you that we will bring the shooter to justice and restore public safety. Thank you." He nodded to the camera and stepped away, bowing his head to converse with another officer who had appeared at his side.

Jason heard a cough beside him and saw that the drunken man was now awake. He looked at the screen, taking in the information. Closing his eyes again, the man muttered, "Asshole. Guy's a freedom fighter." Jason was appalled by the man's callous disregard for murder, and grabbed his shoulder.

"You're okay with people getting killed?" he demanded.

The man's eyes fluttered open and he swallowed, trying to clear his throat. "What? Guy only shoots White people, doesn't he? That's what I heard." He grimaced and turned onto his side, facing away from Jason.

Outside the cell, most of the officers were getting their gear and preparing to head out. Jason caught the eye of the desk sergeant and asked, "Where's everyone going?"

"With the shooting, we're putting as many people out on the streets as we can. A little show of force." the sergeant answered, clearly relishing the idea. Soon the station house grew quiet as all the available officers left the building, leaving only a skeleton crew behind. In the cell, Jason sat thinking while Mateo hummed to himself and Luis lay on the bench, trying to get comfortable despite the hard surface.

Jason was uneasy. The drunk's comments still bothered him; how could he be okay with someone randomly murdering people? He moved closer to Mateo and spoke to him softly, "You see that news report?" he asked.

"Yeah, that's a bummer." said Mateo quietly. "There's no pictures of the shooter or anything, but the story going around is he's Latino like us." Mateo shook his head. "Doesn't make our lives any easier."

Jason agreed; it seemed like all the prejudice and tribalism had only gotten worse recently. Deciding to change the subject, he asked, "How are you and your wife going to handle you getting locked up?" Mateo and Valarie had married just last year, but had been together since high school and had a daughter Matthew's age.

Mateo took a deep breath and said, "It'll be tight, but we'll pull through. This bullshit..." he waved his hands to indicate their current predicament, "...should take about a week to blow over. It did last time, anyway. The foreman's a good guy, and should hold my job for me. Plus, Pablo wasn't caught and he can vouch for me. We'll be okay." Jason hoped this was true, but Mateo's estimate of one week in jail sounded wildly optimistic.

There was a sound from the door, and Jason saw the officer assigned to watch them move to speak with someone beyond the door. He turned to Jason. "You have a visitor." he announced, walking back to his desk.

Hesitantly, a worried looking woman with wavy blond hair that fell down to her shoulders poked her head past the door. "Jason?" she asked uncertainly. It was his wife, and in this moment, she was beautiful!

"Hi Anne." he answered. He was ashamed to have her see him like this, but was very glad she was here all the same. He forced himself to meet her gaze.

Anne turned to talk to the jailer. "I've brought Jason's birth certificate and voter card. Do you need anything else to prove Citizenship?"

"No." he replied. "You can show those to the booking clerk up front. You'll need to pay the bail with her too. He'll need to sign a statement promising to appear in court too, but after that he'll be free to go."

Anne nodded, and said to Jason, "Are you ready?"

Jason looked at Mateo and Luis, who wouldn't be able to get out of here so easily. "Yeah, I'm ready." he told her. He stood, and the jailer opened the cell door to let him out. Jason stepped through, and there was a jarring metallic clank as the bars were locked again behind him.

As Jason and Anne turned to leave, Mateo spoke up, saying, "See you later, brother. Don't forget about us."

"I won't." Jason said. "Take care."

****

The short hallway which led away from the cells was dimly lit, marking the division between captivity and freedom. When they were near the front of the station, Jason caught a fleeting glimpse of one of the skinheads as he walked out the door. He was again frustrated that the group of racist assholes had been processed faster than he and his friends. Scowling, he walked over to a chair and sat down while Anne proved his Citizenship and paid his bail. An officer near the door kept a watchful eye on him, making sure he didn't actually try to leave before everything was settled.

After several minutes Anne returned carrying an electronic pad. She handed it to him, saying nothing. At his touch, the screen lit up showing a 'Promise to Appear' form. Near the top, it listed his name, his Citizenship ID number, and home address. In another box it described the charges against him. *Assault; Disorderly Conduct; Assault with a Weapon; Public Intoxication.* When he'd arrived at the station he had taken a breathalyzer test which would prove he wasn't drunk; that charge would likely be dropped. He hadn't used a weapon, but he wasn't sure how he'd be able to prove that. Maybe someone from the bar would be a witness?

As frustrated as he was with all this, it was worse for Mateo and Luis. As non-Citizens, they were mandated to remain in police custody until their court date. That meant that they couldn't work and had limited options for obtaining legal counsel. The system was very much stacked against them, and Jason felt a twinge of guilt that he was now benefiting from that same system.

He noted the court date, which was set for sixteen days from today, and felt helpless as he recalled Mateo's estimate of one week. Still, he had his own problems to consider. In order to appear in court he'd have to ask for a couple hours off work. It was fortunate that the hearing was scheduled at the courthouse extension here in Aberdeen and not in Cosmopolis; that would have cost him a whole day's work. He placed a reminder on his micro to request the time off, then returned to the Promise to Appear. He scrolled past several pages of dense legalese, down to the end of the document. There he found a place for his thumbprint and a spot next to that for his signature. He pressed his thumb to the square, waited for it to chime its acknowledgment, and then used his finger to write his name. He quelled his annoyance that he had to provide both. They already had his thumbprint; did he really have to give them a signature too? It was overkill, but that was bureaucracy for you.

Jason handed the pad back to Anne, who walked it over to the waiting clerk. The clerk took it, quickly scanned it for completeness, then filed it away while Anne paid the bail. When she was done, Anne turned and Jason stood up.

"Okay. Let's go." Anne said, and together they walked to the front door. Jason nearly crashed into the door, expecting it to open automatically. When it didn't, he grabbed the handle and pulled. The officer stationed near the door nodded to Anne as they left, pointedly ignoring Jason.

Outside, Anne used her micro to summon them a car. "The car will be here in a few minutes." she said. After the climate controlled building, the sudden humidity was oppressive. Jason nodded, letting his eyes adjust to the red-orange sunlight.

"Do you want to tell me what that was all about?" Anne asked, gently touching the bruise on Jason's face. The blood had been washed off, but his nose still throbbed in time with his heartbeat. The look on her face was sad.

"It wasn't my fault." Jason explained a little defensively. "We were at the Rooster like I said when I called. Some drunk asshole crashed into me, and then punched me in the face." Jason smiled wanly, "He seemed to think it was my fault." He could see in her eyes that she believed him and he felt a huge weight lift from his shoulders. "I'm sorry." he said, releasing a breath he didn't know he'd been holding.

Anne hugged him briefly but tightly. "I'm glad you're okay." she said. "Let's just try to get home without anything else happening, alright?"

"Okay." he said as the autonomous car pulled up to the curb. They got in, and Jason recognized the song coming from the speakers as something his father used to play on their music system at home. A wave of nostalgia took him, but after a moment he switched over to a news feed and the car's video screen came to life, showing coverage of the shooting in Cosmopolis. A commentator was saying, "...police believe the shootings are connected, possibly the work of one man. It has been theorized that these attacks are racially motivated, but this appears unsubstantiated as the victims have been people of all backgrounds, both Citizens and not."

"Did you hear about this?" Jason asked, looking at Anne.

"Yeah, it happened as I was coming to the station. The breaking news feed interrupted the show I was watching."

Jason slumped back in his seat. "There was a guy in the cell with us who seemed happy about it. He said that the shooter was only killing White people; I guess he was wrong about that, at least." he said, gesturing at the screen. Anne nodded but remained silent, not knowing what to say.

After a while Jason said, "You heard that the Citizenship vote failed again?"

"Yeah, I heard." Anne replied. "It's not fair, is it?"

"No, it's not." he said, looking out the window. Outside, it was beginning to rain.

CHAPTER 3

It was after midnight when Jason and Anne arrived outside their modest home. The middle of the night had very little meaning on a world where the sun never set, but the human notion of it still remained, and it had been a long day. Jason's eyes felt heavy and gritty, and his nose still throbbed where he had been hit. Overhead, dark rain clouds covered the ever-present sun and washed out the colors, rendering the world in shades of gray.

As they climbed out of the car, Anne said, "Matthew had just gone to bed when the police called. I told him that I had to go out, and that he shouldn't answer the door."

Jason nodded as the autonomous car pulled away from the curb, watching his feet as he climbed the rain-slicked steps. At eleven years old, he knew their son could be trusted to stay at home alone for an hour or two, but it still felt like neglect to him on some level. Parental protectiveness died hard.

Anne was a teacher of five and six year-old children at Lincoln Elementary, a school located near the edge of Aberdeen along the main highway to Cosmopolis. Her students were mostly the sons and daughters of the town's loggers. Citizens could attend the school free of charge, but non-Citizens were required to pay for the privilege. Despite the financial burden this placed on families, the classroom demographics still tilted heavily Hispanic and poor.

Their house was small but Anne's teaching salary meant that they could afford a few modern conveniences, and the door unlocked automatically at their approach. As they entered the home, Jason saw that the video screen had been left on and his son lay asleep on the sofa. The flickering screen on the wall showed a brown skinned man with wild hair dressed in a suit and seated at a desk. He was shouting, "...must change! It must! We are used as virtual..." The room then fell silent as Jason turned off the display. Anne came up behind him and the closet door creaked as she put away her coat. Matthew heard the sound and began to stir in response. He propped himself up on his elbows and blinked at them.

"Dad, what happened to your face?" he asked blearily. Jason was keenly aware of his bruised nose and the two black eyes which were beginning to set in.

"I got hit." he said simply. Then, to change the subject, he asked, "How did your presentation go?", referring to the oral report Matthew had given at school earlier that day.

"It went okay. The teacher didn't say I failed, anyway." he answered casually.

"Do you think you got an A?"

Matthew appeared to consider. "B-plus?" he guessed, hoping that was good enough.

Jason was thoughtful. His son typically did well in school, and a B-plus was good. Still...

"Did you have any homework?" he asked.

Matthew pointed to his micro on the table. "Just the DNA test results. I'm supposed to go over them with you and Mom."

Jason picked up the device and scanned over it. "This goes with the family tree you started last week, right?"

"Yeah, we're supposed to compare the family tree with the DNA results and 'See where we come from.'" he finished, quoting his teacher in a bored voice.

Anne stepped over and took Matthew's shoulder. "Alright, well, right now it's really late. Let's get you to bed. Tomorrow is Saturday. We can sleep in, work on the DNA test and the family tree, and after that we'll catch a bus into Cosmopolis for shopping and dinner. Maybe we'll even visit the capitol building. OK?"

Matthew agreed easily. Anne had grown up in Cosmopolis, only leaving to begin teaching in Aberdeen, and Matthew loved seeing the places Anne had known as a child. He and Anne walked down the hall to his room, Matthew humming a tune as he went. Once their son was tucked in to bed, Anne returned and sat down on the sofa next to Jason. Jason had Matthew's school micro in front of him and was looking over the DNA test results with a furrowed brow.

"Anything interesting?" she asked, looking over his shoulder.

"Kind of..." Jason answered distractedly. He flipped through several pages on the screen, frowning slightly. He then gave Anne a bemused look. "There's no Latino heritage here." he said.

"Did they send him the right report?" she asked, but as she did so she saw Matthew's name prominently displayed at the top.

"Yeah, it's his." Jason confirmed. "Could the test have missed it?" he wondered aloud.

"I wouldn't think so." Anne said. "See, they picked up the Scandinavian ancestry on my side. Shows 7.8 percent."

"Weird..." Jason mused, continuing to study the report. He activated another tab and opened the family tree that Matthew had created previously.

Anne recognized the look on his face and smiled. "Honey, it's late. I'm going to go to bed." she said.

Jason looked up. "No, I'm sorry. I'll put this away for now." he apologized. The exhaustion he had felt as they arrived home had evaporated in the face of this mystery, but he would gladly follow Anne to bed if that's what she wanted.

"No, you'd never be able to sleep until you sorted this out anyway. I'll go get some sleep; that way at least one of us will be well rested tomorrow." She kissed him on the forehead and then vanished down the hallway to the bedroom. Jason hated to see her go, but she was right. This might be a small mystery but he knew it was going to keep him up whether he tried to sleep or not. He might as well not pretend.

Jason stayed up most of the night, researching census records and address information, dates of birth and marriage certificates. The clock showed 5:43 AM when he finally came to bed. Anne stirred next to him as he slid under the sheets, but didn't wake. Jason drifted off to sleep to the sound of rain pattering against the roof.

****

Jason woke alone late the next morning, having gotten almost four hours of sleep. His nose still hurt and he knew he was going to regret the late night, but it had paid off. He finally knew why the DNA test hadn't revealed their family secret!

He slid out from under the sheets and walked unsteadily toward the bathroom. Sensing the movement, the automatic blinds in the bedroom began to open but he stopped them halfway. He saw through the gaps in the blinds that it had stopped raining, but he just wasn't ready for the light yet. His head hurt too much.

Groggily, he showered and then got dressed. Afterward he found Anne sitting at the kitchen table. Still in her slippers, she had her micro out and was reviewing her students' work. Matthew was in the next room, staring at their video screen. The program was loud and looked to be some kind of action-oriented cartoon. A small anthropomorphic chicken with a samurai sword was fighting various farm animals in brightly colored costumes. From what he could tell, the chicken was winning.

"Hey, sleepy head." Anne said, looking up from her micro. "What time did you get to bed?"

Jason smiled sheepishly. "It was before 6 o'clock." he said with mock pride, as though it were an accomplishment.

"So what did you find out?" Anne asked. "About the DNA test?"

Jason had left his micro on the table. He picked it up and opened the session he'd saved. "Take a look." he said, handing her the device. Anne studied it for a few minutes, moving between tabs and following the path Jason had laid out. Her brow wrinkled.

"I thought your great-grandmother Lana was Latina." she said, confused. "You said she had only been married to your great-grandfather for a year when she ran off and left him to raise their son alone."

"That's the story my dad told me." Jason replied, nodding. "I even heard my grandfather mention it once when he thought we were out of the room. He said that afterward great-grandpa Robert had married a White woman to cover it all up and Grandpa was raised with everyone thinking he was a Citizen. No one even questioned it." He smirked. "I guess they just thought he had a good tan."

"What do you mean 'that's the story'?" Anne asked. "If it's not true, then where does the skin color come from?" she asked, pointing at her husband's own golden brown complexion.

"Turns out it's Greek and Italian." he said. He pulled out a chair and sat down. "We didn't ever talk about it because it was supposed to be a secret, but I've known the 'Hispanic story' all my life. My dad kept quiet about being Latino because he was ashamed. My family let the government think we were Citizens to hide the truth; or at least that's what we all thought." Jason took the micro back and looked over the clues again. "But it turns out it's just not true. The answer is right here; the census records show it! Great-Grandma Lana's family was actually from the United States, in North Dakota. A few generations before that they go back to Greece and Italy. There's no Hispanic heritage at all; the skin tone just makes it look that way."

Anne was puzzled. "Wait, that still doesn't make sense. There's a family secret so terrible that no one can know about it, but it's not even true? Why..." she trailed off, baffled by the contradiction.

"It's weird, I know!" Jason said, excited to share the mystery. "I wondered why someone would invent this 'pretend secret'. With the Citizenship problem, isn't the risk too much?" He was smiling now.

"You know the answer?" Anne asked, seeing the look on his face.

"I do." he answered with a grin and handed the micro back to her. "Look at Lana's birth date."

She did, but didn't see anything remarkable. "Uh huh?" she said, nonplussed.

"Now look at the date she married great-Grandpa Robert."

Anne did the math and arrived at a rather uncomfortable answer. "She was barely fourteen years old!" she exclaimed.

"Yeah, and Robert was twenty eight! No wonder they kept that a secret."

Anne checked the birth date of Robert and Lana's son, and then looked again at the marriage date. "She was already pregnant too." she said, looking up at Jason. "He could have been arrested for statutory rape."

"Yeah. I still don't know why that didn't happen." Jason said, taking back the micro. "I looked, but I couldn't find anything about it. I guess nobody took it to the police. Still, I think it explains why she left Robert. I can't imagine the stress she must have been under. Fourteen is way too young to get married and have a kid."

"Yeah." Anne agreed, overwhelmed. It was a lot to digest all at once, and she fell silent as she considered the implications. After a while she asked, "So, are you disappointed you're not really Hispanic?"

Jason took a deep breath and considered. "No; I mean, it's a little disorienting but I'll adjust. It doesn't change who I am. I'm more shook up to find out that my great-grandfather had a kid with an underage girl. That's going to take some time to process."

Anne nodded toward Matthew in the other room. "Are we going to tell him what you found? He still needs to talk with us about the DNA report."

Jason sighed, thinking about what that would mean. "I guess I don't see why not," he said eventually, "but we don't need to add anything about it to his school report. I don't think we need to tell them about a rape in the family, even if it was a hundred years ago."

"Sounds good." Anne agreed.

Jason rose and opened the kitchen cabinets, looking for breakfast. "Do we have any coffee?" he asked.

CHAPTER 4

After breakfast, Jason puttered around the house while Anne helped Matthew with the family tree and DNA results. The constant sunlight and humidity on Ross b had a tendency to make the cheap house paint peel, so Jason spent some much needed time with a paintbrush covering up and repairing a few blemishes.

After painting he washed up in the bathroom. As he did so, he studied his reflection in the mirror. His nose felt a little better than last night, and now only hurt if he touched it. Every time he did, though, it served as a painful reminder of yesterday's events. Most of the bruising had faded from his nose, but the punch had left a mark and the circles under his eyes were still quite pronounced. Some of that was probably due to lack of sleep, he supposed in fairness.

After the night's revelations about his family heritage, he was somewhat amused by his reflection's black hair and golden brown skin. The effect wasn't pronounced, but people would still think he was Hispanic no matter what the DNA test had shown. It was something he had lived with his whole life; it had been part of his identity. This small piece of new information wouldn't change how anyone saw him, and he was fine with that.

He was drying his hands when he heard Anne and Matthew packing a lunch for their trip to Cosmopolis. As he entered the kitchen, Anne asked him, "Could you get us tickets for the bus? I forgot to do that earlier, and my hands are full." she said, piling things into a small insulated lunch box.

"Sure." he said, and pulled out his micro. He accessed

the bus ticket info and purchased three adjacent seats. He also arranged to have a transport car come to their house to take them to the bus terminal. It would have been nice to take the car all the way to Cosmopolis, but the distance charges increased significantly if the car travelled out of town. The bus was much cheaper, and would have to do. "Done." he said, putting the micro back in his pocket. "I also called a car to take us to the terminal. It'll be here in less than five minutes, so we'll need to hurry."

"Thanks." Anne answered distractedly, shifting things around in the small cooler to make room.

"I'll grab the umbrellas and jackets just in case." Jason said, opening the closet. Matthew appeared suddenly in front of him and menaced him with a large toy sword.

"P'KUCK!" he declared, and then pretended to chop his father's arm off.

"Great." said Jason. "Now you'll have to carry the jackets."

"The sword stays here, Kung Pow Chicken." Anne said, coming up behind Matthew and disarming him.

Jason's micro chimed to indicate that the car had arrived outside. He handed Matthew the jackets, took the umbrellas out of the closet and checked to make sure Anne was carrying their packed lunch. "Are we ready?" he asked. His family nodded in agreement. "Alright then, here we go!" he said, and together they headed out the door to the waiting car.

****

The car dropped them off at the terminal just as their bus arrived. Carrying their gear, they piled into the shiny, streamlined bus and found their seats. Anne took the aisle seat, while Jason sat by the window. Engrossed in the program on his micro, Matthew took the middle seat and proceeded to ignore the outside world.

When everyone had boarded, the bus pulled away

from the terminal with a jolt and moved out onto the road. As it gained speed, they passed the lumber yard at the edge of town. The yard operated 24 hours a day and Jason could hear the buzz and clank of the machinery as they passed. Craning his neck, he recognized several of the men working there and as they disappeared in the distance, he was content. He'd worked a long time before earning a regular schedule and it felt good to finally have the weekend off.

On the highway, the trees and undergrowth began to blur past the window. Anne handed him a sandwich. The city of Cosmopolis was about thirty miles away from Aberdeen in a straight line but the road followed the Cosmopolis river and wound around several low hills, which added another ten miles or so. The uneven geography meant that the trip would take almost an hour. Jason checked his micro for the time; it was just after one o'clock. They'd arrive in Cosmopolis about two, which would give them several hours of sight-seeing and shopping before they had to think about dinner.

Jason began to watch the landscape scroll by the window. This close to Aberdeen they were still shrouded by the pale white trees that made up the forest. The star's red-orange light meant that photosynthesis on Ross b was best carried out in the near-infrared part of the spectrum. Accordingly, nearly all visible light was reflected by the leaves, giving them an off-white appearance with speckles of black that produced a pattern similar to birch tree bark on Earth. The resulting foliage was pretty, in a ghostly sort of way. A visitor hoping to see birds or squirrels would have been greatly disappointed though, as Ross b lacked any significant native animal life. According to the early surveyor, there were no native animals anywhere on the planet larger than the end of a finger and nothing found in the ensuing hundred and fifty years or so had done anything to alter that impression.

A little further on, Jason caught a glimpse of ancient stone through the dense trees, which could have been a Pueblo. The word had been borrowed from Earth, but it was an apt description nonetheless. Despite the current lack of animal life, Ross b sported occasional traces of a primitive civilization long past. Whoever they had been, they were extinct long before any humans arrived on the planet. In school he'd learned that scientists thought there might be a link between the lack of animals and the extinct civilization. No one knew for sure what had happened to them, but the mysterious stone ruins they'd left behind had always intrigued him.

As the landscape continued to roll by, he didn't see any more ruins. The trees eventually began to thin and soon gave way to open farmland, filled with plants brought from Earth. The crops were healthy and green, and machinery moved along the rows while huge sun lamps overhead provided the plants with a light spectrum closer to the one they had evolved in. Ross b's native soil was very high in heavy metals and other poisons, so in the early days enormous quantities of soil for farming had been brought from Earth. The dirt was heavy, but the advance of the Higgs-Condensate transmitter had made moving it feasible. Soon after, scientists had isolated those bacteria and nutrients which could be added to the native soil to allow it to support Earth crops. A little further conditioning to remove the toxic elements and it became possible to grow food safely. Ross b's native plants were mostly inedible; at best they couldn't be digested, while at worst they were horribly toxic. A few enterprising individuals had found that one or two of the native species could be processed into recreational drugs but the poisons absorbed by the plants as they grew meant that producing and consuming the drugs was a very bad idea, not to mention illegal.

****

The noise of the bus's motors changed pitch as they began to climb a low hill and Jason woke with a start. The lack of sleep the night before meant he had drifted off. Beside him, Matthew was pointing out the window at a pillar of white smoke which began on the horizon and rose high into the sky. At the peak of the column, Jason saw an incandescent white pinpoint of light. A shuttle had just lifted off from the Cosmopolis spaceport, carrying raw goods to be sent back to Earth. As he watched, the shuttle passed through a cloud and then reappeared a few moments later high above it.

Matthew pressed over into Jason's lap, trying to keep the shuttle in view. "Is it carrying trees?" he asked.

"Probably." Jason answered. Like all the native plant life on Ross b, the trees absorbed heavy elements from the soil as they grew. An accident of nature meant that the trees contained a particular combination of elements which could be processed into effective superconductors. The processing was only done by facilities in the United States, so they sent the trees eleven light years back to Earth to undergo the treatment. Privately, Jason suspected that the United States kept the processing equipment located there so that Ross b could never become economically independent. It served as a way to keep the U.S. territory under control and remind them who's boss. The goods might take eleven years to reach the U.S. but faster-than-light communication meant that the mother country was always watching and ready to impose its will.

The bus passed near the spaceport as it entered Cosmopolis. The port was huge, taking in goods from the surrounding cities and sending them up the gravity well to the Higgs-Condensate transmitter in orbit. Timber was by far the planet's largest export, but other goods were represented as well. A textile mill in nearby Hoquiam produced a variety of fabrics from the native plants, while things as diverse as farm equipment and ceramics arrived from towns located a little further away like Raymond and Lebam.

Outgoing goods were collected in large warehouses and eventually loaded on shuttles and sent to orbit. Once there, everything was transferred to barges and sent through the Higgs-Condensate transmitter, which saturated the barges and their contents with a mixture of exotic subatomic particles which would neutralize their mass and effectively convert them to energy. That energy was then beamed toward Earth at the speed of light. As those added subatomic particles decayed, eventually enough of them would evaporate to allow the mass of the objects to reassert itself. The transmitter carefully calculated how long that process would take, and added just enough of the particles to get the shipment back to Earth. The system had been in use now for over a century and the process had become so refined that shipments typically returned to normal just in time to enter Earth orbit.

Though Cosmopolis was only 30 miles from Aberdeen, the shadows had lengthened noticeably as they approached the day/night terminator. Ahead of them the road forked, with one side skirting the spaceport on approach to Cosmopolis, while the other climbed a hill and continued into the forest. At the intersection, a sign indicated that an army outpost known as Fort Emory lay 15 miles beyond, located just past the terminator on the night side of Ross b. The fort had been established in the early days of colonization to help with exploration and settlement, and had remained active ever since.

The importance of the spaceport had made Cosmopolis by far the largest and most prosperous city on Ross b, and it followed that it had been made the capital city as well. Where Aberdeen seemed old and faded, Cosmopolis was shiny and new. The bus terminal was no different and as they arrived, Jason thought that the building itself fairly sparkled. Excited, he, Anne and Matthew quickly disembarked and walked out onto the street, the city before them gleaming brightly.

Matthew impulsively ran over to dip his fingers into a nearby fountain in the shape of a fish. Jason smiled, watching his son marvel at the sculpture. With no fish on Ross b, Matthew had only seen them in pictures.

"Do you like it?" Jason asked, and Matthew nodded enthusiastically. Turning to Anne, Jason pulled out his micro and got his bearings. Once he was oriented, he pointed and said, "Let's start out down there. We can walk along the river, and it will take us down to the bazaar."

"That sounds nice." Anne agreed. With an effort, they separated Matthew from the fountain and began to walk along the path. Beside them flowed the Cosmopolis River, named by the city's residents in a fit of vanity. The water here was wide and slow. Occasional backwaters swirled near the edge as the river's flow was disturbed by a rock or a tree. Far from shore, a few small boats drifted lazily along with the current.

The family set a leisurely pace, enjoying the day and stopping to examine whatever had captured their son's attention. The path they walked was well maintained and lined by decorative railings. Select native plants had been planted alongside it, with an eye toward symmetry and beauty. Though most native plants were varying shades of off-white, those planted here also displayed mottled grays, blacks and even an occasional light blue countenance.

As they neared the marketplace, Jason began to notice police and security guards tensely watching the crowds. The last time they had come to Cosmopolis it had been a relaxing trip, but now there seemed to be a note of tension in the air. Many of the officers he saw were armed. Jason knew it was likely a response to the recent shootings, but the guns he saw made him feel less safe, not more. Rose Park, the site of the shooting yesterday, was far away on the other side of town and Jason was grateful for this, at least. Still, he felt uneasy and regretted not putting this trip off for another time.

The bazaar was filled with shoppers as they entered, and Jason kept Matthew in front of him to keep him from getting separated. Anne led the way for a while, then stopped to survey the stalls lining the broad corridor around them.

"That one." she announced, pointing to a booth some distance away. Jason nodded and they all set out in that direction. When they arrived, he saw that the seller was peddling beads of various sizes and colors.

Anne pulled up a note on her micro and reviewed it. "I

need 1,000 beads." she told the merchant. "Those small ones there, with the holes in them. 500 of the red, and 500 of the white."

Jason's jaw dropped. "A thousand beads?"

"Yes." she said. "We're going to be making abacuses in class and the school won't buy the materials. I've already got the boxes and sticks, but I need the beads. Don't worry; they don't cost that much. That's why I'm getting them here."

The Hispanic man behind the counter dipped a scoop into the beads and began measuring them out. His electronic scale was marked with notes for converting weight into numbers of beads.

"Wow, with everything that happened yesterday, I didn't even ask how your day went." Jason replied, self-consciously touching his tender nose.

"It went pretty well." Anne told him as she perused the colored beads. "The tests show that there's still a few kids who still haven't learned all their letter sounds. I've arranged for them to get a little extra attention starting next week."

Matthew interjected, saying, "You should get some of the assistants to quiz them."

"That's what we're doing." Anne replied, looking at him. Matthew tended to get wrapped up in his mom's class, reacting to her stories as if he were directly involved.

"And your neighbor?" Jason probed gently, using code to refer to the teacher Anne shared a hallway with. "Is that still an issue?"

Until last year, Anne's grade team in kindergarten had consisted of herself and a young Caucasian man just out of college. He'd been good with the students, but he hadn't lasted very long. He'd come in early, worked late, gone to extra meetings and generally ran himself ragged doing whatever was asked. In just two years, he'd burnt himself out and left.

His replacement was an older woman. She was the wife of one of the loggers in town and to put it bluntly, she was a racist. The demographics of Aberdeen meant that most of the students were non-Citizens whose families had paid the fee so that their kids could attend and this woman's treatment of those children made her feelings about them abundantly clear. If a child acted out, her response was primarily determined by whether the kid was Latino and who their parents were. Discipline was often swift and harsh. Anne had sometimes come home crying after seeing how the students were treated.

Anne's eyes flashed but she kept her voice cool. "No, no changes there. Frankly, I'm not expecting much." Jason could see that she wanted to say more but didn't want to have the discussion in front of Matthew. She took a breath and changed the subject. "I also want to get a new rug for the living room. The one we have still has that stain on it."

Jason shuddered, remembering their one-room apartment on Lewis Street and the night that Pablo's brother had shown up unannounced. "Yeah, okay. That's a good idea."

Anne turned back to the bead seller as he completed the measurements. "That will be eleven dollars." he said brusquely. Jason chose to ignore the cost as Anne used her micro to send the man the money.

"Do you know anyone who sells rugs?" she asked the bead seller.

He pointed past them, further into the bazaar. "Over there, next to the ice cream seller." he said.

The family turned and made their way slowly, fighting against the flow of the crowd. Along the way, Jason again noted that there were a lot of security guards and police watching the market, and each of them had the dark shape of a weapon on their hip. The shootings were making everyone nervous and the police clearly didn't want to take any chances. As Jason, Anne and Matthew reached the rug vendor, the corridor widened into a small plaza and finally provided them some breathing space.

Matthew turned to his parents, eyeing the ice cream for sale in the next stall. "Can I?" he asked.

Anne nodded, expecting this. "Go ahead, just don't over-do it."

Jason watched as his son purchased a double-scoop cone of what appeared to be chocolate & peanut butter. It did look good... Jason forced himself to turn away, telling himself that he didn't need it. Instead, he said, "I'm going to go look for some new work boots. Meet you over there in 45 minutes?" He pointed toward some stone benches set around a decorative fountain.

"Did you want to help me pick out the rug?" Anne asked.

He smiled softly. "No, I trust you." he said. He knew he had no sense of fashion and would only cause problems.

"Okay." she said. "Don't get lost."

"I won't." he replied. Jason turned, getting his bearings. His micro indicated that the closest shoe shop was back the way they had come, so he joined the flow of traffic and allowed it to carry him along to an intersection, where another glance at his micro told him to turn left. Around him the covered bazaar ended and the path opened out onto a public square, with a small park in the middle. A covered gazebo stood on a raised platform at the center of the park, surrounded by a striking combination of plants from both Earth and Ross b.

Small stores lined the public square around the park and Jason followed the sidewalk around to the shoe shop on the side opposite the bazaar. He expected the shop's door to open automatically as he approached, but it didn't. He paused, but the hand painted sign in the window said "Open", so he turned the handle and went in. As the door opened, it jostled a small silver bell mounted to the door-frame. Jason smiled at the incredibly old-fashioned touch.

After some rustling from the back, a tall black-skinned man with close cropped white hair emerged from a short hallway. Clearly the proprietor of the shop, his shirt sleeves were rolled up and he was wearing a heavy leather apron. A variety of tools protruded from the pockets. He smiled as he saw

Jason.

"What can I do for you?" he asked, wiping his hands with a rag.

"My work boots are worn out." Jason said. "I'd like to get some new ones."

"Do you have the old ones? I could try to repair them." the man suggested. Jason noticed the sign above the counter which offered repair services as well as sales.

"No, I don't. I wish I'd thought of that though."

"Well, don't feel too bad. Almost no one does." the man chuckled. "We don't get much repair work these days." The man gestured toward a row of new boots displayed on shelves mounted to the wall. "Something like these?" he asked.

Jason looked at the prices and stifled a gulp. He had once heard a story of a man who could only afford to buy cheap boots. The cheap boots only cost thirty dollars but would wear out in less than a year. Good boots would cost a hundred and fifty dollars, but would last ten years. The story went that the poor man would end up spending twice as much money over ten years, and would still have wet feet. Anne's teaching position paid better than his job at the lumber yard but as he looked at the prices on the boots in front of him, he knew he was going to have wet feet.

Jason pointed to the boots on the far left. "Can I try those on? Size ten." he said. The man nodded and disappeared into the back, then reappeared a few moments later carrying a box.

"Thanks." Jason said as he took the box. He sat down on a low bench and pulled off both of the shoes he was wearing. Anne would have poked fun at him for trying on both of the new boots, but he had always felt that since he was buying both, he should try both on.

He pulled the laces tight and then double-knotted them the way he did in the lumber yard to keep stray branches from untying them. Standing up, he took a few steps, trying to get a feel for the new boots. They were the cheapest pair in the store but he thought that after they were broken in, they would be pretty good. He paced across the showroom and then turned and walked back to where he started.

"These seem pretty good. I think I'll take..." he started to say, but never finished the sentence. He heard a quick series of loud *POPs*, and looked out through the store window into the plaza outside as people started screaming. A woman at a nearby cafe stood to run but just as quickly fell down, a damp spot of blood spreading on her white sweater. The crowded public square suddenly became a solid mass of people pushing for the exits.

The shoe store owner rushed out the door and stood there horrified as he tried to figure out what to do. Through the window Jason saw a flash of something metallic from the gazebo in the center of the park. The store owner had seen it too and began moving forward, keeping low and trying to stay out of sight.

Jason dropped to the floor and crawled closer to the window. By raising his head just a bit, he was able to make out a dark figure standing in the gazebo and pointing a rifle at the crowd. He wore a mask which hid his face and long gloves that covered his hands. As if in slow motion, Jason watched him choose his next target and fire.

By this time the store owner had made it across the causeway and taken cover behind a bench. Unable to merely stand by and watch, Jason saw that the shop door had been left open. He moved cautiously to the doorway, took a breath and then dove through it. He scrambled forward and huddled behind a vending kiosk while he caught his breath. Risking a glance around the machine, he made eye contact with the shoe merchant, who was still kneeling behind the bench. In an unspoken agreement, the two decided they would try to disarm the shooter. They moved at the same time, with Jason running for the bench while the salesman pushed forward, trying to reach the cover of the bushes surrounding the gazebo. Jason was only feet from the bench when he saw the shooter turn the gun toward him. He dove, painfully scraping his hands and knees on the pavement as he landed hard behind the bench. A shot sounded and the report from it echoed through the rapidly emptying square.

Frantic, Jason tried to plan his next move. He craned his neck, trying to see the store owner but the bench blocked his line of sight. From his hiding place, he could only just see the edge of the bushes near the gazebo. He licked his lips and made a decision; he would run toward the bushes and try to regroup with the merchant once he reached them.

Across the square a tall woman burst from a hiding place and ran desperately for the safety of a side street. The shooter whirled, the barrel of his rifle tracking her movements. He seemed to wait, then fired just before she reached safety. She dropped without a sound and did not get up again.

The woman's escape attempt had distracted the shooter and Jason realized that the man was now looking away from him. Fighting back his terror, he seized the opportunity and ran forward blindly. Upon reaching the bushes he threw himself to the ground and lay still, making himself as flat as possible. In light filtered by the low branches overhead, he felt a layer of gritty twigs and leaves, and the smell of dirt filled his nose. As his eyes adjusted to the dimness, he froze. The shop owner lay only a foot away. He was dead, having been killed by a single shot to the head.

CHAPTER 5

Anne browsed among the display racks. The rugs were hung vertically like tapestries, in a layered pattern which rose higher than she could reach. Her head swam as she tried to decide which one would look best in their home. She found it funny that Jason thought she was good at this sort of thing. She couldn't think of one thing in the nearly 15 years they had been married that could have made him think she had any flair for decorating. When they'd gotten married she'd used hardware store paint samples to pick out colors for the ceremony. High fashion, indeed.

She could hear background noise from the ice cream stall next door. The rugs softened the sound, leaving only a gentle murmur punctuated by the occasional squeal of a small child. Matthew was old enough that he'd wanted to sit by himself and eat his ice cream cone. She had allowed it, knowing that she would only be a few feet away. She pretended to examine one of the rugs, peering past the rack to spy on her son.

He was getting tall, showing hints of the man he'd grow to be. His skin was a little lighter than his fathers, but still was several shades darker than her own. He had his father's looks, but she saw something of herself too in his smile. Ice cream coated his lips, and she had to restrain herself from calling out, telling him to get a napkin.

Anne noticed a security guard leaning against a wall behind the stall. He spoke briefly into his lapel, before checking his micro and strolling away in the direction of the entrance to the bazaar. Anne hoped that he hadn't been watching Matthew. Her son might not actually be Hispanic, but she hated the way that the authorities seemed to assume that anyone with brown skin was going to cause a problem. She felt her stomach tighten as she thought about it.

Sighing, she forced her attention back to the rugs in front of her; it was time to make a decision. Fighting the urge to just close her eyes and point, she settled on one with an intricate red and brown pattern, offset with small accents of a deep blue. The dark colors seemed like they'd hide stains better than the other choices. To be honest, she thought it was ugly, but maybe it was less ugly than the other options? She could learn to live with it, anyway. Probably.

She spoke to the seller, and they completed the sale. Afterward she balanced her purchase on her shoulder, the awkward load making her lean to one side. The rolled-up rug was heavier than she'd expected; she'd have Jason carry it when he got back.

As she moved away from the rugs on display, she saw two more security guards. They were huddled together, speaking to a police officer. She watched them out of the corner of her eye, fearing that they might be planning something to do with Matthew. She quickened her pace slightly and called out to her son as she drew near. He was just finishing his ice cream, and the mother in her silently applauded as he grabbed a napkin from the table to wipe his face.

"Come on, Matthew. Let's go wait over where Dad asked us to. He should be back here in a few minutes." she said. Matthew joined her and they moved to the benches near the fountain to wait.

They sat, listening to the water flowing behind them. Then Anne heard something, like firecrackers in the distance. The police officer she'd been watching suddenly looked at his micro. It had made an ugly sound and a portion of the screen flashed a vibrant red. After quickly showing it to the security guards, all three of them set off at a run. Matthew raised his head, looking past the people and into the distance. "Mom, there's something happening down there." he said. As they watched, the crowd reversed direction and began to stampede toward them. There was shouting and screaming, and the sound of people being trampled. As one, a wall of humanity surged toward them.

****

Jason wriggled forward, trying to reach the gazebo. Barely using his legs, he pulled himself along with his forearms. He had no idea how long it had been since he'd left the shoe shop; no idea how long the shooter had been there. The square was empty now. Everyone who could move had fled and those who couldn't now lay on the ground, dead or dying.

The shooter held the rifle across his chest and stood still, surveying his work. When he looked away, Jason seized the moment and rose, charging toward him. He lowered his head, hoping to hit the gunman at the waist and knock him down. Instead, the shooter saw him coming and side-stepped his charge, hitting him hard on the back of the head. Jason dropped to his hands and knees at the impact, and the world swam before his eyes. He felt nauseous and stayed down, dazed and unable to think.

"Well hello there." the man said, his voice unusually high and muffled by the mask. "So glad you could make it!" Frighteningly, the man sounded genuinely pleased. Jason felt terror rise in his throat. He rocked back into a kneeling position and looked up at the shooter. Through the mask, the only feature he could see were the man's cold eyes. They were a dark gray or black, like the color of a storm cloud.

Suddenly, the man's head twitched to the side, as if he were listening to something only he could hear. Jason could see the outline of circuitry under the mask and realized he was wearing a sensor net. The shooter turned his attention back to Jason. "Thank you." he said, and made a little bow. In one swift movement, he shoved the rifle into Jason's arms and pulled something down over his face. Jason was still disoriented, and had the impression of being trapped under a fallen tent. He struggled wildly for a moment, feeling like he was suffocating. After a few seconds he managed to pull the cloth off his head and when his eyes could focus again, he saw that he was alone.

A moment later the sound of feet pounding against hard pavement drew his attention, and Jason turned to see a group of police taking cover at the entrance to the square, pointing weapons in his direction. Several others held their micros around the edges of their shelter, getting tactical information and images of the situation. Jason stood, and expected them to call out, to ask if anyone was hurt, but they remained silent. Too late, he realized he was still holding the rifle.

He quickly tossed the rifle to the ground and raised his hands. "Wait! It wasn't me!" he shouted. The police began to advance on him with guns drawn, moving cautiously toward his position. The ground was strewn with dropped packages and items of clothing. They carefully stepped around the victims, leaving them where they lay and never taking their eyes off Jason.

"Don't fucking move! You are under arrest!" the lead officer shouted, his gun steady in his hand. He'd reached the edge of the park now, and his boots sank slightly into the soft soil. His foot nudged an abandoned backpack, and suddenly two high-pitched electronic tones pierced the air, followed quickly by...

KA-BOOM!

An enormous explosion split the air and the shock wave knocked Jason off his feet. The last thing he saw as he was violently flung onto his back was the roof of the gazebo collapsing down on him. Moments later everything went black.

****

The tide of people surged past the fountain, the bulk

of the concrete structure forcing them to go around. Anne had jumped into the knee-deep water and pulled Matthew in after her, seeking safety against the panicked crowd. Instinctively they crouched low, Anne holding her son close to her in the tepid water. It was only then that she realized the popping sounds she'd heard had been gunfire. Her heart leaped into her mouth as she realized there had been another shooting.

After what seemed like hours, the torrent of people pouring past the fountain dwindled to stragglers. She stood and climbed over the rim, helping Matthew out as well. Their clothes were soaked and they began dripping water onto the floor.

In a daze, they began walking, not sure where to go. The rug lay forgotten on the ground behind them, trampled and partially unrolled. Matthew pulled on his mother's arm. "Mom, what's going on?" he asked.

Anne held on to him tightly, not wanting to lose him. "I don't know, honey." she answered. From behind them, she heard a burst of activity as a cadre of police entered the area. They were armed, and their black uniforms were armored. As she watched, the police began herding the remaining civilians back toward an exit behind them. After a moment a female officer approached them.

"Ma'am, I need to ask you to clear the premises. Please go back that way; there is an exit to your left. Officers stationed along the way will help guide you." the woman said, gesturing back in the direction she had come.

"My husband... He went down there looking for boots." Anne stammered, pointing in the opposite direction; the direction that the sounds of gunfire had come from.

"Ma'am, we've already got officers going down there to check it out. If your husband is there, we'll find him. In the meantime, we need to get you and your son out of here." The officer punctuated her statement by beginning to push them, gently but firmly, toward the exit.

Another officer, a short man with a pale face under his

helmet, approached and the woman handed Anne and Matthew off to him. He guided them quickly toward the door. Anne stumbled as she looked back over her shoulder to where Jason had gone, but the officer caught her and kept them moving to the exit.

After the shade of the covered bazaar, the red-orange light outside was almost blinding. Anne and Matthew stood in a courtyard, staring back at the connected series of buildings and walls that defined the market area. Anne's eyes followed the contours to where the covered bazaar stopped and began to transition into city streets. She jumped as she saw a sudden brilliant flash of light, followed moments later by the sound of an explosion. A distant plume of smoke began to rise above the buildings, silhouetted against the distant shape of downtown. Anne was unable to tear her gaze away, watching the cloud change shape from moment to moment.

Pressed against Anne's side, Matthew spoke softly. "Mom, is Dad alright?" Anne's knees were weak. She quickly found a low bench and sank down into it.

"I just don't know, honey. I'm sorry" she said, brushing his face with her hand.

Matthew sat down beside her. All around them, people milled back and forth. The police were keeping the crowd of civilians together but didn't seem to know what else to do. After a while Anne saw a man approach one of the officers. She couldn't hear what was said, but she recognized the pleading look on his face. He'd lost someone, and needed help. The officer gestured with her hands, seeming to tell the man he had to wait here, that they were doing all that they could. The man stood frozen in place, his expression begging for more, but the officer moved on.

As the officer walked away, her micro buzzed and she picked it up. Anne couldn't read what it said, but she saw a corner of the screen. It showed part of a man's face, with dark hair and brown skin. The officer read the alert, snapped the screen off and put the device back on her belt. She then raised her voice to address the crowd.

"Okay, everyone! We are all going to move further away, back to Friedlander Avenue. We will be walking, so please keep together. Once there, we will begin taking statements and we will have more information available for you. Afterward, we will bring you down to the station as needed to help you find any missing loved ones. Myself and Officer Dover will be coming with you. Please be ready to move."

The stunned group formed a loose mob and began to move slowly along the sidewalk away from the bazaar. Anne looked back and saw the column of smoke and dust still pinned against the sky. Matthew was silent, but there were tears in his eyes. Anne pulled him close, and together they followed the officers down the street.

****

Jason hurt all over. His ears were ringing and his whole body ached. He moaned softly and began to stir. Unseen hands held him down, and a damp cloth rubbed gently at his forehead. It was probably supposed to calm him but instead had the opposite effect and his panic rose quickly. Blinking and trying to focus, he tried to sit up. The pain in his left arm intensified suddenly and he collapsed, breathing hard and sweating. Slowly he realized that his left arm was held in a make-shift sling and tied against his chest.

"Lay down; you are among friends." a voice said, trying to soothe him. Jason's vision finally began to clear, and he found that he was laying on the floor of an old warehouse or factory. The windows lining the walls high above him were broken and clouded, and he could hear the sound of some heavy piece of machinery working far off in the distance. On the other side of the large space a huge door hung partially off its track, leaving a gap large enough to squeeze through.

A group of seven or eight men and women dotted the dirty floor. Their dark hair and skin suggested they were all

Hispanic. There was trash and other items piled haphazardly around, with worn paths meandering among them. Jason slowed his breathing and focused on the man helping him. From Jason's position on the floor, the man appeared silhouetted against the high windows, and his hair and skin seemed to glow in the red-orange light.

"Try not to move. Your arm is broken." the man said gently, checking the sling.

"Where am I?" Jason asked. He felt disoriented, like his head was too light for his shoulders.

"The old glove factory, on the edge of town." the man answered. He dipped the cloth into a small pan of water, wetting it again. "We heard the explosion, and came and pulled you out. Got you away from the police." He smiled and looked into Jason's face. "You are a hero!" he said. "We didn't think you were real."

"What?" Jason asked, slurring the word. Nothing made sense. He shook his head to try to clear it, but the swirl of pain it caused only made him dizzy and nauseous. He blinked, his eyes having trouble focusing.

"You fight the White people and the police! Kill them, even! We have been waiting a long time for someone like you. A long time." His voice was gentle, but there was a fire in his eyes; the eyes of a zealot. "You have started something." he continued. "Already I have spoken to others, and they will tell many more! Word is spreading!" The man wetted the cloth again and wiped some of the blood off Jason's forehead.

Beside him, Jason's micro chimed with an alert. A red band appeared along the top and bottom of the screen, along with the words, "Alert – Armed Suspect! If Seen, Alert Police! Do Not Attempt Contact!" Below that, in high-definition glory, was an image of Jason holding a rifle. The picture must have been taken by the police just as they entered the square, before the bomb went off. On the small screen his dark hair and brown skin somehow seemed to have become more pronounced.

He grabbed the micro and struggled to his feet. "I need to go." he said. "I need to find my wife!" He felt intensely light-headed as he rose, and nearly toppled over. He bowed his head as he steadied himself against a nearby barrel, and realized that he was still wearing the new boots he had been trying on; he'd never gotten the chance to pay for them.

"No, they are looking for you! You must stay here until they give up!" the man pleaded with him. A few of the others had taken notice and came over, with concern showing on their faces.

"But I didn't kill anyone!" Jason protested, and his voice cracked with desperation. He couldn't tell whether any of them believed him.

The man with the damp cloth appeared to consider. "I don't think the police are going to believe you." he said, nodding toward the image on the screen.

The micro chimed again, repeating the alert. Jason's own face stared out at him, seeming to brandish the weapon he was holding. He knew that the man in the image was frightened, but the small screen seemed to distort his face; change it. There, with a rifle raised to his chest, he suddenly became the very image of a freedom fighter. It almost didn't matter what the truth was, it looked bad.

He darkened the screen and shoved the micro into his pocket. "I don't care. I have to go." he said, and pushed his way through the small group. He limped forward, making his way unsteadily to the door and stepped out into the cool red-orange light of the sun.

CHAPTER 6

Anne and Matthew sat together in the police station. Although this was only a satellite office, it was much larger than the station in Aberdeen had been. Anne hated the harsh lighting and uncomfortable chairs, but her thoughts were focused on Jason. Matthew was doing something on his micro, trying to distract himself, but Anne could tell that he couldn't focus on it.

She had forgotten to check the time when they'd arrived at the station, but she knew it had already been over an hour. Men and women in uniform bustled back and forth, moving from one desk to another or meeting each other halfway to stop and consult their micros. It was infuriating. "*Where is my husband?!*" she screamed silently. She was ready to physically grab someone and try to shake the answers from them.

When she saw an officer walking in her direction she tensed, ready to strike if he passed her by. As he drew closer though, she saw that he was looking at her. In his hand he held a large electronic pad.

"Ma'am, please come with me." he said, indicating an open door behind him and to his left. It led into a small office, with windows that looked back into the large open workspace and waiting area.

"What about my son?" she asked, not wanting to leave him alone. Not after today. Not ever again.

"I'll leave the blinds open. You can see each other the whole time. This should only take a few minutes, but I do need to insist you come with me." he answered. His tone was not exactly cold, but it was far from comforting and left her feeling apprehensive. A protective impulse made her hug her son quickly, then, releasing him slowly, she stood.

"Mom?" Matthew asked looking up, his micro forgotten in his lap.

Anne struggled to keep her voice calm. "I'm going to go talk with this officer for a few minutes. I need you to stay here. We're just going into that room over there. You'll be able to see me through the window. If you need something, just come to the door and ask." Matthew nodded silently, and she reluctantly turned to go. She could feel his pleading eyes on her back as she followed the man into the room.

As she sat down at the table in the center of the room, the officer shut the door with a loud thump. A feeling of irrational panic took her, and it was only by force of will that she remained seated. She chose not to look out at Matthew, because she knew she would break down if she saw his face.

The officer appeared oblivious to her discomfort. He calmly took the seat opposite her and set the electronic pad down on the table in front of him. The glare on the screen from the overhead lighting prevented Anne from reading anything on it, and she wondered for a moment if that was intentional.

The man pressed a button on the pad, and spoke. "My name is Lieutenant Michael Putnam." he said, sounding very formal. "You should be aware we are recording this interview. Please state your name."

Anne was dumbfounded, and her mouth moved silently for a moment. "Anne Menounos." she finally said. Her lips felt very dry. "Why are you recording this?" she asked. "I gave you my name when we got here."

"We record everything connected to ongoing investigations." he replied, studying the pad closely. He pushed another button and looked up. "Your ID shows that you live in Aberdeen. What were you doing here in Cosmopolis today?" he asked.

"We were shopping." she said, becoming exasperated.

"We were going to buy a few things, then have dinner. Where is my husband?! Have you found him?" Her voice quivered, the words bursting forth.

Officer Putnam continued to study the pad, ignoring her questions. "Shopping." he repeated. "What were you buying?"

"A-a rug. And some beads." She couldn't understand how any of that mattered. She knew she'd dropped the rug in the chaos at the bazaar, but didn't remember what had happened to the beads.

"And where was your husband? While you were shopping." he asked, looking up at her as if to judge her reaction.

Something inside her snapped. "That's what I'm asking you!" she yelled. Afterward her breath came fast and her stomach was tight. She felt tears beginning to well up in her eyes and, trying to keep her voice under control she said, "He needed boots. He went to go buy boots while I looked at rugs."

"He left you and your son, and went toward the square just outside the bazaar?" Putnam asked, seeming to zero in on something.

Anne nodded her head in acknowledgment. "That's the direction he went, yes. Have you found him? Is he okay?" she pleaded, fearing the answer; afraid they had only found his body.

Lieutenant Putnam sat back in his chair, looking at her deeply for a moment. He pushed a button on the pad, then turned it around on the table so that she could see the screen. "Do you recognize this man?" he asked.

She pulled the pad closer, not picking it up. She instantly recognized Jason's face, but nothing else about the image made any sense. He was standing in what looked like a park, with his black hair a mess. His mouth was partially open, as if speaking or yelling. His eyes were wild, and he held a large black rifle across his chest.

"That's Jason?" she asked. Confusion filled her voice and her head felt like it had been stuffed with cotton.

"This image was recovered from an officer's micro at the scene of the explosion." Putnam said, watching her carefully. "Six of our officers died in the blast and two others are in the hospital. Your husband was responsible."

Anne struggled to make sense of what he was saying. "That can't be true!" and, "Jason wouldn't do that." and, "What?!" all collided and got stuck in her throat. She stared at the picture, at the perverted image of the man she loved. It just couldn't be true!

"Boots." she said softly. "He went to buy boots." She knew it sounded idiotic; that it wasn't a defense or an alibi, but it was the truth.

"Boots." Putnam repeated flatly. Anne nodded.

He reached over and took the pad back. "We'll get you and your son a seat on the bus back to Aberdeen tonight. We are not done with you," he looked at her meaningfully, "but we'll work with the Aberdeen police department to help with the investigation. You will make yourself available to answer any questions they may have. If your husband contacts you, you are required to notify us or the Aberdeen police immediately. No exceptions." He leaned back and keyed something into the pad. "For now," he said, "you are not under arrest, but we will be keeping a close watch." He stood and pushed in his chair.

"We can go?" she asked. Her knees felt weak, and she wasn't sure she could stand.

"Yes. I'll have the desk officer get you the bus tickets." With that Lieutenant Putnam opened the door to leave, but paused in the threshold. "Your husband is a Citizen, isn't he?" he asked.

Anne's face suddenly flashed hot with anger. "Yes he is!" she snapped, glaring at him indignantly. He merely nodded and left, leaving her alone in the room. She looked out the window and saw that Matthew was watching her. A uniformed officer sat in a folding chair in front of him, holding an electronic pad similar to the one she'd seen Putnam with. Her heart sank as she realized they'd been interrogating Matthew as well; checking her story. Upset, she stalked out of the room and rejoined her son.

"Lieutenant Putnam said we can go." she announced, directing the statement to the man seated in front of her son. She still resented Putnam's parting question, and the implications of it left her stomach churning.

"That's okay; we were done here anyway." the man said, smiling. He picked up the folding chair and leaned it against the wall. As he walked away, Anne glared at the electronic pad tucked under his arm.

Matthew slid off his chair and stood, putting his micro in his pocket. Anne wrapped her arm around him protectively and began to push him toward the exit. Matthew stopped and pointed to a sack under the chair where Anne had been sitting earlier. "Don't forget those." he said. Anne looked, and saw that it was the bag of beads. They weren't lost after all.

The reminder of the day's events was simply too much. A sob shook her, and it was like a dam breaking. She picked up the sack and sank into the chair, crying and holding onto Matthew. In that moment it felt like he was the only thing she had left.

They stayed like that for a while, but after a few minutes her micro chimed to let her know that the bus tickets had been purchased and sent to her device. She wiped her face, aware that the eyes of nearly everyone in the station were on her. She stood, carrying the beads.

"Okay, honey. Let's go." she said, wiping her eyes. She guided Matthew to the front of the station and pushed open the door. Together they stepped out into the perpetual red-orange sunlight. She pulled out her micro, intending to summon a taxi to take them to the bus terminal, but as she did so she noticed that her micro was displaying an alert. It must have appeared while they were in the police station, but she hadn't seen it. It was an ugly message, with a red band along the top and bottom. In large print were the words, "Alert –

Armed Suspect!" Her husband's face stared out at her, looking wild; or afraid.

****

The bus dropped Anne and Matthew off at the Aberdeen bus depot just after nine PM and they were home a half-hour later. Anne was exhausted, but didn't think she was going to be able to sleep. On the long bus ride home she'd held Matthew close the entire time. The awkward pose had left her shoulder in pain, and she rubbed at it stiffly.

Matthew had been quiet on the trip, but now that they were home he needed to talk. "Mom, I saw Dad's picture on your micro." he said. His own micro was set up as a child's device and didn't display police alerts, but he had seen Anne's screen when she called for a taxi in Cosmopolis.

"Yeah, I saw that too." she answered tiredly. She didn't know what else to say.

"I don't think that was really him." he said defensively.

"Me either." she agreed. She remembered the officer with the folding chair, the one who'd interrogated Matthew without her permission. Protectiveness flared in her, and she asked gently, "So what did the police ask you about?"

"They wanted to know why we went to Cosmopolis. I told them we were going shopping. Then they asked about Dad, whether I'd ever seen him get angry at people or something. I told them no."

Anne remembered picking Jason up from the police station less than 24 hours before... But no, she thought. She knew the man she'd married, and there was no way he was responsible for this attack. He couldn't be.

Anne suddenly realized that with everything that had happened today, they hadn't had a chance to eat dinner. She wasn't hungry, but she knew that they should eat something. "We should eat." she said. "Do you want to order a pizza?"

Matthew shook his head. "I'm not hungry."

"Me either, but we need something." she replied. She went to the kitchen and opened the cupboards. "I'll get us something small." she said, examining their options.

When she was done their two plates each held a yogurt cup and a handful of mixed nuts. It was a woefully inadequate dinner, but it would do for tonight. She carried the plates over to the table and set them down. Matthew sat looking at his plate, not touching anything.

After a while Anne asked him, "Do you just want to go to bed?"

"I think so." he said, sighing.

"Go get ready and then come back so I can hug you." she said. Matthew wandered out of the room, down the hall and into the bathroom. Anne heard the water come on as he began brushing his teeth.

She sat back heavily in her chair, picking at her food and forcing herself to eat. When she was done, she carried the plate over to the washer and dropped it in. She took Matthew's plate and put his yogurt back in the refrigerator before pouring the loose nuts back into the can. When she was done she wandered absently into the living room and turned on the video screen. The program picked up where they'd left it, with Kung Pow Chicken attacking a cartoon pig. She grimaced and instead selected a music program. The screen shifted to a soothing psychedelic display that flowed and shifted with the melody. She sat down on the couch and closed her eyes, hoping the music would numb her. She was overwhelmed, and felt like she was drowning. She told herself over and over again that Jason was alive and would come home. She *needed* it to be true...

Her eyes were still closed when she was startled by the sound of Matthew's bare feet against the hard floor. They flew open, and her breath caught in her chest as she saw Matthew standing before her. Sometimes he looked so much like his father it hurt. Her throat tightened as she held back a sob.

She muted the music and reached out to hug him, and

Matthew folded himself against her, holding on tight as he began to cry softly. They stayed like that for a while, clinging to each other as Anne cried with him. Eventually though, she let him go and held him steady in front of her, staring into his eyes.

"I will do everything I can to find your dad. I promise." she said solemnly. Matthew nodded and wiped his nose. His eyes were red and puffy, and the look on his face broke Anne's heart. She hugged him again and said, "Okay, honey. Get some sleep, and we'll work on this tomorrow." She let him go, and Matthew began to walk down the hallway toward his bedroom. "I love you." she called after him.

"I love you too, Mom." he answered, and she heard the quiet click as he closed the door to his room.

Alone now, Anne sat very still and waited to see if she would fall apart. She felt like a ghost in her own home, and everything seemed too quiet. She unmuted the music, but kept the volume low. The flickering colors and flowing shapes on the screen were mesmerizing, and she let them wash over her. It felt like time had stopped; like the moving fractals and patterns were the only things in her head.

Harshly, a new sound interrupted the auditory anesthesia washing over her. The amorphous shapes on the screen vanished, replaced by the hard edged image of a newscaster. Visibly reading from an electronic pad in front of him, he said, "We interrupt to bring you this breaking news. Less than an hour ago, this station was sent a message claiming responsibility for today's attack in Cosmopolis. The recent string of mass murders has weighed heavily on the public consciousness and today's events have proven to be the most deadly so far, with at least 22 lives lost."

The man swallowed and went on, "The message claims responsibility for today's attack, as well as others which have occurred over the past month. The message is audio-only, accompanied by a single image. That image is of the Hispanic man, believed to be the attacker, which was released earlier today by Cosmopolis police. We advise discretion in viewing the following message."

The screen shifted to show the inexplicable image of Jason carrying a rifle. The man in the picture appeared wild, and looked so little like the man she had married that it was unreal. Then, over his image, a voice began to speak. It was electronically distorted, with both the timbre and speed changed. There was an echo as well, as if it were made up of many people speaking with one voice. Anne listened, horrified but unable to turn away.

> *"We are The Latino Resistance Front, and we speak for all Hispanics on Ross b. We speak for those who have no voice. Since its founding, Hispanics on this new world have been held down. Subjugated. Beaten. We are the victims of crime, prejudice, and of the State. We have no rights, and we are forbidden from trying to claim them.*
>
> *For over a hundred years, we have been denied what we are owed! Our great grandparents came to this planet with hope. The United States government made them a promise. They were promised Citizenship! They were promised simple human decency! The government has reneged time and again on that promise. Our parents and grandparents have worked and slaved, without reward. Our very humanity has been denied! The United States government back on Earth refuses, to this day, to follow through on their promise! They can no longer be trusted; as if they ever could be trusted.*
>
> *We claim responsibility for today's attack, and the others before it. And those attacks will not be the last. The time has come for violence, and to make a statement for our freedom! Unlike you, we stand by our promises. Today, we promise you this; no one is safe. These attacks will continue. Until there is change there will be more shootings. There will be more bombings. And there will be more bloodshed.*

Our goal is freedom. Ross b can no longer be the territory of a criminal government light years away. We are fighting for independence! Ross b will become a country unto itself, and it will finally make good on the promises which have been empty for so long! We will declare freedom, Citizenship and equality for Hispanics. Because no one else will. God help you if you stand in our way."

The screen held on Jason's image for a few seconds, then faded and resolved to black. The newscaster reappeared, looking stunned and subdued. He glanced down at the pad in his hands, then back up, blinking rapidly. "We now go to Robert Hanson, our analyst for Latino affairs. Robert, what can you..."

Anne switched the screen off. She felt shock, horror, and impending doom all fighting for a place in her chest, with no clear winner. She sat motionless, desperately needing to sleep but unable to make herself get up and go to bed. Her mind raced as she stared at the blank screen. The world would think her husband was a terrorist! She thought of the coming morning, and dreaded it.

CHAPTER 7

Jason walked along side-streets, trying to keep away from everyone. He was scared, and nothing felt right. It seemed that the people who wanted to help him were just as frightening as the police. He'd seen it in the faces of those who'd rescued him from the explosion; they saw him as a symbol of something. Well, he didn't feel like a symbol, and he didn't want to be one. The world around him was rapidly spinning out of control and his mind reeled, unable to make sense of any of it.

A few raindrops hit his face and he looked up, gauging the weather. The clouds above were thicker now than when he'd started out and a serious rain storm appeared to be coming soon. He put his head down and kept moving.

He had to find Anne; he had to know she was alright. He still had his micro but he had turned it off, afraid that the police would track its signal and right now he was unwilling to take that risk. A part of him wanted to go to them and explain, but a glance at his bare arms reminded him that his skin tone was too dark to take that kind of chance. Even under normal circumstances the system was biased against Hispanics, but now? After this? He didn't think he'd get the chance to explain about his Greek ancestry before they started shooting. Or maybe they'd just beat him. Both reactions seemed equally likely. Around him, the light rain was becoming a steady drizzle.

He felt the empty pit of hunger twist in his stomach. He hadn't eaten since lunch the day before. He knew that three blocks to the west the factories and warehouses around him would give way to a commercial district and there were bound to be shops and restaurants there. Until now he'd avoided going that direction because there would be more people and he didn't want to risk being discovered. Now however, the pain in his belly was forcing his hand.

First though, he would need a few things. He followed an alley behind a large, dirty building. The sign on the front of the warehouse had read "Crover Garments" and he hoped to find something inside to serve as a disguise. It didn't have to be great; just good enough to keep people from recognizing him while he got some food. After that he hoped he'd be able to think clearly, and maybe figure a way out of this.

To his disappointment, the warehouse was locked up tight but he found the company's oversize waste bin sitting behind the building. It was a large tan colored container, with ugly rust spots and a heavy steel lid. The bin was sealed to keep people from stealing but the lid was damaged and bent, leaving a narrow gap on one side. He studied the container and decided that if he could find a way up, he should be able to squeeze through the opening.

The rain was falling harder now, and he wiped his face to clear his eyes. The downpour was starting to soften the dirt under his feet and small puddles were beginning to form in the unpaved alley.

The top of the bin was about eight feet off the ground, and his broken arm meant there was no way he was going to be able to climb up the side unaided. Changing tack, he looked around for something he could stand on. He found several large metal pallets scattered nearby, with some laying on the wet ground while others were leaned up against the side of the building. They looked heavy, but each of them was about six inches high. If he could stack several of them in front of the bin they might lift him high enough to get inside. Using his good arm, he grabbed the edge of the nearest one and heaved. The corner raised a few inches and the pallet slid along the ground. His hand slipped and the pallet fell with a wet slap, splashing mud onto his new boots. Undaunted, he continued to work. By alternating from corner to corner, he was able to move the pallet until it was alongside the bin. He then turned to the next one and repeated the process. When he got it lined up next to the first pallet, he braced himself and used his good arm to lift and pull. With some effort he was able to get the edge of the second pallet propped up on top of the first. He then pulled the rest of the pallet up and aligned it with the one underneath. The two were finally stacked, but he would need a few more before the pile was tall enough for what he had in mind.

Moving the pallets had forced him to remain bent over as he worked, causing his back to ache. He stood up straight for a moment, stretching and trying to relieve the growing pain in his broken left arm. The sling was still in place, but the task had caused him to shift and twist awkwardly and his arm was beginning to throb. Still, he needed to stack at least two more pallets before he would be able to get inside the bin. Sighing, he selected a third pallet and slid it along the ground over to the stack. As before, he lifted the edge to the top of the pile and then managed to shove the pallet into place.

The pallets were heavy and despite the cool rain soaking him to the skin, he was becoming overheated. He unzipped his jacket and relived for a moment the memory of Matthew carrying the coats as they went to the bus. A feeling of despair threatened to overwhelm him, but he forced his attention back to the job at hand.

The fourth pallet was smaller and turned out to be somewhat lighter than the others. Once he pulled it over to the pile, he was able to get it on top without too much trouble. Afterward, he sat down on it and pulled his legs up after him. Carefully keeping his balance, he then stood up and the added height brought his head even with the gap in the lid. He jumped cautiously as the pallets wobbled beneath him, trying to catch a glimpse of what was inside.

He was in luck. The bin was mostly empty, but toward the back he saw a pile of broad-brimmed hats. He didn't see much of anything else useful, but a hat would be a good start. Holding on to the lip of the bin with his good arm, he tried walking his feet up the side but his boots slipped and slammed back down on the pallets with a wet thud. Frustrated, he looked again at the side of the bin in front of him, trying to find a solution. He noticed a row of large, evenly spaced rivets which crossed the surface of the bin a few feet up from his starting position. Their rounded tops would make for poor footholds, but they were better than nothing. The pallets didn't give him much room, but he stepped back to gain a small running start. He jumped, grabbing the edge of the bin with his right hand and bringing his feet up to land on the rivets. It took everything he had, but he was able to lift himself up and scrabble over the top.

The bent lid of the bin scratched at his back as he wriggled his way through and fell down heavily into the cavernous interior. His broken arm was pinned under him for a moment as he hit the metal floor and he cried out as the bones scraped together. He rolled over onto his back, breathing hard and whimpering. He gritted his teeth and tried to hold still while he waited for the pain to subside. He lay on his back for long minutes, listening to the raindrops beat against the roof of the container. The pain filled his mind and left him nauseous. Finally, after what seemed like an eternity, his vision began to clear and he could think again.

He slowly raised his head to examine his surroundings. At the far end of the bin were the hats he'd seen earlier. They were white; or rather they were supposed to be white. All of them were splattered with a heavy coating of something thick and purple. He poked at it gingerly, and the glazed substance cracked and flaked at his touch, revealing a deep stain underneath. He wondered if it was some kind of dye. At any rate, it was obvious why these hats had been thrown out.

He picked through them and chose the one with the least purple scale on it. He brushed at it vigorously, then beat the hat against the side of the bin. Most of the crust crumbled away, leaving only the smaller, more stubborn remnants. He eyed it critically, holding it out in front of him. The hat still looked ridiculous, and the wide brim sagged. He frowned at it, trying to decide if it would work as a disguise. Suddenly he laughed out loud as he realized that Anne had a hat just like this for working in the garden! Grinning, he placed it on his head. The fit was a bit loose, but seemed to be the best he could hope for under the circumstances.

Outside the bin, the wind gusted loudly and a smattering of rain was blown in through the opening. He crawled to the other end of the container to keep dry, and found himself resting on something lumpy. As he pulled at it, he realized that he was sitting on top of a jumbled heap of fabric scraps. The scraps had the same glaze of purple dye on them, but they had started out black instead of white as the hats had been. As a result, the purple stains on them hardly showed at all. He had an idea and managed to separate a piece of fabric from the pile that was roughly rectangular and large enough to form a crude cloak. Since his jacket was still soaked through, the fabric might offer some protection from the elements. Also, he thought, it might help with his disguise.

As he draped the fabric across his shoulders, his stomach growled warningly; he couldn't wait here much longer. He still felt a bit sick, but at the same time he desperately needed to find something, *anything*, to eat. He moved back to the opening and tossed the hat and fabric scrap out into the alley, then considered his options for escape. The inner surface of the bin was corrugated, which created a sort of ladder he could climb. By placing his hand on the lip of the bin, he was able to scrabble up without too much trouble. He then swung his legs around and hopped down onto the stack of pallets, which wobbled underneath him as he landed. He kept his balance, but his broken arm twinged sharply as he reflexively tried to windmill his arms. Clenching his teeth, he hopped down onto the muddy ground. The rain was still falling as he gathered up the hat and pulled the fabric remnant over his soaked clothes. He noted ruefully that although the rest of him was drenched, his feet were still dry; it seemed that his new boots were waterproof. He hated having inadvertently stolen them, but that was the least of his worries now. He silently thanked the shop owner and began walking.

Holding the fabric remnant close, Jason left the alley and began to work his way west, keeping his head down and using the wide brim of the hat to shield his face from the rain. As he neared the normally busy commercial district he had worried there would be too many people to avoid, but instead the downpour meant the sidewalks were relatively empty, and those people he did see were hurrying to get out of the weather; they certainly weren't looking at him. The vehicle traffic was also less of a problem than he'd feared, as beaded water obscured the windows of the passing cars. Still, he hurried past them and didn't linger any longer than necessary.

After four blocks, he finally found what he was looking for. It was a small market that appeared to cater to people who wanted a warm meal, selling deli items and snack foods as well as an assortment of other odds and ends. He stood outside and peered through the window furtively, trying not to draw attention.

From what he could see, there were only a few people inside. He guessed that the current time was around eight AM on Sunday, which would explain the relative lack of customers. Should he risk going inside? Probably not; the alert with his face had likely been displayed on every screen in the city. He would almost certainly be recognized. Besides, all his money was tied to his micro. If he turned it back on, then the police might use the signal to locate him. He needed another plan.

He crossed the street and settled down to think while keeping an eye on the store. His stomach ached with hunger; he was becoming desperate and the only option he could think of was to steal, but he needed a way to do it without getting caught.

Overhead, the rain began to slow and the sky became a lighter shade of gray. He was grateful for the change, and shook the beaded water off his hat and cloak. Under the fabric though, he was still very wet. His clothes clung to his skin and pulled awkwardly as he tried to get comfortable.

A few minutes later he noticed a woman walking his direction and he looked up, alarmed. She was clearly heading to work; her uniform marked her as an employee of a local second-hand store. As she came closer her lips parted in surprise and Jason quickly pulled his hat down over his face, terrified that he'd been recognized. She stopped in front of him and knelt down to see his face. Her brown Latina eyes held no sign of fear as she looked at him.

"Wait here. I'll bring you something." she said, and then stood and crossed the street. As she went inside the market, Jason's mind raced. He considered getting up and fleeing the area; it would be the smart thing to do. She was probably on her micro right now, telling the police where he was. Still, he thought, she hadn't been afraid, and he was so very hungry. Instead of running, he waited, watching her through the store window.

She emerged a few minutes later carrying a large sack. The weight of its contents made it swing as she hurried back across the street. Jason stood up uncertainly as she approached.

Upon reaching him, she opened the bag. "Here." she said, pulling out something hot and offering it to him. It was a corn dog, and his mouth began to water. He reached out with his good arm and took it from her.

"Thank you." he said, and began to devour it. It was greasy, but it tasted delicious. She waited as he finished eating.

"It's the least I could do for you." she replied. "I got you some other things as well. Mostly it's food and a credit chip. I couldn't spare much money to put on the chip, but it's better than nothing. Also, I thought you'd want these." She opened the bag and pulled out some scissors and a disposable razor. Jason took the razor from her with a silent question on his face. She smiled and explained, "You're going to need a better disguise than that god-awful hat. Maybe shave your head? You need to do *something* to look different or they'll catch you!"

So she *had* recognized him... He knew she was right, but he still felt guilty as he accepted the bag. "I'm not who you think I am." he protested. "I just want to get home."

"Aren't you the guy from The Resistance?" she asked. He could hear her capitalizing the words as she spoke them.

"What?" he responded, clueless. The world seemed to be spinning out from underneath him, knocking him off balance. She took out her micro and her fingers danced quickly across the screen. Turning the device toward him, she asked, "Isn't that you?"

On the screen was the by now familiar image of Jason holding the rifle. His heart sank as he said, "Yes, but..." The woman interrupted him and pressed another button on the device. Jason listened with growing horror as a disembodied voice began to speak over the image.

> *"We are The Latino Resistance Front, and we speak for all Hispanics on Ross b. We speak for those who have no voice. Since its founding, Hispanics on this new world have been held down. Subjugated. Beaten. We are the victims of crime, prejudice, and of the State. We have no rights, and we are forbidden from trying to claim them."*

The woman stared at him intently as he listened to the recording, and Jason saw the same unsettling fire in her eyes as he had seen in the man who'd saved him after the explosion.

> *"We claim responsibility for today's attack, and the others before it. And those attacks will not be the last."*

Jason suddenly realized the seriousness of his situation. He wasn't just being used as the face of an attack; he was being made into the icon of an entire movement! His knees went weak and he was forced to lean against the wall behind him to keep from falling over.

> *"Until there is change there will be more shootings. There will be more bombings. And there will be more bloodshed. Our goal is freedom. Ross b can no longer be the territory of a criminal government light years away. We are fighting for independence! Ross b will become a country unto itself, and it will finally make good on the promises which have been empty for so long! We will declare freedom, Citizenship and equality for Hispanics. Because no one else will. God help you if you stand in our way."*

Jason's jaw dropped; it wasn't over! This 'Latino Resistance Front' was going to keep killing and killing, and they were making him the face of it all!

He looked at the woman, still holding her micro out to him. He could see in her eyes that she needed it all to be true. She needed him to be a hero, or at least what she thought a hero was. But it wasn't right; he couldn't fill that role for her or for anyone else. He wasn't even Hispanic! As the message ended, a heavy silence hung in the air as she waited for him to say something.

"I'm not a murderer." he told her quietly. She stood silently for a moment, studying his face. He didn't know what she hoped to find there. Eventually though, she seemed to reach a decision and her face became unreadable.

"Keep the bag." she said. "You'll need it. If you can, try to make it over to 1st street. Maybe Jonah can help you." With that, she began walking away. Before disappearing though, she paused. Fixing her gaze on him, she said, "Our people will have justice." and then she was gone.

Jason felt like he'd just fallen off a cliff. He knew he couldn't stay here any longer, but his feet seemed rooted to the ground. As someone entering the store across the street glanced his way, he forced himself to begin placing one foot in front of the other. He didn't know where he was going, but he did know that the woman had been right about one thing; he needed help. Instantly his thoughts turned to Anne. She was his lifeline. Calling her was a risk, but he couldn't put it off any longer.

First though, he needed a plan. Turning his micro back on was probably going to alert the police to his location, so he needed to come up with a way to avoid them. Carefully trying to consider everything that might go wrong, he eventually came up with something that might work. It would be risky, especially if he were recognized, but it seemed manageable. He set the bag down and rummaged through it, looking for the credit chip. He didn't know how much money was on it but he hoped it would be enough for what he had in mind. Suspended above him and running parallel to the road was the pneumatic tube used by the city trams. It led westward, away from the industrial district. He followed the tube, hoping to find a boarding terminal as he headed deeper into the city.

He kept his head down as he walked, using the hat to hide his face. The rain had mostly stopped and he was finally beginning to dry out, but the better weather seemed to be drawing more people out into the streets. He began to feel incredibly conspicuous, afraid that his ridiculous hat and makeshift cloak would give him away. He kept his eyes fixed on the sidewalk, only occasionally looking up to make sure he was still following the tram tube.

When he located the boarding terminal, he was dismayed to find himself surrounded by more people than he was comfortable with. He entered the square cautiously, keeping to the periphery and away from the commuters gathered at the stairs which led to the boarding platform above the street. He settled down against a wall to wait and watched the people come and go, knowing he would need to pick his moment carefully. He pulled the fabric cloak tightly around himself, hoping to pass for a beggar while he waited.

A large Caucasian man, slovenly and dressed in a stained coat and dark pants appeared nearby. The man clearly did not belong with the better dressed people who stood waiting for the tram. Instead he kept to the shadows of the surrounding buildings, and seemed to be looking for something. Jason lowered his head until he could just see the man's feet below the brim of his hat. His heart leaped into his throat as he saw the feet turn and approach him.

"Hey, you buyin?" the man asked him casually.

The words "Buying what?" escaped Jason's lips before he could stop them. He knew what the man was selling.

"Rush. Or Helium. Got both. You interested?" The man patted the pockets of his large coat as he spoke, as if to prove he had the goods.

Jason shook his head, keeping the hat down over his eyes. "No, man. Not my thing. I stay away from that stuff."

The salesman nodded approvingly. "Smart. This shit will ruin you." He sat down next to Jason, not even asking whether he wanted company. "Helium is fun, makes you see pretty lights and shit, but it makes you stupid too. Someone says you should do somethin', you do it. Don't even ask why. Shit, sometimes you even think it was your own idea!" The man stopped, then chuckled as a new thought occurred to him. "What it does to your voice is funny as hell though, I gotta say. I guess that's why it's called Helium, ain't it!"

Jason turned away, hoping his body language would convince the man to leave, but the dealer went on, oblivious to the signs that his audience wasn't interested.

"The Rush ain't any better. Makes you real paranoid; you think everyone's out to get you. I knew this guy who really went in for that shit. One night he freaked out and went off on his girl. She called the cops, yellin' that he was gonna kill her." The man stopped for a long moment. Jason risked a look at him and saw that the man's face had turned somber. He seemed to study his hands as they rested on his knees. "He did too. Damn shame; she was real nice."

A moment later though, the man's friendly demeanor returned. He clapped Jason on the shoulder, using him as leverage to stand up. "Well, can't stay. Got shit to sell. Nice talkin' to you." he said, and moved off. He surveyed the crowd gathered at the terminal and seemed to decide that he wasn't going to make any sales here. He strode off north, looking for someplace where people had disposable cash and a distinct lack of good judgement.

Jason turned his attention back to watching the terminal. The crowds seemed to come in waves, every fifteen minutes or so. He figured he could wait for a lull, then get over to the kiosk and buy two tram tickets before too many people took interest.

He stood up as his moment came. Keeping his back to anyone who might be watching, he hurried over to the kiosk and activated it. The credit chip connected wirelessly and the screen showed him a balance of ten dollars; it was barely enough, but it would do. The price of a ticket was $4.50 no matter his destination, so he selected a station on the far west side of town. His plan also required a return trip, and he remembered the woman's mention of someone on 1st street named Jonah. He added an eastbound ticket back to the 1st street station, which brought the total to nine dollars.

It was tempting to call Anne now, but he just couldn't risk it. He finished the transaction, and the machine printed out two small paper tickets. If he'd used his micro, the tickets would be stored digitally but using the credit chip meant he had to rely on physical tickets. That alone would be a little suspicious, but he hoped that anyone who noticed would take him for homeless and not give him any further attention. He stuffed the tickets into his pocket and faded back, keeping his distance from anyone else waiting for the tram.

Ten long minutes later he heard the whoosh of the pneumatic tram as it slid into position at the terminal. The doors opened and a group of passengers filtered out, each going their own way. Thirty seconds later a chime sounded, indicating that the waiting passengers could now begin boarding. A line formed and Jason fell in, doing his best to fit in despite how he was dressed.

Jason found the crowd waiting to board the tram to be a diverse mix of people from the working class neighborhood he found himself in. In line behind him was a woman in a janitor's uniform, while ahead of him was a man who appeared genuinely homeless. Jason watched as most of those in line entered the tram without even pausing, letting their micros handle the transaction. Very occasionally, someone would present a paper ticket to the bored looking attendant. The man would pass the tickets over a panel built into a small pedestal where he stood, accepting the ticket and letting the passenger board.

The line moved forward quickly and the homeless man was next to board. He presented a paper ticket to the attendant, who took it and waved him through before the panel had even chimed its approval. Jason did the same, keeping his eyes down until the chime sounded again. He then stepped on board the tram and took a seat.

'So far, so good.' Jason thought. No one had even looked in his direction. A video screen too small for the job was mounted to the ceiling of the tram car, and showed what appeared to be a soap opera. The sound was turned off and everyone ignored it.

Soon after he sat down, the tram doors rattled closed and a yellow "Stay Seated" sign illuminated near the overhead video screen. With a sound like sucking air through a straw, pneumatic pressure began to push the tram toward the next terminal. Jason slid down in his seat as they built speed, using his hat to hide his face.

Several passengers had still been standing as the tram began to move and now had to scramble to find seats. A large Black man sat down heavily next to Jason, leaning on him and pressing against his broken arm. Jason gritted his teeth and squeezed closer to the window, trying to take the pressure off his injury. The man didn't say a word, so Jason closed his eyes and pretended to sleep and the man got off two stops later without giving him a second glance.

It took the tram over an hour to reach the last station on the west side of Cosmopolis. This was a wealthy area, with high-end apartment buildings and small manicured gardens with bright open areas. The red sun was actually shining overhead as Jason descended from the terminal and stood near the foot of the stairs.

Once he was alone, he began to put his idea into action. He pulled the micro from his pocket and stared at the dark screen, running the plan through in his mind. As soon as he turned it on, he was pretty sure that the police would immediately begin tracking his location. The micro would automatically encrypt his call, but the police would still be able to see the signal. He figured he would only have a few minutes before they arrived to arrest him. A nearby sign showed that the return tram would arrive in fifteen minutes. He waited for ten, then activated the device.

The screen flickered to life as the machine powered up, showing white first and then cycling through all the colors of the rainbow as a progress bar crawled along the bottom. The process took less than 30 seconds, but it seemed to take much longer. He didn't know at what point the police would be able to track the signal and the uncertainty made him nervous.

After what felt like an eternity, the device was finally ready to go. He opened the contact menu and touched the entry for Anne with trepidation. Up to this point he hadn't allowed himself to think that maybe she had been hurt, but now that fear gripped his heart and squeezed tight. Steeling himself, he held the device out so that the micro's camera would capture his face and waited to see if Anne would answer. He had not quite four minutes left until the next tram arrived.

Two small beeps sounded in quick succession as the call connected and suddenly Anne's face filled the screen. Her eyes widened in shock as Jason smiled in relief. "Hi Honey." he said.

"Jason?!" she breathed. She swallowed as if her mouth were dry. "Are you okay? What's going on?"

He decided that his broken arm didn't matter right now. "I'm fine." he said. "I don't have much time. I just needed to know that you and Matthew were alright."

"We're okay, but we saw the police alert! You were holding a gun!" She was desperate, pleading for answers. "Did you..."

"No." he interrupted. "I didn't shoot anyone or blow anything up. It wasn't me." He spoke firmly, and to his relief he saw that she believed him. Jason glanced at the call timer running in the corner of his screen. "I'm sorry, for all this. I just had to see you. Look, I need to go; tell Matthew that I love him. I love you, too." he said.

"I love you." she answered immediately. They stared at each other in silence for a moment, then she blurted, "Don't go!"

Jason paused, not wanting to end the call. "I'm coming home." he promised her. "I don't know how I'll get there yet, but I am coming home."

Two minutes left.

"We'll be waiting." she said. She looked into his eyes. "I love you."

"I love you too." he replied and then closed the connection. His eyes burned with tears as he locked the micro and powered it down once more. After making sure no one was watching, he dropped the device to the ground and stomped on it. The small block of plastic and metal was sturdy, but he felt it give way under his boot. He kicked at it several more times, distorting the case, and breaking the screen. Finally, he peeled it apart and ground the internal electronics under his heel, leaving small fragments embedded in the pavement.

With 30 seconds to spare, he dropped the remains of the smashed micro into a nearby waste bin and then joined the line to board the eastbound tram. He filed forward nervously, expecting the police to overrun the area at any moment. But as he gave his ticket to the attendant and took a seat, the scene outside remained peaceful. The doors closed and the tram began to move, carrying him toward 1st street and Jonah.

His anger flared as he wondered who this 'Jonah' was. The woman on the street had said he might be able to help, but she had also been willing to give aid to a man she thought was a terrorist. Was Jonah somehow connected to The Resistance? Was he the one who'd made him the face of a terrorist attack?

A small, tinny sound interrupted his thoughts and he looked around in confusion before realizing it had come from overhead. The video display above him was set to a news-feed and the audio was just loud enough for him to hear. On the screen, a blonde woman was saying, "...two new shootings today, with a total of 19 victims. At least one of the perpetrators appears to have been Hispanic."

A divided image appeared, showing each of the attackers. The pictures had obviously been extracted from security-camera footage. One was of a man with obviously brown skin and dark hair. The second appeared to be of a woman, and Jason noticed with horror that she was wearing the same kind of mask and gloves as the shooter at the bazaar. They both stood as if they were posing for the camera, as if they had wanted to be seen.

"The Latino Resistance Front has issued a statement to the media claiming responsibility for these new attacks." the blonde reporter continued. "Cosmopolis Chief of Police Michael Edgars has been quoted as saying, 'This is now a war.' In related news, a Hispanic owned business has been set ablaze in the commercial district near 36th street. Firefighters are on scene to keep the fire from spreading. Sadly, the fire is believed to have been set deliberately in response to the recent attacks."

Jason slumped in his seat, feeling overwhelmed. His head pounded with the rhythm of the tram as it sped along the tube. The world was coming undone all around him, and somehow it felt like it was his fault.

CHAPTER 8

The tram wheezed to a stop at the 1st street station, and when the doors opened Jason stepped out and made his way down to the street. Before him stood a mix of worn apartment buildings and small shops. The shiny buildings of the city's busy downtown towered in the distance, a contrast that made it clear development had begun to pass the tired neighborhood in front of him by decades ago. He remembered with irony just how bright and shiny Cosmopolis had seemed yesterday as he and his family walked along the river. Now a musty odor drifted in the air that he couldn't quite identify; maybe it was just age.

Halfway down the block in front of him a gap in the buildings marked the location of a small vacant lot. Tufts of pale white weeds grew along the edges but the center of the lot was barren and open. The space had drawn a group of six or eight children who were all gleefully running after a dirty ball. There was no goal that Jason could see; rather than an organized soccer match, it appeared to be a game of chase where a ball was only incidentally involved. The children laughed and shouted to one another, each trying to take the ball from the leader.

Before setting out, Jason shifted the ill-fitting hat on his head, trying in vain to make it sit comfortably. The morning's rainsquall had moved on and left everything wet, but a warm, dense humidity remained and he knew it wouldn't be long before he started to sweat. He began walking north as he considered how to find Jonah. Preoccupied with his thoughts, he stumbled over a patch of uneven sidewalk and felt the bag he carried swing and bounce against his leg as he caught himself. He silently thanked the woman who had given him the supplies; he'd eaten most of the food on the tram ride but had saved a small package of jerky for emergencies. The way things were going, he was pretty sure he'd need it sooner or later.

The bag of supplies didn't only contain food; it also held scissors and a disposable razor. His encounter this morning outside the store had been unsettling, but the woman had been right about one thing; if he was going to make it back to Aberdeen, he would need a better disguise than a woman's gardening hat.

He watched the storefronts carefully as he walked, while at the same time trying to remain inconspicuous. His plan for a better disguise meant shaving his head and if it was going to work, then he couldn't be noticed beforehand by anyone who might matter. He hoped to find a restroom with a locking door, as that would give him the privacy he needed to cut his hair. He surveyed the options as he went, looking for a likely place. A restaurant? Too busy. The coffee shop? Fewer people, but the owner was standing out front and she didn't seem friendly. The Latino Outreach center? Better, but the lights were off and the gray stone building didn't look open.

By now he'd walked several blocks from the tram and the neighborhood he found himself in had slowly transitioned from working-class poor to outright seedy. The people he saw on the street kept to themselves, only glancing his way furtively. Distantly he heard the wail of a siren and froze. The sound gently grew, then faded without coming close. He shook himself, hoping that no one had noticed his nervous reaction. He knew the police had to be searching for him, but so far he appeared to be in the clear.

A door opened across the street, causing him to quicken his pace. A short time later he came upon an establishment which seemed likely to be what he needed; a run-down convenience store. A partially broken 'OPEN' sign flickered behind the barred windows. It was perfect; nothing about the place looked inviting at all. He cautiously watched the door for several minutes, but he didn't see anyone enter or leave in all that time. Then, bracing himself for what he might find, he went inside.

He heard the music before he even opened the door. The sound was loud and abrasive, like someone cutting through a metal trash can with a chainsaw. A young woman with vaguely Asian features and purple hair stood near the register, talking into her micro. A faint chime sounded and without turning to see who had come into her store, she aimed a middle finger over her shoulder in Jason's direction. He saw the words "Fuck You!" tattooed vertically along her finger in case he'd missed the message, forcing him to stifle a smile.

Her shoulders fell as she realized that Jason hadn't left. Sighing into her micro, she said, "I'll have to call you back.", set the device down and then turned a baleful eye toward him. She very pointedly did not turn the music down.

"What?" she demanded, somewhere between angry and bored. The name tag clipped to her jacket read 'Brodie'.

"I'd like to use the restroom." Jason said, raising his voice to be heard over the music.

"Customers only." she replied curtly and then picked up her micro, assuming he'd leave.

"What can I get for a dollar?" he asked quickly.

"Goddammit." she muttered. "Here. One of these." she said, grabbing a small, cheaply made flashlight from a bucket next to the register. It was bright pink and looked like it would probably break the first time he tried to use it.

Jason agreed and pulled out the credit chip which held his sole remaining dollar. He passed the chip over the register and it beeped, completing the transaction. He then took the light from her and shoved it into a pocket. Their business concluded, Brodie again turned to her micro while at the same time pointing toward the rear of the store. In seconds she had returned to her call, her first words being, "Fucking customers..."

Jason walked the direction she had indicated, hoping she had been pointing him toward the restroom. In a back corner he found a darkened doorway with an ancient mop stored inside. A glance into the shadows also revealed a stained toilet and sink. Relieved to have found what he was looking for, Jason stepped inside and carefully moved the mop out of the way so that he could close the door.

With the door closed, the room suddenly fell into total darkness. After a moment his questing hand found the switch and the light came on with a loud buzz. Around him, decades of graffiti had been carved into the pale green walls, most of it obscene. He set his bag down beside the sink, avoiding a large puddle of scum-filled water which had pooled there.

The man he found staring back at him from the mirror looked exhausted, which made sense as he hadn't gotten any real sleep in over 24 hours. He wondered for a moment if being unconscious counted, then decided probably not. He lifted the hat off his head and was dismayed to find a long cut on his forehead which began high above his right eye and travelled horizontally before disappearing into his black hair. He hadn't even realized it was there. He probed at it gently, and was relieved to find that it didn't hurt too much. His eyes had dark bags under them, which could be due to lack of sleep but were just as likely left over from being punched in the nose. His face was dirty, and he needed a shave too. All things considered, he looked like hell.

He pulled the fabric remnant from his shoulders and let it fall to the floor where it lay in an uneven heap. In the mirror, the cloak's absence revealed the dirty and stained sling which held his broken left arm. The pain was dull and ever-present but the sling had been well made and he had no way to replace it now anyway. Besides, he needed to focus on what he came here to do. He reached into the bag and pulled out the scissors.

Doing his best despite his injured arm, he began to hack at his hair. The scissors didn't cooperate at first and got caught, pulling the hair instead of cutting it. He worked the handles back and forth carefully and eventually found a technique that worked. After that, the work went quickly and his hair fell in clumps onto the sink and floor. When he was done, he examined his newly shorn head in the mirror. He barely recognized himself; most of his thick black hair was now less than a quarter inch long, but he wasn't done yet. He took a breath and braced for the next step.

He returned the scissors to the bag and fished out the disposable razor. After considering his reflection for a moment, he decided to leave the day-old stubble on his chin in place. Instead, using water and a bit of liquid hand-soap which dribbled from a yellowed dispenser, he worked up a lather and smeared it over his head. Careful of the cut on his forehead, he pulled the razor over his scalp in long strokes and tried to avoid giving himself any new injuries. When he was done, he examined himself critically in the mirror and scowled at his newly bald reflection. He thought he looked ridiculous and he worried what Anne would think, but he had to admit that he could barely recognize himself. He hoped it would be an effective disguise.

He knew the store clerk, Brodie, would probably have questions, so he made sure to clean his hair out of the sink before gathering his things and once again donning the hat and cloak. He took one last look in the mirror to confirm that the hat hid his transformation. Once he left the store he planned to toss both the hat and the cloak into the nearest trash can, but until then it would be best to maintain the pretense that nothing had changed.

His next goal was to find this Jonah person, whoever he was, and asking the woman behind the counter about him seemed as good a place to start as any. He braced himself for her particular brand of caustic customer service and went back up to the register.

Brodie's back was turned as Jason approached her. She was kneeling on the hard floor as she fiddled with the music player, and seemed frustrated. She cursed softly as the music cut out, then smiled in victory as a new song began to blare over the speakers. To Jason the new song didn't sound any different than the last one, but he figured that maybe he just didn't have the ear for it. Brodie rose and began to nod her head in time to the music's triphammer rhythm, and was startled as she turned to find Jason standing near the counter.

"What the fuck?!" she demanded, the ambiguous question as much a greeting as an exclamation. She stood glaring at him, waiting for an answer. Jason hid a smile; a part of him wanted to like this woman. He decided to try the direct approach.

Raising his voice to be heard over the music, Jason said, "I'm looking for someone named Jonah. Do you know who that is?"

Brodie calmed somewhat. "Yeah, he runs the El Rey Latino Outreach Center up the street." she said. "I don't know if he's there today though."

Jason remembered the outreach center he'd passed on his way here. "Okay, thanks." he said, and turned to leave. As he opened the door, Brodie called out to him loudly, saying, "You know your hat looks like ass, right?" He kept moving, letting the door close behind him.

Outside, the day had continued to warm. At a trash can along the sidewalk he quickly pulled off the fabric remnant and tossed it in, followed by the purple hat. It was like shedding a skin, and the new breeze across his freshly shaved head gave him goosebumps. He felt self-conscious about his new appearance but logically he knew that to a stranger he wouldn't stand out any more now than he had in the ugly hat.

Rummaging through his bag of supplies, he pulled out the package of beef jerky and placed it in his jacket pocket next to the cheap flashlight, then threw the bag and its remaining contents into the receptacle as well. With his transformation now complete, he made peace with his new look and began walking south toward the outreach center.

The El Rey Latino Outreach Center was located four blocks from the convenience store and now that he knew where he was going, it didn't take him long to reach it. In front of the building, he stood on the sidewalk and weighed his options. A sign above the door read 'El Rey Latino Outreach Center', underscored in smaller letters by the words 'Strengthening Lives and Securing Futures'. The place seemed innocent enough, but if this Jonah had framed him for the attack at the bazaar... One way or another, he had to learn the truth. He climbed the stairs to the door but couldn't see anyone inside and a halfhearted tug on the handle revealed that the door was locked. Returning to the sidewalk, he wondered what to do next. He needed answers and, thin as it was, Jonah was his only lead.

A loud rattle followed by the sound of voices began to echo from the alley next to the building. Trying to appear casual, Jason moved to investigate and saw a delivery truck parked there. Two Black men were lifting boxes out of the back of the truck and carrying them through a large roll-up door in the side of the building. A third man, Hispanic and dressed in a gray wool suit, was laughing and making conversation with them. He was older, with gray hair and wearing a pair of old-fashioned spectacles. When the truck was empty the workers presented the older man with an electronic pad and he scanned it briefly before pressing his thumb to the screen and formally accepting the delivery. With calls of, "See you next week!" the two men climbed into the back of the truck which then drove off toward the other end of the alley. The older man had remained behind but as Jason watched he stepped through the wide door and prepared to lower it behind him. Without thinking Jason sprinted down the alley toward him, shouting, "Wait!"

The door paused in its descent and then raised again. The man in the gray suit stepped out and looked toward him.

He seemed curious rather than afraid and he waited while Jason ran down the alley toward him.

Upon reaching him, Jason was breathing hard. He had acted on impulse and was now torn between making accusations and thanking the bespectacled man for waiting. Instead, he said, "I'm trying to find someone named Jonah. Do you know him?"

The man nodded. "Jonah Rodriguez? I do; that's me." he said. "Can I help you?"

Jason stood in stunned silence for a moment. His lips moved soundlessly as he fumbled for the right words, then in a rush he couldn't stop, he blurted out, "The Resistance used my picture for their speech! I was there, I saw the gunman shooting people! They died right in front of me! Was that you; are you The Resistance?!" There was a manic edge to his voice that he hadn't expected. His breath still came hard and his body was tensed as if expecting a fight. This was stupid, he thought; even if it's true, did he expect the man to admit it right here on the street? He gritted his teeth and considered running back out of the alley and away from everything.

Jonah appeared taken aback as he stared at Jason for a long moment and then an expression of shocked understanding spread over his face. Jason felt like the ground had collapsed under his feet as he realized that Jonah had recognized him! Quickly, Jonah reached out and grabbed Jason's jacket. "Come with me!" he said, pulling at him. Jason tripped on the edge of the door and stumbled as he tried to regain his balance. Jonah put out both hands to steady him, bumping against Jason's broken arm in the process. An involuntary gasp of pain escaped before Jason could stop it and Jonah pulled back, apologizing.

Once they were inside Jonah leaned back out the door, checking the alley for anyone who might have seen them. Satisfied, he pulled the door down and locked it, sealing them inside. As Jason's eyes adjusted, he saw that the room was cluttered with shelves and boxes showing labels like 'Coats' and

'Detergent'. Near the door, an area just large enough to park a truck was the only open space.

The two men stood together in the cool storeroom, evaluating each other silently. After a moment, Jonah asked gently, "So you are Jason Menounos?"

Jason's guard went up instantly. "How do you know who I am?" he asked warily.

"Every micro in the city was sent an alert with your name and face. They say you are armed and dangerous." Jonah glanced up at Jason's bare scalp. "Shaving your head was smart but I'm good with faces; I still recognized you, though not many would." He gave a wry smile and studied Jason as if trying to make a decision. "So have you come to us to find a place to hide? To see if we will keep you safe until the police stop looking for you?"

Jason didn't quite know how to respond; he had come here looking for answers but the soft-spoken man in front of him didn't seem like a terrorist. Still, he knew that evil often hid behind a bland exterior. His eyes met Jonah's and his voice was quiet but hard. "Did you use me as the face of your so-called revolution?" he asked.

Jonah held his gaze for a moment, then sighed as his features softened. "No." he said sadly. "I did not. That was others." He shivered suddenly and hugged his arms close about himself. "It's cold in here. Please; let's go up to my office and we'll talk some more." he said and turned to go. He reached the doorway and paused, turning to see if Jason was following. Reluctantly, Jason moved to accompany him through the door.

As they made their way through the building they walked through a dining room with two long folding tables and an attached kitchen before passing by a common room with a video screen and reaching a sort of lobby space near the front door. Everywhere the floors were covered with the kind of hard tile used in schools because it was durable and cheap, and every room was painted the same shade of industrial off-white. Posters hung on the walls advertising various community plays, potluck dinners and social services. Upon reaching the front of the building they climbed a flight of stairs to the second floor and reached Jonah's office at the end of a short hallway. A small plaque on the door read 'Director'. On entering the room Jason noted a half empty mug sitting on the cluttered desk and walls that had been painted the same off-white color as everything else.

A pair of chairs stood near the desk and Jonah motioned for Jason to sit down. As Jonah took a seat at the desk, he paused, frowned and said, "Unfortunately I have to ask; did you attack those people at the bazaar?"

"No, I didn't." Jason answered him firmly, keeping his voice steady.

Jonah nodded. "I thought not," he said, "but all the same, I had to ask. Just to be sure."

"What's going on?!" Jason demanded. "If you didn't do this, who did?! Why me?!"

"Probably, you were just convenient." Jonah explained gravely. "You were in the wrong place at the wrong time. You've heard of The Latino Resistance Front?"

"Not till this morning. I only heard the name when I saw the announcement they put out with my picture."

Jonah nodded again. "From what I can tell, The Resistance is pretty much exactly what they say they are, but they also have a dark side." He paused. "Well, a *darker* side, anyway."

Jason snorted in disgust. "Darker than mass murder?" he asked darkly.

Jonah looked uncomfortable. "Did you know that this center is not the only place to go in this city for those in need of a hot meal?" he asked, placing his hands on the desk. "Others do outreach as well."

Jason was confused by the seeming non-sequitur. "I didn't know that, but I guess it makes sense." he said hesitantly.

"In the last year a new organization calling themselves Casa Preciosa has shown up. Like us, they offer food and other services and also like us, they focus on the Hispanic community. Sometimes, the people we serve will make use of both places, taking help where they can get it." Jonah picked up the mug from his desk and took a sip before continuing. "In the past few months I have been hearing things from people who come to us from Casa Preciosa. They talk of freedom, revolution, and of violence. Sometimes someone will leave our care entirely and go there, only to completely disappear soon after. No one will say where they have gone."

Jason listened, hearing the man's concern but not understanding what bearing it had on his own problems.

Jonah went on, looking down as he spoke. "The rumor is that some of them have become the attackers we've heard about. I don't have any proof but frankly, what I'm hearing is frightening."

Jason still didn't see how it all fit together. "So why did The Resistance use my picture?" he asked hesitantly.

"My guess is that it was just opportunistic. It might have been a coincidence, but that image does make you look like a dangerous revolutionary. It was probably too good for them to pass up."

'So it's not even personal...' Jason thought. He wanted nothing more than to escape this; to run away and to go home. Thoughts of Anne and Matthew swelled in him, pushing any other concerns aside. "I need to get back to Aberdeen, to my wife and son." he said, his throat tight. "Will you help me?"

Jonah gave a tired smile. "In this world, we have to stick together. Of course; I'll help you as much as I can." he agreed.

Jason thanked him profusely, then saw the nameplate on his desk which read 'Director – El Rey Latino Outreach Center'. A little awkwardly, he said, "You said 'We have to stick together'. I have to be honest; despite what it looks like, I'm not actually Latino." He hated to bring it up, but it felt wrong to gain Jonah's help under false pretenses.

"This center helps Hispanics because they tend to be

the ones in the most need. If you need my help, then that's good enough for me." Jonah replied. He stood and frowned, seeming to notice Jason's broken arm anew. "First though, let's see if we can get that fixed."

CHAPTER 9

Jonah reached into the pocket of his suit jacket and removed a battered old micro. Judging from the scratches and wear marks, it had been well used. He slid his round wire-rim glasses down on his nose and peered over them as he poked at the device and selected a contact from the address book.

"I'm going to call Courtney Damiya; she is a paramedic and has access to some medical equipment. I just hope she's not out on a call." Jonah said, frowning down at the micro as the call was made. The 'Waiting' icon flashed slowly, then after nearly 30 seconds the icon vanished and a woman's face filled the tiny screen. Her bleached blonde hair hung limply over one eye and she looked tired, but she smiled when she saw Jonah's face.

"Jonah! Haven't seen you in a while; things must have been quiet at The Center for a change." she said.

"A little," he replied, "but I doubt it will stay that way. How's your daughter?"

"She's fine, I guess. She never tells me anything anymore. She's working right now; sometimes I think she only comes home to sleep."

"She's certainly got spirit. Tell her we miss her volunteering down here."

"I will. Now, I doubt you called just to chat. What do you need?"

Jonah hesitated. "Ah, I was hoping you could make a private call down here at The Center. We've run into a small medical issue and I think that your special touch is just what we need."

"Huh." Courtney replied, an odd look on her face. "Should I bring the van?" Her tone gave the words added meaning that made Jason curious.

"Yes, I think that would be a good idea." Jonah answered. Jason could tell he wasn't exactly comfortable making this kind of request, but also that he'd done it before. He began to wonder what life was really like in this neighborhood.

"I have something to take care of first, but I can be there in about an hour or so. Will that be okay?" she asked.

"That should be fine. We can hold things together until then." Jonah looked very sincerely into the screen as he said, "Thank you, Courtney. You are more help than you know."

Courtney smiled softly and said, "I know." as she closed the connection.

Jonah set the micro down on his desk and leaned back in his chair. "Courtney and her daughter are old friends of The Center. They volunteer here sometimes, helping serve food or doing any number of other things. They have been a godsend for us! I understand that her daughter has recently been accepted to the medical degree program at The University of Cosmopolis. Between the two of them, they have helped more people than I can count."

Jason wasn't sure he liked the idea of getting anyone else involved, but wasn't in a position to object. Realistically, if this woman could fix his broken arm, he'd take it in a second.

Jonah stood, tugging his suit back into place. "Well, until Courtney arrives we're the only ones here, so we may as well try to get comfortable. Can I get you something to eat?"

At the mention of food, Jason's stomach growled loudly. "Yes," he said. "That sounds great."

****

After finishing his first real meal in over 24 hours Jason sat with Jonah in the dining room, feeling as if he was forgetting something. He couldn't place it, but something just felt off. The clock on the wall gave a soft chime, followed less than a second later by a similar sound from Jonah's micro. The off-balance feeling crystallized as Jason realized that somehow it was already six PM; Ross b's constant sunlight sometimes made the days feel endless, but nearly eleven hours had simply evaporated while he was out walking the streets or riding in the trams. Six o'clock... at home it was dinner time. He wondered what Anne's day had been like; it couldn't have been easy for her. For the millionth time, he wished he was home with his family.

Jason was pulled from his reverie as Jonah's micro buzzed with an incoming call. He picked it up and Courtney Damiya appeared. Her face was drawn and she looked worried.

"Jonah, I'm almost there. Can you have the loading door open when I show up? I want to get this thing off the street."

Jonah nodded. "Sure, I can do that. What's wrong?" he asked, his brow furrowed.

"I'll tell you when I get there." she said, and broke the connection.

Jonah turned to Jason. "I'm going to go open the door for her. You should go upstairs and wait for me to come get you. I don't know what's going on and it might be better for you to stay out of sight until we know."

Jonah departed toward the storeroom while Jason returned to the lobby and climbed the stairs. Once he reached the second floor, he considered where to hide. Jonah's office lay to the right at the end of the hall, but there were several closed doors to his left. He opened the nearest one and found that the room held a variety of canned goods stacked in boxes. The next door revealed a sort of lost-and-found, with coats, shirts, and pants hung on hangers or folded and stacked neatly on shelves. The third room turned out to be a bathroom with a toilet, sink and small shower, and the last door was locked. Choosing among the doors he was able to open, he decided that the canned food room would provide the best cover. He stood in the doorway, listening intently. If he heard trouble he could quickly hide among the boxes to avoid being seen.

The distant clatter of the storeroom door being opened echoed up the stairwell, then less than two minutes later the sound came again as the door was pulled closed. Jason edged close to the top of the stairs, listening for trouble. Soon Jonah's disembodied voice came from below. "Jason, all clear." he called, his voice slightly raised. "Courtney is here. With all that is happening, she brought her daughter too." As Jason cautiously descended the stairs, he found Jonah speaking with a tall Asian woman with blonde hair; this must be Courtney. Seated a short distance away was a young woman in a black jacket, sporting a shock of purple hair. Jason recognized her as Brodie, the clerk from the convenience store! She lifted her head in response to his stare, a question on her face. He could see that she didn't recognize him.

Courtney was telling Jonah about the drive over. "...since then they're everywhere, setting up checkpoints. They started up north but they're working their way south."

"Wait, who's coming south?" Jason asked, interjecting.

"The Army." she said. "There was another bombing; this time they blew up the bridge on Ashford Avenue. The Resistance hasn't claimed the attack yet, but it looks like one of theirs. People are saying the governor is going to declare martial law. The Army is already locking down Hispanic neighborhoods; I saw that myself on the way over here. They're keeping people off the streets and enforcing a curfew on Latinos. I didn't see any checkpoints around here yet but I did see them further north. It won't be long until they're everywhere."

Feeling paranoid, Jason glanced through the window to the street outside. Nothing seemed any different, but he suddenly felt exposed and wished he were somewhere less visible.

Jonah nodded to Courtney, showing that he understood. "We'll I'm glad you made it here." he said. "We should be okay until this blows over; we have supplies and food as well as beds if need be. You and your daughter aren't Hispanic, so the Army isn't likely to bother you but I'm still happy you're off the streets tonight." Turning to Jason, he seemed to remember something. "Courtney, can you take my friend Jason here down to your van? His arm is broken and I'm hoping you can help him."

Courtney looked critically at Jason's left arm which was resting in the dirty sling. "I'll see what I can do. Let's go out to the van." she said, gesturing for Jason to accompany her. As they began walking toward the rear of the building, Brodie lifted herself from her seat and followed.

The van had been wedged into the same storeroom that Jason and Jonah had used to enter from the alley. The large vehicle seemed comically out of place inside the small room, as if an elephant had decided to move into a closet. Upon closer inspection, Jason realized that the van was in fact an ambulance. The words "Samaritan Hospital – Cosmopolis" were written in large block letters on the side, indicating that the vehicle belonged to them.

"Wow." Jason said. "How did you get an ambulance?"

Courtney opened the back and began setting up the equipment. "I'm a paramedic, so I'm always on call." she explained. "They let me take the ambulance home with me so that if I get sent out on an emergency call, I don't have to go get the ambulance first."

"Then I guess I'm lucky you weren't called out for the bridge bombing." Jason remarked.

Courtney shook her head. "Wouldn't have happened. Ashford Avenue is in the northeast part of the city. That's another hospital's district; Bennett Memorial, I think. Samaritan covers the southeast corner."

As her mother worked, Brodie watched over her shoulder, double checking everything and making a few small adjustments. After one too many intrusions, Courtney paused and asked her, "Do you want to be doing this?"

"Yeah." she answered, smiling. Jason wasn't sure he liked the idea. The 'Fuck You' tattoo on her finger wasn't visible at the moment, but the memory of it didn't exactly inspire confidence.

Her mother smirked. "Well, you're the one who's going to be a doctor." she said, and stepped down out of the ambulance. She turned to Jason and said grandiosely, "The doctor will see you now." More seriously, she added, "It's okay. She's been trained on the fuser, it'll be fine." Against his better judgment, Jason climbed into the ambulance and sat down on the gurney which was locked into rails on the floor.

Brodie's demeanor was suddenly vastly different than it had been in the store. She was calm and steady, projecting an air of competence that seemed to change everything about her. Her purple hair was tied back and she pushed the sleeves of her black jacket up to her elbows. She turned her attention to a squat, beige colored machine mounted to the wall of the van. From a rack next to it, Brodie selected a vaguely cylindrical object nearly three feet long and attached it to the box by a way of a coiled black cable. The device was made up of four connected plates and was hollow, forming a long tube. Jason could see all the way through it as Brodie examined it. Satisfied with what she saw, she powered on the box and the interior of the plates began to glow a soft blue.

She set the device down and began untying Jason's sling. "Okay," she said. "I'm going to need you to slide your arm inside the fuser." The hole in the middle of the device was only about three inches wide; too narrow to fit Jason's whole arm. He was about to object but Brodie pressed a button on the wall mounted box's control screen and the plates which formed the cylinder separated and spread apart with a clicking sound. The space in the middle had now more than quadrupled and Jason gingerly eased his broken arm inside up to the shoulder. Brodie reached over to adjust the sleeve, positioning his arm precisely where she wanted it. She clearly knew what she was doing and had an air of calm and purpose about her that he would never have imagined previously.

Once she was certain everything was in place, she pressed another button on the control screen and the four plates contracted around his arm. They squeezed tightly as a series of inflatable bladders expanded inside the device, holding his arm securely in place. The increasing sense of constriction began to feel uncomfortable, but there was no way to remove his arm now even if he wanted to.

"Have you ever had a bone fused before?" Brodie asked.

"No." Jason answered.

Brodie nodded. "This will take about fifteen minutes. You're going to feel some discomfort and afterward you'll need to wear a cast for about two hours while the osteo-polymer sets. After that the bone will be strong enough to use and will reach full strength within 24 hours. The polymer is completely biologically neutral, so you don't need to worry about allergy or rejection. There will probably be some residual bruising at the site of the break and some slight bleeding caused by the fuser's arthroscopic needles, but it shouldn't be too bad."

Jason took a deep breath. "Okay, let's do this." he said, and Brodie keyed the activation sequence into the control screen. The device on his arm began to give off a slight vibration, with the sensation pulsing rhythmically up and down his arm. It was almost pleasant.

As the machine worked, Brodie began to describe what was happening at each step. "Right now, it's scanning the bones to determine the location and nature of the break. It does this several times, and from different angles to be sure it hasn't missed anything."

The vibration stopped suddenly and for a moment it seemed as if nothing was happening. Then his arm was briefly cold, giving him goosebumps. He jumped as he felt a rapid series of small stings which surprised him more than they hurt. He gave Brodie a questioning look.

"That was the anesthetic injection. You don't want to feel the next part without it." she said.

Jason began to feel a little sick to his stomach and forced himself to sit still. Again the machine seemed idle but Brodie continued to watch the screen on the control box, unconcerned. She pressed a button and the image on the screen shifted, but it didn't seem to affect the treatment. As she brushed a loose strand of purple hair back from her face, he again saw the tattoo on her finger and wondered what he'd gotten himself into.

A sudden click drew his attention back to the device on his arm and he felt a growing pressure which seemed to come from all sides. The sensation continued and after a while his arm began to feel oddly warm. The feeling quickly went from warm to intensely hot. Instinctively he wanted to pull his arm from the device but it was stuck fast. After a long minute, the heat began to subside and he could breathe again. Then the feeling of pressure began to build again, this time slightly further up his arm. As before, the area went from warm to hot and stayed that way for far longer than was comfortable. He gritted his teeth as he waited for the sensation to pass.

Brodie continued to explain the procedure. "That's the arthroscopic needles." she said calmly. "They carry microscopic tools that help position the bones and make other repairs. Once the bone and any fragments are aligned, they inject the osteo-polymer which glues everything into place. The heat helps it cure and afterward your body treats it like your own bone."

Eventually the excruciating heat passed and the feeling of pressure on his arm diminished. His arm flashed hot again briefly before suddenly becoming unusually cool. A series of beeps emanated from the control box and Brodie studied the readout for a moment. "Everything looks good." she reported. "The break has been repaired and the arthroscopic incisions have been sealed." She pressed a series of buttons on the screen in rapid succession. A new sound like an electric pump began to come from the box and an odd feeling engulfed his arm from the elbow to the wrist. "Now it's creating a temporary cast." she explained. "It'll need to dry for a few minutes before the fuser can come off, but basically you're done." As if in response, a five minute countdown appeared on the screen.

During the entire procedure the previously acerbic Brodie had been nothing but calm and professional, and Jason could scarcely believe that this was the same woman he'd encountered before. "Thank you." he said. "I have to admit, you seem a lot different now than you did earlier."

She looked at him curiously. "Do I know you?" she asked.

He gave her a small smile. "We met at the store this afternoon. You said you didn't like my hat."

Brodie broke into a broad grin. "Oh! That was you? I just thought you were some asshole!"

The curse word fell easily from her lips and suddenly she seemed more like the woman he'd met before. Behind them, Brodie's mother didn't even react. She must have been used to it.

"The hat really did look like shit, though." Brodie confided with a smile.

An unexpected alert suddenly sounded, the noise coming from both Brodie's micro and her mother's. Courtney pulled hers out of her pocket and studied the screen with a frown.

"Well, the governor's fucking done it." she announced acidly. Suddenly Jason could see where her daughter's vocabulary had come from.

He started to ask what she meant but Brodie beat him to it. "Done what?" she asked.

"Fucking declared martial law, that's what. All non-Citizens are ordered to stay off the streets and everyone has to obey an eight PM curfew. The Army has been ordered to set up checkpoints in Latino neighborhoods and the micro network in those areas will be shut down and restricted to emergency use only."

They were all quiet for a moment, then Jason said, "You and Brodie aren't Hispanic. Maybe you should go home while you can?" Mother and daughter looked at each other while a rapid succession of thoughts, fears and excuses played over their faces. When it had passed, they were no closer to a decision.

A long tone from the fuser's control box startled everyone and Brodie turned to examine the display. Satisfied, she touched a button and the device suddenly released Jason's arm. He pulled himself free of the metal sleeve and revealed a pale blue cast that was hard and dry to the touch. Brodie took the fuser from him and inspected it before placing it gently onto a cradle mounted next to the control box.

Jonah's voice came to them from the kitchen. "Come back inside. I think you all should hear this."

****

Jonah led them into the common room, where they found a small receiver tuned to a police channel. Police communications were generally encrypted to prevent interception but apparently the device on the table was able to listen in anyway. Jason didn't know whether such a receiver was legal, but it seemed shady at best. Jonah saw his look and explained sheepishly, "I have occasionally found it useful to know what the police are doing."

The voices coming from the speaker painted a confusing picture, but overall it was one of trouble. The word 'riot' was uttered more than once. Over Courtney's shoulder, Jason watched the connection status indicator on her micro go dark. The authorities had shut the network down, as she had said they would. The endless police chatter was unaffected however; it was hosted on a separate network and continued unabated.

Things seemed to be getting worse; the voices they heard overlapped at times, making the chaos difficult to follow. Jason's ears strained to make any sense of it.

Jonah suddenly reached for the receiver. "Did you hear that?" he asked. "They mentioned something on Third Avenue." They all leaned closer, trying to follow the reports flooding in. A man's voice called for the fire department to report to a grocery store. In the same breath, he asked for additional officers to be dispatched to his location. Other voices soon joined in, calling for crowd dispersal and potential riot control.

Jonah looked at the three of them gathered around the table, a worried expression on his face. "It sounds bad out there." he said. "I think you should all stay here tonight. Perhaps things will be more settled in the morning." Courtney and Brodie nodded in reluctant agreement, and Jonah added, "We'll put out some cots for you in the dining room and I'll stay in the apartment upstairs." Jason realized that the apartment must have been what was behind that locked door he'd found upstairs. As for himself, he had no objection to staying here; it didn't sound at all safe outside.

Working together, they cleared the tables from the dining room and brought out the folding cots. Afterward, they spent some time getting to know one another and Jason told them about his family and home. Courtney divulged a few risque stories of her paramedic duties and Brodie related a very off-color tale about a customer she'd had to serve at the store, as well as talking more seriously about her interest in medicine. It amazed Jason that she could be so abrasive one minute and so earnest about her studies the next. The two sides were almost irreconcilable. Still, she had been competent while using the fuser; maybe she would make a good doctor.

When Jason's temporary cast was ready to come off, Courtney used a small saw with a spinning blade to cut it free. At the same time, he could see that she was checking up on her daughter's work with the fuser. She seemed pleased and asked him how his arm felt.

"Good." he said, working his elbow and fingers. "The skin's still a little tender though."

"That should pass in a day or so. The polymer is still setting, but the bone should be okay for light use. Just don't lift anything heavy. By tomorrow afternoon it will be at full strength and you'll be able to use it like normal."

As they readied for bed, Jonah made the bathroom and toilet upstairs available to them and Jason took a hot shower, trying to wash away the events of the past two days. It didn't work very well but he did feel a little better; cleaner, at least. He borrowed a set of shorts to sleep in and made his way downstairs, passing by Jonah who was on his way up. He had just set the sentry system for the building, which would alert them if anyone was prowling around outside while they slept. The two men nodded as they passed and afterward Jason heard the soft click of the apartment door closing.

As Jason settled into a cot in the darkened dining room, he thought about Anne and Matthew. Whatever it took, he would make it back to them, by any means necessary. He drifted off to an uneasy sleep as half-formed thoughts rose and fell in his head.

CHAPTER 10

The next morning Jason woke early. As he opened his eyes in the dark he was confused and for a moment he didn't know where he was. Sounds from the street outside began to slowly drift in; occasional shouts or the blaring of a horn. Soon he remembered he was at the El Rey Latino Outreach Center and his breathing slowed. He didn't know the time; there were no windows in the dining room and the room was still dark. Following the meager light that filtered in through the crack under the door, he moved to the exit and opened it, quietly closing it behind him.

He stopped and put on his boots just outside the door. Now in the lobby, he could see the street outside through the window. Several people walked past briskly, followed a few moments later by a police car rolling slowly along behind them. He couldn't tell if the officers inside the car were watching the people, but the sight made his pulse quicken. He stood frozen until the car had moved out of view.

As he came back to himself, he realized that Jonah was sitting at a small circular table nearby, drinking something steaming from a ceramic mug. The table in front of him held a pile of clothing and a pair of shoes. Eyeing the mug, Jason asked, "Is that coffee?"

"This is just hot water, actually." Jonah replied. "The coffee's in there, and I didn't want to wake anyone." he said, nodding back toward the dining room where Courtney and Brodie were still sleeping.

Jason examined the clothes on the table and picked up a button-down shirt from the top of the pile. The thin cloth felt cheap and the images printed on the fabric were a confusing mixture of parrots and cactuses, neither of which could be found on Ross b. He looked at Jonah with a question on his face.

"The Center has a supply of second-hand clothes for those in need. The clothes you were wearing when you arrived were torn and dirty; I thought you could use a change. These all seemed about your size." Jonah said, sipping at his water.

"Thank you." Jason replied. The shirt was not his style, but he was hardly in a position to be picky.

Jonah set the mug down on the table and leaned forward. "Do you have a way to get home?" he asked.

Jason sighed. "Not yet. We took the bus to get here; maybe I can take the bus back home?"

Jonah considered. "You could try that. But don't you think it's a little risky, being seen in public like that?"

"Yeah, a little, but it's still the best idea I can think of." he replied.

Jonah sat back and took a pensive sip from his mug. "Let me think about it for a while." he said.

Jason picked up the pile of clothes. "Do you mind if I get dressed upstairs?" he asked. "Down here is a little... public."

Jonah nodded. "Sure; I didn't lock the apartment. Go on up." Jason thanked him and carried the clothes up the stairs.

In the apartment, Jason dressed himself. Miraculously, the pants fit perfectly. He didn't even need the belt which Jonah had provided. The shirt was a little large, but it wasn't too bad. He caught his reflection in the mirror and the ridiculous pattern made him smile. Parrots and cactuses? Who had thought this was a good idea? Still, at least the clothes were clean. He studied his reflection and self-consciously ran a hand over his bald head. He hardly recognized himself; hopefully that meant no one else would either.

Jason picked up the shoes and inspected them. It had

been thoughtful of Jonah to include them, but they had obviously seen better days. They were a worn gray color, thin and designed to slip on or off without trouble. His gaze then went to the still-new boots he'd been wearing when this all began. The toes had gotten scuffed but otherwise they were no worse for wear. He decided to keep them; after all, they had served him well so far. He pulled them on and double-knotted the laces out of long habit.

Back downstairs in the lobby, Jason saw that Courtney and Brodie were now up. With the dining room and kitchen no longer off limits, everyone had gotten coffee and Jason gratefully accepted a cup.

Courtney and Brodie sat around the table, drinking drowsily for long minutes as they slowly woke up. Suddenly a loud chime rang out and everyone raised their heads, wondering what it meant. Over by the front door, the green light of the sentry system changed to amber and a small screen flickered to life. Jonah rose from his seat and went to the monitor. On it was an overhead view of two Caucasian men in army uniforms as they stood outside the front door. The nearest one looked up and spoke directly into the camera. His mouth moved silently for a moment before Jonah activated the microphone.

"...need to speak to someone in charge. Please come to the door." The man spoke in the firm, clipped tones of someone who clearly expected to be obeyed. The expression on his face was somewhere between bored and frustrated.

Jonah turned to Jason with concern on his face. "Perhaps you should wait upstairs while we sort this out. There is another sentry terminal on the wall inside the apartment; you can watch from there to see if this is going to be a problem."

Jason didn't like the idea of being trapped upstairs but they didn't have time to come up with a better plan. He set his drink down and hurried up the stairs, ignoring the butterflies in his stomach. Once inside the apartment, he closed and locked the door behind him. Next to the door, the sentry terminal was already active. He enabled the audio and video feeds and watched on the small screen as Jonah opened the front door.

"What can I do for you?" he heard Jonah ask in a voice pressed thin by the system's small microphone. The two men took half a step forward but Jonah subtly moved to block the door, keeping them outside.

The older of the two men spoke. "I am Sergeant Sharp. This is Corporal Dilley. We are with the 18th Infantry Division of the United States Army, assigned to Fort Emory. When the governor declared martial law last night, the Army was given the task of keeping the peace in Cosmopolis. To that end, we are setting up checkpoints and command posts throughout the city. I am here to inform you that we will be commandeering this building for command post duty. You are required to give up use of this facility until such time as we return it to you. I have been authorized to allow you two hours to vacate the premises." He finished speaking and leveled his gaze at Jonah, daring him to object.

Jonah was caught flat-footed by the sergeant's demands. "Is that really...?" he started, but Sergeant Sharp moved in close, interrupting him.

"Shut the fuck up and get out, *José*." he said, just loud enough for Jonah to hear. The words were nearly lost but the system compensated and amplified them for Jason's ears. He caught his breath; using José as an insult was almost comically old-fashioned but the meaning was clear. He saw a brief flash of anger cross Jonah's face and Sergeant Sharp's hand moved casually to the holstered side-arm on his hip. The implied threat wasn't subtle.

Jonah cleared his throat and without stepping back from the doorway, turned to speak to Courtney and Brodie. "I'm afraid we'll need to pack up and leave." he said with a little too much cheerfulness. "These gentlemen will be taking over The Center for the time being." He nodded significantly toward Sergeant Sharp. "They have generously given us two hours to get our things together." Addressing the Sergeant directly, he said, "We'll see you again in two hours then." and moved to close the door.

Sergeant Sharp caught the door, forced it open and stepped inside. Corporal Dilley followed him in, glowering threateningly. "I think we'll wait here." Sharp said and swaggered over to the small table where Courtney and Brodie were sitting. He pulled out an empty chair and sat down next to them with a smile on his face. "Hello, ladies." he said as he picked up Jason's abandoned coffee mug. He sniffed at it guardedly, then took a sip. The corporal took up a position near the door, keeping an eye on everyone.

Watching the soldiers from the corner of his eye, Jonah said, "Courtney and Brodie, would you gather your things from the dining room? I'm going to go get a few things from upstairs."

In the apartment, Jason was panicking. After the two men had moved inside, the camera and microphone had been unable to follow them. A knock at the apartment door made him jump and he cast around desperately for a hiding place. Before he could move however, the door burst open and Jonah hurried inside, closing the door rapidly behind him. He grabbed a raincoat and various odds and ends from a closet and began stuffing them into a small gray duffel bag. As he moved, he whispered urgently to Jason.

"I think we can get you out of here, but it's going to be close." he said. He moved on from the closet to the tiny kitchenette and added a small box of crackers and a few tins of something Jason couldn't identify to the bag. With the duffel nearly full, he turned to Jason. "When I leave, hide in the supply closet just down the hall. In a few minutes, I'll try to bring the men up here for a tour. While they are in the apartment, you'll be able to get down the stairs. Try to get to the ambulance. You can hide in the back and we'll drive you out with us when we go."

Jason nodded, afraid to speak. Jonah whispered, "Good luck." and patted him on the arm before vanishing back downstairs, leaving him alone in the apartment.

His mind was a blank; he felt completely out of his depth, but his feet took over where his brain failed him. As instructed, he quickly left the apartment and hid in the supply closet down the hall. He waited there, crouching behind the stacked boxes and trying not to breathe.

Jonah descended the stairs with the duffel bag thrown over his shoulder. Sergeant Sharp eyed him intently as he came near.

"I'm going to go check on Courtney and Brodie." Jonah informed him, and moved smoothly into the dining room.

Sergeant Sharp looked suspiciously at the dining room door as it closed behind Jonah. After a moment, he spoke to Corporal Dilley. "Corporal, stay here. I'm gonna go see what they're doing". He went to the dining room door and shoved it open, more forcefully than necessary. In the large room, Jonah and Courtney each held the end of a folding table as they maneuvered it into place. Brodie stood at the counter behind them, placing supplies into a small box. They all looked up in surprise as the sergeant barged into the room.

"Is something wrong?" Jonah asked as he set down his end of the table.

"Just making sure there aren't any surprises." Sharp said, contempt and suspicion playing across his face.

"Maybe I should give you a tour? So you can see we aren't hiding anything?" Jonah asked.

Sergeant Sharp considered this, then nodded. "Yeah, I think that would be a good idea. Let's start upstairs." he said. Jonah agreed, and stepped forward to follow the Sergeant. As he reached the door, he turned and spoke to Courtney.

"Courtney, don't forget to put your duffel bag into the ambulance. You don't want to leave it here." he said, indicating the bag he had left propped up against the wall. He and Courtney exchanged a pair of brief glances, then Jonah led the sergeant back through the door. Together they moved into the lobby, pausing at the foot of the stairs near Corporal Dilley's post. "Let's have the Corporal come too." Jonah said. "That way we don't have to do this twice."

Corporal Dilley looked to his sergeant. Sergeant Sharp considered for a moment, then said, "Dilley, take a look around down here while we're upstairs. I don't want anything happening while my back is turned." He gave Jonah an innocent smile. Gesturing at the stairs, he said, "Shall we go?".

From inside the supply closet, Jason heard the two men as they climbed the stairs. Apparently Jonah had been unable to keep the soldiers together; that complicated things. As Jonah and the sergeant proceeded past the closet and on to the apartment, he heard Jonah mumble, "Now, let me just get this unlocked." Raising his head just above the boxes, Jason watched them disappear into the dimly lit suite, leaving the door open behind them. When they could no longer be seen, Jason seized the moment and moved as quietly as he could to the stairs. As he crept downward he found to his relief that there was no one around, but froze when he heard voices coming from the next room. The dining room door had been left open so Jason slowly eased closer, pressing himself against the wall to stay out of sight.

From the depths of the dining room, he heard Courtney's voice saying, "Through there is the storeroom and the garage. I've got my ambulance parked there for now."

"I'd still like to see for myself." answered a man's voice. Jason heard the door to the storeroom open and as he peered around the doorframe he saw Courtney and Brodie follow one of the soldiers into the storeroom and toward the ambulance. Courtney held Jonah's duffel bag in one hand as she closed the door behind them.

To Jason's relief, this left the dining room empty. He crept inside, searching for a place to hide until he could get to the ambulance. He found that the room offered very little cover, but after a moment he remembered the narrow closet along the far wall which held the cots from the night before. Opening the door, he carefully climbed over the folded beds inside before pulling the door closed once more and listening intently for his chance.

After what felt like an eternity, he heard the storeroom door open once more, followed by footsteps which crossed back through the dining room. As they continued on into the lobby, Jason's beating heart marked the seconds as he waited until he was sure they wouldn't return.

As quietly as he could, Jason opened the closet door and peered out. In front of him, the dining room was only dimly lit; they had turned off the lights as they left. Holding his breath, he emerged from the closet and made his way to the storeroom door.

Inside the storeroom, the interior lights of the ambulance were on, giving the room a yellowish hue. Ignoring this, Jason hurried to the back of the vehicle and climbed inside. He then let out a strangled scream as Brodie's voice came to him unexpectedly from the front compartment. She shushed him emphatically and climbed over an awkward hump in the floor to join him in the rear of the ambulance.

"Jesus, shut up!" she said, holding a finger to her lips. "Here, we've got to put you in this." She unfolded something large and black from its packaging, and Jason knew without asking that it was a body bag. He hated everything about this idea, but he clenched his teeth and let her help as he wriggled his way into it. Once inside, Brodie helped him to lay down on top of the padded gurney. As she zipped the bag up over his face, he tried to dismiss the notion that this would be the last thing he ever saw.

He lay there in tomb-like darkness as he waited for something to happen. Brodie spoke near his ear, her voice a loud whisper. "My mom gave me the code to start the ambulance. She and Jonah are going to keep the Army guys busy while we get the fuck out of here. Hang on." He felt her pat what she must have thought was his shoulder, then climb back into the forward compartment. He heard the driver's door open and a rustling sound told him she'd gotten out of the vehicle. He was confused until he heard the rattle of the garage door opening and felt the ambulance sway gently as she got back in. There was a clicking sound as she entered the ignition code, and then a high-pitched whine as the ambulance's systems came online. The vehicle lurched sharply, causing him to reflexively grip the gurney's rails from inside the body bag and soon he recognized the sounds of tires against pavement; they were in motion.

A minute passed, then Brodie called out to him, raising her voice to be heard over the vehicle noise. "We can talk now; we're out." she said. "Mom told those fuckers from the Army that I'm taking the ambulance back to the hospital for her, so we're free to go. Jonah said your plan was to take the bus back to Aberdeen, so I set our destination as the bus station on the north side of town. I'll buy you a ticket, and you can ride the bus home."

Jason felt odd talking from inside the bag, but forced himself to answer. "Aren't there supposed to be checkpoints everywhere?"

"Yeah, there are, but I have a plan for that." she answered. He could hear the smile in her voice and it worried him. The ambulance swayed slightly from side to side as they took a corner, and he chose to concentrate on not getting seasick. They drove on in relative silence, leaving Jason alone with his thoughts.

After a while he felt the ambulance slow and heard Brodie tapping at the navigation controls. "What's going on?" he asked as the vehicle came to a stop. "Checkpoint?"

"Not exactly." she said. "You know those riots we heard about? We just found one."

Jason fumbled with the zipper on the bag, managing to get it open part way. His left arm twinged with a ghostly residual ache as he propped himself up and carefully peered out the window.

About a block in front of them a group of protesters had erected a barricade built of trash, rubble and anything else they could find, using it to mark their battle line. They stood behind the makeshift wall in loose groups, chanting and yelling at the soldiers who had lined up across from them on the other side of the intersection. Many of them wore bandannas covering their faces, but their exposed skin and hair hinted that most were Hispanic.

They cheered as someone approached from the back, pulling a cart piled high with wood and scraps of metal siding that had been pulled from a nearby building. The wood was used to shore up the barricade while the siding was fashioned into makeshift shields that were quickly distributed among the unruly crowd.

As Jason watched, the protesters' chanting grew louder and he could feel the tension began to build. There was a commotion near the front line as someone hurled an object across the gap toward the troops. The missile fell short, but all eyes watched as it hit the road and shattered into pieces.

On the other side of the intersection the Army troops stood in ordered ranks; each soldier wearing heavily padded armor and carrying riot shields. Armored military vehicles idled behind them, ready to be brought to bear. Even at this distance Jason could see how the race, ethnicity and color of those involved defined the conflict. The protesters were brown, while the soldiers were White. The troops were all Caucasian because non-Citizens weren't allowed to join the Army, and the Hispanics were protesting because no one would listen to them. The government had broken its promises and now the Army had been brought in to keep these people in their place. There was no overlap between them and it was a microcosm of everything wrong with this world.

At a shouted word from their commander, the troops tensed visibly. Jason got the sense that action was imminent and he didn't want to be here when it happened.

"Can we go around?" he asked Brodie.

Brodie tore her eyes from the protesters, brushing a strand of purple hair out of her face and refocusing her attention on Jason's question. "Shit. Yeah, I think so." she said, and began to access the ambulance's navigation interface. A map of the local streets appeared on the screen and she traced a finger along a route from their current location, turning down an alley and along a side street. In response to her instructions, the ambulance began to move along the path she'd laid out.

As they turned west, the red-orange sun was blocked by the buildings as the ambulance navigated down the alley. The shadows deepened, then retreated again as they emerged and made a right-hand turn onto an adjacent city street. Overhead a section of the pneumatic tram tube cast a strange semi-translucent shadow onto the pavement.

They drove slowly north but the scene they now faced wasn't any better than the one they'd left behind. The street in front of them was strewn with debris and the people they found looked bewildered and beaten; the aftermath of a riot. Everywhere military vehicles rolled implacably forward, water cannons spraying seemingly at random. White clouds of smoke drifted close to the ground. Jason couldn't tell if it was tear gas or smoke from fires set by the protesters.

Here and there, a few people had managed to regroup and were trying to fight back. Someone stuffed a rag into a bottle and lit it from a torch; a molotov cocktail. The man threw the bottle against an approaching armored truck where it shattered and spread fire over the windshield. The truck was unfazed and kept rolling slowly forward while the roof mounted water cannon knocked the man brutally to the pavement. All around them, Jason could hear a cacophony of sirens, shouting, and wailing.

In the midst of the chaos, Brodie found a path. She leaned back in her seat so Jason could hear her, saying, "Okay, I think we can get through here but you probably should get back down just in case. You don't want to be seen."

Jason lay back onto the gurney and wriggled his shoulders as he pulled the body bag back up around him. The zipper was difficult and caught a few inches from the top, refusing to go any further; it would have to be good enough. Beneath him, the gurney jolted and the world tilted slightly around him. He was about to ask what was going on when the ambulance's siren blared loudly to life. The piercing tri-tone note rose and fell, the pattern changing unpredictably. Over the siren, he heard Brodie shout, "Hold on!", followed by a severe rocking and bumping. The motion calmed quickly, but the shrieking siren continued unabated. In the darkness of the bag, he could just make out the high-pitched whine of the ambulance's motors as they began to pick up speed. Brodie had been silent for a while now, and he began counting his heartbeats as he tried to mark the passage of time. When he reached 250, he called out, raising his voice to be heard over the siren.

"Did we make it through?" he shouted.

"Mostly." Brodie called back, her voice nearly drowned out. "There are still a few army vehicles around, so I'm gonna keep running the siren. I should be able to turn it off in a minute."

Jason realized that she was using the siren in the hope that no one would dare stop them. Maybe it would work; as long as the siren was on, they looked like they were racing to an emergency call. He was actually kind of impressed.

"Good idea about the siren." he told her.

Brodie accepted the compliment graciously, then said, "I think we'll be okay for now. My mom works for Samaritan, which is in the southeast part of the city. As we get further north, hopefully no one will look too close."

Jason forced the zipper on the bag back down, trying to get some air. He considered, then said, "Keep the siren on and drive fast. Maybe no one will look twice if they have to get out of the way."

From the opening in the bag he saw Brodie smile and reach down to toggle the speed limiter off. "Way ahead of you." she said as the ambulance sped up. After a moment she pulled out her micro and frowned. "Fuck. I forgot the network is down. I wanted to see if I could get any info on where the riots are; see which roads are open."

"Just do your best." he said, struggling to be heard over the siren's wail.

The noise level inside the vehicle made continued conversation difficult, so the two of them spent the rest of the trip in relative silence. Twice they encountered military checkpoints, but the siren worked as they had hoped and each time the soldiers waved them through without question. Eventually Jason unzipped the body bag further and stretched, working his arms and shoulders free before sitting up and swinging his legs off the gurney. Minutes ago, he had felt the vehicle change direction and now, through the window, he could see that they had slowed. Brodie sat in the front compartment, studying the electronic map unhappily. When she saw that Jason was watching her, she sighed and pushed a button to bring the ambulance to a halt. As the vehicle pulled over, she angled the navigation display toward him.

"We're fucked." Brodie informed him bluntly. "The Army is all over the bus station. They must be using it as a goddamn command post or something."

Jason was confused. "How do you know? I thought the network was down." he asked.

"Because I fucking saw it!" she replied acidly, her frustration flaring. She pointed to a thin gray line on the map. "This is the road we were on a minute ago. See how it goes right to the station?" Jason nodded, seeing the line approach the bus station from the south. An orange line showing their path was overlaid on top of the gray one. This line made a left turn a block before the station and continued west a short distance before ending at their current position.

"I saw their damn tanks or whatever parked out front." she continued, looking even more pissed than usual. Jason studied the screen and saw that the northwestern part of the city was defined by the river which flowed through it heading west. A large city park took up most of the riverfront along the southern bank.

"Could you get me to the river?" he asked. He realized to his own surprise that he was thinking of walking back to Aberdeen.

Brodie stared at him, not understanding. "Yeah. Why?" she asked cautiously.

"I can hike. One way or another, I have to get home." he said, standing up in the cramped space. As he did so, his foot struck something soft. He reached under the gurney and pulled out the duffel bag that he'd seen Jonah packing back in the apartment. He looked questioningly at Brodie, but she shook her head.

"Jonah said it was yours." she said simply.

He'd seen Jonah stuff a variety of clothing and food into the bag. Had Jonah realized what would happen? After the Army took over The Center, maybe Jonah knew they'd probably be at the bus station too. Somehow he'd guessed that it might come to this and had done what he could to help. When this was all over, Jason knew he would owe Jonah a big favor.

Brodie drove the ambulance to a secluded area along the river. Carrying the duffel bag in one hand, Jason fumbled open the rear door of the ambulance. Once outside, he went around to the driver's compartment and rapped on the window to signal to Brodie that he was ready. Brodie mouthed "good luck" as she waved goodbye, then turned to the controls and the ambulance drove away. In the silence that followed, Jason took a deep breath and stepped forward into the woods.

****

Jason woke up on a bed of dry, brittle leaves with the unyielding red-orange sun filtering down through the tree branches. The spare shirt he'd placed over his face to block the light had slipped off and now lay on the ground above his head. He groaned and pulled it back into place.

The darkness returned, but after a moment he was forced to acknowledge that he was irrevocably awake. He lay still, trying to relax and ease the stiffness in his legs and feet. He hadn't stopped walking since he left Cosmopolis. Outside the city he had skirted farmland for hours, staying out of sight. Eventually the landscape had transitioned into forest, with uneven terrain under foot. He no longer had to worry about hiding, but the going became more difficult. He had been thoroughly exhausted by the time he lay down to sleep.

He pulled the shirt from his face, uncertain how long he had been asleep. The position of the sun in the sky offered no clues; it remained fixed in the same place it had been when he went to sleep. After some thought he guessed that it was probably Tuesday morning. Assuming he had walked for a full day yesterday, that meant that he still had another day's travel left to go.

He had spent Monday largely following the Cosmopolis River as it flowed toward Aberdeen. The river's course curved and wandered, so where he could, he had strayed from the riverbank and cut through the woods in as straight a line as possible. So long as he didn't get lost, taking shortcuts like that would help shorten his trip.

Groaning, he sat up, leaving a deep depression in the duffel bag he had used as a pillow. His stomach growled, prompting him to rummage through his supplies for one of the meal-bars that Jonah had packed. He chewed it absently, ignoring the dry, gritty taste. When he was done, he made his way down to the riverbank and filled an empty can with cold water, then added a tablet which fizzed as it quickly sank and dissolved. The tablet would neutralize the heavy metals and other poisons in the water, rendering it safe to drink. When he was sure the tablet had done its work, he raised the can to his lips and took a long drink. The water still had an odd taste, which he sincerely hoped wasn't from toxins the tablet had missed. Most likely it was because the can had previously held last night's dinner.

His thirst slaked, he stood and stretched to loosen his joints for the journey ahead. His calf muscles were almost painfully sore, so he braced himself with his hands against a nearby tree, keeping his left foot planted flat on the ground. He counted to sixty, then reversed his feet and stretched the other calf. Afterward, he wasn't sure he felt any better, but decided that it would have to be good enough.

He was traveling light, so breaking camp was simple. He'd turned the duffel bag into a pillow by removing all the hard or lumpy objects; now, he simply reversed the process. He was ready to go in under two minutes.

He set out again, continuing to follow the river's westward flow. He'd only been hiking for a short time when he noticed a patch of gray stone through the branches ahead. He smiled; he'd hoped to come across a Pueblo. He had no way of knowing if this was the one he'd seen from the bus window, but it could have been. He approached it curiously and quickly discovered that only a single wall of the structure remained. Made from two large stone slabs, time and erosion had not been kind and now they leaned precariously, as if ready to fall.

The Pueblo ruins were the last remains of some alien civilization that had vanished thousands of years before humans ever came to this world. As a kid he'd been fascinated and had read everything he could about them, but really almost nothing was known for certain. A few sharpened stone points and the Pueblos themselves were all that had ever been found. There were no bones or fossils, and no hints of a written language or even any carved images. Who they were and where they had gone remained an enigma locked in the planet's deep past, offering few easy answers.

Jason stepped reverently among the stones, trying to imagine what life here had once been like. The mystery pulled at him. The rubble and dry leaves crunched under his boots, the only sound in the forest until a distant echo of thunder pulled him back and he reluctantly stepped out of the ruins.

The thunder had come from a bank of dark clouds to the east, back toward Cosmopolis; that was good. Through the white leaves above and to the west he could still see reassuring wisps as thin clouds drifted eastward. Hopefully the storm would stay behind him. Using the river as a guide, he once again set course toward home.

Hours later, he was forced to stop and rest his feet again. The new boots were good, but they could only do so much. He sat down on a wide stump and pulled off the boots and socks. His shirt had stuck to his chest and he plucked at the thin fabric, pulling it free. The humidity had only gotten worse as he hiked, and he welcomed the opportunity to rest. He sat, watching as the trees slowly swayed in the breeze.

The trees which grew around him were skinny and widely spaced, while the stump he sat on was old and damp. He guessed that the tree it came from had been cut down maybe ten or twenty years ago. Dozens of black stumps just like the one he sat on dotted the forest floor here and lumps of something like a white fungus grew on them, burrowing beneath the decaying bark. This whole area had once been clear cut, but was now recovering. The young trees growing here were spread thin, but they too would eventually have their day. It was the circle of life on this planet. He pulled his boots back on and began to once again push himself over the uneven landscape.

He lost track of how long he'd been hiking. For hours the river or his footfalls were the only sounds in the forest, but he stopped suddenly as that all changed. The noise he heard was a high percussive whine, followed by the snapping of branches. It echoed around him, followed by a slow motion *WHUMP*. It was the sound of trees being felled and it meant he was nearing Aberdeen! He might even know the men cutting the trees, but he quickly decided to stay hidden. He didn't need that kind of attention right now; he had to get home.

The sound seemed to be coming from along the river, so he climbed a rocky hill and skirted around the area instead.

This added distance and time to his journey, but he kept going and rejoined the river once he was past the logging site. As he did so, he found a muddy logging road that paralleled the river and made eager use of it, following it down out of the hills. The relatively smooth surface allowed him to make much better time, but even so he remained cautious. Every twenty minutes or so a large truck would emerge from the woods behind him, carrying logs back to the yard to be milled. As the trucks passed, Jason ducked into the pale brush lining the road and hid until they were gone. After an hour, the mud finally gave way to pavement and the town of Aberdeen came into view.

Once in town, he no longer had much chance to hide. Instead he hoped his changed appearance would be enough to allow him to escape notice. He felt naked out in the open, but it would have looked even more suspicious to be darting behind bushes and sneaking past mailboxes. He brushed the mud and dirt off his clothes as best he could and tried to appear nonchalant as he went, holding his shaved head high. It seemed to work, as no one paid him any attention as he walked through downtown, past the library and on to the residential parts of town.

With his feet aching, he finally reached his neighborhood. He forced himself to put one foot in front of the other and keep going. At last he turned onto the street where his small house stood and his heart sank; the porch light was off and he could see that no one was home. He wanted nothing more than to get inside, to sleep in his own bed, but with Anne and Matthew gone it suddenly didn't feel like a victory.

He stood at the foot of the small path which led to his front door, uncertain what to do. He could still get inside using his passcode, but he was more worried about his family. Where were they? His heart raced as horrible possibilities flooded his mind.

With an effort he pushed back the fear; it wouldn't help him. He needed a plan. Maybe Mateo or Pablo would know what had happened to his family? Their houses weren't too far away. He turned and began walking back the way he'd come. After two blocks he shifted direction and walked along a side street, past a series of houses that were smaller and rougher than his own.

He'd been on the go for so long. He let his eyes close for a moment and fatigue hit him like a wave. He had been walking for two days straight, and he suspected he wasn't thinking clearly. He needed a place to rest. Maybe... An idea arrived fully formed in his head. If he hadn't been so tired he never would have considered it, but suddenly he knew where he should go. Less than a block later he made a left turn onto a small dead-end street.

When a work site was too far from home, the logging company would sometimes rent small mobile trailers for their employees to stay in. Among the loggers themselves, these trailers were known as campers. The campers were cramped and uncomfortable, and only offered basic facilities; a bed, a toilet, a tiny kitchenette and a table. There just wasn't room for much more. They were only meant to be used as temporary shelter, and years of hard use over rough terrain quickly wore them out. At the end of their useful lives, the campers were often sold and rebuilt. Refurbished and improved, they were bought as homes by those who couldn't afford anything more.

The homes lining the small dead-end street Jason now walked had all started their lives as campers. Ahead of him the street ended in a tangle of off-white bushes and weeds. Regretting his decision with every step, he finally stopped in front of the last camper on the left. He considered knocking on the thin door, but in the end he decided against it. He was exhausted, and didn't want to have this particular encounter without his wits about him.

Behind the camper he could see a shoddily built shed and even from the street he could see that the door didn't close properly; he decided to risk it. As he crossed the yard to the shed he furtively watched the camper, but didn't see anyone behind the small windows. As quietly as he could, he opened the shed door and went inside.

The shed had no windows, but with the door closed light shown through numerous cracks in the structure. After a minute his eyes began to adjust and he was able to make out the clutter which dominated every available space. In the end, there was only just enough room for him to lay down on the floor, provided he curled up a bit. He set down the duffel bag and converted it for pillow duty. Ready to collapse, he laid his head down and was asleep almost instantly.

He woke the next morning to a loud grinding sound, followed by an electric whine as an old privately owned car came to life somewhere nearby. Jason was pulled from the depths of slumber, listening as the sound slowly receded into the distance. He shifted uncomfortably on the floor, desperately needing to pee but not wanting to get up. He struggled against the inevitable and tried to think; was it Wednesday now?

Losing the battle with his bladder, he stood and peered cautiously through the door before darting behind the shed and relieving himself onto the ground. Afterward he went back inside to gather his things, regretting his decision to come here. Unfortunately, it was too late to change his mind now.

He stepped back into the yard and heard a creaking sound from the camper as someone moved around inside. Well, he thought, time to get this over with. He felt a small knot in his belly as he went to the camper's door. He hesitated, then knocked quietly, as if he hoped no one would hear. A moment later the door was opened and he stood face to face with an older man. His iron gray hair held only hints of the black it had once been, but the scowl on his brown lined face was the same as he remembered it.

"Hi Dad." Jason said.

CHAPTER 11

It was the morning after the attack on the bazaar, and Anne had woken up alone for the first time in years. She wandered through their home, feeling lost. It was Sunday; she always did housework on Sundays, but now she found it hard to concentrate. The world seemed to swim around her, just out of reach. The events of yesterday played over and over in her mind. The bazaar and shopping; the confusion as the crowds started to run; the officer's face as he told her that her husband was a murderer. Everything was blurred, as if she'd only seen it from the window of a moving car, but it was all she could think about.

When she got up, Matthew was already in front of the video screen, but as she entered the room she saw that it was turned off. Matthew's eyes were red; he had been crying, but he tried to hide it when she came near. She hugged him, then sent him off to get some breakfast and get dressed. While he was gone she busied herself with little things. She hardly noticed when Matthew sidled past her and went outside.

An insistent beeping drew her attention. She found she was sitting in a chair at the dining room table, with a mop leaning against the wall. She didn't remember getting it out and the floor was still dry. The beeping began again and she realized it was an alarm she'd set so that she wouldn't forget lunch. She heard the front door open and close, and for a moment her heart leapt. Jason's name was on her lips, but died when she saw Matthew turn the corner. She swallowed her husband's name without speaking it.

"Can I make you a sandwich?" she asked instead, putting the mop away.

Matthew shrugged, going to the refrigerator and getting a lunch pack. "I'll just have this." he said, and pulled the seal off the top. Inside was some sliced fruit and a yogurt cup, along with some crackers. Anne's stomach rebelled at the sight of it; she wasn't hungry.

"What have you been doing?" she asked.

"I went over to Mark's house. He and I just kind of walked around the neighborhood."

"See anything good?"

"Not really." he said. "There were some guys in trucks driving around. We saw them yell at some people, so we stayed off the street."

The revelation frightened her; The Latino Resistance Front was using her husband's image to push their rebellion. Was this some kind of response? "I don't want you going outside for a while." she said. "I'm not sure what's going on, but I want you to stay here." Matthew didn't argue.

Later, when Matthew had gone into his room to play, she checked the local newsfeeds on her micro. There was nothing new, but she did see an opinion piece written by someone she didn't recognize. The title was "Citizens Against Violence", but the content preview read, "In the past 24 hours it has become obvious that the Hispanics we have taken in only want to hurt us and our children..." She didn't have the stomach to read the rest. She set the device down next to her on the couch and closed her eyes. A moment later she was startled when the micro chimed with an incoming call. The icon on the screen showed it was Jason!

Almost unable to believe it, she picked the micro up and accepted the call. "Jason?!" she breathed. Her tongue felt thick and her voice seemed to catch in her throat. "Are you okay? What's going on?"

On the small screen Jason looked exhausted, but his tired smile was wonderful. "I'm fine." he said reassuringly. "I don't have much time. I just needed to know that you and Matthew were alright."

"We're okay," she told him, "but we saw the police alert! You were holding a gun! Did you..." She couldn't finish the question. She knew it wasn't true, but needed to hear him say it.

He answered quickly, knowing what she was asking. "No. I didn't shoot anyone or blow anything up. It wasn't me." Anne's heart swelled. It was everything she needed to hear.

Jason glanced briefly to the side and then back. "I'm sorry, for all this. I just had to see you." he said. He frowned apologetically. "Look, I need to go. Tell Matthew that I love him. I love you, too." he said.

"I love you too." she echoed. She didn't want to end the call; it would be like losing him all over again. After a moment of awkward silence, she blurted, "Don't go!"

On the screen Jason paused, needing her as much as she needed him. "I'm coming home." he swore. "I don't know how I'll get there yet, but I am coming home."

She heard the unshakable vow in his voice. He would do it, no matter what. "We'll be waiting." she said. "I love you."

"I love you too." he replied, and then the call ended. She stared at the blank screen as the realization sank in; Jason was coming home! Through all of her worry and anguish, she smiled. "Matt, come here!" she called loudly. "I just heard from Dad!"

The mood at dinner that night was almost light. They smiled and laughed, still feeling stressed but daring to be hopeful. Afterward Anne and Matthew passed the time playing something they called the Dictionary Game; one person would secretly choose a word, reveal the first letter, and then read the definition. The other person would try to guess what the word was. It was a simple game, but it was one they had often played together as a family. It felt good.

When it was time for bed, Matthew brushed his teeth while Anne sat on the couch reading. Her finger slid over the micro's screen, turning the pages lightly. As she began another chapter, the machine chimed loudly, startling her. Her stomach tightened as a news alert appeared on the screen. There had been another bombing in Cosmopolis, this time a bridge. In that instant her fears came rushing back. Had Jason been there? She had no way of knowing.

Matthew came out of the bathroom in his pajamas, and Anne quickly darkened the screen. She didn't want him worrying when there was nothing they could do. Her son saw the look on her face, and could tell that something was amiss.

"What's wrong, Mom?" he asked.

"Nothing, honey." she answered evasively. She pulled Matthew down to the couch beside her, and he curled up on the cushion. His lithe body was warm and alive as he snuggled against her and they stayed like that for a while. A few minutes later though, the silence was broken again by the micro, and she felt a flash of anger at it. She reached over to turn the device off entirely, but Matthew leaned over her shoulder and read the message on the screen.

"Martial law?" he asked curiously. "What does that mean?"

Anne read the alert carefully before answering. It seemed that the governor had issued an order mobilizing the Army, sending them into Cosmopolis to help keep the peace.

"It means that the government is going to use the Army as police." she said. It wasn't exactly right, but it was close enough.

Anne's father and grandfather had both been in the Army, but this order felt wrong somehow. She wanted to trust the government to do what's right, but she also knew that many people did not share her optimism. Hispanics especially carried a deep distrust of the Army. The government claimed that the Army was kept on Ross b to help explore the cold, dark side of the planet, but to the Hispanic community their role was to keep Latinos in their place. On some level, the governor's new martial law decree seemed to prove their point.

Matthew seemed to consider her answer for a moment, then gave a non-committal, “Huh." Anne powered the micro off and hugged her son close.

“Why don’t you go to bed; I’ll see you in the morning. It’s school tomorrow, for the both of us.” she said. Matthew groaned loudly, but smiled up at her. After one last squeeze he disappeared down the hallway and she rose to get ready for bed herself. After all, she had school tomorrow too.

It was early the next morning when the car dropped them off at the shared campus. The schools consisted of three similar buildings, all built close together on the same patch of flat ground. As Anne and Matthew entered the courtyard, she patted her son’s arm as they went their separate ways.

They had arrived a little early, and Anne knew that she had time to get some prep work done before the students arrived. She entered the building and made her way through the halls to the staff room. Inside was a refrigerator, and also some scissors, a die cutter, paper and other supplies. Anne put her lunch into the fridge and then began to gather a stack of thick colored paper.

She was stacking sheets of orange paper together for the die cutter when she heard the door open. One of the second grade teachers had stopped halfway through, with her mouth hanging open. Anne said, “Hi...”, but the woman was gone before she could say anything more. Anne returned to her work, but a strange sensation crept up her spine. She had arrived at the school early, but even so there should have been other teachers in the staff room by now. With a dread certainty, she realized that everyone must have seen the announcement from The Resistance. They had seen her husband branded as a terrorist. Suddenly she felt very self-conscious; was everyone going to treat her like this?

She finished her task and carried the stack of die-cut shapes back to her classroom. On the way there, she only passed a few people in the halls. When she offered a greeting, she got a stiff ‘hello’ in return, but nothing more. No one seemed to know how to talk to her, or even wanted to. The specter of Jason and the attacks were just too much, and they poisoned everything. She understood their fear, but it hurt all the same. She entered her classroom and closed the door behind her. Class would begin in twenty minutes, and she wanted to be ready.

The students arrived and the morning passed quickly, which helped to keep her mind busy. As she took attendance, Anne realized that her few White students were among those who were missing. She didn't comment on it, just recorded the absences and moved on. She let the busy day keep her mind occupied. She taught reading, then writing, followed by a short recess so the kids could play outside. After that came math and she started the lesson, building on last week's material.

Just after ten o'clock there was a knock at her classroom door. She opened it to find the principal, Mrs. Connolly, standing there. Her blonde hair was pulled back into a severe bun which seemed to stretch the skin on her face tight. "Mrs. Menounos," she said, avoiding eye contact, "these men need to see you for a moment." For the first time Anne noticed the two police officers standing in the hall.

"Of course," Anne replied, worried about her husband, "but I don't have anyone to watch the class at the moment. Would you mind...?" She gestured toward the classroom, and Mrs. Connolly nodded and stepped through the door, closing it softly behind her.

Anne turned to face the police officers. "What can I do for you?" she asked. Behind them, she noticed a face watching from the classroom across the hall. It vanished from the window almost as soon as she looked, leaving her to wonder if she had imagined it.

"I am Officer Shale, this is Officer Anderson. We need to ask you a few questions in private." one of the men said. "Mrs. Connolly said we could use her office." Anne nodded, and followed Officer Shale as he led the way. Anderson took up a position behind her. She wondered if that was merely coincidental, and decided probably not.

She felt as if she were on parade. They were marching her through the school, and though the halls were conspicuously empty, she was certain that everyone was watching. Upon reaching the office, Officer Shale stood aside and let her open the door. She took a seat at the large desk while the two men remained standing. The walls around them were adorned with inspirational posters and a variety of quotes from the Bible, the Vedas, and Martin Luther King Jr. Shale and Anderson projected a faint air of intimidation, and the decor suddenly seemed very out of place.

Shale took his micro from his belt and consulted the screen for a moment. Looking up from it, he said, "You received a call yesterday." He wasn't asking.

Anne's blood ran cold. They knew. Of course they knew. "Yes, I did." she agreed, her mouth suddenly very dry. She carefully clenched her hands in her lap to keep them from shaking.

"Who called you?" he asked. Anne could tell he already knew but was giving her a chance to make a mistake; to catch her in the act. She wondered if telling only most of the truth was still a lie.

"It was Jason; my husband." she said. She felt lightheaded.

"Now, I've spoken to Lieutenant Putnam in Cosmopolis. He told me that you are required to let us know if your husband attempts to contact you. Do you remember that?" There was a hint of something dangerous in his voice. Anne couldn't quite tell what it was, but she had no other choice and pressed ahead.

"Yes, I do. I was going to call you after school today." In her head, she quickly readied the rest of the lie. *I got up late. I was busy getting my son ready for school. I simply haven't had the time yet.*

"The tracking on the micro network shows that the call originated near a tram terminal in west Cosmopolis. Did he say anything about what he was doing there, or where he was going?"

"No." she answered, almost truthfully. "He just called to make sure we were alright." He'd also said he was coming home, but Anne didn't volunteer that information. Surely they already knew.

Shale lowered his micro and looked up, letting the device hang loosely in his hand. "I'd like you to provide us with a copy of the call." he said. Anne was confused; couldn't they just pull a copy from the network?

Shale must have seen the look on her face and spread his hands in a calming gesture. "With the martial law decree, the networks in Cosmopolis are locked down and re-routed for military use. I've submitted an official request for a copy of the call, but frankly we aren't their top priority right now. This will all be a lot simpler if you could just give it to us yourself."

Anne nodded almost imperceptibly as she understood what they were asking. Privately, she found it almost funny that the martial law decree was making this harder for them, but suddenly she saw that it also gave her an opportunity. She pulled out her micro and began scrolling through menus. "Just a minute. Let me find it." she said. Subtly, she held the device so that the screen was hidden from their view. Then, as quickly as she could, she brought up the call and moved it to the editing toolbar. From there she jumped to the end of the recording and scrolled backward, swiftly highlighting the section she wanted to remove. She then snipped the recording, deleting the last 19 seconds of the call. She then saved the modified file and sent it to Officer Shale's micro.

Shale's micro chimed as the file arrived and he queued up the call. He watched the recording, and Anne listened carefully for any mistakes, hoping she'd done it right. Jason's voice sounded thin over the small speaker, saying, "...tell Matthew that I love him. I love you, too." Then her own voice answered, "I love you." as the file ended. She held her breath as she waited to see how the two men would react.

Officer Shale tapped a button to save the file, then clipped the micro back onto his belt. “Thank you for your help.” he told Anne. “You can go back to your class now; we’ll find our own way out." With that, he and Anderson departed, leaving the door open behind them. Anne stayed seated for a moment, trying to slow her heart. ‘Well,’ she thought, ‘there is no going back now.’ She tried to feel strong, as if she hadn’t just doomed her family by lying to the police. She forced herself to put on a neutral expression, ignoring how thin it was. She just hoped it would be enough to get her through the rest of the day. She stood and walked through the long halls back to her class.

At the midday recess, Anne stood near the school while her students ran wild, playing in, on, and around the playground equipment. The weather was good, with a slight breeze blowing her hair, and for a moment it felt wonderful; a break from the stress of the day.

After a while it became obvious that Sandra, the other kindergarten teacher, was not going to bring her students out to recess. This happened occasionally, but Anne couldn’t help but wonder if today it was because she was out there. She looked at the red-orange light reflected off the distant hills and pushed the thought away. After this morning, her only goal was to make it through the day. Nothing else mattered.

A distant bell announced that it was lunch time over at the middle school. Her own school’s lunchtime had been 30 minutes ago, and her kids only had another five minutes to play. Across the playground she could see a small group of students playing rough. She began to wander that direction, ready to step in if needed.

Her attention was focused on watching the group of rambunctious children, so when she felt a tugging at her sleeve she jumped, momentarily startled. She bit back a few choice words, and turned to see who had pulled at her coat. Her brow knitted in confusion as she saw that it was Matthew.

She calmed herself and asked, "What is it, honey?" He had walked across the campus, away from his own school and no one seemed to have noticed. The realization troubled her.

"Mom, I want to go home." he said miserably. From the way he avoided looking at her she could tell that this was more than feeling ill. She put her hand on his forehead anyway.

"Are you getting sick?" she asked.

He hesitated, then said, "No, I just want to go. Everyone is acting weird."

Anne was silent for a moment. She was pretty sure she knew what he meant; she'd felt it too. "People don't want to talk to you?" she guessed.

"Yeah, but it's not just that." he said. She could see his frustration in the way he clenched and unclenched his hands. "The White kids..." he started. She knew that everything on this world seemed to come down to race and ethnicity, but it still hurt deeply to see her son affected by it. "They're being mean. Not just to me, but to the Hispanic kids too. I saw someone trip Marco in the hall and shove him against a wall. No one did anything about it."

Anne was suddenly very much aware of the color of her son's skin. She wanted to help him; to keep him safe, but she didn't have many options. "Do you think you can make it through the day?" she asked quietly, caressing his black hair with her pale hand.

"Even the Hispanic kids won't talk to me." he went on, seeming not to hear her. "Nicholas and Penelope said 'Hi' but they didn't sit with me at lunch. Everyone just stared at me."

Anne's heart ached. It sounded like his day had gone about as well as hers had. "For now, go back to class." she told him soothingly. "I'll see if I can get the rest of the day off, and I'll come get you if I can."

Matthew nodded, agreeing silently. He hugged her, then started back toward the middle school. Anne watched him until he was out of sight. Suddenly remembering her students, she checked the time and muttered, "Shit." under her breath. She'd let recess go on too long. Quickly, she called the children together and lined them up. Then, as a group, they filed inside.

Once everyone was back, it was time to send them to music class. Again Anne lined the students up at the door, and the music teacher arrived just as they finished. After a brief greeting, he led them away down the hall.

The children wouldn't be back for 35 minutes, and it was finally Anne's prep period. Normally she would use the time to set up for the next lesson, but instead she went off to find the principal. She had a few hours of personal time coming to her and she hoped to take the rest of the day off. It would let her pull Matthew out of class, and she suspected that everyone would be happy to have them gone anyway.

As soon as she stepped out of her classroom, however, she heard, "Anne, do you have a moment?" Principal Connolly stood in the hallway, only a few feet away. Her hair was still pulled back tightly, though a few stray hairs floated free around her head. Anne held the door open for her, and together they went back inside.

Anne sat on the edge of her desk and seized the opportunity to speak first. "I was actually just coming to find you..." she began, but trailed off as she saw the serious look on Mrs. Connolly's face.

The principal hesitated, choosing her words carefully. "Anne, I'm sorry to have to tell you this." she said, keeping her tone professional. "You've been a good fit here, and you have been good with the students. But this morning's visit from the police has made it clear that your husband is going to be a distraction." That might be true, but Anne could also hear her unspoken words. *You are a distraction too. We don't know what to do with you. Are you working with your husband? Are you guilty too?* Mrs. Connolly swallowed, and went on. "I need to ask you to take some time off; at least until the situation with your husband is resolved." she finished flatly.

Anne's throat was tight, but her eyes were dry. To her

surprise, she felt cool and empty. “Are you firing me?” she asked.

“We’re suspending you.” Mrs. Connolly clarified. “Until the situation with your husband is resolved, you are to remain off-campus.”

“You’re firing me, then.” Anne said, nodding as she stood up. Somewhere in her subconscious, she suddenly felt free. She took a few steps, her mind racing. “The students are with Mr. Marcab in music class." She pointed to the display monitor on her desk. “My lesson plans for the week are filed, so you should have no trouble there." She felt it was important to tell her everything she could think of about the students; this wasn’t their fault. The principal at least had the grace to look uncomfortable as Anne went on, outlining anything she thought needed attention.

After a minute though, Anne’s thoughts ran dry. She looked around the classroom, realizing that she had personally bought almost everything in the room except the desks. A part of her hated to leave it all behind, but she was suddenly done. It was over. Without even saying goodbye, she walked out the door. Her shoes clicked against the tile floor as she made her way down the hall to the exit.

Over at the middle school, Anne walked resolutely past the front office and continued on to her son’s class. It was just after one o’clock, and she knew he would be in the science lab. She reached the door and knocked. A moment later the teacher, a confused man in his late 50’s, answered the door. He recognized her and called back over his shoulder to Matthew. Anne saw her son scoop up his micro and walk hurriedly to the door. Without speaking to anyone, mother and son left the school campus together.

On the car ride home, Anne couldn’t bring herself to tell Matthew that she’d been fired. Ruefully, she guessed he’d figure it out when she started staying home more. Still, she didn’t plan to send him back to school tomorrow. She needed time to think; they both did. What was their life going to be like from now on?

The car took them through a middle class neighborhood, and they saw a large home with two empty police cars stopped out front. They didn't see the officers, but the home's front door hung open. A few people stood in the street, keeping their distance but clearly curious. Anne noticed that the bystanders stood in two different groups, separating themselves by skin color. It was hard not to see it as a microcosm of everything that was going on. As the car carried them past, she caught a fleeting glimpse of a brown-skinned man being led out of the home with his hands cuffed behind his back. They disappeared into the distance before she could see anything more.

At home, Anne struggled. As the day ended, she lay in bed unable to sleep. Her mind was numb, but it also clung to the thought of seeing Jason again. She lay there a long time, and when her alarm sounded in the morning, she couldn't say whether she had slept at all.

Tuesday morning felt strange. For the first time she could remember, she had nowhere to go and no schedule to keep. In some ways it felt like a weekend. Matthew played games on his micro for a while, then later they sat in front of the living room screen and watched a few programs. When one ended, they would switch to another. She let Matthew choose the shows, but as he flipped from feed to feed, they would sometimes catch part of a news report before moving on. It seemed that Cosmopolis was tearing itself apart. There were some peaceful protests, but there were also riots and bombings. The Army was doing its best to keep order, but it was doing it at gunpoint. She tried to push the images of violence from her mind as she prayed that Jason was okay.

She was napping in her room when the chime came. She jolted awake, confused for a moment in the darkened room. The noise came again, louder this time, and she realized it was her micro. She bounded out of bed and picked the device up from the dresser. Hoping Jason was calling, she accepted the call without even looking to see who it was.

"Anne?" a female voice came. Anne shifted the micro, changing the call to video mode. A woman's face appeared on the screen, with brown skin, and a thin pointed chin.

"Valarie!" Anne said. Valarie was Mateo's wife. Anne remembered that Mateo had been arrested along with Jason for fighting at The Rooster. As a non-Citizen, he was still in jail. Mateo and Valarie had been good friends to her and Jason, and she was glad to see a friendly face.

"Anne, I'm sorry, but I didn't know who else to call." Valarie said. She sounded distraught and her image kept moving, sometimes putting her out of frame.

"That's fine; what's wrong?" Anne asked, becoming concerned.

"There's some sketchy looking guys driving around the neighborhood." Valarie explained. "They're going around harassing and threatening people."

It sounded like the same group Matthew had seen around their house on Sunday. "Do you want us to come over?" she asked.

On the small screen, Valarie nodded. "Yes, please." she said, sounding relieved.

"We'll be over as soon as we can." Anne assured her and ended the call. She used her micro to summon a car as she called out to Matthew. "Matt, get your shoes on. We're going to go visit Valarie."

The car carried Anne and Matthew sedately through the neighborhood surrounding Mateo and Valarie's modest home. Along the way they didn't see anyone out in the streets, threatening or otherwise, but Anne still felt better coming to check on her friend. They needed to stick together and support one another, now more than ever.

The car parked itself in front of the house, and Anne and Matthew went up to the door. Valarie cut hair out of her home, and the small porch sported a cheerful sign that directed her customers around to the rear of the house. Anne knocked instead on the front door and after a moment Valarie answered. She was dressed in a baggy white shirt and black pants, and her curly hair hung wildly around her face. Her eyes were rimmed with red, but she smiled when she saw them.

"Come in!" she said gratefully. Once they were inside, she quickly closed and locked the door behind them.

Though Valarie's home was small, it was well decorated. The end tables sported white lace doilies and displayed cherished family photos held in gilded frames. Mateo and Valarie had met in high school and had been together for years before getting married. A collection of their wedding photos hung prominently on the wall across from the sofa. The smell of baking cookies filled the air, and Anne's mouth began to water in spite of herself. Making an effort to be a good hostess, Valarie got them all some tea as they sat down on the sofa. As they made conversation, Matthew began to look increasingly bored, slouching into the overstuffed cushions.

Mateo and Valarie had a daughter about Matthew's age, and Anne suddenly wondered where she was. "Where is Arabelle?" she asked, concerned.

"She's in school." Valarie said. "She should be home soon though."

Anne blushed; she should have known that. "I pulled Matthew out of school yesterday." she explained apologetically. "I guess I forgot what day it is."

"That's okay. I understand." Valarie answered quickly. Anne realized that her friend hadn't yet asked about Jason, though she must have seen his face on the news. What did she think? Did she think he was a terrorist? A freedom fighter? Just an innocent man? Anne wasn't sure she wanted to know and as the conversation moved on, she decided not to bring it up.

A short time later they heard the front door open as Arabelle returned home from school. The girl froze for a moment when she saw Anne and Matthew, but relaxed when her mom asked, "Aren't you going to say hi?"

Arabelle nodded to them shyly before slipping away

into the kitchen. They heard her squeal excitedly upon seeing the cookies, followed by silence. Anne guessed the girl had gone to her room.

In the living room, Valarie suddenly noticed something through the large picture window. Anne followed her gaze out to the street and saw a converted truck with an open bed rolling slowly through the neighborhood. It was the kind of vehicle the logging company would use to ferry supplies out into the woods. Three men stood in the back, holding on to the frame for balance. Their faces didn't look friendly and the truck seemed to take forever to move out of sight.

Anne looked at Valarie with sympathy in her eyes. "Are those the same guys you saw before?" she asked.

"Yes." Valarie confirmed. "They've been by at least four times today. Earlier, they caught my neighbor while he was outside. They yelled horrible things at him, and threatened to run him over with the truck. They said this was '*their town*', whatever that means. They only left when the police showed up."

Anne thought about the men that Matthew had seen in their own neighborhood. The world was turning ugly everywhere.

"Do you want us to spend the night here? In case they come to the door?" Anne asked, leaving unspoken the hope that her fair skin might be an advantage in dealing with them.

Valarie smiled and nodded, almost in tears. "Yes!" she said, the word coming out in a rush of air.

"Okay." Anne agreed. "Where do you want us to sleep?"

The guest bedroom was done up in lace and pastel colors. Matthew looked embarrassed to even be in the room, but the bed was comfortable and that seemed to compensate for the decor. He and Anne shared the large bed without complaint, and Anne drew the blinds on the window to block the light. Together they lay in the darkness and waited for morning.

CHAPTER 12

Jason's father had been a logger his entire life. It was a tough way to make a living; tougher even than working at the mill as Jason had. The old man had once been tightly muscled but time and retirement had softened him, and his still tanned skin now hung loosely from his frame.

While his father's given name was Lawrence, Jason couldn't remember anyone ever calling him that. He was always just Larry. As Jason entered the camper, he took in the false wood paneling and the clutter strewn around the camper, and he couldn't imagine anyone named Lawrence living there. The detritus of a lifetime was stacked on every available surface, and there was a faint sour smell in the air. A few empty beer cans were scattered on the small table, along with an unwashed bowl. Larry didn't seem to notice the mess, as if it had been there so long it had become invisible to him.

When the camper had been converted for use as a stationary home, it had gained an addition that could only be generously called a living room. The added area measured a modest four feet by five feet, and held a video display tilted toward a small chair. Somehow, the additional space managed to only highlight the claustrophobic nature of the camper.

Jason saw that the video screen had been left on, though the sound had been muted. The program it showed was a newsfeed from Cosmopolis, focusing on the riots. As the image shifted, he saw a street filled with protestors, with written commentary and a series of alerts scrolling along the bottom of the screen. His father ignored the silent program as he cleared off a chair for Jason near the cluttered table. Jason took the offered seat while his father turned the camper's only other chair away from the video display and sat down in it heavily.

"Well, don't see much of you these days." Larry began, then coughed. "What have you been up to?" The old man paused and Jason caught a glint in his eye. "Do I need to call the cops?" Larry asked, gauging his son's reaction.

"I'd rather you didn't." Jason answered carefully. He loved his dad, but knew that explaining this would be tricky. "So, I guess you saw the broadcast? The one with my picture?"

Larry nodded. "I saw it. Nice picture by the way. Very 'Che Guevara'." he said, making a reference that Jason didn't follow. Larry paused, looking his son up and down. "You know, I think you looked better with hair." he said finally.

Jason ran a hand over his scalp self-consciously. It had been several days since he shaved it and the stubble there now felt like sandpaper. He tried on a smile but a frown quickly took its place. "Dad, you know I didn't do it, right? I couldn't do that." he said earnestly, but his father was already nodding, dismissing his concern with a wave of his hand.

"I know. We may have had our differences, but I know this wasn't you." Larry reassured him. On the newsfeed, people were now marching in the streets and carrying signs. The Army watched them impassively with rifles held rigidly across their chests. Larry waved a hand at the display. "It's these fuckers. They poison everything." he said, blaming the protestors.

The view changed suddenly, and now showed masked men brandishing improvised clubs. As one, they charged forward, battering themselves against a line of soldiers in riot gear. One of them got in a lucky hit and a soldier went down. The rest of the soldiers closed ranks immediately, protecting their fallen comrade. Larry sighed, shaking his head sadly. "You see how our people act? They're like animals."

'Our people'... Jason was quiet for a moment as he absorbed the latent self-loathing contained within that state-

ment.

"Dad, Matthew did a project in school last week." Jason began softly. His father looked at him expectantly, waiting for him to continue. "He built a family tree. The school gave him a DNA test too, so that he could trace the family further back." At the mention of a DNA test his father looked concerned but Jason pressed on before he could interrupt. "They didn't find anything." he said. "There was no Hispanic DNA."

His father seemed to sink into himself. He could see the old man weighing this new revelation against his whole life; the family story, the secret shame, the harassment due to his skin color, Citizenship or not. Jason himself had lived through much the same thing and knew what it was like. Despite the struggle though, the truth never stood a chance.

"I don't buy it. I know what I know." Larry said firmly. He had believed these things his whole life and being told something different now wasn't going to change his mind. Jason felt off balance, as if he'd thrown a punch that didn't connect.

"Okay." he said awkwardly, letting the issue drop.

An uneasy silence followed, and Jason's eyes began to wander around the small camper. The clutter had an organic quality to it, as if it had always been there. Near one of the small windows he found a single framed photograph. It was an old image of his parents standing together in a field or park, and they both looked young and happy. That had been a long time ago; Jason's mother had left Larry shortly after Jason graduated from high school. Jason had kept in touch with her as best he could, but she had always asked that he keep it secret from his father. Last he heard she was living in Hoquiam, on the other side of Cosmopolis.

Jason glanced back at his father and was again struck by how tired the old man looked. The weight of the passing years had fallen heavily on him, and Jason began to worry that if he stayed here much longer it would cover him as well. He took a deep breath and sat forward in his chair. "I can't stay long, but I was walking by and had to stop in. You've been okay?", he asked, changing the subject and trying to work toward a graceful exit.

His dad smirked and seemed to draw himself up. "I'm too ornery to keep down." he said with mock bravado. After a moment he deflated and gave Jason a small smile. "I'm glad you came. You should do it more often, if you can." he said, trying to hide the tremor in his voice.

"If I can." Jason agreed. He nodded toward the screen, still reporting on the trouble in Cosmopolis. "Look, Dad. I'm sorry, but I've got a lot of things to take care of. I need to get going."

Larry nodded sadly. "I understand." he said. "Once you get this sorted out, let me know. I'll buy you a drink."

Jason smiled, "Thanks, Dad. I love you."

"I love you too son." Larry answered awkwardly, and stood to push the door open. Jason sidled past him and stepped out onto the hard packed dirt. The old man waved a brief goodbye before letting the door bang shut again.

Blinking in the red-orange sunlight, Jason adjusted the duffel bag on his shoulder and began walking back toward the main road. At the intersection he paused, then decided to check one more time whether Anne and Matthew had returned home. He began walking back toward his house, his feet only aching a little.

As he walked along the street, Jason kept to the side of the road to avoid any cars. His feet straddled the division where the pavement met the dirt and gravel alongside it, giving his steps an alternating *pat, crunch, pat, crunch* rhythm.

It had been a quiet morning, so when he heard the sound of a motor and noisy tires on the road behind him, Jason drifted further to the right and began to walk entirely on the unpaved shoulder. When the vehicle slowed without passing him, his heart began to race. Was it the police? He turned his head to look without reducing his pace.

Instead of a police cruiser, he saw a dirty and abused

truck. The vehicle pulled in front of him and then came to a stop in front of a green house with a short white fence. Three men jumped down from the back and began to saunter menacingly toward him. They didn't seem to recognize him, but they were definitely looking for trouble. Jason stopped walking, keeping his hands visible.

"Hi." he said, keeping his tone bright and friendly. "Did you need something?"

Another man, slightly shorter than the others, climbed down from the truck's driver's seat. His blond hair had been combed diagonally across his head but a faint breeze caught it and blew it across his face. He absent-mindedly flipped it back up and out of his eyes as he walked toward Jason. His right cheek was red and showed a hint of a developing bruise.

"We were just gonna ask you the same question." the man said, his voice a mix of condescension and threat that Jason found very easy to understand. "We're out here patrolling. Lookin' for troublemakers." He spread his arms out wide, taking in the whole world. "With everything that's going on, we've got to keep our streets safe."

Jason stayed focused on the blond man but kept the others in his peripheral vision as they spread out, taking positions on either side of him. The blond man took a few steps forward.

"Now, from the look of you, you might be trouble. I'm gonna strongly suggest that you get off our streets. Now, roach." he ordered in a disgusted voice.

'Roach', huh? That was a new one. Jason felt adrenaline tighten his gut. "I'd like to." he said. "My house is just a few blocks that way. I'm headed there now." He knew they weren't going to let him go, but there was a form to these things.

"No you're not." the blond man retorted harshly. "You don't live here. This is *our* town."

Jason's feet were kicked out from under him and he fell back hard, the impact knocking the air from his lungs. He gasped, struggling to regain his breath. The four men loomed over him and he curled up as one of them kicked him viciously in the ribs. He tried to cry out, but just couldn't seem to breathe. The blond man hung back as his friends kicked Jason again in the stomach. Jason closed his eyes, helpless to stop them.

"Hey!" came a shout, followed by the commanding blast of a gunshot. The men kicking Jason stopped and whirled to face the new threat. "Get the fuck out of here!" the voice ordered them, moving closer. Jason unfolded slightly and opened his eyes. He saw a Caucasian woman with short brown hair in dirty coveralls standing near the gate in the white fence. She was aiming a shotgun at his attackers. Suddenly submissive, they held their hands up and walked backward toward their truck. She held the gun on them until they drove out of sight.

When they were gone the woman came over to Jason. "You okay?" she asked, offering him her hand. Jason took it and was surprised at the callouses he felt there. Despite the stained coveralls, the woman was surprisingly pretty, with large green eyes in a face lightly smudged with grease. Jason exhaled painfully and let her help him up.

"I think I'll be okay." he said, wheezing slightly. His back hurt and he expected his ribs would bruise, but nothing felt broken. "Thanks for your help."

The woman nodded, her gun pointed down at the ground. "Those assholes have been making trouble ever since the riots in Cosmopolis started. They're trying to keep anyone like you," she waved her hand up and down at him, "scared and in your place." She frowned. "Look, you really should get off the street if you can. Where are you going?"

"Just a few more blocks. I live on Juniper Street."

"I'll let you go, then." she said. "Those guys have been 'patrolling' every couple hours. After this, they'll probably be back sooner." With that, she walked back through the gate, calling out, "Good luck." before she entered the house, leaving

Jason standing bewildered on the street. Ignoring the ache in his ribs, he started again for home.

****

When Anne woke the next morning, Matthew was already out of bed. Her shirt and pants had twisted during the night, with the folds leaving red lines on her skin. Uncomfortable, she rolled out of the overly plush bed and tugged her wrinkled clothes back into place.

She used the toilet in the hallway, then crept into the living room, rubbing the sleep from her eyes. Valarie was slumped in an armchair with her eyes closed while Matthew and Arabelle sat on the floor in front of the sofa, watching something bright and colorful on the video screen. The volume was low but she heard a distinctive "P'KUCK!" and looked just in time to see Kung Pow Chicken attack a confused pig.

Her brain was still fogged with sleep but something just didn't feel right. She should be at school... no, she was done with that now; Matthew too. But what about Arabelle? She glanced at Valarie's softly snoring form and decided not to wake her. Anne took a seat on the sofa instead and watched the cartoon with the kids.

After a while, Kung Pow Chicken seemed to win his war against the pigs and the program took a break. The children paused it, then got up and went to the kitchen. The noise seemed to wake Valarie and, seeing Anne on the sofa, she smiled and sat up in her chair.

"Good morning." Valarie said, greeting her in a voice thick with sleep.

"Good morning." Anne replied. "You didn't sleep there, did you?"

"No, I got up with Arabelle and came out here with her. Matthew joined us a few minutes later." Valarie blinked rapidly, forcing the sleep from her eyes. "Thank you for staying here. Every time a car passed last night, I woke up terrified."

"Do you need any help getting Arabelle ready for school?" Anne asked, but Valarie shook her head.

"I thought about how you decided to keep Matthew home. Until this blows over, I think I'm going to keep Arabelle home too. I don't want her out of my sight right now."

Anne nodded in agreement. "I understand. It's weird out there right now." She shifted on the cushions and frowned down at her rumpled clothes. "After breakfast, Matt and I are going to go back home and get some fresh clothes. Do you want to come with us? We could use the company."

"That would be great." Valarie said. She pulled herself up from the chair and stretched. "How do you feel about french toast?"

****

After breakfast Valarie used her micro to summon a car. It wasn't scheduled to arrive for a few minutes but they all waited outside anyway, breathing in the fresh air and enjoying the mild breeze. Anne was relieved; on some level she had felt trapped inside and it felt good to be under the open sky.

To her left, Anne heard the sound of a vehicle coming down the road and froze when she recognized the same truck that had been circling the neighborhood yesterday. Her anger rose and she held her ground as the truck came closer. Valarie and the children subtly moved behind her.

Menacingly, the truck began to slow, then came to a stop. The driver, a man with blond hair combed across his head, got out and swaggered toward them while three other men jumped down from the back of the truck and joined him.

"Hello there." the blond man said, talking past Anne to Valarie and smiling obscenely. "Whatcha doing?" Behind the children, the summoned transport car pulled up quietly and parked in front of the house. No one looked at it.

"We were just leaving." Valarie said stiffly, gathering the children close to her. Anne moved to put herself between the man and Valarie.

"That's a good idea. Don't come back." the man said, and spat on the ground.

Valarie's lips moved silently, at a loss for words. Finally she found her voice and said in cold fury, "This is my house! Get off my property!"

The blond man didn't back away. Urged on by his friends, he slowly walked forward. Anne's hands balled into tight fists. "What are you going to do about it?" he said to Valarie, taunting her as he came closer.

Anne swung hard, hitting him with everything she had. Her fist connected solidly with his cheek and his head snapped to one side. He staggered back a step, raising his hand to his cheek. Anne was disappointed; she'd been aiming for his eye. "Bitch!" he exclaimed, rubbing the injury. His friends were suddenly at his side, and they began to circle her.

At that moment, a neighbor's car turned the corner and began to drive past the house. "Hey, Ryan..." one of the blond man's friends cautioned, pointing it out. The car slowed, watching the confrontation.

Grudgingly, Ryan decided he didn't want an audience. "Come on." he said to his friends. As they stalked back to the truck, he turned and shouted to Anne and Valarie. "This isn't over! Count on it." With that, they all got in the truck and left. A moment later, the car in the street sped up and drove away without stopping.

Anne massaged her hand gently as she turned back to Valarie and the kids. Matthew stood with his mouth open while Valarie and Arabelle looked shocked and scared, the daughter a mirror image of her mother.

"Let's get going." Anne said quietly, and everyone piled into the waiting car without another word.

As the car neared Anne's house, Valarie finally spoke. "That was bad." she said.

Anne nodded, not knowing what to say. She could see the fear in Valarie's eyes. "Do you want us there again tonight?"

she offered. “In case they come back?”

“Yeah, I think so.” Valarie answered, but her concerned expression didn’t fade. “What are we going to do?” she asked in despair, not expecting an answer.

Anne leaned over and hugged her close. “We’ll stick together.” she said, hoping it would be enough. A small jolt signaled that they had reached their destination and Anne released her. With heavy hearts they climbed out of the car and went inside.

****

Hope flared in Jason when he saw the empty car parked in front of his house. A dark silhouette slid past the window and he couldn’t hold back anymore; his walk became a run. Upon reaching the front door, he heard the bell chime as the system alerted those inside that someone was there. It seemed to take an eternity but eventually there was a click as the door was unlocked. And then it happened; he was finally face to face with Anne, the woman he loved. Anne stared at him in shock, then whispered, “Jason?”, not believing her eyes. He smiled and pulled her close, hugging her tightly and not wanting to ever let go. His tears welled up as he held her.

“I’m home.” he whispered.

CHAPTER 13

Matthew was in his bedroom when he heard the commotion at the front door. Cautiously, he poked his head around the corner and then charged into the room as fast as he could.

"Dad!" he called, tackling his father around the waist and wedging himself between his parents. The reunited family held each other in a long embrace before Jason finally separated himself enough to close the door. He made his way over to the couch and sat down stiffly.

"Oooh..." he exhaled as the weight left his feet. Anne and Matthew sat on either side of him and Jason relaxed for the first time in days. Matthew ran a hand over the coarse stubble on his father's head and Jason smiled. He turned to Anne and said apologetically, "Sorry honey. I had to do it."

She smiled ruefully at his bald head, saying "It'll grow back." She was overjoyed to have her husband home, no matter how he looked.

They sat there together as a family, but after a moment Jason noticed Valarie and Arabelle were standing awkwardly nearby. He stopped himself from asking about Mateo, remembering that Valarie's husband was still in jail, and instead greeted them with, "Hi Val; hi Arabelle." Valarie and Arabelle returned his greeting a little uncomfortably and he waved for them to sit down in the remaining chairs.

Jason's ribs were still sore where he had been kicked and Matthew was eagerly leaning against him with sharp elbows. It hurt, but he didn't push his son away. It felt so good to be home. He closed his eyes, letting the feeling of relief wash over him. He knew it couldn't last, but right now he needed it desperately.

After savoring the moment for as long as he could, he forced himself to break the spell. He turned toward Anne and asked, "So how's it been here?"

Anne fell silent for a moment, uncertain how to answer. They had only been apart a few days, but so much had happened. "It's been tough." she admitted. "I pulled Matthew out of school on Monday; I quit my job too." Matthew looked up at his mother in surprise; he hadn't known that part. "And the trouble in Cosmopolis has caused problems here too." Anne explained. "Last night we stayed with Valarie and Arabelle because there were some guys harassing people in her neighborhood. They're still out there too; we had some problems with them this morning on our way over here. We were going to pick up some fresh clothes and then stay with her again tonight."

Jason looked at Valarie and Arabelle. He'd been friends with Mateo since middle school, and he'd known Valarie for almost as long. They'd become like family. "We can still do that." he said. Anne nodded, agreeing.

An unexpected chime broke the silence and everyone appeared confused for a moment as they tried to discern its meaning. Valarie checked her micro, but shook her head; the chime wasn't for her. Anne patted her pockets, then realized she'd left her micro on the kitchen table. The chime came again from across the room, confirming that the noise had come from Anne's device. She stood and walked over to get it.

When she returned, she was staring down at the device with a puzzled look on her face. "Hey, take a look at this!" she exclaimed. With a touch, she transferred the news alert on her micro to the video screen on the wall. The screen came to life, displaying an article with the headline '*Martial Law Decree Lifted*'. The article contained an embedded video and Anne started it playing.

A round-table style discussion group appeared, with

three people in suits gathered together and arranged to face the camera. A middle-aged woman, her obviously bleached hair pulled back into a tight bun, spoke first.

"Under pressure from civil rights groups and the federal government on Earth, Governor Halton has today lifted the martial law decree he imposed just three days ago. We now turn to our regular contributors Georgia Kneely and Kenneth Wright for comment."

Kenneth spoke first. "Thank you, Allison. I think this just goes to show how inappropriate Governor Halton's declaration was in the first place. Without even attempting to understand these people's grievances, he marched the Army into the city and used them to enforce his own agenda at gunpoint. It was never going to work."

Georgia made a face and began to reply even before Kenneth had finished speaking. "Ken, that is just wrong, plain and simple." she declared loudly. "We took these people in and gave them a home, and how do they repay us? With killings and bombings. You would have us show sympathy for these terrorists? They are animals! They have no concern for human life; there are even reports that some in the Hispanic community have turned on one another! There are places in the city where they have killed more of their own kind than Citizens! Ken, these people do not deserve our sympathy; they need to be stopped by any means necessary."

The two argued back and forth for several minutes, talking over one another without ever honestly addressing each other's arguments. Mercifully, it finally drew to a close and the host again addressed the camera.

"Well, right or wrong, the martial law decree is gone, at least for now. Cosmopolis Chief of Police Michael Edgars has issued a statement saying that his department is more than capable of keeping the peace now that the Army has pulled back out of the city. I'm sure I speak for everyone here when I say, I hope he is right. Thank you for watching, and we'll see you tomorrow."

Jason and the others stood motionless as the program ended, weighing what they had just heard. After a moment Valarie breathed out heavily. "Wow. I guess that's good." she said, but she didn't appear convinced. She hesitated, then looked at Jason out of the corner of her eye. Something was clearly troubling her, but she didn't want to bring it up in front of the children. Turning to her daughter, she said, "Arabelle, can you and Matthew go out back to play for a few minutes?" she said. Arabelle looked confused, but agreed. She and Matthew departed, leaving the adults alone.

Once the kids were out of the room, Valarie spoke hesitantly. "Jason, if you're going to be helping us, I have to know. Did you do it; the attack? Are you part of The Resistance?" Jason watched her choose her words carefully, and he couldn't tell whether she wanted it to be true or not. It dawned on him that he might be explaining the past few days for the rest of his life, and he didn't relish the prospect.

Resigning himself to it, he began to describe what had happened. He told Valarie about the shooting and the bombing; how The Latino Resistance Front had stolen his image and used it to spread their message. At first it was hard to find the words and he felt clumsy as he told the story, as if he were making excuses. He worried too that she wouldn't believe him; that no one would. To his surprise though, Valarie understood. She relaxed, and as the burden lifted, the words began to come more easily. He felt lighter, and once the children came back inside Valarie offered to fix them all lunch.

Jason and Anne went back into the living room to talk while Valarie stayed in the kitchen to make sandwiches. Their conversation was interrupted mid-sentence when they heard Valarie cry out in horror. Jason dashed back into the kitchen, followed closely by Anne. They found Valarie staring at her micro. She looked up at them, her face pale as she held the device out for them to see. The display showed Valarie's home monitoring system and a flashing yellow badge along the top of the screen showed that the system had seen a prowler. Valarie touched the screen again and brought up an overview of her home and property, with the camera and sensor locations highlighted. She selected a camera and an image of her front yard appeared. There, parked haphazardly across her walkway was a truck; *the* truck. One tire was propped up on the curb, and the dirt was churned up where the treads had dug into the soil. She quickly switched to another view, this one showing her front door. From there it was clear that the frame had been broken and the door itself hung open. Someone was in her home!

The screen blurred as Valarie began to shake. Jason couldn't tell if it was in anger or fear; perhaps both. She was being violated as they watched and part of him wanted to look away, as if he shouldn't be seeing it. Anne touched her arm, a look of determination on her face. "The car is still out front." she said.

They dropped what they were doing and ran to the door. Anne and Valarie got the car ready while Jason made sure the children were following. The five of them piled into the car, lunch forgotten on the counter. Jason slammed the car door while Anne set the navigation for Valarie's home. Slowly the car began to move and Anne frustratedly kept pushing buttons, trying without success to override the speed limiter.

In the back seat, Valarie cycled through her home's interior cameras. Theoretically, the system had already called the police, but she didn't have much faith they'd show up any time soon. Even before the events of the past few days, people like her were left to fend for themselves and that was unlikely to change now.

Valarie's house was now less than 15 minutes away, but it may as well have been across the planet. Beside her, the kids leaned over to see the screen. "Mom!" Arabelle cried out, pointing. They watched as the man with blond hair led his friends through the house. They all carried long pry bars and were using them to smash anything and everything. Windows were broken and family portraits lay where they fell, the frames destroyed.

Valarie watched in horror as one of the men went back to the truck and retrieved a portable welding torch. He brought it inside, then back into the bedrooms. He set the torch down and began ripping the linens off the beds and throwing them into piles. Then he lit the torch and used it to set the piles alight. As the flames rose, he stepped back and surveyed the rooms for anything else that might burn.

His friends had already made similar piles in every room and methodically each one was set on fire. The carpet beneath the pyres began to smolder lazily, resisting the flames as best it could while the air became hazy with smoke. On the small screen the men smiled and laughed, finally seeming satisfied. Valarie was powerless to stop them as they climbed back into the truck and sped off. Jason glanced at the car's navigation display; they were still two minutes away.

****

As the car came to a halt in front of the house, everything seemed fine at first. Then, slowly, the details began to sink in. The broken front door; the smoke beginning to escape through shattered windows; the soft yellow light of flames from deep inside. Valarie stood at the foot of her walk with her hand over her mouth, her shock not yet turned to tears.

Jason turned to the children. "Stay here." he ordered, and set out for the house at a run. The movement jolted Valarie into action, and she ran to follow him in. Anne started to come as well, but thought better of it. She returned to the car to keep an eye on Matthew and Arabelle.

Inside the house, bits of broken glass crunched under Jason's boots and the foul air reeked of smoke. The wall which had displayed Mateo and Valarie's wedding pictures now bore a wide scar of broken wood and plaster where they had hung. A pile of ashes lay at the base of the wall where a fire had burned and gone out, leaving a thick black smear which reached toward the ceiling.

Valarie arrived next to Jason and paused for a moment, overwhelmed to see her home in ruins. Jason looked around in a panic, trying to decide how to help. The smoke seemed thicker toward the back of the house and he heard a noise from down the hall as something shifted. He ran to the kitchen and began opening cupboards until he found what he was looking for. He pulled out a large cake pan and began filling it with water from the sink. Behind him Valarie turned and ran toward the bedrooms.

Trying not to spill, Jason carried the pan of water down the hall and to Arabelle's room. A glance inside showed charred embers but no actual flames, so he moved on to the master bedroom. The wood native to Ross b didn't burn very well and most of the fires the men had set had gone out, but the fire in the master bedroom was stubborn. It had been fueled by the linens from the bed and those burned much better than the wood. The carpet where the pile stood was charred and the ceiling showed an ugly black mark directly above it. Jason threw the water he was carrying into the flames, where it disappeared without much effect. He needed a better plan.

Valarie had watched Jason toss the water at the flames and understood the problem. She turned and ran from the room, leaving him alone. He was about to go back to the kitchen to refill his makeshift bucket when he heard a noise from outside the shattered bedroom window. As he watched, Valarie climbed through, avoiding the broken glass and pulling a garden hose in after her. Before she was even properly on her feet, she squeezed the handle and began spraying water toward the center of the room. The flames sputtered and fought, but after a moment they began to die back. She kept spraying until the cinders stopped sizzling and then sagged back against the wall, her adrenaline spent. She was shaking visibly, so Jason came over and hugged her for a moment. Releasing her, he said, "Let's go check on the kids." Valarie sniffed and nodded, wiping a tear from her cheek.

They emerged from the house in an exhausted daze and walked to the curb where Anne and the children waited. Jason grabbed Anne and pulled her close, putting his arm around Matthew as well. Beside them, Valarie hugged her daughter tightly. Afterward they leaned against the car, staring at the damaged home. The danger had passed, but it was obvious that nothing was okay.

For some reason Jason's thoughts eventually turned to Jonah and the outreach center. Even in the midst of Ross b's endemic injustice, Jonah had managed to create a safe place for people. There was nothing like that here in Aberdeen. Still, it gave him an idea that he couldn't shake.

"We should go to Cosmopolis." Jason said out loud. Anne looked up at him, uncertain what he meant. "We should all go. Valarie and Arabelle too." At the mention of their names, they turned to listen. Jason leaned forward, making his argument to all of them. "There's nothing left in Aberdeen for any of us." he said. "We could make a fresh start in Cosmopolis, and I met some people there who could help us get set up. It has to be better than staying here."

Anne was quiet, wondering what the future would hold if they stayed. She'd lost her job, or quit; whichever it was, she had nothing to hold her here anymore. She looked up at her husband and nodded, agreeing.

Valarie wore a haunted look. Like Jason, her whole life had been spent in this town, with these people. She frowned at the ruined house in front of them and realized that some of those same people had done this. The world felt like it had changed overnight. Her husband was still in jail, and Aberdeen just didn't feel like home anymore. "I need to call Mateo." she said finally. "To let him know where we're going, so he can find us when he gets out."

Jason hesitated. "Let's have a plan first." he suggested. "Don't call him until we know what we're going to do." Valarie nodded, reluctantly accepting Jason's advice.

Anne asked, "How *are* we going to get to Cosmopolis?" Giving her husband a rueful smile, she added, "You probably shouldn't take the bus this time, and I don't want to walk if we don't have to." Jason may have disguised himself by shaving his head, but public transportation was hardly a risk she wanted to take.

Jason pondered for a moment. "Could we take the car?" he asked hopefully.

Valarie shook her head. "No; I'm the one who called the car in, and I'm only registered for in-town usage. The nav won't even let me enter an out of town destination." she said, spreading her hands.

They were silent for a while, staring at the house. In the distance, they could hear the sound of traffic on the highway. The highway! Jason turned to Valarie. "Can you call Pablo?" he asked.

****

The day's light breeze had suddenly turned into something stiffer and now began to pull at their clothes. To get out of the wind, they entered the parked car and closed the door behind them as Valarie made the call to Pablo. When he answered, the small screen made his face appear pinched, as if he were squinting at a bright light. The sounds of the lumber yard around him echoed loudly, and an orderly stack of stripped logs filled the space behind him. Valarie carefully framed herself in the camera, keeping Jason out of view.

"Hi Pablo; do you have a minute to talk? It's kind of private." she asked.

"Yeah..." he answered distractedly. "Just a second." His eyes shifted away and the image bounced and moved as he found a quieter place to talk. After a minute the image steadied again and he turned his attention back to Valarie. "What do you need?" he said.

"You're alone?" Valarie asked, wanting to be sure.

"It's just us." he assured her, curious but starting to become worried.

Valarie tilted her micro and Jason leaned into frame. "Hi Pablo." he said.

Pablo's eyebrows rose and a whispered curse escaped his lips. The image shook again as he pressed even tighter against the wall behind him, eliminating any chance of anyone seeing Jason's face on his screen.

"Shit, man. Good to see you!" Pablo said in a heavy whisper. He smirked, then added, "I hear you've been busy."

Jason fought back a flash of frustration. He hated this; the assumption that maybe he *was* a revolutionary. He forced a tight smile and said, "Sorry, but that wasn't me." He stopped, not wanting to take the time to explain further. "We can talk about it later. Right now, I need to ask you a favor."

"Anything." Pablo answered without reservation.

Jason hated to drag him into this, but he had no choice. "We need to get to Cosmopolis." he explained. "It'll be the five of us; me, Anne, Matthew, Valarie and Arabelle." Pablo was quiet as he listened intently. "I'm hoping you could talk the shipping crew into taking us." It was Wednesday and the crew would be scheduled to pick up a shipment of logs to take back to Cosmopolis today. The timing would be tight, but they should be able to make it work.

Pablo hesitated. "That might be tough." he said. "The crew is here right now, loading up. They're supposed to head back to Cosmopolis as soon as they're done." He thought for a moment, then said, "I think I can switch with the driver, though; he owes me a favor. I'll take you guys myself. Can you be ready in about an hour?"

Jason felt relief wash over him. "We'll be there! Thank you." he said.

"No problem." Pablo replied with a smirk. "I'll meet you guys at the bridge on the way out of town."

"Sounds good." Jason said and nodded to Valarie, who cut the connection a moment later. He took a deep breath and leaned back. “It’s going to be tight, but this should work.” he said, trying to sound confident. His ribs still ached where he’d been kicked earlier and he rubbed at the sore spot absently. “Unfortunately, I don’t think there was anything left in the house we could use. From what I saw, all the clothes and things were burned.”

Valarie’s face fell as the realization set in that she’d lost everything. She started to speak, but something caught in her throat.

“You can borrow some of my clothes, at least until we can get you some new ones.” Anne offered gently.

“Thank you.” Valarie said, her eyes glistening. Beside her, Arabelle was pale.

Anne took the girl’s hand and said, “We’ll figure something out for you too. It’s only until we get set up in Cosmopolis."

She trailed off, the silence hanging briefly in the air. Anne gave Arabelle’s hand one last squeeze and said, “We need to get going." She reached forward and keyed a destination into the car’s navigation. They needed to hurry back to Jason and Anne’s home to gather what they could before they left. The vehicle pulled away from the curb, gently gaining speed.

****

Minutes later, the car rounded the last corner and accelerated toward its destination. As soon as they drew near, Jason and Anne both saw that something was wrong. Police cars lined the street on both sides, with a dense cluster of them parked in front of their home. Jason quickly ducked down and Anne overrode the navigation, causing the car to continue past the house without slowing.

Anne put an involuntary hand to her mouth as she took in the scene. The front door to their home had been forced open and officers in bulletproof armor were moving around inside. Outside, men in similar gear paced the small yard as they methodically searched the area.

Incredibly, the car made it by without drawing attention, leaving their home and the police vehicles behind. Anne pressed a key on the nav screen and the car turned left at the next intersection and headed back across town. After a few blocks, Jason cautiously raised his head, then sat upright in his seat. His breath came fast and he closed his eyes tightly for a moment. His chest heaved as he bit back an inappropriate giggle borne of stress and fear. Anne put a comforting hand on his knee.

"Well," Jason said, "it looks like we won't be able to bring anything with us either." He was quiet for a moment, then felt a cold pit form in his stomach. "Anne, do you still have your micro?" he asked urgently.

Anne nodded and pulled the device from her pocket. She handed it to her husband while giving him a curious look. Jason gazed back at her apologetically.

"We need to get rid of it." he told her. Anne realized in a flash; the tracking! The police could use the signal to find them.

"Let's pull over." she said, entering a command on the car's dashboard. She leaned back to Matthew and asked, "Matt, do you have your micro?" In answer, he held up his device. Anne took it from him and said soothingly, "We'll get you a new one as soon as we can, but right now we have to get rid of it." She wondered how much of this madness made sense to him, but he nodded in mute agreement. Feeling guilty, she handed Matthew's micro over to Jason.

The car came to a stop along the roadside as Jason locked the micros down and powered them off. Opening the car door, he stepped out and placed them on the ground. Then, as he'd done with his own micro, he proceeded to kick at them until they broke open, and then destroyed the sensitive electronics inside. Afterward, he swept the remnants into the ditch and got back into the car. Anne pressed another button and they drove away, leaving the broken devices behind.

****

The Cosmopolis River flowed along the northeastern border of Aberdeen and the highway crossed the river just outside the city limits. The riverbank held a small city park and the car dropped them off there before driving itself away. They only had twenty minutes until Pablo was to meet them, and the deserted park was as good a place to wait as any.

Above their heads the sky had turned gray and overcast, but it didn't look like rain yet. The breeze had returned, causing the branches of the off-white bushes to sway gently. Matthew and Arabelle found a small playground and together they climbed up to the highest point and sat down. It looked to Jason like they were talking, but he couldn't hear what they were saying. The adults sat on a bench nearby to wait and keep watch. Jason lay down with his hands folded over his chest, putting his head in Anne's lap. The sense of peace was intoxicating and he felt his eyes start to close despite the stress of the day.

When Valarie spoke, the sound of it startled him. His eyes fluttered open and he sat up, unsure if he'd actually been asleep. "How did the police know you were back in town?" she asked again, her brow furrowed.

Jason thought about it for a moment as his fatigue receded. "I don't know." he admitted. "I called Anne a few days ago but I destroyed my micro afterward. Besides, I was still in Cosmopolis then. They shouldn't have been able to track me here."

Anne raised her eyebrows in surprise. "That must be it!" she exclaimed. Jason and Valarie stared at her uncomprehendingly, so she elaborated. "The police came to see me at school. They knew you had called, but they didn't know what we said. They couldn't get a copy of the call from the network for some reason. They asked me to give it to them and I panicked! I cut off the part where you said you were coming home.

Maybe they got a copy of the whole thing somehow!" Her mouth hung open as she realized what that meant. “Now they probably think I’m part of the conspiracy or whatever too!”

Valarie frowned as she considered the implications. “I need to call Mateo at the jail, but I don’t want to lead the police here.” she said, obviously torn. She knew the risk but couldn't leave without letting her husband know where they were going.

Jason had a realization. “Wait, they’re just looking for me and Anne, right? They don’t know you’re with us, so they shouldn’t be tracking you. Just don’t mention us on the call; we don’t know who might be listening.”

Valarie agreed and took out her micro. Jason and Anne moved away, out of the camera’s field of view. When they were clear, Valarie placed the call. They listened as Valarie was connected to the police station and then negotiated with the desk clerk. After several agonizing minutes, she closed the connection.

Seeing their curious looks, Valarie explained, “I have to wait for Mateo to call me; he’s not allowed to receive calls from the outside." She waited, and after a few minutes her micro signaled an incoming call from the jail. Valarie answered it quickly and was relieved to see Mateo’s face appear on the screen. In the background a guard could be seen, monitoring the exchange. Clearly, Mateo had no expectation of privacy.

Valarie smiled warmly at the sight of her husband. “Hi honey!” she said, almost shyly. Mateo smiled broadly in response.

“Hi Val!” he said. He was clearly happy to hear from his wife, but didn’t feel like he could speak freely with the guard watching over his shoulder. She knew as well as he did the restrictions he was under and was sympathetic. After an awkward pause, Mateo said, “I talked to an attorney yesterday. She seemed to think I might be released sometime next week; after the hearing.”

Valarie nodded, wearing a strained smile on her face. "That's great!" she answered.

"Luis is still in here too." he continued. "He hasn't gotten to see the attorney yet. There's only one and her schedule is pretty packed. He told me that he'll probably get to see her on Friday." Mateo smiled thinly. "At least Jason got out of here quickly. Thank heaven for small wonders." he said. Out of sight of the camera, Jason frowned.

Valarie tensed at the mention of Jason's name. "Did you hear about what happened with him?" she asked, keeping her tone neutral.

"Yeah, I did! It's weird, right? None of us thought he was into that stuff!" Mateo answered. Jason caught the skepticism in his voice and was glad to hear it. "Actually it's been big news here. Earlier today Luis and I overheard a couple of the officers saying they thought that Anne was in on it too. They rushed out to their house but no one was home." The officer behind Mateo frowned. Sensing he was treading on sensitive ground, Mateo decided to change the subject. "So, what's going on with you?" he asked.

Valarie knew she had to tell him they were leaving but couldn't bring herself to do it. Mateo could see she was struggling with something, and asked, "Val, what is it?"

The words were caught in her throat, but finally broke free. "Mateo, someone broke into our house. They tried to burn it." she said. She saw the shock on his face and wished she had found an easier way to tell him.

"Jesus! Are you and Arabelle okay?!" he asked, leaning closer to the screen.

"We're fine." she said. "We weren't there when it happened. But I'm scared." Even on the small screen, Mateo's anguish was obvious. Valarie continued. "We're going to Cosmopolis. There's some people there we can stay with; people I trust to keep us safe." Mateo's mouth moved silently, at a loss for words. She tried to comfort him, saying, "I'll send you the address as soon as I can."

Mateo nodded, unable to speak. His eyes shone as he found his voice. "Tell Arabelle that I love her." he said softly.

"I will." Valarie answered. She started to touch his face on the screen, then pulled her hand back. On the verge of tears, she managed to hold her voice steady. "I love you." she said.

"I love you too." he answered. Knowing his time was up, he nodded to the guard who reached into view and ended the connection.

Valarie held perfectly still, as if she might fall apart if she moved. Anne came over and hugged her, holding her for a long time while Jason stood awkwardly a few feet away. At last Anne let go and stepped back.

"Well," she said. "I guess we're as ready as we're going to be. Now we just have to wait for Pablo and hope the police don't know where we are."

Behind her, Matthew and Arabelle had returned from the playground. From their looks, Jason could tell they had been listening. Matthew's young face was grim and Jason could tell he was terrified.

"Come here, son." he said, folding Matthew into his arms. "We'll get through this, one way or another." He held his son close and Matthew hugged him back fiercely. Anne joined in, wrapping her arms around them both.

It was almost time to go, and it wasn't long before they saw a large truck creeping down the short incline leading to the bridge, pulling a trailer piled high with logs. As it came closer, the truck slowed, then eased to a stop on the shoulder. As a group, the five of them left the park and walked over to meet Pablo, who climbed down out of the cab to meet them.

"Good to see you!" Pablo said, embracing each of them warmly.

"Did you have much trouble?" Jason asked.

"Naw." Pablo answered dismissively. "Michael was driving this run, and he owes me. I got the rest of the crew to stay behind too; said I was picking up my own crew." He looked at the assembled group. "I wasn't lying about that!" he said with a laugh. "Now come on. Let's get everyone inside."

Pablo shepherded them toward the truck, opening the door as they got close. The trucks which hauled logs to the spaceport were much larger than any car, but they hadn't been built with passenger comfort in mind. The oversized tires were nearly as tall as Matthew and sported rows of deep treads. The cab had been formed from sheet metal and the shape studiously avoided anything that could be called styling. The spartan design tucked the motor beneath the cab, placing the passengers several feet off the ground. A small ladder hung below the open door, offering a way up. The cabin contained two rows of bench-style seats and was roomy enough, if only barely.

Jason helped Matthew and Arabelle up into the cab, then watched while Valarie and Anne climbed in after them. He took one last sentimental look at Aberdeen, then pulled himself up as well.

CHAPTER 14

The first drops of rain appeared on the windshield only a few minutes after they set out, and the hydrophobic glass began shedding the drops almost as soon as they appeared. The wind pushed the beaded water aside easily, leaving only thin trails behind. Jason moved closer to the door, trying to make room in the seat for his son, who was wedged between Pablo and himself. Matthew's head was on a swivel, taking in the passing scenery as if he'd never been out of town before.

The cab had been designed to seat six, so theoretically there should have been enough room but somehow it still felt cramped. As the miles rolled by, they filled Pablo in, letting him know what they had been through the past few days. Pablo listened intently, all the more curious now that he was a part of it.

Valarie told Pablo how she'd been harassed and her house had been burned. Pablo's face darkened as she spoke, and he took a moment to call his boyfriend to warn him. Afterward, Jason told of the El Rey Latino Outreach Center and meeting Jonah Rodriguez. He explained how he had escaped Cosmopolis during the riots and how Jonah and the others had helped him. For her part, Anne told them of the horrible aftermath of the attack on the bazaar and how she had been fired from her job at the school. As she spoke, Jason's face turned red and he had to look away. This was his first time hearing most of the details, and he struggled to stay calm. He hated feeling helpless, and hated that he hadn't been there for her.

****

Eventually the buildings of Cosmopolis came into view, rising above the trees just as the rainfall began to ebb. To their left, the spaceport filled the landscape. The port was littered with warehouses surrounded by unitized shipping containers stacked in long rows. Launch towers for the shuttles dotted the tarmac, staggered and separated so that an accident at one wouldn't shut down the entire port. Jason leaned closer to the window, looking skyward and hoping to see the firetrail of a shuttle, but the sky was empty for the moment.

Pablo touched a key on the nav screen, telling the truck to pull over about a half-mile before they reached the spaceport gates. A few minutes later the heavy vehicle eased to a stop along a section of road lined with trees. The wind blew the pale branches, making them sway and revealing a clearing beyond them which opened toward the city. Pablo unlocked the doors and the small group climbed down out of the cab and onto the roadside. Though the rain had subsided, the soil had been saturated and their feet splashed in the puddles that still dotted the ground.

Pablo called down to them from inside the cab. "Good luck, you guys. If you need anything, call me. I'll do what I can."

Jason nodded his thanks. "How are you going to get all this unloaded?" he asked, pointing with his thumb at the stack of logs that filled the trailer almost beyond capacity.

"I'll get the dockworkers to help. They'll be pissed about it, but if they don't help they'll fall behind. I'll just tell them my crew got sick." Pablo finished with a chuckle, saying, "They'll probably think I'm running drugs or something! Hell, they'll probably want in on it!"

"Well then, good luck! We couldn't have done this without you. Thank you so much!" Jason called, stepping back from the truck. Everyone waved as Pablo closed the door and started down the road toward the spaceport. As the truck pulled away, he turned to Anne, Valarie and the children. By blood or by choice, they were all family now. Resolutely, he pointed through the underbrush to where the trees were replaced by a field of low, damp scrub, and said, "That's the outskirts of the city over there. Let's get moving."

****

It took almost a half-hour to push through the tangled brush and their clothes were wet up past the knees by the time they reached the city. They emerged from the pale thicket and onto the sidewalk through an empty lot and began to make their way out of the residential area they found themselves in. The sky overhead remained dull and gray but the breeze was warm and their clothes began to slowly dry. Jason hoped they didn't appear too out of place; that they simply looked like family and friends out for a walk. Cars had begun to pass by more frequently, and he judged that the regular workday must have ended and people were now heading home for dinner.

As they walked, Jason told them again about Jonah and the community center he ran. Anne and the children seemed hopeful, but Valarie appeared cautious. She quietly gestured for Jason to slow his pace, so they could talk without Matthew and Arabelle listening in. He did so, and Anne fell back with him, wanting to hear what Valarie had to say.

"What if Jonah isn't there?" Valarie asked, keeping her voice low. "You don't know what happened to him during the riots."

Jason breathed out heavily. "I don't know," he admitted, "but I think it's a good place to start. We'll check the outreach center first and if not, we'll think of something else."

Jason thought about mentioning the other community center he had heard about, but quickly decided against it. Jonah had thought they were tied to The Resistance, and Jason knew he couldn't bring his family there, no matter what. His expression darkened and he scowled for a long moment, lost in thought. Finally he returned to her question, saying, "Jonah is pretty much the only reason I made it out of the city before. He has good friends too. I'd bet he made it through okay."

Valarie had seen the shadow cross Jason's face and it didn't make her feel any more confident. Still uncertain, she turned to Anne and asked, "You grew up here, didn't you? Is there anyone you know who could help? Family, maybe?"

"Not anymore." Anne answered, shaking her head. "My parents have both been gone a long time, and my brother moved away a few years ago. I lost touch with everyone else when I moved to Aberdeen to start teaching."

Valarie still appeared wary, but decided not to push the issue any further. "Okay..." she said. "I just hope Jonah is everything you say he is."

****

The city around them eventually transitioned to a commercial area, with shops and kiosks lining the street. A savory smell began to fill the air and a short time later Arabelle spoke up. "Mom, can we get something to eat?" she asked. Upon hearing the suggestion, Matthew suddenly looked very interested and nodded enthusiastically.

Jason's own stomach growled at the mention of food but there was nothing he could do about it at the moment. "The outreach center is still a ways off, but if we push on until we get there, they should have something we could eat." he said.

"I could buy us something." Valarie offered. She was the only one of them who still had her micro, and this meant that she still had access to her money. "Tell you what," she continued. "I'll buy us something to eat and then we can get tram tickets so we don't have to walk all the way there."

Jason's stomach growled again, louder this time. He saw the looks his family were giving him and realized there was no way he could say no. They stopped at a small food cart, operated by a man in his early thirties, with Filipino features. As they approached, he greeted them with an incongruous drawl. The food smelled amazing and consisted of a selection of skewered items sizzling over a hot grill. Hungry and excited, they each chose something from the cart. Valarie completed the transaction as Jason eyed the 'food on a stick' in his hand. The man had called it isaw, and Jason had been afraid to ask the details. He'd always had an aversion to street food, and the thing in his hand did little to change his mind. Eventually however, hunger compelled him to try it and to his relief it was much better than he expected. The taste was hot and smokey, with a hint of vinegar and garlic. It was only afterward that he noticed he was the only one who got the isaw. Everyone else hid their smiles as they nibbled on more mundane looking items. Taking another bite, Jason thanked the proprietor and they walked on toward the nearest tram station.

A few minutes later they stood at the ticket kiosk while Valarie used her micro to buy them five tickets to the station on 1st street. When she was done they joined the group of people waiting on the platform and soon they heard a hiss of compressed air as the tram halted at the station above the street. They boarded and found a group of empty seats together near the back of the car. As the air hissed again and the car began to move, Jason was reminded of the last time he'd ridden the tram. Hopefully this day would turn out better than that one had.

Jason stared out the window, watching as the city passed by beside and beneath him. What he saw told the story of the past few days. There were areas where all of the windows for entire city blocks had been smashed and were now being boarded up. Walls that had been graffitied with protest slogans were now being painted over or washed away. Even the military checkpoints were in the process of being dismantled; some permanently while others were being handed off to the police. Everywhere he looked, it seemed that the city was in active denial. He was watching them sweep the problem under a rug, and the willful ignorance it showed left him shaken.

He fell quiet as he considered their next move. The last time he'd seen Jonah, the Army had evicted him and taken over The Center. The martial law decree that had allowed it was now gone, but he still didn't know for sure where that left Jonah. He hoped that Jonah had been able to return to The Center, but wondered what options they had if he had not. His thoughts again turned to the other shelter, the one that Jonah had said seemed somehow tied to the terrorist attacks. The city he saw outside the window was a fertile place for something like that to take root. If they were offering violence and revenge in the guise of help, it would be too much for some people to pass up, and the cycle of bloodshed would continue.

****

At last they approached the 1st Street station and the sprawling cityscape scrolling past the window slowed. The pneumatic tram hissed to a stop and the doors opened, releasing them onto the elevated platform. They descended to the street and Jason recognized the same worn buildings he'd seen there before, now marked by traces of the violence of the past few days. Keeping a watchful eye, he signaled to the others to follow him as he set off down the sidewalk toward The Center.

Fragments of glass and stone littered the ground, crunching under their feet as they walked. Clearly, the neighborhood around them had not escaped the riots. A small chunk of debris became lodged in the tread of Jason's boot and he kicked at the ground, trying to free it. It made a clicking sound as it came loose, bouncing and rolling until it came to rest near a patch of scarred and blackened pavement.

All around them, the buildings appeared wounded. The cafe he had seen just a few days ago was now boarded up, its windows shattered. The people they passed avoided eye contact and the atmosphere felt brittle, like an argument between lovers where one partner had gone too far. It was a dangerous feeling and it left Jason on edge.

Several blocks later they stood in front of the large gray stone building which housed the El Rey Latino Outreach Center. The traces of the riots were fewer here, though Jason didn't know if it was respect for The Center or fear of the Army which had protected it. There was litter on the steps, but the windows were intact. Hope bloomed as Jason saw lights on inside. Cautiously, he pulled the door open and they entered the building.

Instantly Jason could tell that the Army was gone, but their presence had left deep scars. The floor was marked and scraped where heavy objects had sat before being dragged away, and several holes had been left in the walls. Posters had been ripped down and now lay torn on the floor. He got the impression that this was more than just waste caused by a hasty order to leave; the damage seemed to have been done deliberately.

Despite this however, there was hope to be found as well. Everywhere he looked he saw people from the neighborhood taking stock and trying to push the mess back. It was an obviously heartfelt community gesture; people who usually depended on The Center for help were now taking the chance to give something back. The people laughed and talked as they worked, and the atmosphere in The Center felt light despite the wreckage left behind by the Army.

Jason and his family moved away from the door, letting it close behind them. They stood there for a few minutes, watching the activity around them in amazement. People who were too busy to stop and chat still smiled amiably as they passed. Finally Jason caught sight of Jonah, locked in conversation with a short, formidable looking woman.

Seizing the moment, Jason called out, "Jonah!". Upon hearing his name Jonah looked up, and there was no hint of surprise in his broad smile as he acknowledged Jason. Jonah briefly finished speaking to the woman, then made his way over to Jason and his family.

"Jason! Glad you made it back here! As you can see, we could use your help!" Jonah's expression made it clear he was joking; almost. "And who are these lovely people?" he asked, though it was obvious he had a pretty good idea already.

Jason made the introductions. "This is my wife Anne, and my son Matthew. These two are friends of the family; Valarie and her daughter Arabelle."

Jonah shook each of their hands warmly. "Welcome to the El Rey Latino Outreach Center." he said. "At the moment, we don't have much to offer, but what we do have, we gladly share." A quick series of chirps emanated from his micro and he glanced down at it briefly. "We're just about to break for dinner." he said. "Would you join us?"

****

Dinner was a communal affair, served on a collection of folding tables erected in the dining room. As word of food spread, over twenty people filed in, filling the seats to capacity. A crew of five men and women had been working to prepare the meal, using whatever ingredients they had available. As they laid the food out on the tables, Jason saw that it largely consisted of sandwiches and other simple items. They had clearly done the best they could with what they had, and the results were actually fairly impressive.

Jonah took a seat and invited Jason, Anne and Valarie to sit next to him. As they ate, Jason filled Jonah in on his escape in the ambulance and subsequent walk to Aberdeen. Anne and Valarie only listened at first, but eventually described the harassment they had experienced and the attack which had burned Valarie's home. In turn, Jonah told them what it had been like in Cosmopolis during the riots.

"After the Army moved in, I stayed with friends; Courtney and Brodie." Jonah explained. "The Army had set up checkpoints and they were patrolling the neighborhood pretty heavily, so we stayed put in their apartment for the duration. When the governor rescinded the martial law order, no one told me whether I could return to The Center, so I took the initiative and came anyway. When I got here, the Army was gone." He glanced at the damage around them. "They did leave their mark, however."

He fell quiet for a moment, frowning down at his plate. When he looked back up, he said, "Although the riots and the military checkpoints were bad, from what I've heard the worst of the violence wasn't done by protesters at all; it was gang related. Apparently one gang took the opportunity to slaughter another one and take over their territory. The police are far too busy to do anything about it, so I guess they got away with it." he said sadly.

Jonah sighed, looking exhausted, and Jason wondered when he had last slept. "The Army has almost completely pulled out of the city now." Jonah continued. "Most of the checkpoints have been removed too. A few have been left in place, but now they're manned by the city's police." He smiled tiredly, saying, "I guess that's an improvement. The people are able to move around more freely now, and there haven't been any new riots." He waved a hand at the wreckage littering The Center. "Now, all that's left is to clean up."

Jason saw the bags under Jonah's eyes and hated that what he had to say next would only add to his burden. "Jonah," he began reluctantly. "I need to ask a favor. After the attack on Valarie, we decided to leave Aberdeen. We're hoping you and The Center could help us to start over, here in Cosmopolis." He paused, searching Jonah's face for a reaction, but the man's tired countenance betrayed nothing. Jason continued to make his case, extremely conscious of The Center's limited resources, and that he was asking Jonah to expend those resources on a group of virtual strangers.

"I know it's a lot to ask, but I think it could be good for The Center too. Anne is a teacher, and Valarie can cut hair. We can all help clean up..." he trailed off as he could see Jonah considering his response. "I know I'm not Hispanic," Jason added, quietly pleading, "but we are absolutely willing to help out in any way you need."

The statement seemed to shock Jonah. He shook his head, his expression serious and maybe even a little angry. "That doesn't matter." he said firmly. "I said before that I would help you, no matter your heritage. I stand by that now." He softened a little, and said, "Of course I will help you. After dinner, come to my office upstairs. We'll get something figured out."

****

The rest of the meal passed quickly, with most of the volunteers filing out and returning to their tasks as soon as they were done eating. As Jonah finished his sandwich, someone tapped on his shoulder and held a micro out for him to see. Jonah peered at the small display, nodding vaguely. "Excuse me," he apologized to his guests as he pushed away from the table. "I need to take care of this." To Jason, he said, "Please come upstairs when you are done." He nodded to each of them and then left the room.

Jason, Anne and Valarie were nearly the only adults left in the room now. Matthew and Arabelle left the table they had been seated at and came over to join them. Jason looked at each of them in turn, and asked, "So, what do you think?"

Valarie spoke first. "So far, so good." she said. "This seems like a good place, and with so many people from the community turning out to help, that speaks well of Jonah. I like him."

Anne nodded, agreeing. "This could work." she said hopefully.

Around them, a few people emerged from the kitchen and began to clear the tables. Valarie stood, moving to help them. Arabelle followed suit, and soon mother and daughter disappeared into the kitchen. Jason looked at Anne for a moment, then said to Matthew, "Son, how about you help out in the kitchen too. Do whatever they ask you to, and if you don't know what to do, ask Valarie for help. Your mom and I are going to go talk to Jonah some more." Matthew didn't argue and grabbed a plate to carry into the kitchen.

"Will he be okay?" Anne asked, a little concerned at letting Matthew out of her sight.

"He should be. Valarie will be with him." Jason reassured her. "Well," he said, standing up. "let's go see what Jonah has to say."

****

The door to Jonah's office stood open as Jason and Anne reached the top of the stairs. Jason recognized Courtney sitting in front of the desk. She smiled and stood as they entered, offering them seats in front of Jonah. Jason and Anne sat down together while Courtney moved to an extra chair near the back of the room.

In front of them, Jonah straightened in his chair and folded his hands as if he were about to make a presentation. When he spoke, it was with the air of a man delivering an important business decision. "As I said before, we can help you." he began. "You two are a special case; normally we don't help criminals," Anne tensed at that, but Jonah smiled to soften his words, saying, "but I don't believe that either of you have actually done anything wrong."

He opened a desk drawer and removed two micros. "The main problem we need to solve for you is the police. To do that, you will need to become someone else. These micros are yours to keep. They contain the details of your new identities." For a moment, Jason felt like he was in a spy movie, and his head swam. "I have a friend at the police department who helps us out like this from time to time," Jonah explained, "but he can only do so much. Courtney acted as courier, delivering them here from my contact." Jonah suddenly became very serious and locked eyes with them. "Please don't test how good these new identities are. Basically, it's just a new name and a little bit of money. The identities should be good enough to get you work and let you rent an apartment, but that's about it."

Behind them, Courtney shifted in her chair as she spoke up. "The police department has a cache of false identities they use for witness protection. We borrowed two of those and deleted them from the database so they won't know they're gone." she elaborated. Leaning forward and placing her elbows on her knees, she added, "Until you get settled, you can stay with Brodie and me." Her tone was friendly, and it seemed she was trying to take the formality out of Jonah's offer.

"What about Valarie and Arabelle?" Anne asked.

"Fortunately, they are in a little better position." Jonah said, taking Courtney's hint and softening his demeanor somewhat. "The police aren't looking for them, so there's no need for them to hide while they get set up here."

A momentary silence fell as Jonah sat back and mentally reviewed everything he had told them. "The new identities should be enough to get you started." he concluded eventually, gesturing to the micros. "We'll continue to help you where we can, but you're going to have to do a lot of this on your own."

"That's okay. Honestly, it's more than I'd even hoped. Thank you." Jason told him as he picked up the micros. He handed one to Anne and said, "Honey, can you go let Valarie know where we stand? I need to talk to Jonah alone for a minute." Anne's face clouded over. Reluctantly, she stood and left the room, eyeing him from over her shoulder. He knew he'd have some explaining to do later. Courtney stood and followed her out, leaving the two men alone.

When they were gone, Jason fidgeted in his chair for a moment, then rose and began to pace, unable to sit still. He had something big on his mind and was unsure how to frame it. Still seated at his desk, Jonah patiently waited for him to find the words.

"The Resistance..." Jason began, finally giving voice to his jumbled thoughts. "They framed me for their attack, and they used my picture to spread their message. They're terrorists, and they made me the face of it all." He spoke slowly as his thoughts came together like beads on a string. "I know that things are bad for non-Citizens, but The Resistance just doesn't make sense! What they're doing isn't about justice; they've killed as many Latinos as they have Citizens! It's..."

He stopped himself, then started again. "You told me about the other shelter..." he said haltingly, trying to remember its name.

"Casa Preciosa." Jonah prompted, and Jason nodded.

"Casa Preciosa." he repeated carefully, as if testing the words in his mouth. "You told me that some of the people who went to them for help ended up as attackers for The Resistance." Jonah nodded slowly, wary of where this might go. "So there's a connection there; a place to start." Jason went on, speaking as much to himself as to Jonah. After a moment's silence, he said quietly, "I want to go there. I want to try to bring down The Resistance."

"Are you sure?" Jonah asked, beseeching him to reconsider. "The Resistance is dangerous, and they've killed so many. What about your family?"

Jason lowered his head, hating his answer but unable to change it. "I haven't told Anne yet," he admitted, "but I will. She deserves to know." Meeting Jonah's eyes, he added, "They made this personal for me. I have to do this."

Jonah shook his head sadly. One man crusades rarely ended well. "I don't like it," he said, "but I won't stop you." With an air of finality, he offered his hand and Jason shook it gratefully.

"Thank you." Jason said. "I wanted to let you know. You know the city far better than I do, and I'll probably need your help to get it done."

Jonah sighed and looked down. "I just hope it doesn't get you killed." he said softly.

PART II:

DUMETELLA CAROLINENSIS

CHAPTER 15

Three AM on Ross b was weird. By planetary custom it was the middle of the night, yet the red-orange sun still hung in the sky, locked in place and bright as ever. It may as well have been noon, yet most business on the planet was done during the more 'civilized' hours of six AM to ten PM or so. Jason had never understood why people didn't just ignore the clock and take care of things whenever it suited them.

Some businesses did operate around the clock; the lumber mill in Aberdeen for example. He'd heard that the factories here in Cosmopolis often did the same, but these establishments were the odd ones out. Businesses which catered to customers, like stores or cafes, still clung to the idea of 'business hours', and Jason found that infuriating. With an enormous effort, he stifled a yawn. To be fair, there were some diners, bars, and the like that also stayed open 24 hours a day. Maybe he was just grumpy because he needed coffee, and there weren't any of those places around here. Goddamnit.

After three months, he'd hoped for something better than this. Jason, Mateo, and a large, unrepentant felon named Marcus Ortiz stood near the entrance of a run-down apartment building in one of the worst neighborhoods Jason had ever seen. The street around them was empty. Every decent person in the area was home asleep; if any decent people lived here, anyway. The buildings towering over the street cast long fixed shadows, creating a permanent twilight that matched Jason's mood. Good, he thought. Crime is best done in the dark.

Jason watched Marcus eyeing the building. "Do you expect trouble?" he asked.

Marcus answered him with a sneer. "Don't think so, but I'm packing anyway. Guy's just an Anglo asshole who thinks he's hot shit." Marcus had a deep seated hatred of those he called 'Anglos' and wasn't afraid to show it. "These fuckers just need to know to pay up. It ain't that hard." he finished dismissively.

Mateo patted his over-shirt near the waist, checking his own weapon. In their new line of work, you couldn't be too careful. Jason had known Mateo for years and in all that time he'd always been law abiding and honest. It was a little disconcerting how easily he'd taken to his new role.

Jason felt the weight of the pistol in his own pocket, comforted to a degree by the protection it promised, but not enough to make him stupid. Guns hadn't changed much in centuries; explosive chemical propulsion was still the cheapest and most efficient way to drive a metal slug through a person. A gun's inherent threat commanded immediate attention, no matter who was holding it. "I guess we're ready." he said. "Let's do it."

The front door to the building wasn't locked. In a better neighborhood there would have been a computer system in place to screen visitors to see if they had any legitimate business there, but the building they entered was battered and broken. There was no system in place to ask questions of anyone.

The worn and stained carpet in the entryway did little to deaden their footsteps as they headed for the elevator. Eleven steps took them across the lobby; two more put them inside the lift. The doors closed and Marcus keyed their destination into the pad. With a distant squeal, the elevator began to rise.

The ride was slow, and the lift seemed to shudder occasionally as it climbed up the worn building. Jason's attention began to wander, his gaze drawn to the wall beside him. It had once been polished to a mirror finish, but time and neglect had covered it with an uneven fog. He leaned closer and made out his reflection looking back at him.

After all this time, he had finally come to accept that the man he saw there was actually him. He kept his head shaved out of necessity now; the look had become a commitment. To augment it and to offset the lack of hair on his head, he'd grown a short beard that to his surprise was flecked with gray. Beside him, Mateo looked pretty much as he always had. Shorter than Jason and slightly stocky, he carried himself well. He'd grown a goatee and cut his hair short but overall, he looked much the same as he had since high school.

At long last, the elevator chimed and came to a stop. The doors squeaked open, revealing that the lift had not quite aligned itself with the floor outside. Stepping over the lip carefully, they exited the elevator and entered a long hallway.

Marcus and Mateo began to walk toward a door some distance away, but Jason asked them to wait. "Hold up. I need to fix my boot." he explained. The laces had started to come loose and he knelt down now to re-tie them.

These were the same boots he'd been wearing when his life had changed forever. They had been new at the time, but now they were dirty and scuffed. Still, they were comfortable like no other pair he'd ever worn. For a moment the face of the man who'd tried to sell them to him swam before his eyes... Pushing the memory of the attack away, he pulled the laces tight and double-knotted them.

Several steps away, Marcus was growing impatient. "Come on, Lucas!" he growled. "Get your ass up! We've got work to do."

Jason stiffened, but only a little. His name was 'Lucas' now, and would be for as long as he was living this life. Learning to answer to that name had been an adjustment, but it was the name Jonah had given him. He stood up and straightened his shirt; Marcus was right. 'Lucas Mendoza' had work to do.

They reached the apartment as a group, and Marcus knocked loudly on the door. It was opened a moment later by a large, threatening looking Black man, openly carrying an automatic pistol. He glowered and said nothing, his hand firmly gripping the weapon; not pointing the gun at them, but also not *not* pointing it at them.

"We're here to see Jock about the money." Marcus said belligerently. Jason heard the smile behind his bravado. A born street-tough, Marcus actually liked this kind of thing. The doorman stared at them for a tense moment, then stepped aside so they could enter.

In another life, Jason would have been both amazed and disgusted by what he saw. The place was dark, filthy, and stank of body odor and harsh chemicals. One of the walls had been crudely demolished to make the space bigger, and the mess spilled over into the next apartment. He wondered how they'd gotten away with that, then realized that nobody who mattered cared.

The armed man who had let them in drifted back toward the wall, keeping watch while simultaneously giving them a little space. Jason noticed too that the guard was not the only armed man in the room, and he felt the compact weight of the pistol in his own pocket. If it came to shooting, it was going to be ugly.

A group of men and women were clustered around a large video screen mounted to a back wall. Images shifted and flickered across the display, almost too fast for Jason to follow. The flashing lights were accompanied by the heavy throb of loud music and the resulting cacophony struck him as guaranteed to cause headaches.

In one corner of the room, two men and a woman sat huddled close around a small portable stove. On the cooking surface several brown-gray chunks had been heated until they began to give off a thin blue smoke. The vapor wafted up and they brought their heads close, breathing deep and trying not to choke. They laughed then, their voices unnaturally high and light; an unsettling contrast to their dilated pupils and bloodshot eyes.

A skinny Caucasian man dressed entirely in white

pushed his way through the people gathered around the video screen, shoving them aside as he asserted dominance. He looked like he was trying to make a fashion statement, but only had a pile of dirty laundry to pull from. The wrinkled clothes might have looked good once; now they just looked stained and slept in.

He approached Jason, Mateo, and Marcus, and said just loud enough for them to hear, "Come on. Let's go talk in the back." He led the way, not waiting to see if they followed. Marcus scowled, but fell into step behind him. Jason and Mateo followed suit, and a pair of armed men materialized behind them, bringing up the rear.

They were led into what might have once been a bedroom, but was now missing a bed. Instead, the room was dominated by a white leather sofa and their guide sat down on it, spreading his arms wide and propping his legs up on the cushions so that no room was left for his guests. Marcus, Jason and Mateo remained standing while the two guards moved to either end of the couch.

"Welcome to my castle." the man in white said expansively. "My name is Jock. What can I do for you?" From his body language, Jason could see that they were supposed to be impressed, but all he actually saw was a bit of bad playacting.

Marcus took a half-step forward. "The Brotherhood sends their regards." he said. With an effort, Jason managed not to roll his eyes; there was a fair bit of bad playacting here too.

"I hear you've had a good couple of weeks." Marcus continued. "Sales are up; business is good." Jock nodded in agreement, looking down at his fingernails. Jason wasn't sure, but he thought he caught a bit of nervousness. The armed men standing near the ends of the couch continued to stare impassively.

"Couldn't have done it without your product." Jock replied, his tone almost, but not quite, resentful.

"You know the rules. You get paid, we get paid. That's

how it works." Marcus said firmly. Jason knew Marcus hated Jock, but he was trying to sound reasonable, as if the rules mattered.

"I had some unexpected costs I had to cover." Jock said, managing to maintain his bravado. He must know this wasn't going to work, but he was trying anyway. Jason had to give him credit for that, at least. "I have most of the money, and I'll have the rest of it by the middle of next week."

Marcus stared at him, his gaze hard. Jason and Mateo both kept quiet and did their best to look tough; that was their job.

"The Nortown Crew understood the situation." Jock asserted. "They knew there were costs, but they were patient and they always got paid." He scowled up at Marcus, trying out defiance. "Then *you* fuckers took over, and you don't know shit! You don't know how this racket works. Nortown took a fair cut and let me and mine do our work. They..."

Marcus exploded. "Shut up, you Anglo fuck!" he shouted and kicked at the sofa, shoving it backward across the bare floor. In that instant Jason and Mateo pulled their guns and pointed them at the guards. The guards started to raise theirs but froze halfway, unwilling to test Jason and Mateo's resolve. Marcus let the tension hang in the air, using silence to intimidate where words hadn't worked.

At that moment there was a knock at the door and Marcus' face flashed in annoyance as the spell was broken. Reluctantly, he stepped back and Jason and Mateo lowered their guns. The guards relaxed slightly and Jock's voice cracked as he shouted, "What!"

The door opened a few inches and a dark-skinned man with a shiny shaved head poked his head through. "Hey, Jock? We found 'em." he said. "They're bringing them up now."

Jock rose from the leather sofa, his bravado returning. "Excuse me, fellas. Got to tend to my other business for a moment. It shouldn't take long."

Jock shouldered his way past Marcus and his guards

followed him out. They returned to the main room, leaving Marcus, Jason and Mateo alone. Jason and Mateo exchanged glances, then followed Jock out through the door. Marcus joined them a moment later.

The number of lackeys and hangers-on standing around the large room seemed to have doubled. A group of them had formed a rough circle around Jock, leaving an open space in the middle. In the center, Jock stood pacing back and forth in front of two small kneeling figures that were gagged and had their hands and feet tied. Marcus and Jason pushed forward for a better view, while Mateo hung back, alert for trouble.

The dark-skinned man stood close to Jock, talking fast and pointing at the two bound forms. Jason could only catch fragments of what was said, but Jock appeared pleased. He moved a little closer, angling for a better look, and his heart sank. The two shivering figures were children. Boys, both maybe eleven years old; the same age as Matthew.

The boys knelt on the floor, tied and unable to move. One boy was of Asian descent, with dark hair and eyes that contrasted with his pale skin. The other was clearly Latino, with a dark golden brown complexion. Both boys showed evidence of violence, and the skin around the Asian boy's right eye was swollen and purple.

Jock stepped toward the boys, squatting to bring his face level with theirs. "Now, I'd say you learned a lesson here." he told them. His tone was threatening, trying and failing to masquerade as sweetness. He reached out and shoved the Latino boy, sending him toppling into the other one. Standing back up, he searched the crowd. "Marcus!" he exclaimed. "This actually works out just fine. Come up here and we'll talk business."

The crowd quickly thinned as Marcus stepped forward, making themselves scarce. As he reached the center of the circle, Jock tried to throw an arm over his shoulder but Marcus blocked him angrily. He glared at Jock and the man's momentum faltered.

"I'm trying to help you, asshole." Jock insisted, sounding insulted. "You're here to get paid for the Helium, right?"

"I thought you had 'unexpected costs'?" Marcus sneered.

"A business investment." Jock said. "I bought these two and six others from the Sepulchers. Cost me a bit, but I can resell them at nearly twice the price; double my money. I have a buyer for the others, but these two ran." He yelled the last words at the children. They might have cowered if they had been able. He leaned in close to Marcus then, as if they were friends. "I can give you ten thousand now. Take these kids as payment for the rest. That should clear my debt to you."

A few steps away, Jason held his face immobile. Christ… What had he gotten himself into?

Marcus turned to the boys, considering. "It's not right, holding a Latino kid like this. He ain't supposed to be a slave." he said quietly.

"You can do whatever you want with him." Jock said dismissively, waving his hand. "I just want my debt to The Brotherhood settled, nice and square."

Marcus seemed to reach a decision. "Let's see the money." he demanded. Jock pointed and one of his men stepped forward, holding a micro in his hand. Marcus pulled a similar device from inside his jacket and pressed a few keys. Both micros chimed and their screens lit up; Marcus' in green, the other in red. Marcus nodded, seeing the transfer of funds register on his device. He looked at Jock and said, "Alright, now the kids."

At Jocks direction, the boys' restraints were cut and they rose unsteadily to their feet. A man started to cut their gags as well, but Marcus stopped them. "Leave those on." he said firmly. Jason wondered if it was just to keep them quiet, or if Marcus was trying to silence his conscience. Jason's own sense of morality was screaming at him, but he forced it down. All around him there were armed men, Marcus included. If he spoke up now, he was dead. He felt empty as he realized he may never get the chance to make this right.

The mood in the dingy apartment changed as everyone realized that the deal was done and the danger had passed. Jason marvelled at how they could pay such close attention while at the same time very intentionally ignoring everything. He hated these people. Most of them were here for the drugs, or just to hang out with 'the right people'. It was a shitty way to live, and apparently they were slave traders on top of it. He reflected unhappily that now he was one too. Fantastic.

Jason and Mateo kept an eye on the children while Marcus finished his conversation with Jock. Jason assumed it went something like, "We're square for now, but next time we want cash." For Marcus, that would pass as being polite.

Eventually, Marcus rejoined his companions. "Alright. Let's go." he announced. He led the way out the door, with their new slaves trailing behind him while Mateo and Jason brought up the rear. They rode the lift in silence as they descended toward the street. This time, Jason avoided looking at his reflection in the elevator wall.

****

They exited the building and stepped out onto the sidewalk, their eyes taking a moment to adjust to the sunlight. It was creeping toward four AM now, but the streets around them remained empty. They had only gone a few steps when Marcus turned and glared up at the building to where he thought Jock's apartment might be.

"I really hate that Anglo fucker." he growled angrily. "He's a lying sonofabitch, too! He doesn't get to use The Brotherhood's money on some bullshit 'business investment'. Someday, I'm going to teach him that." He stopped mid-rant, his hard face becoming pensive as his gaze drifted down to the two children standing next to him. Pulling a knife from inside his jacket, he flicked it open with a soft click. Carefully, he cut the gag off the Hispanic boy, leaving the Asian boy's restraint in place.

"There. What's your name?" Marcus asked him.

"Daniel." the boy answered quietly, raising his eyes to meet Marcus'. Jason could see that he was terrified, but was trying to hide it. He watched the boy carefully, waiting to see if he would run. If he did, Jason knew he wouldn't try too hard to catch him.

Marcus put a hand on the boy's shoulder. "Let's go." he said, almost paternaly. He then struck the other boy on the back of the head hard enough to send him stumbling forward. "You too, dipshit." he said. There was no trace of warmness in his tone now.

Jason couldn't stop himself. "Come on, man!" he called out reproachfully. He knew even that was a risk, but he couldn't keep quiet.

Marcus whirled, his broad face unreadable. "What?" he demanded irritably. "I cut the Latino kid free. I'm not gonna keep him, but we have to take him down to the shelter and let Gabe and Angel know about this."

"What about him?" Jason asked, nodding toward the Asian boy.

"What about him?" Marcus answered, anger growing in his voice. "Kid's not Latino. I don't give two shits what happens to him and neither should you. He's money in our pocket! If I can make a little something extra from him, then great; that's how we fund the revolution!" Marcus still held the knife and was using it to point. Jason saw the hint of a threat in his eye and realized he had to let this drop. He raised his hands to show he was backing down. He had no power here and Marcus knew it. Jason couldn't stop him without killing him or getting killed himself. Ignoring the pit forming in his gut, Jason gently prodded the Asian boy in the back, pushing him toward the road and the waiting car.

Marcus had parked his car just down the street. Unusually, this was his personal car; he owned it. In Jason's old life, everyone he knew had subscribed to on-call car services. In his new one though, he'd met a certain class of people who preferred to own instead of rent. They would modify their cars too, removing anything the police might use to track them and adding an assortment of performance parts; different gearing, larger capacitors and higher amp motors. They generally avoided flashy paint jobs as that would make them too easy to identify, but Marcus had bucked that trend. His car, a low, dark purple brick with a matte black roof, would have stood out no matter where he parked it.

As they reached the car, Marcus popped open the trunk and began rooting around inside. Jason was afraid for a moment that Marcus intended to shove the kids into the tight space and was less than relieved when he pulled out a length of rope instead. Untangling it, he began roughly tying the Asian boy's hands and feet.

"Should have just left them tied up." Mateo observed.

"That fucker" Marcus said, meaning Jock, "had the ropes cut before I could say anything. At least we didn't have to carry them." Once the boy was bound, he stuffed the rope back in the trunk, leaving Daniel free. Marcus nodded to Mateo, who then lifted the Asian kid over one shoulder while Marcus opened the car door. With a grunt, Mateo deposited his burden into the cramped back seat and then climbed in after him. Daniel tentatively opened the front passenger door and sat down while Marcus circled the car and got into the driver's seat.

Marcus' customized car now posed a problem; there were only four seats. They could probably all squeeze in, pressing Daniel or the Asian kid between them, but it would be tight and Jason needed some air anyway. He stood next to the car, frowning as Marcus twisted to glare at him. Seeing Jason's hesitation, Marcus commanded, "Lucas, get in the fucking car!"

"Look, it's too tight in there." Jason said quickly. "I'll just walk to a tram station. I want to go see my girl anyway." he said. The fact that it was mostly true made the lie come easily.

Mateo saw an opening and leaned forward in his seat. “I’ll hang back too.” he said. “I need to find some coffee anyway. I’ll catch up with you back at the shelter." Without waiting for an answer, he exited the car and stood on the sidewalk next to Jason.

Marcus was obviously pissed at having to deal with the kids all by himself, but he warmed to the idea that he’d be the one to bring them in. “Fine.” he said. “You two do what you want. I need to get the micro back and get it unloaded." He pointed with his thumb at the child bound in the back seat. “I guess I’ll take the credit for this too.” he said gruffly.

He drove away without waiting for an answer, the modified car emitting a sound like an arc welder as he accelerated hard, leaving a strong smell of ozone behind. Jason and Mateo watched as Marcus disappeared in the distance.

When he was gone, Mateo said, “This is how we fund the revolution, huh?" The disgust in his voice was unmistakable.

“Fuck.” Jason said, stretching the all-purpose expletive to its fullest potential.

****

It was five blocks to the nearest tram station. At first Jason walked in silence, wrestling with his conscience and by no means winning. Mateo let him stew, giving him the time he needed to sort his mind out. By the time they reached the station and boarded the pneumatic tram, Jason had begun speaking again.

“What the fuck are we doing?” he asked. Mateo knew it was a rhetorical question, but one that needed an answer nonetheless.

“We’re trying to bring down The Resistance.” Mateo reminded him. “They killed a whole lot of people and the police don’t seem to give a shit since the attacks stopped.”

Jason nodded, only somewhat reassured. It was true the attacks had stopped; there hadn't been any since the riots, but it didn't make sense! To begin his investigation, Jason had gone to the Casa Preciosa shelter as 'Lucas Mendoza'. As a non-Citizen, Lucas had led a hard life, one that had left him homeless. Jason had sought help from the shelter, hoping that by doing so he'd be able to discover more about The Resistance. Casa Preciosa had been his only link, but what he found there only added to his confusion.

In his first days at the shelter he had met Benito Reyes. The diminutive man was an unapologetic revolutionary; he would pace determinedly around the dining hall, preaching violence, subversion and change. His audience were the shelter's clients, the homeless who had nowhere else to go. Not all of them were interested in his message but many were, and Benito would work tirelessly to win over anyone who would listen.

However, Jason quickly found that Benito's presence was merely tolerated by those who held the real power at the shelter; The Brotherhood gang and its leaders, Gabe and Angel Batista. The brothers were criminals and drug dealers looking to carve out an empire for themselves. They had no interest in revolution. Over the course of weeks Jason had watched young men come in off the street to talk with Gabe and Angel, always in hushed tones and often behind closed doors. Occasionally, the men would be armed, their weapons holstered in deference to the brothers.

As Lucas Mendoza, Jason had slowly moved himself into their orbit. At first he just relayed messages and delivered packages. He never asked what he was carrying, but he wasn't a fool. Later, when they needed muscle, the brothers had asked Lucas to come along. He had proven himself competent and able to follow directions, and in this line of work those were valuable commodities.

When Mateo got out of jail and made his way to Cosmopolis, he had immediately wanted to help. Jason urged him to stay away, as it would be dangerous. But, against his wishes, Mateo began frequenting the Casa Preciosa shelter. Eventually, the brothers connected Mateo with Lucas and Jason was forced to vouch for him. As much as he hated to let Mateo get involved, it felt good to have a friend there with him. Mateo fell into his new role easily, and Gabe and Angel started using them both as backup for Marcus as he collected money for the gang.

Marcus Ortiz was one of the worst people Jason had ever met, and also one of the most racist. As a poor Hispanic, Marcus had seen the worst Ross b had to offer and it had taught him to hate Citizens in general and White people in particular, with a singular passion. He was one of the very few members of The Brotherhood who took the revolutionary rantings of Benito Reyes seriously. But although he often quoted the man's defiant rhetoric, Marcus' true love was crime. He was brutal and could be cruel to the point of sadism. He loved the lifestyle and the respect being in the gang gave him and he wasn't above using violence to get his way.

As the tram flew through the tube, the night's events continued to weigh on Jason. They were still several blocks from their destination when he rose and impulsively pressed the 'Next Stop' button by the door. Immediately, the tram began to slow. Mateo came up behind him, his eyebrows raised in a question.

"I want to walk the rest of the way." Jason explained darkly. "I'm pissed off and kind of tired. I figure the walk will help clear my head."

At the next station they descended to the street and entered a posh commercial district lined with shops but devoid of people at this odd hour. The sidewalk took them past windows displaying jewelry and small boutiques advertising fancy clothing and accessories. Jason ignored the scenery; he had other things on his mind.

They had only gone a block when Jason noticed that Mateo wasn't at his side. He stopped and turned to find his friend staring into a shop window. As Jason rejoined him, Mateo asked distantly, "Did I tell you Valarie's pregnant?".

Jason stood dumbfounded, caught completely off guard. "No?" he ventured, uncertain how to respond. He wondered what had drawn Mateo's interest and saw that he had stopped in front of a shop selling designer baby clothes.

"Won't be getting the kid anything from here, I'd guess." Mateo said, smiling ruefully.

"Probably not." Jason agreed. After a moment, he asked, "How's Valarie taking it?"

"Good and bad." Mateo answered as they started walking again. "You know she's never liked our new line of work..." he trailed off, not finishing the sentence.

Valarie had taken Mateo's decision to follow Jason undercover badly. She'd screamed at him and blamed Jason for his choice. It had been bad for a while but things between them had eventually gotten better. Still, it remained a sensitive subject.

"How far along is she?" Jason asked.

"Just two months."

"Wow, so you guys just found out."

"Yeah. She wants me to quit all this." Mateo said. "I haven't agreed to it yet, but I might. She makes good sense, you know?"

"I know." Jason said, leaving it at that. He hadn't wanted Mateo to follow him into this hell, but he also couldn't imagine surviving it without him. Still, it was Mateo's choice to make; he wouldn't add to his friend's burden by asking him to stay. They walked on together, lost in thought.

After a while they left the richest part of the city behind, moving into the denser downtown area. After the riots, these were the parts of the city that Jason had thought would never be the same. Now, over three months later, it was like the riots had never happened. The city had martialled its resources and put them to work, erasing the scars and burying the memory. The Latino Resistance Front was in the past as well. Their threats and attacks had ended with the riots and everyone had moved on, choosing to forget or ignore the problems which had caused them. The city around them was clean again, bright and tender like newly healed skin.

It was all a lie, of course. The racism and inequality still persisted, and if anything, was worse now than it had been before. Though most people carried on like the riots had never happened, a lot of people had been hurt, both Citizens and not, and those who had been hurt still sought revenge. The violence was usually small and personal, easy for the authorities to ignore, but it was there just the same. *Nadum cambiam*; nothing changes.

They stopped as they reached a street corner and Mateo pointed across the intersection, spying an all-night diner that occupied the first floor of a brown three story building. "Hey, that place is open! Let's stop and get some coffee." he suggested.

Jason could barely think straight anymore; coffee sounded great. He agreed readily, and they quickly crossed the street and went inside.

There was only one other customer in the building. Ignoring the counter seating, they chose an empty booth near the back and settled in. Mateo stripped off his coat, wadding it up and placing it on the seat next to him. An old-style menu screen was mounted to the wall just above the table. It lit up at Jason's touch, but didn't seem to work right. He fought with it, trying to access the drinks menu. After a minute Mateo leaned over and pulled it up for him. A few button pushes later, their order was placed and a bored looking waitress came over with a pot of black liquid and two cups. She filled their mugs and left again without a word.

Jason took a cautious sip of the black liquid, nearly burning his tongue. The taste was bitter, but it would do. He added some sugar from a small jar on the table and looked around for something to stir it in. Not finding anything, he gently swirled the cup while stifling another yawn.

Sleep pulled at him like gravity, but he couldn't rest yet. He took another cautious sip of coffee, willing himself to stay awake. He was anxious to see Anne again; he didn't get to see her nearly often enough these days. The time on his micro read 4:47 AM. He sighed; she wouldn't be there yet. He still had a few more hours to wait.

CHAPTER 16

Anne quickly checked herself in the restroom mirror before going on shift. The tag she wore clipped to her pocket displayed her new name, announcing to the world that she was 'Lena' now, the letters appearing reversed in the mirror. Anne liked the name; Lena was short and simple, like her old one. She felt lucky; she hadn't had any choice in her new identity, but Lena was a name she might have chosen for herself.

Her new last name, however, was something else. 'Anisimova' was a mouthful to say the least. She still had to get a running start in order to say it properly. At least the ungainly name wasn't printed on her name tag.

A woman's raised voice came from outside the door. "Are you ready? I'm going to unlock the front doors." This was Brodie, and they were about to go on shift together. She straightened her shirt and opened the door.

"I'm ready." Anne told her as she emerged from the restroom. Brodie went to the front door and used the control pad beside it to set the store to 'Open'. At her touch the system came to life, readying itself for the business day. The door unlocked with a clicking sound and the darkened glass behind the barred windows cleared, letting in the red-orange sunlight from outside. A lurid collection of colored advertisements hanging in the windows lit up with a faint hum, letting the world know they were open for business.

When she and Jason had fled Aberdeen for Cosmopolis, Anne hadn't considered what her life would be like after the transition. She had been a teacher, with training and an education that was suited to that life. She hadn't realized how little of it would be useful now.

For a while she'd tried tutoring, both at Jonah's El Rey Latino Outreach Center and privately. In the end though, it hadn't been enough. As Lena Anisimova, she didn't have the credentials to attract many students, and Jonah could only pay her so much for her efforts at The Center. To her frustration, she discovered that tutoring just didn't pay enough to live on.

She'd hoped to save enough money to get her own apartment; one that she and Matthew could share. Since the beginning, she and her son had been living with Courtney and Brodie Damiya. She'd met Courtney at The Center and Jason had introduced her and her daughter as the ones who'd helped him escape Cosmopolis before the riots. They were good people and she liked them a lot, but even so, she wanted a space to call her own.

After struggling for a few months to get by as a tutor, Anne had become disheartened. Brodie could see the stress she was feeling and wanted to help. She sat down with Anne one night to talk. Brodie listened as Anne explained how useless she felt, and that she didn't see a way forward. Brodie nodded, saying little and letting Anne vent her frustration. When her words ran out, Brodie pulled out her micro and opened a page for taking notes. At the bottom of the screen, she used her finger to write 'Teacher'. Anne watched, curious as Brodie moved back to the top of the screen and paused.

"So, how did you become a teacher? What were the steps you had to follow?" Brodie asked. She could guess the answer, but knew it would help Anne to say it out loud.

"I went to school; college." Anne answered dubiously.

"Okay. College costs money, so you'll need to get some." Brodie said as if thinking out loud. On her micro, she wrote 'College' near the middle of the screen and then wrote 'Money' just above it. "You've been tutoring, but you also said it doesn't pay enough. What else could you do for money?"

Anne sighed. "That's just it; I don't know. All my training is teaching related. It's not good for much else."

"What about a job you don't need training for?" Brodie asked, keeping her tone neutral.

Anne thought about a job like that. She hadn't even considered it; doing something she didn't care about just to make ends meet. Nodding slowly, she admitted, "I could do that. It would pay the rent, at least." A menial job would be progress so long as it paid well enough, but still a part of her resisted the idea. She'd been a teacher all her life. It was what she'd always wanted to do.

Brodie wrote 'Simple Job' at the top of the screen and then wrote 'Pays Rent' below that. She connected Job to Rent with an arrow and in a flash Anne saw the path that had been laid out before her. It might only be a subsistence existence, but it would be better than what she had now. Anne continued to stare at the screen, but Brodie wasn't done. Next to 'Pays Rent', she wrote 'College Fund' and drew another arrow down from 'Simple Job' and connected it there. Anne's mind sparked again, seeing the connection that should have been obvious. It would be hard, but the idea was so simple she really should have thought of it before.

Brodie raised her eyes to Anne, speaking to her as if she were a slow child. "So you'll just have to work for it..." she said gently.

God, it would be hard, Anne thought. The concept was simple; work a regular job, save money for school, then go to college and become a teacher again. It was a long-term plan to say the least, but she'd done it before, so maybe she could do it again. She would truly be starting over, but the way forward finally seemed clear.

Anne took a deep breath and said, "I guess I need to look for a job." Feeling a little guilty, she added, "And if you and your mom will let us, Matt and I could keep living here to save money." Brodie nodded, happy that Anne understood what she had told her. It was the same path Brodie herself was following; she planned to leave for medical school in the fall.

The idea changed Anne's world overnight. She didn't entirely give up tutoring, but the next day Anne accessed the help wanted postings and began her search while Brodie went off to her own menial job at a corner store downtown. Anne's search was thorough and she sent inquiries on several listings. Each time she did, she imagined what the job would be like; warehouse worker, garment maker, janitorial service. None of the possibilities were glamourous in the least, but whatever job she got, she would use it as a means to reach her goals.

A lucky break came when Brodie got back home later that day. The door to the apartment opened and Brodie's voice echoed into the small living room. "Hey Anne? Want a job?" she announced.

It turned out that the guy who normally worked the morning shift at the store hadn't shown up. Two and a half hours after his shift was to have begun, he'd sent the boss a message which simply said, "I quit." When Brodie arrived for her own shift, she was forced to get the store ready to open by herself as well as get her own work done. She hadn't been happy.

Now, two weeks later, Anne had a name tag and a uniform. The uniform was more of a vest really, but the employee handbook said she still had to wear it. Brodie, who somehow never wore the required vest, had handled all her training. Anne had never even seen their boss. Idley, she wondered if he really existed at all.

With the store now open, Brodie moved behind the counter and turned on her music. In deference to Anne, she kept the volume reasonable, but it was still a cacophony of electronic terror that set Anne's teeth on edge. For her, it was far too early in the morning for that kind of noise.

As she straightened and stocked the shelves, Anne thought about Valarie and Arabelle. The two had established their own routine over the past few months, and Anne didn't see as much of them as she used to. Jonah had given Valarie a space to work, which she used to cut hair and offer other cosmetic services. Her customers paid her directly, so she didn't have to rely on a salary from The Center. The income was decent and had enabled her to rent an apartment. Additionally, she had been able to afford to send Arabelle to public school. Anne desperately wished she could enroll Matthew as well, but the fact that she and Jason were wanted criminals made the risk too great. She continued his education by tutoring him at the center along with her other students.

Matthew... Anne didn't relish the idea of being away from her son, especially early in the morning, but it was necessary. They'd fallen into a pattern; in the mornings Anne would go to work while Matthew would help Jonah out at The Center. After her shift, Anne would join Matthew at The Center, including him in her tutoring sessions while also teaching any other kids who showed up. In the evenings, they would return to Brodie and Courtney's apartment for dinner and family time. It wasn't perfect, but it was the best they could do under the circumstances.

The store had been open for twenty minutes without a single customer entering the building. Anne was using the free time to try and organize the small storeroom when the door chime sounded to let her know someone had come in. She yelled, "Just a second!" as she shoved the final boxes into place. Brodie was around somewhere, but Anne had learned it was best if she dealt with the customers instead.

Anne emerged from the storeroom and was brushing the dust off her uniform when she saw Jason. She smiled instantly; she loved any chance she got to see him. He reached out to take her in his arms and she ran around the counter to meet him. They held each other close for a moment, relishing the physical contact which happened all too rarely these days. The last few months had been so very hard, for both of them.

At last his arms loosened and he stepped back to look at her. She looked different than she had three months ago; Jason wasn't the only one who'd had to change in this new life. Anne had cut her hair to less than half its previous length and dyed it black. She had also begun wearing glasses, the frames a delicate purple, though only for cosmetic reasons. The look was strikingly different from her old one, yet Jason still found her irresistible. The need to be near her was an almost physical ache. The sad fact was that Lucas Mendoza and Lena Anisimova weren't married, they were only dating. To maintain the necessary fiction, Jason had a separate apartment where he lived alone. The Brotherhood knew he had a girlfriend, but he couldn't let them know how important Anne was to him. The gang was far too dangerous to put his family at risk that way. Keeping Anne separate from his new life hurt him deeply, but he had to do it in order to stay sane. He needed her to be his island of stability.

Slowly, Anne became aware that Mateo stood a few paces behind her husband. "Hi Mateo!", she said, greeting him with a smile.

Brodie had heard the door chime and now finally emerged from the back of the store to investigate. Seeing Jason and Mateo, she greeted them both warmly. "How's it going? Still criminals?" she asked, her tone friendly despite the confrontational words.

"Still criminals." Mateo assured her as they embraced. Brodie had bonded closely with his daughter Arabelle and Mateo had come to think of her as family.

Behind them the door chime rang again as a shabbily dressed woman entered the store, her walk a little uneven. Mateo let Brodie go and the four of them stood around awkwardly while the woman wandered toward the back, presumably looking for the alcohol.

Brodie eyed her suspiciously, but then turned to Jason and Anne and said, "I can cover the store for a while if you two want to go get some breakfast."

Jason looked at Anne, who quickly took Brodie up on her offer. "Yes, thank you!" Anne said. "We'll get something nearby. I'll be back in less than an hour!" She then reached behind the counter to grab her coat and they left together, leaving Brodie and Mateo alone with the customer. Mateo inclined his head toward the woman, who now seemed to be taking an awfully long time to come back from the wine section, and raised his eyebrow questioningly.

Brodie shook her head, a determined look on her face. "She comes in here all the time; I can handle her. We have an understanding." she told him cryptically.

Mateo took her at her word, giving it no further thought. He pulled a bag of something salty from a nearby rack and Brodie operated the register as he paid for it. With that done he leaned against the wall, opened the package and began eating. "If you don't mind," he said, "I'll hang out here till The Center opens and I can go see Valarie."

Brodie nodded absently, her attention focused on the woman in the back. "That's fine with me." she said. Keeping an eye on her target, she muttered quietly, "What's your play gonna be this time, bitch?".

****

Jason and Anne walked side by side down the sidewalk, almost completely alone due to the early morning hour. They held hands too, something they hadn't done in years. The world around them thought they were dating and for the moment it really did feel like it was true. Anne couldn't stop smiling; she felt the butterflies in her stomach which came from being close to someone she loved. She saw Jason so infrequently these days, but the rarity of it only made things feel that much sweeter when she did.

She looked up at him, trying to take in every detail. She'd gotten used to his shaved head, and the short beard he now wore actually looked good. Still, she saw the dark circles under his eyes and knew he was exhausted. He should have been asleep, but he was making time for her. His willing sacrifice made her feel good, but she wished it didn't cost him so much.

Jason caught her looking at him and smiled. "So where do you want to eat?" he asked. His voice was a little raspy with the need for sleep, but it was great to hear it nonetheless.

"There's a 24 hour diner on 4th street." she said. "It should be open."

Jason chuckled. "That'll be the second diner I've been in today."

"We can go somewhere else if you want..." Anne said, hoping to find something that would suit them both.

"It'll be fine." Jason replied soothingly. "I only had coffee before. Some real food will be good."

At the next intersection they made a left turn and began working their way toward 4th street. Jason's steps faltered a few minutes later as he saw a police checkpoint two blocks ahead. The checkpoint was manned, and augmented by a series of interconnected steel plates and sandbags that narrowed the exit, leaving only enough room for people to pass through one at a time. To avoid suspicion Jason forced himself to resume walking, but he slowed his pace enough to give them time to think. Anne matched his shortened stride and stayed by his side.

"Do you want to try another way?" she asked quietly.

"I don't know. If they've seen us, they might take a closer look if we try to leave." Jason kept his voice low, though there was no way the police could have heard them at this distance.

By this time their steps had taken them another block. A side street appeared to their left, giving them an opportunity to turn and avoid the checkpoint. Jason considered moving toward it, but a pair of police officers were now looking in their direction. They appeared disinterested, but that would quickly change if he and Anne tried to vanish. They had no choice now; they would have to pass through the checkpoint.

It was still too early in the morning for rush hour to be in full effect, so the line of waiting people was short. Ahead of them, everyone's credentials were scanned and checked against the database. Jason saw a few people in line who looked like Citizens, but the majority were brown skinned men and women like himself. He bit back a flash of bitter amusement to see that the Citizens were having their identifications verified like everyone else.

The men running the checkpoint were efficient and the line moved quickly. When it was his turn, Jason brought his ID up on his micro's display.

"Name?" asked the nearest officer without much interest.

Jason handed him the micro to be scanned. "Lucas Mendoza" he said. His ID had been checked several times over the past three months without trouble, but each time the process made him nervous. The bored officer read the ID information on Jason's micro, visually matching it to the man he saw in front of him as well as checking it against the records they had on file. The process only took a moment before he was waved through; Lucas Mendoza had passed inspection once again. He waited while they repeated the verification process for Anne. In no time at all 'Lena Anisimova' joined him on the other side of the barrier and the two of them resumed their interrupted walk down the street.

A few blocks further and the checkpoint was lost behind them. Jason hated the checkpoints, but he had to admit that the police were handling them better than the Army had. The difference might only be one of tone, but at least it was something.

Ahead, they were approaching a construction site. The boundary was marked by a tall fence with the entrance gated and locked, but the bars at the corner of the fence had been pulled open and laid back, allowing access. From inside they heard a violent commotion, and with a sinking feeling Jason hurried forward to investigate. As he reached the hole in the fence Anne grabbed his coat and pulled him to a stop as she came up behind him.

Inside they saw two men, white-skinned and shouting

racist epithets, kicking at the bloodied and curled up form of a Latino man as he lay on the ground. Jason started to rush toward them, but again Anne stopped him. He looked at her in disbelief and she made a small motion with her head, indicating something behind her. A quick glance revealed that they weren't the only ones who had heard the men. A small group of people gathered behind them, silently witnessing the brutal display. At least one of them had pulled out a micro and was using it to record the attack. If he got involved now, Jason would be caught on video too.

One of the men turned and saw that they were being recorded. "Get the fuck out of here!" he shouted furiously at the assembled onlookers. When the group didn't disperse both men ignored the bloodied man on the ground and instead began to advance on the crowd menacingly. Behind them, bleeding and in pain, their victim pulled a gun from his waistband. His hand shook as he pointed the weapon and fired.

He only managed a single shot, but it echoed loudly. The bullet hit the closest man in the shoulder, his body twisting forward as he fell. The other man reacted quickly, pulling out his own weapon and returning fire in a rage. Shots rang out six, seven, eight times before Jason lost count. Then it was over; the brown skinned man in front of them lay dead.

As silence returned, the shooter looked up with wild eyes. Perhaps realizing there were too many witnesses, he threw the gun into a nearby bush and ran, forcing his way through the crowd.

Beside Jason, Anne grabbed at the nearest woman and pulled her close. "Go! Get the police! There's a checkpoint back that way! Hurry!" she shouted, forcibly pushing her toward the checkpoint. Terrified, the woman fled. Help would probably arrive too late, but it was all they could do; it would have to be enough. In the chaos that followed Jason and Anne melted away, disappearing down the street before the police could arrive.

****

They sat together in the diner without speaking; the violence they had witnessed was just too fresh. Anne shivered and Jason reached across the table to take her hand in his. Her face was pale and she looked more than a little shaken up.

"How are you doing?" he asked her gently. Truthfully, he was just as unsettled as she was, but he'd deal with it later.

"I don't know." she answered uncertainly. "I think I'll be okay." He saw the haunted look in her eyes but he saw strength there too, and anger. "The riots came and went but nothing really changed, did it?" Anne said bitterly.

"I don't think so." Jason conceded quietly. "People fixed all the damage to the city and then just pretended it was nothing. No one even asked *why* the riots happened. The goddamn Resistance..." His voice began to rise, but he stopped himself mid-sentence. He didn't really know what he was feeling except frustration. The racism and oppression that every Hispanic on Ross b dealt with was all too real, but he couldn't accept that The Latino Resistance Front was the right solution. To him, they weren't any better than the government. They were worse, even; they were killers.

Anne let the silence linger for a moment, trying to read her husband's dark expression. He was visibly angry but she could see that it wasn't directed at her. A passing shadow crossed his face and for a brief moment she caught a glimpse of 'Lucas'. In that instant he looked very much like the violent criminal he pretended to be. Then the moment passed and 'Lucas' was gone. In his place sat the man she loved, looking exhausted.

"You should really try to get more sleep." she said, squeezing his hand. He squeezed back, and after a moment she asked, "Are you getting anywhere?"

Jason was confused by the apparent change of subject and for a moment the expansive question was lost on him.

Then he realized she was asking about his work with The Brotherhood and trying to find The Resistance. What could he tell her? That he hadn't found anything? That despite trying desperately to find a connection between the two, all he'd really done was go into business with drug dealers? That this morning he'd met with a slave trader and become one himself? Despair overwhelmed him and he bowed his head, nearly broken by it all. Christ, he needed to sleep...

"I don't know." he murmured, failing to keep the weariness from his voice. "There's been a few hints, but I haven't found anyone actually connected to The Resistance. There's one guy at the shelter who goes on about revolution like he's reading from a Resistance pamphlet, but everyone just ignores him." He let out an exasperated sigh. "The Brotherhood is a bunch of criminals and drug dealers, but it's all just gang stuff. They're not interested in revolution." He ran a hand over his bare scalp, feeling the tiny hairs bristle against his fingertips. "I keep thinking that I'll find a connection if I stay a little longer, but I just don't know anymore. I feel lost."

Anne leaned back in her seat and Jason raised his eyes to meet hers. When she spoke, her voice was quiet but steady. "Is it time to move on?" she asked.

The question hung in the air, setting off an avalanche of objections in Jason's mind. Inevitably though, they all rang hollow. Anne was right; he was done. It was time to get out.

"I think so." he said slowly, breaking the words off one by one. Anne knew how hard this was for him. He'd begun this crusade hoping to reclaim their lives and no one could claim he hadn't given it his all. To give up now was no small thing, but the time had finally come. "I'll need to do it carefully, though." Jason continued, thinking out loud. "I can't just disappear or they'll come looking for me. I'll talk to Gabe or Angel, see if they will let me go. They won't like it, but I can't leave without their say-so. Not without more trouble following us."

Anne hated the life Jason had gotten himself into, but

she understood. She hadn't liked the idea from the start, and now there were consequences they hadn't even thought of. Still, they were a team. She eyed him mischievously, trying to lighten the mood. "They'll have to get past me first." she said with comic bravado.

Jason laughed a little. "I don't like their chances, then." he said.

Anne's stomach grumbled and she reluctantly turned to the menu screen. "We'd better get something ordered if we're going to get back in time." she said.

Jason closed his eyes for just a moment and felt sleep pulling at him seductively. Forcing them open again, he agreed. "Just make sure to order me some coffee."

****

Afterward they returned to the store, taking a different route to avoid the checkpoint as well as the scene of the attack they had witnessed. The door chime sounded as they entered, and from behind two rows of shelves they heard Brodie's exasperated voice shout, "Goddamnit, lady!". Mateo greeted them as Anne took off her jacket and Brodie emerged looking ready to fight. She relaxed as she saw that it was only them.

"Shit. I thought it was her again!" Brodie said.

"Her?" Anne replied.

"Better that you don't ask." Mateo advised somberly. "I saw the whole thing. It was ugly."

"I don't think we fared much better." Jason told Mateo with a sour look on his face. "I'll tell you about it later." He paused, thinking about the conversation he and Anne had had. "Actually, I think I've got a lot to tell you, but not now. I need to sleep on it first." Mateo would have to hear about his decision to leave The Brotherhood sometime, but he didn't look forward to telling him.

Mateo gave him an odd look, but didn't push the issue.

Instead he said, "That works out okay anyway. The Center is almost open and I'm going to go meet up with Valarie." Like Jason, Mateo took any chance he could to see his family.

"Say hi to Matthew for me." Jason told him. He desperately wanted to see his son but felt like he was going to collapse if he didn't get some rest soon. "Tell him I'll try to come by this afternoon and see him." He hated being a part-time parent but he tried to keep Matthew as far away from his new life as he could.

Turning to Anne, he said, "I'll see you then too.", knowing that she would be tutoring at The Center. "I really need to go get some sleep." He felt the wired, shaky exhaustion that meant a crash was coming soon.

Anne leaned in and kissed him. "I'll see you then." she said, and watched him go.

Outside the store Jason rubbed his eyes, trying to clear his head. He needed to get back to his apartment. He knew the neighborhood around him well but was so tired it took him a moment to get his bearings. Fixing the direction firmly in his mind, he crossed the street and was halfway to the tram station when his micro chimed. He ignored it at first but the insistent sound came again and he pulled the device from his pocket angrily to see who had contacted him. The message was from Marcus, text only. It read, "Come back to Casa Preciosa. Right now."

"Fuck." Jason swore tiredly.

CHAPTER 17

Jason stepped out of the car into a dirty neighborhood on Ocosta Way. Since coming to Cosmopolis he'd largely relied on the tram network to get around the city, but Marcus' message had been urgent, leaving him no time to wait for one of the pneumatic trains. He closed the door and the car drove itself away, leaving him with a throbbing headache swelling behind his eyes as he approached the Casa Preciosa shelter.

Casa Preciosa was in one of the older parts of Cosmopolis and the buildings here were somewhat shorter than those in the towering downtown. The shelter itself stood a mere two stories high, with a mottled stone exterior in various shades of brown and an entrance that faced away from the unmoving sun. The ancient double door was marked by years of use and neglect, and was covered by peeling paint a shade darker than the rest of the building.

Jason shivered involuntarily as he neared the door, a sudden breeze chilling him as he reached for the handle. From the steps he couldn't see the little camera he knew was watching; The Brotherhood kept a close eye on anyone who came to their door.

Movement from the street caught Jason's eye and he heard the soft crunch of tires against pavement as another car came to a halt in front of the building, delivering someone else to the shelter. When the vehicle's door opened to reveal Mateo, Jason realized that Marcus must have summoned him to this urgent meeting as well.

Mateo slammed the door closed as he got out, his anger and frustration unmistakable. Instead of continuing inside,

Jason walked over to meet his friend.

Mateo greeted him with a frustrated nod toward the shelter. "Goddamn Marcus!" he swore, waving a hand toward the building.

Jason rubbed at his eyes, trying to clear the feeling of packed cotton inside his head. He knew they were standing in view of the camera and that someone could be watching them. He subtly reminded Mateo of this fact, and they casually drifted down the sidewalk until they had moved beyond the device's field of view. When they could talk privately, Jason said, "So Marcus called you here too?".

Mateo nodded, frowning. "Some cryptic bullshit about, 'Come back right now.'"

"He sent me the same thing. Any idea what's up?" Jason asked.

"No idea." Mateo replied bitterly. "It's fucking bullshit though! I was literally just saying 'Hi' to Valarie when my micro beeped. All I could do was hug her and go." He was still upset but was visibly trying to calm himself. He took a breath before starting again. "I hate having to jump whenever Marcus gets a bug up his ass." he said, looking at the ground.

The Brotherhood was fiercely hierarchical. In practice that meant that a lower ranking member had to do whatever anyone above them said. There was a strict pecking order, and Jason and Mateo were at the bottom of it. Unfortunately, Marcus was the one above them. If they disobeyed him they would have to answer for it. The Brotherhood was harsh and gave no second chances; they would likely be killed, no questions asked.

"Yeah. I know." Jason said bitterly. He didn't know what else to say.

Mateo looked at him, noting the bags under his bloodshot eyes. "You didn't get a chance to sleep, did you?" he asked, and Jason shook his head no. "Shit." Mateo said sympathetically. They stood together in silence for a while, but then Mateo sighed and looked back toward the shelter. "Well, let's get this over with." he said, squaring his shoulders as if readying himself to do battle. Together they walked back to the entrance and Mateo opened the heavy doors, revealing the dimly lit space inside.

****

The interior of Casa Preciosa showed its age even more clearly than the outside did. Jason didn't know it, but the shelter had been among the first structures ever erected on Ross b. It had started life as a storage facility, been expanded for use as a barracks and mess hall, and then had been pressed into service as a medical clinic. As Cosmopolis grew up around it and the city-center shifted further to the east, the building had become less and less important and its history had been forgotten in the process. It had been well over thirty years since this part of town had been a vibrant community, and with the passage of time the building had effectively been abandoned.

Later, as often happens with abandoned properties, the building had been broken into and used as a sleeping place by those who had nowhere else to go. A nascent charity eventually purchased the building, reasoning that since the homeless already used it, it only made sense to convert it into a proper shelter. Unfortunately though, the new owners underestimated the enormity of the task and the endeavor quickly found itself underwater financially. The newly renovated shelter closed its doors shortly after they opened, leaving its mission unfulfilled. Those it had been meant to serve were left to seek help in other parts of the city. Despite the loss though, many of them chose not to move, preferring instead to stay in the neighborhood they considered their home, despite the hardships.

It was into this vacuum that The Brotherhood was born. Gabriel and Angel Batista had grown up in the Ocosta area, and they came of age alongside many of those who lived on the street. On occasion the brothers had been homeless themselves, and they quickly learned to do whatever was necessary to survive. As non-Citizens they lived at the margins of society, getting work when they could, and stealing or worse when they couldn't. It was a life familiar to everyone around them, and they were good at it. Over time they amassed a loyal crew and gained money and power.

The Brotherhood soon held sway over an increasingly large area; at first a few city blocks, then more. They acquired the shelter building as a base of operations, taking care to make the purchase in the name of a false organization which they controlled as silent, anonymous partners. They called the building Casa Preciosa, an ironic reference to its bland stone exterior. Eventually they reopened the shelter to the homeless, not to give back to the community, but because doing so gave cover for their activities and helped hide the comings and goings of their members. It was an awkward arrangement, but one that worked.

Gabriel and Angel had no interest in Casa Preciosa as anything more than a front and so had done little to improve it in the time since they took possession. They invested the bare minimum needed to keep the building standing and the shelter functioning, nothing more. As a result, the place was worn and dirty, carrying on as best it could despite the neglect.

Jason and Mateo stood just inside the double doors, waiting for their eyes to adjust to the dim lighting. In front of them the cafeteria took up nearly half of the first floor. It was here that the needy and the homeless could come for a free meal. The shelter rules dictated that this generosity was supposed to be limited to one meal a day, though Jason knew that some of those he saw furtively eating at the low tables would be back again for lunch, and maybe dinner too.

A blur of swift movement caught his eye as a scruffy orange cat jumped up on one of the tables; an actual cat! He had been amazed when he had first seen it. A few weeks after Jason began visiting the shelter, the animal had simply shown up at the door and wandered in, to the delight of everyone who saw it. It was young, but he was amazed it had lived even that long. Pets on Ross b were a rarity; not because people didn't want them but because they often had such short life-spans. It was a sad fact that no one could stop an animal from eating pretty much anything it found laying on the ground, and on Ross b things on the ground were often tainted by the toxic metals this planet was known for. It was not a recipe for a long life. Jason watched the cat, even now expecting to see the spasms that were a symptom of such exposure. It strolled carefully along the tabletop, sniffing at each plate as it passed by. Despite the odds, it appeared healthy, if a little scrawny and disheveled. Somehow, the cat had avoided the poisons so far, and Jason wished it continued luck. Maybe it couldn't avoid death forever, but it had made it this far and that alone was an achievement.

The cat paused in front of a small Hispanic girl, her skin colored as much by dirt as by heritage. The animal lowered its head and took a cautious bite from her plate, never taking its eyes off her. The girl giggled and reached out her hand to touch it. Seeing the movement, the animal pulled away, staying just out of reach. It quickly swallowed the stolen morsel and moved on down the table. For the cat this was a buffet and there were still many more entrees to try.

The little girl appeared to be alone and Jason couldn't help wonder where her parents were. She was flanked on either side by two men, one Hispanic and the other Caucasian. Both men ignored her, focusing instead on the food in front of them. Jason could see in their eyes the bloodshot red that indicated either a lack of sleep or drug use. It could easily be both, he knew. It seemed that at least a third of those who frequented the shelter had a drug habit. The smarter ones used as little as possible, trying to minimize the accumulating toxins, but even they eventually succumbed to the poisons in the drugs. Once some critical threshold was crossed, the user's remaining life was short and painful.

On Ross b, Helium was the drug of choice, though Rush too had its users. The homeless population was especially vulnerable and made up a large number of the addicts in the city. For those living on the street, Rush could seem like a good thing at first. The stimulant kept them alert, a valuable thing when sleeping might result in being attacked unaware. The crippling paranoia which came from prolonged use was only an extension of that effect, and the transition from help to hindrance was almost seamless.

Helium too was a staple of the homeless community, though it also saw some use in the club scene as a party drug. It was a mild hallucinogen and people used it simply to have fun or as an escape. The hallucinatory effects were quite pleasant most of the time, and once those faded the user was still left euphoric and quite suggestible for hours afterward. Sometimes this was taken advantage of, and had unfortunately led to its use as a date-rape drug. Still, the lasting high and associated pliability was the sought-after effect for some people and there were those who took it voluntarily for that express purpose. The resulting high-pitched voice which gave the drug its name was just one of the more comical side-effects and tended to fade over time.

Both drugs were derived from plants native to Ross b. Nearly all of the life that had evolved on Ross b was incompatible with that of Earth, but the early settlers of the planet had experimented, hoping to find novel compounds and medications locked inside the chemistry of their new world. These endeavors had produced limited results, but did lead to the disastrous discovery of these two drugs. All plantlife on Ross b inevitably contained dangerous amounts of poisons in the form of heavy metals absorbed from the ground and which acted in the body like mercury or lead. In the case of Rush and Helium, the metals were an integral part of the chemistry which produced their effects, and so removing the toxins was impossible. Extended use of the drugs caused the poisons to accumulate in the body and disrupt the nervous system, causing spasms, uncontrolled shaking and eventually death. It was an ugly way to go, and was the main reason these drugs had been declared illegal.

After seemingly rising from nowhere, The Brotherhood now controlled the narcotics trade in a large swath of the city and was the gang's main source of income. Jason hated that his personal mission had made him a part of the system which supplied these poisons. All around him he saw vulnerable people being sold a slow death, and it tore at him. For a while he'd been able to justify it as necessary to bring down The Resistance, but now he knew that it was time to get out.

A thin, strident voice suddenly demanded attention, and Jason saw the small form of Benito Reyes pacing back and forth among the tables. Today he wasn't finding his audience to be very receptive; those nearest to him averted their eyes and tried to finish their meals quickly. The man's voice was ragged and Jason could tell he must have been preaching all morning to deaf ears.

"...see that nothing has changed!" Benito was shouting. "*Nada ha cambiado!*" The words meant nothing to Jason but he could guess the meaning from the tone. It must have been Spanish, and he could see the pride on Benito's face as he spoke the words. Benito was the only person Jason had ever met who spoke much Spanish. As the original Latino settlers tried to assimilate to United States customs and values, they had consciously chosen to forego teaching their children Spanish in favor of English. Almost in the space of a single generation, the language largely disappeared from the planet. Jason didn't know where Benito had picked it up, but he privately suspected that the man didn't actually speak it all that well.

Benito's use of broken Spanish wasn't the only thing which set him apart; his manner of dress was also unique. He wore a loose-fitting white shirt with a brightly colored vee-shaped stripe around the neck comprised of repeating geometric patterns and black pants with white filigree along the outside edges. Missing today was another item he commonly wore; a rainbow striped poncho which would hang down below his waist. Jason had seen pictures of Hispanic people from Latin America on Earth and Benito's outfit seemed more like a parody or a costume. His entire persona was defined by a sort of cargo-cult Latinoism that even Jason found a little insulting, despite not being of the culture himself.

Benito's rant had turned to current events, and Jason found himself listening despite knowing better. "Go look on the net, you can see for yourselves! *Ver!* Early this morning another one of our proud brothers was murdered in cold blood! *Asesinado muerto!*" Benito held up his micro for the people to see, the screen small but clear enough. To his dismay, Jason recognized the construction site from this morning and watched again in horror as the man was shot to death. He turned away, feeling slightly nauseous. He'd known someone had filmed the attack, and now, just hours later, he was seeing it happen again.

"The riots were ended too soon!" Benito shouted as the clip ended. "Our people are still their victims, day after day! We need retribution! We need revenge! We must ask The Latino Resistance Front to come back; to pick up the sword and fight again! *Lucha con una espada!*"

Benito's rhetoric was incendiary but all around him the people only stared at their food, avoiding eye contact. Unlike those Benito had already won over to his cause, these people were using all their energy just to survive; they didn't have anything more to give in the service of a revolution. Still, the man kept going, performing for an audience that wilfully ignored him.

Jason watched Benito's continued exhortations fall flat and looked away. He began to search the room for Marcus; it was time to find out why he and Mateo had been called to the shelter. Not seeing him in the cafeteria, Jason guessed that Marcus was probably upstairs, so he motioned to Mateo and together they headed toward the back of the building.

The building's sole staircase was old and narrow,

forcing Jason and Mateo to ascend single-file. At the top, the cramped landing led immediately into a room that was littered with mismatched furniture and tables. At one end of the space a sturdy plastic box about a foot high had been overturned long ago and left there for use as an impromptu platform. High windows along one wall let in Ross b's red-orange light, which filtered through the dirty glass and gave everything it touched a fiery glow.

The room was filled with perhaps a dozen men, all of whom Jason knew as fellow members of The Brotherhood. To his surprise, he saw that everyone Marcus had gathered here was Latino and the realization left him unsettled. Hispanics admittedly made up the majority of The Brotherhood's membership, but they didn't account for everyone. The lack of anyone else in the room didn't bode well.

After a moment Marcus appeared in front of the unruly crowd and mounted the plastic box. The assembled men grumbled loudly, apparently no happier to be here than Jason or Mateo. As Marcus raised his arms petulantly and called for attention, Jason and Mateo found a place to stand near the wall and tried to keep out of the way.

While Marcus tried to quiet the group, Mateo quietly nudged Jason and pointed to a spot in the front row. Jason saw that Daniel, the slave boy they had taken as payment for drugs, was sitting cross-legged on the floor in front of Marcus. The boy looked overwhelmed but at least he appeared free. Jason could see no sign of the second boy though, and wondered what had become of him.

Growing frustrated, Marcus raised his voice. "Alright, shut the fuck up!" he shouted, calling for quiet. His audience slowly began to settle down, waiting dubiously to see what he had to say. "Alright!" he repeated, trying to build up some verbal momentum. "Now, you all heard Benito talking downstairs..."

At the mention of Benito's name, voices in the crowd began to groan derisively. Marcus wasn't any good at public speaking but he plowed ahead doggedly, trying to win them over. "You may not believe the things he says, but you all saw the video!" he bellowed accusingly, his face turning red. "What do you think we should do about it?! Should we keep quiet? Should we stay in our fucking place?! Benito says we should fight and I say he's right! I say we track down the Anglo fuckers who did this and kill them!"

The men gathered in front of him were unmoved, and unlike Jason and Mateo they were Marcus' peers in the gang; they weren't bound to do his bidding. Marcus had misjudged his audience and now he was losing them. Jason watched the rage smoulder in his eyes. His goal had apparently been to organize a lynching but it wasn't going the way he had planned.

"No way! He wasn't in The Brotherhood!" someone shouted, shaking his head. "He wasn't one of us!"

"Yes he was!" Marcus shot back. "He was Hispanic, just like you! That makes him our brother!"

Everyone in the gang had heard him go on like this before, and it wasn't a winning argument. The fact was, Marcus was the only one in The Brotherhood who took Benito Reyes' revolutionary rhetoric seriously and buying into it had made him something of an outcast. The men gathered here largely respected him; he was a dangerous fighter and a good man to have at your back in a brawl, but they could only be drawn so far. A wild hunt to avenge the death of a man who wasn't in The Brotherhood was just asking too much and Marcus should have known better.

Marcus' frustrated voice grew louder but as he kept arguing, Jason's attention was drawn toward the door as Benito Reyes quietly slipped in and found a space in the back to stand and watch. Jason was surprised and confused; despite seemingly living at Casa Preciosa, Benito was very much *not* a member of The Brotherhood. It was unheard of for him to be allowed to witness gang business, and his presence in the room now was unprecedented.

Jason watched him for a while but eventually turned

his attention back to Marcus, who by now had lost the crowd entirely. Amid a general murmur and a few shouted curses, the meeting broke up and the men wandered off in search of something, anything, better to do. Jason and Mateo stood and waited as the room emptied. Scowling, Marcus jumped down off the box and stalked over to them. The boy Daniel followed him timidly, like a forgotten puppy. Jason was revolted to see how the boy watched Marcus, as a son might watch his father.

"Fucking cowards." Marcus spat as he approached them. "Scared motherfuckers!" He yelled these words toward the now empty doorway, and the shout echoed down the stairs. Afterward, quieter but no less angry, he said to Jason and Mateo, "They're fucking scared. We're just going to have to do this ourselves." He scowled malignantly at nothing, his thoughts turned inward.

"Come on man, what they said is true; the guy who got killed wasn't in the gang! It's not our business." Mateo said, trying to talk him down.

In response Marcus suddenly lunged forward, rage radiating from him. "I'm making it our business!" he said, grabbing a fistfull of Mateo's shirt before releasing it violently and shoving him back. "It fucking *is* our business. Some Anglo fucker kills one of our own, we fight back! That's justice!" Marcus was breathing heavily now, as though his anger carried a physical weight.

Jason could see clearly where this path would take him, and knew he couldn't go through with it. He'd been careful these past few months; he'd had to intimidate and even sometimes hurt people, and yet somehow he'd made it this far without having to kill anyone. He worried he would no longer recognize himself if that changed. If he was going to have any chance of getting out of The Brotherhood with his soul intact, he needed to do it soon. Marcus hadn't even asked whether Jason and Mateo wanted to come with him; he'd made it an order. As far as Marcus was concerned, this was a gang matter and his underlings would damn well do what they were told.

"Now, I'm going to go get some things together." Marcus said, quieter now but still seething. "Be ready to go when I get back." With one last hard look at Mateo, he turned to go, leaving Jason and his friend to exchange looks. Daniel fell into step behind Marcus as he left, a boy following his adopted father. Jason watched them leave together and felt the tension in his body grow tighter. There was nothing good in that boy's future if he followed in Marcus' footsteps, and Jason couldn't see a way to help him. The sounds of their feet on the stairs mingled and overlapped as they descended.

A sudden voice from behind startled Jason and he whirled, ready to fend off an attack. He found Benito standing there, looking solemn. "Marcus is right, you know." he said, standing his ground. "Not because he's doing what *I* said, but because he's doing what is right for his people. *Si.* He is a good man; a warrior."

Jason was momentarily at a loss for words. Finding them again, he pointed after Daniel, saying, "What about the boy? Marcus is just teaching him how to hate."

"Of course." Benito said calmly, closing his eyes. He opened them again and held Jason's gaze unnervingly. "You *should* hate injustice! You should be willing to kill to end it! *Muerto!* Marcus has learned that, and if he's half the man I think he is, he'll teach it to Daniel as well."

Jason was left dumbstruck, unable to answer. There was a horrible twisted logic to what Benito said, and it repulsed him. It *was* right to fight injustice, to hate it even. But there was a difference between hating an injustice and hating the people who perpetrated it. It was a vanishingly thin and difficult distinction, but it was an important one and Jason clung to it with both hands.

Benito still stood in front of them, his face pensive. "Marcus rescued the *niño* from a life of slavery, did you know that?" he asked softly.

Jason found his voice and answered. "Yes; I was there. There were actually two boys; Daniel and an Asian kid." Jason hadn't seen the second boy since he'd been thrown into Marcus' car, and that probably wasn't a good sign. He decided he would ask Marcus about the boy the next chance he got.

At Jason's reply, Benito's face lit up. "That's right! I'd forgotten that you work for Marcus now! *Bueno!*" He smiled, but then his face fell and he continued. "It is a travesty, the Sepultures holding a Latino boy as a slave. *Tragedia!* They are as guilty as all the Anglos who beat and kill us!"

The diminutive man's countenance had shifted suddenly; he was becoming angry now. Jason was getting a personal dose of the fire Benito usually reserved for haranguing the masses. "We need The Resistance again!" he declared emphatically. "We need to fight for our freedom and if that means killing to get it, even the Seps, so be it! *Luchar!*"

As his voice died away, Benito grinned as if amused by his own outburst. He then leaned in toward Jason, lowering his voice conspiratorially. "I asked Gabe to get a message to them for me." he confided. "The Resistance is truly still needed! They inspire us to fight against the oppression and to rise above the Anglos! I begged them to come back!" As the words escaped his lips, he paused and straightened back up, suddenly uncomfortable. With a quick half-smile, Benito retired from the room, leaving Jason and Mateo alone.

Jason felt stunned, like someone had blinded him with a searchlight. Benito thought that Gabe knew The Resistance? He suddenly felt weightless, and it was the best feeling he'd ever had. There *was* a link to The Resistance! It was Gabe Batista, and Benito had asked him to pass along a message to them! It was the connection he'd been looking for all this time, and now he finally had it!

Beside Jason, Mateo put his hands in his pockets. "Guy's kinda nuts, isn't he?" he said cooly, nodding toward the doorway Benito had disappeared through. He too had noticed Benito's slip but was playing it cool, gauging his friend's reaction.

"Gabe knows The Resistance!" Jason breathed. "Holy shit! He said that Gabe can get a message to them! Gabe's the connection!"

Mateo smiled. "Been a long time coming, getting that out of them, hasn't it?" he said. "So now what? We start working Gabe for info, try to infiltrate from there?"

Jason didn't know yet; he needed time to think this through. He was about to answer when they heard the sound of footsteps on the stairs and a voice called out to them.

"Mateo; Lucas. You guys need to come back downstairs." a member of The Brotherhood said. "Gabe and Angel are putting something together with Marcus. They say they want you there too." Without waiting for an answer, the man turned and vanished back the way he came.

Jason raised his eyebrows, while Mateo pulled his hands from his pockets.

"Let's go see what they want." Jason said.

****

Jason and Marcus descended the narrow stairway and turned toward Gabriel and Angel's office on the far side of the cafeteria. Along one wall they passed a storage room filled with folded cots and other bedding material. In the evenings, the tables were put away and most of the first floor was converted into a dormitory. The patrons were expected to do this themselves and they often fought amongst each other for the best cots and places to sleep. Over time a kind of system had developed where the strong prevailed and the weak were pushed to the margins. In some ways it served as a training ground for up-and-coming members of the gang. The contrast with Jonah's El Rey Latino Outreach Center was striking, and was something that Jason tried not to think about.

Breakfast was drawing to a close as they crossed the room and the scene was chaotic. As people milled around them gathering their belongings and clearing tables, Jason saw Marcus framed by the open office door. Marcus gestured to them impatiently, urging them to hurry. They moved quickly past the tables and people blocking their path, and joined Marcus inside the private room.

Gabriel and Angel Batista tightly controlled access to their office, and Jason had never before been invited inside. As Mateo followed him in, Jason gently closed the door and then turned to take in the sparsely appointed room. There really wasn't much to see; the furnishings mainly consisted of a cheap wall-mounted screen and two black couches at right angles, with a low table in front of them. On one of the couches sat Gabe and Angel, the eponymous brothers who had founded and defined The Brotherhood. They wore their black hair long, but tied back and held out of their faces. Both were muscular and bore numerous tattoos, the blue markings seeming to crawl from beneath their shirts. Gabe was the elder brother, and was slightly taller than Angel. When he spoke, his voice sounded gruff but also somehow musical.

"I'm putting a stop to Marcus' bullshit revenge idea right now." Gabe informed them flatly as Marcus, Jason and Mateo sat down opposite the brothers. Jason spared a glance at Marcus and the impotent scowl he found there said that the big man had already been told. "We've got bigger things to take care of anyway." Gabe continued, ignoring Marcus' sulking. "Thanks to your deal with Jock, we learned that the Seps are doing business in our territory. They should know better than that by now, but apparently they're just stupid."

It was the oldest grievance in human history. People had fought over territory since the beginning of time and things were no different on Ross b. In Cosmopolis, the Sepulchers territory traditionally covered the northeast corner of the city, while The Brotherhood controlled a sizable area in the southwest. As each gang tried to expand their influence, conflicts were inevitable.

When Gabe finished, Marcus turned to Jason and Mateo, clearly trying to regain some face by taking control of the discussion. When he spoke though, he sounded like he was repeating someone else's words. "Now that we know the Seps are selling slaves in our territory, we have to do something." he said, echoing much of what Gabe had already told them. "The Seps are tough, but we can't let them walk all over us. Gabe and Angel are sending us to go talk with them; offer them a deal. Deal is, they can sell in our territory but we get a cut."

So this was about the Sepultures selling their slaves in Brotherhood territory? From the sound of it, Gabe and Angel didn't want to shut them down either, they just wanted them to pay for the privilege. After what Benito had said about the Seps enslaving Hispanic kids, no wonder Marcus is pissed, Jason thought. It was obvious that Marcus was trying hard to convince Jason and Mateo, and by extension himself, that the offer was a good idea. It wasn't working though, and the conflict was evident on his face.

Out of the corner of his eye, Jason saw Gabe nod. "We're sending Marcus to do the talking," he confirmed. "and he's going to bring you two along as muscle. You've done good for us so far. Don't let us down." he said, a loose strand of hair falling over his face.

Jason felt trapped. He didn't want to go on some bullshit mission. He wanted out but now he found he couldn't bring himself to say so. He had finally found a connection to The Latino Resistance Front, and it ran right through Gabe and Angel. If he backed out now, he might never get another chance.

"Marcus is our brother." he said, the words tasting like ashes in his mouth. "We'll back him up." Inside, Jason despaired. Would he ever find a way out of this?

The meeting was at an end. Marcus stood up, shaking hands with Gabe and Angel. "We'll go talk to the bastards; see if we can make a deal. If not, well, we can handle that too." he reassured them.

"Just go talk to them for now." Angel said. "We don't want a war, at least not yet. We've got a few things to put in place before that." He smiled, but Jason heard the ghost of something ominous in his voice.

Marcus, Jason and Mateo left the office together, and Jason saw Daniel sitting near the door. Upon seeing him, Marcus seemed to make up his mind about something. “Look,” he said, “I’m going to go get Daniel settled at my place and then I’m gonna fucking sleep. I’ll be back here tonight at seven. We’ll go see the Seps then. Be here and be ready to go." He strode purposefully toward the door and Daniel rose to follow. The two of them left the shelter side-by-side.

“Getting ready won’t take much.” Mateo said once Marcus had gone. “I’ve still got my gun and ammo from this morning.”

“Me too.” Jason replied, sighing. “I guess we’ll just be ready early then." He made a herculean effort to stifle a yawn, and failed. He hadn’t slept in over twenty four hours now, and he just didn’t have anything more left in him. At least they weren’t leaving till tonight; the delay would let him get some shut-eye. Later he’d go back to his apartment to shower, but right now he was too tired to move. Looking for a place to lay down, he found one of the long tables that still filled the cafeteria. Heedless of the mess, he pushed aside a few plates and lay flat on the tabletop, closing his eyes for a moment. He told himself he was just resting, but he began to drift off almost as soon as he was horizontal.

Mateo sat down on a nearby bench, deep in thought. When he finally spoke he sounded hesitant, as if he didn’t want to wake Jason but had no choice. “You had something you were going to tell me, before. What was it?”

Jason jumped at Mateo’s question, starting guiltily from a deep sleep he hadn’t meant to take. “Hmm...?” he mumbled, his tongue feeling thick in his mouth.

Mateo chose his words carefully. “You said you had to think about it first. That’s a hell of a thing to say and leave me hanging. Did you want to talk about it now?" He felt bad for waking his friend, but it had been weighing on him ever since Jason had brought it up.

With an effort, Jason propped himself up on his elbows. He regretted having said anything earlier. The past several hours had been wild and terrible, swinging from drug deals and slavery, to witnessing a murder, to *finally* discovering a lead on The Resistance. He felt overwhelmed and burned out, but now he had a sliver of hope. He had to see this through, no matter the cost.

"No. I mean, yeah I did, but then things changed. It doesn't matter anymore." he said eventually.

"Okay." Mateo answered noncommittally. Jason suspected that his friend knew more than he let on, and was grateful when he didn't pursue the issue further. With his body aching from exhaustion, Jason lay back down and sank into a dark, dreamless sleep.

CHAPTER 18

Seven hours later, Jason sat alone in his apartment. He had continued to sleep on the table at Casa Preciosa until eventually someone asked him to move so they could set up for lunch. With his back aching from the hard surface, he'd rolled off the table groggily and decided to go back to his apartment to finish sleeping in a proper bed.

His plan had been to rest for a few hours and then go visit Anne and Matthew at The Center. He'd been absolutely crushed when he finally woke and realized that it was too late to make that happen. He'd called Anne immediately to apologize. She had said she understood, but even on the tiny screen he had seen the hurt on her face.

So much had happened since they'd parted ways this morning! He wanted to share the excitement he'd felt at finally finding a clue to the link between The Brotherhood and The Resistance. He wanted to explain to her that his time away hadn't been for nothing! Twice he almost interrupted her mid-sentence, but each time he held back. He knew that revealing what he'd found would also mean telling her that he'd changed his mind about leaving The Brotherhood. He knew she wanted him to come home, to try and build a new life for the both of them, and for Matthew too. Deep down he knew she was right but he just couldn't do it yet. He had a real chance now to fix things, to reclaim what The Resistance had stolen from them. In the end he kept quiet, shamefully promising himself he'd tell her later, in person. She deserved that much, and more.

Near the end of the call Anne had passed the micro to

Matthew. As hard as it had been to keep things from her, in some ways talking to his son had hurt him more. He should have spent the day with Matthew instead of making do with yet another video call. Like his mother, Matt seemed distant on the small screen and Jason could feel his son's unspoken disappointment just below the surface. Still, he persevered and kept talking. As the call came to an end, he made a point of telling Matt that he loved him. It was so little, but it was all he had to give.

After the call was over, he sat alone in his room with no one to talk to. Time passed slowly until his micro beeped softly on top of the dresser, reminding him that he had to go meet Marcus. He stood ruefully, mourning the time he'd lost. He'd spent almost the whole day asleep, but in spite of the consequences he had to admit that the rest had done him good. His head felt clear for the first time in days and the ever-present headache had finally receded. Still, the prospect of going to make a deal with slave-dealers held no appeal at all.

Sourly, he showered and dressed before calling in a car and making his way back to Casa Preciosa. The traffic he passed on the way carried people who looked like they were getting ready for a night out on the town. He chuckled bitterly; while these people had been working, he'd been sleeping. Now that he was going to work, it was past their dinnertime. As the cityscape slid by outside, he longed wistfully for a life more like theirs, or at least one less like his.

****

Upon arriving at Casa Preciosa, Jason saw that most of the dining tables had been folded up or pushed out of the way. Those few patrons who remained in the shelter were gathered in small groups playing cards or listlessly watching one of the portable screens they occasionally brought in with them. The murmur of overlapping conversations was dull and lethargic, matching the people themselves.

Jason was pouring himself a cup of room-temperature coffee from the communal pot when his micro beeped again. He'd set an alarm for 6:45 PM so that he would have some warning before Marcus arrived. He had a hunch that their visit to the Seps wouldn't go smoothly; they were known to be dangerous and the prospect of meeting them in their own territory weighed heavily on his mind.

He silenced the alarm and sat down to wait in an unoccupied chair against one wall. He had only been sitting there a few minutes when Mateo entered, carrying a small box under one arm. Mateo nodded to Jason and adjusted his grip on the package. Jason assumed it held donuts and he was proven right when Mateo walked over to a table where four men sat playing cards and tossed the box on top of the meager pile of chips in the center of the table.

"Here you go." Mateo told them generously as he grabbed a donut for himself and returned to take up a chair next to Jason. Mateo had a habit of providing sweets for those who used the shelter, bringing in a new box every few days. It had made him very popular among the patrons and Jason guessed that it made Mateo feel better too; a simple recognition of their shared humanity in an inhumane place.

"Did you sleep here all day? You were still out when I left." Mateo teased as he sat down. His tone was light but Jason could see that if he said yes, Mateo would believe him without question.

"For a while. Eventually I went home to sleep in my own bed, and to take a shower. What did you do all day?"

Mateo nodded while chewing on his pastry. "I actually got to spend the afternoon with Valarie!" he said, a smile in his voice. "We hung out at The Center while she worked. I tried to get her to pick out baby names with me, but she's not ready for that yet." He paused mid-bite. "Actually, I kind of expected you to show up there too, to see your family."

Jason again felt a harsh stab of guilt. "I overslept." he admitted bitterly. "By the time I woke up, there wasn't time to go see them. I called them, but it's not the same."

Mateo was sympathetic. "That's rough." he said. He took a last bite of donut and wiped a bit of glaze from the corner of his mouth. Jason was lost in his own thoughts and didn't have anything more to say. They sat together in silence, neither one speaking.

A few minutes later the shelter door opened again and Marcus entered with an exaggerated swagger. Jason knew it was affected because he forgot to do it as often as not. The man was such a collection of stereotypes and fake machismo it was ridiculous. It would have been funny if it hadn't been so toxic.

Jason was about to stand up and signal to Marcus that he was ready to go when a small figure entered a few steps behind him. It was Daniel. The boy had changed clothes since this morning and appeared to have washed. His hair was trimmed and combed up into short, spiky rows. He now looked like any of a dozen kids Jason might see in the neighborhood everyday, but with an edge that suggested Marcus had been the one to choose the look. Still, the boy appeared determined to make Marcus proud and wore a tough look on his young face. Marcus whispered something to him and pointed, and the boy sauntered across the room and sat down at the card table. Those already seated there shot disbelieving looks at Marcus, but he ignored them.

"You guys ready?" Marcus asked Jason and Mateo gruffly.

Jason considered asking what he planned to do with Daniel but decided against it. The boy seemed safe for now and Jason reluctantly chose to let the question drop. Whatever answer Marcus gave would probably be nonsense anyway. Jason had learned to pick his battles, and this one would gain him nothing good.

"Yeah, we're ready." Mateo answered. Jason nodded in agreement as they both stood.

"Then let's go." Marcus said impatiently and turned to leave.

They followed him out the door to where Marcus' garish purple vehicle sat waiting for them by the curb. Jason hesitated at the memory of its nearly vestigial back seat.

"Hey, let's call in a car instead." he suggested. "One with a real back seat." Marcus looked disgusted at the idea.

"Lucas, I am not riding in one of those rented shit-mobiles." he sneered.

"So which one of us gets crammed in the back, then?" Jason asked.

"I don't give a shit..." Marcus began, as Mateo forcibly called out, "Front!"

Jason was taken aback and ruefully shook his head at Mateo's wide grin. Grudgingly, he opened the car door and climbed into the vehicle's claustrophobic rear seat.

"You can sit up here on the way back." Mateo said graciously as he settled into the comparatively enormous front seat. He stretched his legs dramatically, wiggling his feet to draw attention to the extra room he now enjoyed.

****

Jason craned his neck to see the sky through the car's tinted windows. When they left Casa Preciosa the clouds overhead had been a steel gray. Since then a stiff breeze had arisen and a series of strong gusts pushed at the car as they travelled through the city. Jason pressed his knees into the back of the seat in front of him as he fished out his micro and brought up the weather report. He made a face as he read the screen, then verified with another source. The results were the same; no storm was forecast. He raised his eyes back to the window and a far distant flash of lightning put the lie to the predictions in his hand. Expected or not, a storm was coming and it looked like a bad one.

Jason returned the micro to his pocket and leaned forward to study the path Marcus had laid into the car's navigation system. The route it showed was straightforward, taking the shortest possible path with the exception of two quick detours. Jason quickly realized that these excursions were there to skirt police checkpoints. Marcus had no more interest in talking to the cops than any of them did and had planned accordingly.

He frowned as he saw how little their path was altered by the deviations and marvelled to himself at how worthless the police checkpoints really were. Most of them had been dismantled since the riots and those that remained formed imperfect rings around the city center and Ross b's capitol mall. Ostensibly they protected the crowded downtown, the governor's mansion and other official buildings, but in reality they were nothing more than theater. As their current route proved, in most cases the checkpoints could be avoided entirely simply by taking a parallel street. They were laughably ineffective and were yet another sign that the city had moved on and no longer took The Resistance threat seriously.

No one spoke as they continued into the denser part of the city, giving Jason time to think. He remembered the danger The Resistance posed even if no one else did, and now he had a clue how to find them. A faint smile played at his lips; he just had to follow the breadcrumbs.

Despite his elation at learning Gabe and Angel had a link to The Resistance though, something about the revelation troubled him. He'd been in The Brotherhood for months; why had it taken him until now to find this out? It didn't help that Benito Reyes was a less than reliable source of information either. If anyone at the shelter was going to be suddenly revealed to have connections to The Latino Resistance Front, wouldn't it have been him?

Jason turned the question over in his mind, but made no progress. Suddenly however, he realized that if he was careful in how he asked, Marcus just might reveal whether Benito himself was the link, rather than Gabe or Angel. Feeling clumsy and obvious, he raised his voice over the car's aggressive electric whine. "I saw that Benito came up to watch your speech this morning." he commented casually.

Leaving the driving to the car's automatic systems, Marcus twisted in his seat to face Jason. His expression said he couldn't decide whether Jason was actually interested, or if he was trying to pick a fight.

"Yeah." Marcus answered guardedly. "He wanted me to try and get you and the other guys to go out looking for that Anglo asshole. I guess he came up to see how it was going." There was a darkness in his expression that said not to push him.

"Afterward he stopped and talked to Mateo and me." Jason went on, trying to draw him out.

"Huh. What about?"

"He talked to us about how justice was important, and that sometimes you just had to grab it because no one is going to give it to you." Jason paused, watching Marcus' face for warning signs. "He said he wanted The Resistance to come back. Couldn't he just ask them himself?"

Surprisingly, Marcus actually relaxed at the question. He chuckled a little and said, "You might think so. Actually, I don't think he knows anyone in The Resistance. The way he tells it, he was preaching revolution before they ever showed up. I guess when he was young he read a lot of history on things like the Irish Republican Army and something called FARC. He liked the idea of fighting back, but he's not a tough guy. So he started making speeches instead, trying to spread the word." He paused a moment and tried on a knowing look. "A few of us listened to him. When The Resistance showed up, he thought they were perfect. They were just what he'd been preaching about."

The look in Marcus' eye made Jason wonder for a moment if maybe *he* was the connection to The Resistance, but the more he thought about it the more he decided that didn't make sense. Jason knew that Marcus didn't have any friends outside the gang, and none of his fellow gang members cared much about revolution. He decided to change tack and see if

Marcus knew anything about Gabe or Angel's supposed connection to The Resistance.

"What about Gabe and Angel?" he asked. "Benito said he asked them to get a message to The Resistance."

Marcus' mouth twitched but his expression didn't change. "Gabe and Angel run the gang; that's all they care about. They don't give a shit about any revolution."

With that he turned back around in his seat. It was clear that the conversation was over and it left Jason right where he started; with a possible connection between The Brotherhood and The Latino Resistance Front that no one except Benito seemed to know anything about. He resigned himself to the fact that this was never going to be easy. He'd have to keep digging and hope the pieces he found eventually fit together.

A few miles later a spattering of rain began to collect on the windshield. Jason passed the time as he often did, by thinking of his family. He hated the way he'd left it with them, especially Matthew. He missed them so much...

Eventually thoughts of family led Jason to wonder about the relationship between Marcus and the slave boy Daniel. Unable to stop himself, he again leaned forward.

"So what's the deal with the boy, Daniel?" he asked Marcus. "You planning to adopt him?"

Marcus didn't turn around. He answered over his shoulder, as if it were the most normal question in the world. "Maybe. He doesn't have any real family left alive that he knows of."

Jason knew that Daniel must have come from a bad situation, but the blunt words still hit him in the gut. The other one, the Asian boy, couldn't have been any better off. "What about the other kid?" he asked before he could stop himself. He knew that Marcus' attachment to Daniel was at least partly due to their shared heritage. The big man had already made it clear that he didn't care about the other kid, but Jason was still unprepared for his cavalier response.

"Gabe took him." Marcus explained dismissively, as if it were answer enough. His tone was flat and uncaring, and it gave Jason chills.

In the front seat, Marcus had already moved on. "There's the club. We'll pull over here." he said, the matter already forgotten.

****

The Sepulchers operated out of an old abandoned nightclub called The LV, located across the street from one of the city's many open-air markets. The Seps had been in operation far longer than The Brotherhood but in the end their tactics and goals were the same; to meet those needs society left unmet, to make money, and to control territory.

Despite these similarities though, there were differences too, and The Brotherhood and The Seps each specialized in filling different niches. While The Brotherhood manufactured and distributed narcotics, The Seps instead made their money from human trafficking. It was a lucrative endeavor. The key to their success was in securing a supply of 'product' to exploit, and The Seps maintained deep connections and utilized a variety of methods to obtain it.

The largest number of their victims came from what was called the frontier areas; places far beyond the boundaries of Cosmopolis. While the capital city and its suburbs were surrounded by the dense forests that supported their local economies, not all of Ross b was so lucky. As pioneers and settlers continued to push outward in search of new and different resources, they sometimes established outposts in regions where the valuable trees didn't grow. Settlers were often forced to live in very harsh conditions, too hot or too cold depending on their exposure to the unmoving sun. Without the reliable economic base provided by logging, many of these new towns failed, leaving their inhabitants destitute and struggling to get by.

The Seps had built their empire by preying on these people. They would lure them back to the city with offers of work, but once they arrived the promised jobs would vanish and the victims were then sold to the highest bidder. It was a horrible system of forced labor, prostitution and disposable people, and because the Seps kept the right people happy, nothing was done about it.

As Jason stared at the dreary nightclub through rain covered windows, he had to fight the impulse to get out and just walk away. He felt dirty just being on the Seps' turf, and he didn't think that going to talk to them would make him feel any better.

In the front seat, Marcus studied the building for a moment. Then, as if reaching a decision, he opened his door and got out. Mateo followed, joining him on the sidewalk. The wind blustered and pulled at their clothes, forcing them to squint and turn their backs to the driving rain. Realizing that Jason hadn't joined them, Marcus glared impatiently into the car's dry interior. Jason gritted his teeth and grudgingly pushed his door open, bracing himself against the weather.

As his boots splashed into a shallow puddle Jason reflexively glanced around, nervously checking for trouble. He didn't see any warning signs, but their absence didn't change anything. They were deep in enemy territory and the wide open street around them left him feeling exposed. Uneasily, he closed the car door and met with Marcus and Mateo as they walked swiftly through the rain toward the club.

As they made ready to go inside, they took cover from the unyielding rain under the club's ancient marquee, which read in faded and stained block letters "Closed for Remodeling". This was supposed to be a peaceful mission but each of them checked that their weapons were ready; stowed out of sight, yet still within easy reach. Afterward, Marcus took a moment to lay down the ground rules.

"When we get in there, I don't want to have to explain anything you fuckers might say, so just keep quiet. I'll do the talking." he growled. "Personally, I'd just as soon shoot them but Gabe and Angel say that's not the plan. I'm just gonna tell them that if they do business in our territory, then we get a cut."

With that Marcus fell silent, and after a moment Jason and Mateo realized that he wasn't going to add anything else. That was just as well, Jason thought; he didn't want a pep-talk. After receiving a pair of nods, Marcus pulled open the door and led the way inside.

****

They were intercepted almost immediately. Upon entering the lobby a short Asian man and a large Black woman leveled their automatic weapons and pointed them at Marcus' chest. The guards each displayed identical tattoos on their right hands; an unusual image somewhere between a ghost and a genie that appeared to serve as the Sepultures' mark of membership. The mark was the man's only visible tattoo, but the Black woman also sported two words spelled out in large gothic letters that spread across her chest. Though the text was partially obscured by her shirt, it seemed to read "Uber Alice." Jason strongly suspected that he didn't want to know what the phrase meant.

Despite the weapons trained on him, Marcus tried to appear calm and in control. He held up his hands, saying, "We're with The Brotherhood. We're here to see Billy." Jason heard a bravado in the big man's voice that he knew from experience was fake. He held his breath and waited for the worst, momentarily certain that 'Uber Alice' would simply pull her trigger.

Without changing her expression, 'Uber Alice' gestured with the barrel of her gun, indicating that they could proceed. She pointed them to an open door and Marcus walked through it into a room that was lit in a lurid red. Mateo and Jason followed, keeping close to Marcus. The two guards fell in behind them and Jason imagined he could feel the tip of a gun being pressed into his back.

The red room held a tall man whose job it was to frisk each of them for weapons. Marcus made no attempt to hide what he carried, and Jason was surprised when the man merely called out what he found without confiscating anything. Afterward, Marcus was waved forward and the process was repeated for Mateo and Jason. The whole thing left Jason feeling off balance; was it a gesture of respect to let them keep their guns? Maybe, or maybe it was an indication that the Seps just didn't consider them a threat. Afterward, they were allowed to proceed through a second door on the other side of the room and out into the club's main hall.

The space they entered was large and oddly shaped, with walls that were angled and slightly concave. The entire room was covered in the ornate decorations of a bygone era, and their combined effect was to draw attention toward a raised stage that lay at one end. Perhaps a dozen men stood scattered around the floor. Their placement seemed random at first, but Jason noticed that each of them had unobstructed lines of sight on each of the exit doors as well as their guests. The carpet under his feet was torn and uneven, and the stained floor sloped gently toward the stage. He realized this must have once been a performing hall, though with all the seating removed the cavernous space felt hollow and tomb-like.

A thin Caucasian man sat perched on the edge of the stage, theatrically positioned and surrounded by several guards, all of them armed. He was clearly the one in charge; Billy, Marcus had called him. The man was far older than Jason had expected, with thinning hair that had been swept back over his scalp in a vain attempt at fashion. The lines on his face revealed that he'd lived a hard life, though his satisfied scowl said it had been one of his own choosing. As they came closer the man grinned and spread his arms dramatically, saying, "I'm Billy Ghoul. Welcome to my club!" He paused, keeping his arms aloft as if waiting for a reaction. When none came, he let them drop lifelessly back to his side. Disapointed, he demanded peevishly, “So what the fuck do you want?”

Marcus had been caught off guard by the man’s capricious demeanor. Sounding like an actor who’d forgotten his lines, he stammered, “We’re The Brotherhood...”

“I fucking know that!” Billy snapped. “Gabe sent me some bullshit message. Said he was sending some guys to come talk to me. Said he wanted to make a deal. I told him not to waste my fucking time." He paused, looking Marcus up and down. “I guess he sent you anyway.” he finished awkwardly.

Marcus tried to rally, oblivious to Billy’s cold stare. “You recently sold some ‘goods’ to Jock on Boone street...” he began. Jason winced at the euphemism for slaves; even to him it sounded awkward. Not for the first time, he seriously questioned Gabe’s judgement in choosing Marcus to play the diplomat.

On the stage, Billy Ghoul raised his head as if just remembering something. Ignoring Marcus’ attempts to negotiate, he said, “You know what, nevermind. I’m glad you came. I want you to see something.”

The wiry old man hopped down from the stage and spoke a few quick words to a thin, pale man with red hair. The man nodded and disappeared through a previously unseen doorway, only to return moments later leading a young woman by the arm. Her blue eyes were dilated and darted wildly around the room, her legs nearly buckling as she was urged forward. She appeared terrified and huddled close to her guide, pressing her head against his chest and hiding behind her thick brown hair.

The man stopped while still several feet from Marcus and lifted the woman’s chin so that she was forced to look directly at him. He spoke and she listened intently, then gave a small nod and turned toward Marcus. In front of their very eyes, her body language seemed to change completely. Suddenly sure of herself, she stepped confidently away from her guide and strode forward, projecting an air of manic purpose only just held in check. Marcus drew back involuntarily as she approached, uncertain how to react.

"Simon tells me that you wanted to see me." the woman announced a little too loudly. Her voice carried the oddly high-pitched tone that was a telltale sign of Helium use, but there was clearly something else going on as well. Her intensely focused gaze told Jason that whatever was going on inside her head, she wasn't hallucinating now. He shivered involuntarily, becoming almost irrationally nervous.

Marcus kept his eyes trained on the woman as he called out to Billy. "What the fuck is this?" he demanded.

"I thought you'd recognize it!" Billy responded sardonically. The woman's head snapped around as Billy spoke, and she glared at him accusingly.

"Does he know me?" she asked her guide, Simon, suspiciously. "I don't know him! How does he know me?!" Her speech seemed pressured and she was quickly becoming hysterical. Simon grabbed her arm gently and at his touch her demeanor changed again. She desperately threw herself against him, shaking. Simon whispered to her softly and after a moment she again turned toward Marcus, somehow projecting an eerie calm and frightening mania all at the same time. When she spoke, Jason could hear the tight restraint in her voice.

"Simon says you wanted to see me. Here I am!" It was an odd thing; she seemed to think that her purpose here was only to be seen, nothing more. She held still in front of them, putting herself on display. There was nothing sexual about it, she simply stood there to be observed. Marcus had no idea what to make of it and turned his attention back to Billy, his face a mask of confusion and disgust.

Billy let Marcus stew for a long moment before shouting, "You see how she is? Weird as fuck, to say the least! We sold her about a month ago and had to pick her back up from the buyer last week. Normally we don't do refunds, but this guys sort of a special case. Anyway, look at her! She's irrational! Dangerous, even! We're lucky she bonded with Simon here;

she won't do fuck-all anyone else tells her!"

Marcus looked lost. He'd come here to deliver a message, not deal with whatever the fuck this was. Gamely, he tried to wrest control of the conversation back. "So what? She's not my problem, and it's not what we came here to talk about." he said.

Billy went on as if Marcus hadn't spoken. "You see, this one here, she's got a drug habit." he explained. "We knew that when we sold her, of course. A lot of our merchandise does. It can be useful at times too, the Helium anyway. Problem with her though, is she likes Rush. Far as we can tell, she'd never done Helium before we gave it to her."

Jason saw a spark of understanding flicker across Marcus' face. Jason however, didn't have a clue. In front of them, Billy had grown agitated and was now pacing back and forth. Clearly, he didn't care whether his guests understood or not; he had a presentation to make and was going to see it through.

"You ever mix Rush and Helium? Do you know what happens?!" he asked, heavily stressing each word. He sounded like an abusive father, the tension building toward violence. When Marcus didn't answer, Billy turned on him. "You get all fucked up!" Billy roared, his voice breaking with outrage. "I can't sell this! If she won't do what she's told, she's not good for anything!" As the echo faded he nodded to Simon, who grabbed the woman and led her out.

Billy focused on Marcus now, sliding up close and getting in his face. Marcus stiffened but held his ground, refusing to give an inch. Billy spoke, and a quiet threat coated his words. "It was your shit that fucked her up, so you are going to pay me for the damages."

The events of the past few minutes had left Marcus on uncertain ground. Nothing Gabe or Angel had said had prepared him for this, and now he would have to improvise. "I'll need to take that back to Gabe and Angel." he ventured, hoping it was the smart move.

Billy stared at him menacingly for a moment before

backing off and nodding his head. "Makes sense. Those two can't let a little pissant like you make this kind of decision. Tell them I want you back here with my money in two hours. If not..." he trailed off menacingly. It was clear that he was talking about a war.

He then turned his back on Marcus dismissively and hopped back up onto the stage. It was obvious he considered the meeting to be at an end. Around them, most of the men began heading for the doors while Uber Alice and the Asian man tried to herd Marcus, Jason and Mateo toward the exit.

"Wait!" Marcus bellowed. On the stage Billy paused, his frustration clearly evident. "We still need to talk about territory!" Marcus said, trying to make the plea sound tough. It was what Gabe and Angel had sent him to do, and he couldn't go back to Casa Preciosa without trying.

"Yeah?" Billy said, just barely willing to humor them. From outside came a distant howl as a gust of wind shook the building, driving the heavy rain into the walls and windows.

Marcus relaxed somewhat as the conversation turned to more familiar ground. "Boone street is in our territory, and we know you sold some merchandise to Jock." he said. "The Brotherhood can't just let that pass, but we're willing to make a deal." Jason heard the strain in Marcus' voice, and the bluster that failed to cover his nervousness. "We're willing to let you sell in our territory, but The Brotherhood needs a cut. Thirty percent."

Billy smiled as if a child had just said something cute. "Your territory..." he repeated slowly. His smile faded, then returned as a twisted parody of itself. "Look, The Brotherhood is into drugs, I get that. You guys came from nothing and muscled your way into the business. Fucking good for you!" he said, feigning generosity. "But that's all." he added sharply, turning mean. "You're good at keeping people high, but not at shit-all else. 'Your territory'..." his tone was mocking now, and dripping with acid. "Fucker, when it comes to slaves, the whole city is *our* territory! We're the only game in town and we'll sell wherever the fuck we want! Now get the fuck out of my club before I have you shot."

At that moment Jason felt a heavy hand come down hard on his shoulder and watched as the same thing happened to Marcus and Mateo. For a surreal moment Jason studied the unusual gang tattoo on the hand that held him. He came back to reality just as the situation began to spin out of control.

Marcus twisted out of Uber Alice's grasp, looking angry. "Hey!" he shouted indignantly.

On the stage, Billy Ghoul had finally had enough. "Fuck it. Shoot them." he ordered flatly.

For Jason, the next few moments happened in slow-motion. Marcus was quick and had his gun drawn before Uber Alice could bring hers to bear. He shoved the barrel deep into her stomach and pulled the trigger. Muffled by her body, the shot was surprisingly quiet but the impact shoved her back as the bullet lodged in her abdomen. Jason and Mateo were only a moment slower than Marcus in drawing their weapons and both dropped and rolled away from the men who had grabbed them. Quickly getting back to his feet, Jason scanned the room, looking for cover. Two more shots rang out but Jason ignored them as his adrenaline began to spike and his breath came fast. All around them, chaos erupted.

A sudden absence at his side told Jason that Mateo was already moving. Following his friend, he and Mateo made a crouching run toward the nearest exit, blind-firing their weapons to keep Billy Ghoul's people at bay. Mateo dove through the open doorway and into the club's lobby, and Jason followed him a moment later. Still inside the main room, Marcus was dashing erratically toward an exit a little further away than the one Jason and Mateo had found. A rapid series of shots followed his movements as Billy's guards turned their fire toward him.

In the lobby, Jason and Mateo ducked behind a wall. They were out of the line of fire for the moment and Jason had time to watch as a spot of blood slowly expanded under the fabric of his pant leg. He poked at it gingerly but felt no pain; whatever the damage was, he'd worry about it later.

He shook his head and tried to assess their options. Looking toward the front of the club, Jason realized that he could see the door which led outside. Getting there would mean passing the entrance to the main hall again and opening themselves up to the still escalating gunfire, but it still offered the surest route of escape. He signaled to Mateo and got ready to run.

Before they could dash for the exit there was a sudden commotion from the other end of the lobby as Marcus burst through a set of double doors and dove to the ground. He half rolled, half crawled until his back was against the wall and then sat there for a moment, panting. There was a dark smear of blood on his arm but the hand that held his pistol still looked strong. As his eyes scanned the lobby, he seemed to look right through Jason and Mateo.

Jason tried to signal to him but the big man was already up and running. He sprinted past them without slowing and leapt for the exit door, crashing through it and out onto the street. Knowing they might not get another chance, Jason and Mateo ran after him.

As soon as they left their cover, staccato gunfire began to echo all around them. Desperate and unable to turn back, Jason lowered his head and ran hard for the door, with Mateo trailing just a few steps behind. Together, they burst out into the torrential rain.

A flash of movement showed that Marcus was already at the car. Before they could join him, Marcus threw the door open and dove in, the electronics coming to life even before the door closed. Jason watched in shocked disbelief as Marcus gunned the motor and raced away down the street without them, leaving a billowing cloud of spray behind.

A wet arm was thrown over Jason's shoulder and he heard Mateo whisper, "Shit!" in awe at what Marcus had done. Still, they'd have to deal with that later. Right now he knew they had only moments before Billy Ghoul's people followed them outside.

Jason's mind raced as he considered their limited options. Could they run for it? It seemed like their only choice. He was trying to decide which way to go when he realized with horror that Mateo had begun to sag weakly against him. A quick look at his shirt showed a spreading bloodstain near the waist. "Holy fuck!" Jason exclaimed. He held Mateo's arm in place to keep it over his shoulder and hefted him up. "Come on." he urged. "We can't stay here."

Mateo nodded, though there was no way he would be able to go very far like this. Across the street Jason saw the open-air market and began helping Mateo in that direction. As they reached the bazaar, they found that it was empty. The day's driving rain had kept customers away and the stall's owners had covered their wares before closing for the day to protect them from the storm.

Looking for a place to hide, Jason helped Mateo hobble deeper into the market. When he thought they'd gone far enough, he pulled Mateo down behind a stall and leaned him against the counter. There, Jason gently tried to assess his friend's wound. Mateo hissed and flinched at his probing fingers but was otherwise still.

In the end, all Jason could tell was that it was bad. Somehow, he needed to get Mateo help, and fast. Awkwardly, he reached into his pocket and took out his micro. His hands were shaking as he made the call and twice he was forced to start over. Carefully, he tried again and watched the screen intently as the call connected. When a face finally appeared, he didn't even wait for a hello.

"Courtney!" he said in a panicked whisper. "I need your help, right now! It's an emergency!"

CHAPTER 19

"...Apply pressure! Hold it... no, keep it there!" Courtney told him forcefully. Her own stained hands were busy as she dug through a medical kit looking for more gauze. Jason did his best to keep the pad pressed against Mateo's wound but the blood was somehow sticky and slimy at the same time, making his fingers slip...

"How long till we get there?" Jason asked over the unending wail of the siren. His fingers had gone numb and his leg ached from crouching awkwardly beside the gurney which took up most of the space inside the crowded ambulance.

With a glance, Courtney checked a display mounted to the wall behind him. "We're probably ten minutes out. I already let them know we're coming." she answered distractedly. Frowning, she returned to watching Mateo's vital signs. Jason struggled to stay upright as they rounded yet another corner and the light slid across Courtney's face as the ambulance changed direction. Beneath them, the electric motors buzzed and hummed as the vehicle accelerated again...

Jason was thrown forward violently as the ambulance came to a sudden stop. At almost the same instant the back doors were flung open and a small cluster of men and women appeared. They surrounded the gurney as it slid out, their white uniforms tinted pink by the red-orange sunlight. Each doctor and nurse played a tightly choreographed role as they assessed the patient, calling out numbers and spouting acronyms faster than Jason could follow. Their expressions were serious, missing the frantic shock and worry that Jason knew was written all over his own face. After a quick consultation with Courtney they hurried away, dragging Mateo along with them. In a rush they disappeared through a double set of automatic doors and were gone...

****

Jason sat in the emergency room with Courtney by his side. Mateo had been in surgery for over an hour now and the wait so far had been interminable. Courtney was as frustrated and worried as Jason was, but there was simply no news yet. All they could do was wait.

Jason shifted uncomfortably in his seat. His leg still hurt and the pain only seemed to be getting worse. He rubbed at it gently, trying to soothe the ache. As his hand passed over his shin, he found a small tear in the black fabric and realized that below the hole the pant leg felt oddly stiff and heavy. With a sudden rush of adrenaline, he remembered seeing the blood spot on his leg during the fight at the club. Grimly, he slipped a finger through the hole and probed gingerly at his leg. A sharp pain shot through him as he found a small puncture wound, just beside the prominent shin bone. Drawing his finger back, he saw that it was spotted with a dark clot of blood. "Uh, Courtney?" he said, keeping his voice steady with an effort.

Courtney turned her attention from staring at the intake desk and looked at Jason as he held up the crimson digit. "Shit! What happened?" she demanded, immediately shifting into diagnosis and treatment mode.

"It's my leg. I think I was shot too." he said, feeling a little lightheaded.

Without a word Courtney got up and went to the nurses' station, returning a moment later with a small tub of supplies and a pair of scissors. She quickly repositioned her chair so that it faced his and gently lifted his leg into her lap. With the scissors she quickly cut away the trouser leg just above his left knee and then pulled a damp cloth from the tub. Skillfully, she began cleaning the wound.

"It doesn't look too bad," she said after a minute, appraising the damage cautiously, "but I'm a little worried about the nerve. I think the bullet is still in there." She worked quickly, giving him an injection to help dull the pain, followed by a localized short-acting vasoconstrictor and coagulant to help staunch the bleeding. Next, she produced a tool similar to a pair of scissors, but with an end designed for grasping instead of cutting. She positioned the forceps and began to gently probe the wound. Adjusting her grip on the handle, she glanced up at Jason apologetically, saying, "This might hurt a bit. I'm sorry." He gritted his teeth and nodded, giving his permission for her to begin.

She went to work with the forceps, her hands gentle but efficient. Jason's leg had been numbed to the pain, but he still felt a series of strange tugging sensations that left him queasy. After a long moment she managed to pull the small bullet free and held it up for inspection, studying it closely to make sure it hadn't shattered. Satisfied that it remained intact, she dropped the bullet into the waiting tub. "Okay," she sighed, smiling faintly. "now for the easy part."

She then turned her attention to closing the wound, cleaning it thoroughly before covering it with a small textured appliqué and spraying the area liberally with a liquid polymer that puckered and turned a delicate white as it dried. Jason couldn't help frowning at how the resulting bandage contrasted conspicuously with his brown skin.

Courtney saw his face and gave him a concerned look. Not wanting her to feel bad, he forced a smile and asked a little too brightly, "So that's it?"

"That's it." she told him with a nod. "Later, we should have somebody take a look at the nerve. If it's damaged, we'll need to repair it. That's not something I can do myself but a doctor should be able to, no problem."

"Thank you." Jason said, looking curiously at his bare leg. It still felt odd; the anesthetic was mostly keeping the pain at bay but the numbness left him feeling as if his lower leg belonged to someone else. He decided not to say anything about it, reasoning that it was probably normal and that the sensation would pass as the anesthesia wore off.

As he again tried to get comfortable in his chair, Courtney returned the tub to the nurses' station and then chatted with a white-coated doctor as he passed. Their conversation seemed friendly enough, but Jason couldn't help but feel uneasy. He and Mateo had arrived here with suspicious gunshot wounds and on top of that, 'Lucas Mendoza' wasn't who he appeared to be. If anyone became curious, it was only a matter of time before the police would arrive to ask questions he'd rather not answer.

He was still turning that thought over in his mind when Courtney returned and sat down next to him. Jason leaned in close so they could talk without being overheard.

"So what did you tell the hospital about how Mateo and I got shot?" he asked softly.

"I told them it was a Latino gang shooting." she replied in a voice just above a whisper. "Unfortunately, that kind of thing is really common. You both look Hispanic and, believe it or not, that means they usually don't call the cops. They don't typically do that unless the shooting involves a Citizen."

Jason tried and failed to hide his shock at the callousness that showed. "Because it'd be a waste of taxpayer resources?" he asked sourly.

"Something like that." Courtney admitted with a sigh. He could see in her eyes that she agreed with his assessment of the morals involved, but in this case society's neglect worked in their favor. If the cops weren't coming, then he wouldn't have to try to explain things to them. Thank goodness for casual racism, he thought bitterly.

His micro chimed for attention and, frowning, he

pulled the device from his pocket. The display flashed a message from Gabe, asking where he was. In his mind's eye he again saw Marcus' car driving away, leaving him and Mateo to the Seps, and he clenched his teeth. No, he wasn't ready to talk to Gabe yet.

He thumbed ignore and began to return the device to his pocket, but paused halfway. "Shit! I need to call Valarie!" he said out loud. He'd been so caught up, he hadn't thought of it until now. Beside him, Courtney overheard his exclamation and nodded. Valarie's going to be pissed, Jason thought. Well, he added, she certainly has a right to be.

****

Mateo was going to be okay; the doctor had said so. He was still sedated, and had been for several hours now, but the doctor had said he would recover. Jason clung tightly to that fact, using it to help weather the storm he now faced.

In front of him, Valarie had finally run out of steam. She was past yelling at him now. Her eyes were red and puffy from crying, and she stared at him angrily before finally taking her daughter and going to sit at Mateo's bedside. Hatred for Jason radiated from her like a supernova, and he carefully kept his distance. She hadn't banned him from the room, but probably only because she hadn't thought of it yet. Jason understood her anger; she was in the right here and he knew it. He had put Mateo in danger and of course it was his fault that this had happened. He knew he deserved every ounce of the venom he had gotten.

He quietly reached for the door and let himself out into the hallway where his own family waited sombrely. At his approach they stood and embraced him, Matthew's arms tightly encircling his chest just below Anne's. Anne began to sob quietly, overcome by emotion. Jason held her close, knowing that it was all he could offer her right now. A blue gowned orderly quickly hurried by, graciously pretending not to see them. After a long moment Anne let him go and stepped back. With a sniff she wiped her eyes and the three of them sat down on the chairs that had been placed against the wall.

The thin cushion did little to soften the seat as Jason sank down into it. He adjusted, trying to ease the strange feeling the anesthetic had left in his leg and to assuage the persistent numbness in his foot. He saw Anne watching him and offered her a tired smile, but the pain in her eyes brought him up short. She leaned close and laid a delicate hand on his arm, and the simple physical gesture nearly broke him. Despite his best efforts he felt tears begin to well up.

Jason fought to keep control. He averted his eyes and tugged self-consciously at his clothes, and Anne followed his gaze. She seemed to notice his pants for the first time, the truncated fabric of the left leg ending just above the knee. She moved her hand to his exposed leg, gently touching the white polymer bandage near his shin.

"What happened?" she asked with heartsick anguish.

Jason knew that she was worried about his leg, but the question was far broader than just that. Answering should have been easy, but he struggled to find the words to explain it to her. Haltingly, he recounted the events of the day and told her how he and Mateo had ended up here. Her eyes grew wide as he went on and he desperately wanted to stop; to just hold her. He could tell she didn't understand and he hated putting her through this.

When he was done, Anne stared at him uncomprehendingly. She seemed suddenly sad and distant. After a long moment she said in quiet protest, "I thought you were getting out..."

He couldn't avoid telling her any longer. She had a right to know.

"I know, but I can't. Not yet." he said, looking down at his hands. "I finally found a clue, and I'm close. I have to see where it goes." Anne gaped at him, left bewildered and speechless by his response.

Jason raised his head as he felt the silence between them start to crystalize. He pressed on desperately, explaining everything. He told her about Benito Reyes and how he'd finally found a connection between The Brotherhood and The Latino Resistance Front. He needed her to understand why he was doing this, and why he couldn't stop now.

Anne listened to her husband's words but found herself struggling to accept them. Deep down, she loved him above all else but staying with The Brotherhood just felt like madness. She couldn't understand his need to fix things, to try to get back what they'd lost when they could choose to move on instead. Slowly though, she decided that whether she understood wasn't the most important thing. He was still the man she loved and despite the insanity of the past few months, she found that she did still trust him. Swallowing hard, she found her voice.

"Okay."

The word hung in the air between them and Jason could sense how hard it had been for her to say. She had given her permission for him to continue, but doing so had taken everything she had. This was his one, last chance. If it failed, he wouldn't get another.

Grateful, he reached out a hand to her and she took it, letting him pull her close. She rested her head on his shoulder and was surprised to feel a tear run down his cheek and land on her forehead. Quietly, she heard him whisper, "Thank you."

****

It was several hours later. Hunger had started to gnaw at Jason and Matthew had expressed an interest in food as well. After Anne agreed, Jason went to the hospital cafeteria to get them all something to eat. As he returned carrying the food, he could feel the dull ache in his leg beginning to come back. It wasn't quite the same as before, but it throbbed and hurt all the same. His steps slowed and he walked carefully, trying to ease the pain in his leg and the strange numbness in his foot.

The cafeteria had turned out to be located on the other side of the hospital, quite far from the corridor where he'd left Anne and Matthew. As he carried their food back through yet another endless hallway, he leaned against the wall to rest his leg for a minute. A moment later his micro chimed for the third time in an hour and he felt a hot frustration bloom in his chest. With his hands full he couldn't pull the device out to check, but he knew it must be Gabe calling again. The gang leader had been trying to reach him for hours now, but notably Marcus hadn't tried even once. He almost wished that fucker *would* call; after the way he'd abandoned them, Jason very much had a few things he wanted to tell him.

Eventually the micro's insistent chime fell silent again. Wincing at the pain in his leg, Jason pushed off from the wall and continued down the winding halls toward his family. He'd nearly made it back when he realized he was in trouble. His steps had become leaden and it felt like his left boot was pulled too tight. There was an odd pressure-like feeling against the top part of his foot, and yet somehow it still seemed numb. He looked down as he walked and saw that with each step his left foot wasn't swinging as far forward as his right, causing him to limp. He tried to equalize his gait by force of will, but found that he couldn't.

Suddenly, a nurse rounded a corner in front of him and they collided heavily, the impact knocking the food from his arms and sending the nurse careening into a nearby wall. Reflexively, Jason reached out to try to catch her but the attempt left him overbalanced and his aching leg finally collapsed. Seemingly in slow motion, he landed in an undignified heap on the floor.

"Are you alright?" the nurse asked, having caught herself using the wall's railing.

"I don't know..." Jason answered in confusion. His leg tingled strangely and he wasn't yet sure what to make of it.

From down the hall they heard a commotion and then the pounding sound of rapid footsteps. Anne flew around the corner a moment later, with Matthew close behind.

"Jason!" Anne exclaimed worriedly at finding her husband on the floor.

Jason panicked reflexively when she called his name; his *real* name. He could hardly fault her for it, but it was still a risk. Still, the nurse hovering over him showed no sign of recognition, so it seemed that their secret remained safe for now.

Anne reached his side as he rolled onto his hands and knees and laboriously began to get his feet under him. The tingle in his left leg worsened immediately and he could feel how tremulous and weak it was. He managed to stand up but the leg held for only a moment before giving out again and sending him crashing back to the floor.

Immediately the nurse was at his side. She assessed the situation quickly and, noticing the white polymer bandage on his leg, examined the area carefully. Realizing what it meant, she asked in a serious tone, "Who is your doctor?"

Jason shook his head. "I haven't seen one. An EMT, Courtney Damiya, is the one who worked on me." The nurse remained focused on his leg but was obviously listening closely. Jason went on, saying, "I was shot. Courtney did what she could, but said she was worried about the nerve. She couldn't fix it herself, so she said I'd need to have a doctor look at it later."

The nurse nodded. "The superficial peroneal nerve. She's right." She touched a panel on her lapel, activating a voicelink to the nurses' station. "Hi, this is Katy." she told them calmly. "Can you send someone over to me near room 212 in the recovery wing? I'm in the hallway with a collapsed patient. He's okay for now but I need someone as soon as possible." The voice on the other end of the link confirmed her request and she touched the panel again, ending the connection.

She then nodded to Anne and together the two of them helped Jason into a nearby chair. As Anne sat down beside him

Jason could feel her eyes on him, her face a perfect mix of concern and anger that he hadn't told her how serious his injury was. He hadn't been trying to keep it from her; they'd just had so much else to talk about that he had simply forgotten.

The nurse stayed to keep an eye on him and ten minutes later a white coated doctor appeared, pushing an empty wheelchair. She parked the chair in front of them and then sat in it as she began to examine Jason's leg. The doctor asked what had caused the injury and he told the story again, making sure to keep it consistent with the only-slightly-fictional tale Courtney had already told the hospital. The dark skinned doctor frowned as he spoke, but stayed focused on his injury. When he was done, she produced a narrow pen-like device from a deep pocket. With his leg resting in her lap, she asked him to look away and report when he could feel a touch. After a moment he jumped involuntarily, as if she'd stabbed him!

The doctor felt him stiffen and commented wryly, "I guess that part's okay." She asked him to look away again and she methodically probed several more areas up and down his leg and foot. When she was done she returned the device to her pocket and said, "Unfortunately, there does appear to be some damage to the superficial peroneal nerve. We can treat it but recovery will be slow. You'll likely be limping for several weeks."

Jason nodded, oddly relieved at the prognosis. Something about the idea of nerve damage made his stomach churn but he was relieved to learn he could recover from it, even if that recovery might take weeks.

"I want to take you down to an exam room." the doctor said. "We can perform the treatment right away. Really, it's just a short series of injections, so your family can wait for you here. We should only be gone a few minutes."

"Sounds good to me." Jason agreed as the doctor rose. He levered himself out of his seat and over to the now empty wheelchair, putting as little weight as possible on his damaged leg. Once he was settled, the nurse took up a position behind him to push while the doctor made ready to follow them.

Before they set off, Jason asked, “Wait just a minute?”. When the nurse paused, Jason turned to Anne. He hated to leave her behind and yet he was doing it again. As sincerely as he could, he told her, “I promise I’ll be back.”

Anne gave him a small smile. “I know.” she said.

With that the nurse began to push the chair down the hallway. A moment later they turned a corner and Anne vanished from his sight.

****

In the exam room, the doctor placed a scanner over Jason’s leg to confirm her diagnosis. The machine hummed softly as it self-calibrated, the pitch shifting and becoming more rhythmic as it began carefully tracing the paths of the nerves inside his leg. The doctor studied the readings, evaluating the results as they appeared on the attached display.

“Okay, I don’t see any surprises.” she said, looking up. “The regeneration treatment should be pretty straight forward.”

She quickly removed the scanner from his leg, then turned to a compact pharmaceuticals dispenser mounted under a cabinet behind her chair. Her fingers danced smoothly over the controls, selecting the medication and then authorizing the machine to dispense it as a collection of small colored syringes. Laying the syringes out on the counter, she then prepped his leg by briskly wiping down the area with a strong smelling disinfectant.

The regeneration treatment consisted of eight deep injections at a cluster of sites around the bullet wound, followed by six more along the outside edge of the shin, following the path of the nerve. The doctor said the injections were a cocktail of Schwann cell precursors, myelin protein fragments and a few other things Jason couldn’t pronounce if he tried. The needles didn't really hurt but he wondered if that might be due to the creeping numbness he still felt.

When the last injection had been completed, Jason stood and tested the leg cautiously while leaning against the exam table. He discovered that if he was careful it could hold him up, but only just barely. He was a little disappointed to find that the treatment hadn't produced much change yet but reminded himself that the doctor had said a full recovery may take weeks.

"You should begin to notice incremental improvement soon, but the medication is only just starting to do its work." the doctor said. "Give it a day or two and you should begin to notice a real difference. If it's not significantly better in two weeks, come back and we'll give it another look."

While the doctor spoke, Jason tried taking a few steps around the room. He found that he could walk again, but it was exhausting and, despite his best efforts, a tremor quickly developed. Grimacing, he grabbed onto the exam table for support while he waited for it to subside. After a moment he lowered himself into the wheelchair with a new understanding of his limits.

He sighed; the treatment was an improvement but he knew he wasn't yet ready for the long walk back to his family. "Could I keep the chair for a while? At least until I'm ready to leave?" he asked, shifting the wheels back and forth to get a feel for it.

"Of course. I'd advise staying off your feet for at least an hour anyway." she said.

Jason thanked her. Seeing that he was anxious to return to his family, the doctor then stood and held the door open for him. As he rolled out into the hallway, she said, "If you need me, ask for Doctor Katz. They'll come find me."

Jason said that he would, and they parted ways. He was grateful for her help, but right now he had a promise to keep; he needed to get back to Anne and Matthew. The chair moved easily over the smooth tile and as he gained confidence he began to pile on more speed with each push against the wheels. Soon he came to a long stretch of empty hallway where the floor sloped modestly downward. He was already moving pretty quickly, so he let his momentum carry him down the incline. Near the bottom he placed his hands against the wheels and felt the heat quickly rise, the friction nearly burning his palms as he slowed. As he finally came to a stop, the chair spun around, facing him back the way he'd come. He rested there a moment, letting his hands cool before continuing.

He was preparing to turn the chair back around and go when his micro chimed insistently for, what, the fifth time since he'd been here? The sixth? Angrily, he pulled the device out and glared at it. As he suspected, the call still wasn't from Marcus; instead it was yet another request from Gabe. The preview image showed the gang leader's face prominently centered in the frame, but Jason's jaw clenched as he saw who stood in the background; it was Marcus! The treacherous fuck had a bandage wrapped around his arm, but was otherwise fine!

Jason sat absolutely still for a moment, letting the micro continue to bleep while he studied Marcus' smug face. He couldn't imagine how it was that Gabe or Angel hadn't already killed that fucker after what he'd done. It didn't make sense! Eventually though, the micro's continued ringing became too much for him to ignore and he reluctantly accepted the call.

Gabe began to speak the moment the connection became active. "Lucas! Christ man, where have you been?!" he exclaimed, sounding both relieved and exasperated.

"I've been in the hospital. You should ask Marcus about that." Jason replied flatly.

Gabe nodded, but his expression was dismissive. "We've already talked about it. So you made it out okay?" Behind Gabe, Marcus looked up and then wandered out of frame.

"I got shot in the leg. Kinda fucked me up, but the doctors helped. Mateo's hurt pretty bad, though." On the small screen Gabe's face appeared to show some real concern, surprising Jason. He went on, explaining, "He was shot in the stomach. I don't really know what the damage was, but he was in surgery for quite a while. He's sedated for now."

Gabe wore a sympathetic expression as he listened, but when he spoke it was clear to Jason that he'd missed the point. "That's too bad, but we're going to get the fucking Seps back." Gabe said. "We've already got something in motion. Get back here as soon as you can." There was a sudden noise from offscreen and Gabe leaned out of frame for a moment, shouting unintelligibly. He then leaned back into view, saying, "That's an order. Get back here ASAP." The unseen commotion rose again and Gabe abruptly ended the call.

Alone in the empty hallway, Jason was left feeling deeply worried. It didn't look like Marcus was in trouble at all for what he'd done, and that was a bad sign. Did he pin this fiasco with the Seps on him and Mateo? If Marcus was using them as a scapegoat, he needed to put a stop to it fast. Gabe and Angel were brutal and they couldn't be trusted to seek retribution from only him, either. Just as often they took out whole families.

Jason had a sudden moment of clarity and a chill ran down his spine; Marcus knew he had a girlfriend. If The Brotherhood turned on him, they might eventually track Anne down, and Matthew too. There was no way around it; he had to find out what Marcus had told them and the only way to do that was to go back to Casa Preciosa.

He put his hands on the chair's wheels and gave them a heavy push, overcoming inertia with an effort. He hated this life that did nothing but tear him from his family. He didn't want to leave them again, but he at least had to say goodbye.

Before long he rounded the final corner and found Anne and Matthew sitting right where he left them. As he came closer, Anne locked eyes with him and she knew instantly that something was wrong.

"You've got to go?" she asked, her voice tight with apprehension.

Jason nodded sadly. "I'm sorry. Yes, I've got to. It's important." He maneuvered the wheelchair up against the wall and slowly stood, careful not to put any more weight on his injured leg than it could bear. Anne watched him, tensed to leap forward and catch him if he fell. He took a few wary steps, but didn't stumble. He found that if he was deliberate in his movements and didn't try to hurry, he could walk.

"I wish you didn't have to go." Anne said sadly, knowing he wouldn't leave unless he had to.

Matthew stood up and came over, his face flush with worry. "Stay safe, Dad." he said as he threw his arms around his father.

"I will." Jason replied, holding him close. Anne reached out and took Jason's hand in hers. She held on tightly, and he returned the gesture with all his heart.

"I'll call when I can, to let you know how I'm doing." Jason said, fighting back a lump in his throat.

"I know." Anne replied, trying to hide her tears.

He didn't want to leave things like this but he had no choice. With his goodbyes said, Jason turned and with a slow limping gait, made his way down the hallway and out of the hospital alone.

CHAPTER 20

Although Gabe had ordered him to hurry, Jason didn't actually go directly to Casa Preciosa. Instead, he first went to his cluttered studio apartment to replace the pants that had been ruined while treating his wound. There, he sat down on the unmade bed and struggled to remove the old pants before tossing them into the trash. The persistent weakness in his leg made the task awkward and afterward he lay back on the bed to rest and catch his breath.

When he felt a little stronger, he sat back up and examined his injury. He had to concede that it looked surprisingly good, all things considered. There was some bruising and the whole area remained tender, but the all-consuming ache that had radiated up and down his leg had faded into the background. It may have been his imagination but he even thought there was some improvement to the numbness in his foot.

He slid carefully down off the bed and took a few unaided steps around the room. His leg was still noticeably weak, but it did seem like the treatment the doctor gave him was having an effect. A moment later though, he knew he had pushed himself too far. His leg began to shake and he sagged against the counter which divided his living space from the small kitchen. He supported himself with his good leg and then worked his way along the counter to a nearby chair while he considered his options.

His leg really did feel better than before, but apparently feeling a little better didn't mean he had no limits. Rest would help; now that he was sitting it already felt a little better, but he just didn't have the luxury of time. What he really needed was a crutch or a cane.

His eyes settled on the thick curtains he habitually kept tightly drawn to block out the unyielding sunlight. A better apartment would have had dimmable glass instead of curtains, but this was decidedly not a 'better apartment'. The curtains were held in place by a stout-looking rod which more than spanned the width of the window frame. When he felt strong enough, he rose from the chair and shuffled closer, examining the curtain rod critically. Bracing against the wall to keep the weight off his injured leg, Jason reached up and lifted the curtains down, blinking rapidly in the blinding red-orange light that suddenly poured through the uncovered glass.

Turning his back to the window, he weighed the rod-curtain assembly in his hands. After a contemplative moment he unscrewed one of the decorative ends and tilted the rod, letting the heavy curtains slide off and fall into a pile on the floor. He left them where they lay and focused instead on the sturdy rod still in his hands.

The rod consisted of two sliding halves, with the smaller part fitting inside the larger one and allowing the whole thing to extend as needed. He pulled at it experimentally and the two halves began to slide apart, lengthening the rod. He kept pulling until the pieces separated entirely, then discarded the thicker, more awkward half.

The thinner portion still sported its decorative ball-shaped finial, which he found fit neatly into the palm of his hand. Using the finial as a grip, he tested the half-rod as a makeshift cane and was pleased to discover that the length was perfect, supporting him without forcing him to stoop. He disliked needing its help, but using it would be better than collapsing in front of Gabe and Angel after only a few steps. He would just have to get used to it.

Cautiously, he made his way over to the full-length mirror that hung from the apartment's front door. As he studied his reflection he was pleased to find that the modified curtain rod didn't look too ridiculous in its new role. Indeed, if he didn't know its origin he might have thought it was actually a store-bought cane.

Suddenly, Jason's eye caught sight of the ruined pants which lay crumpled on the floor behind him. He swallowed hard and felt a sudden spasm of guilt for what had happened to Mateo. As he relived the memory of that night, his face flushed hotly and he felt his anger rise.

He had to deal with Marcus. Marcus was the reason Mateo lay suffering in a hospital bed, and now he might be putting Anne and Matthew in danger too. The thought was more than Jason could stand. One way or another, he had to find a way to keep his family safe.

Angry and frustrated, he pulled a new pair of pants from the dresser and eased them on, careful not to aggravate his injury. He couldn't put it off any longer; he had to go to Casa Preciosa and confront Marcus.

****

Down on the street in front of the building, Jason considered how to get to Casa Preciosa. He'd have preferred to take the tram but the station was several blocks away and he wasn't sure just how far he could walk, even with the cane. Instead he chose to ignore the mounting costs and used his micro to summon yet another automatic car to take him to the shelter.

The car arrived quickly and as it came to a stop in front of him, he suddenly noticed that the sky overhead was clear and nearly cloudless. Even the faint breeze against his bare scalp was only barely perceptible. The calm was a jarring contrast to the unforeseen storm of yesterday; or was it last night? Between the chaos at the Sep's LV club and the drama at the hospital afterward, he'd lost track of time.

The storm may have passed but the day still felt warm and humid, leaving him glad he hadn't tried to walk to the tram station. He opened the car door and settled in, glad to feel the air-conditioning begin to pull the moisture from the air.

The ride from his apartment to Casa Preciosa seemed to take forever, though in reality it was only a few miles away. He used the time to try to push aside his simmering anger at Marcus so that he could be in control when he faced him. He focused instead on what he had to do next; find out what lies Marcus had told the gang and do whatever he could to protect his family. He fixated on this, repeating it like a mantra until he felt at least a little calmer.

When the car dropped Jason off at the shelter though, he immediately sensed that something was wrong. The street out front was usually lined by the various personal cars belonging to the gang members, but now only two or three such cars were present. The vehicle nearest the door belonged to Marcus and sat empty, low and foreboding.

The sight made Jason's stomach tighten and the fragile calm he'd achieved on the way over evaporated, replaced by a seething anger that twisted inside him. He took several deep breaths and tried to regain his temper; if he went charging in like this he'd probably just get himself killed. He pushed the anger down and made it stay there; not to be forgotten, but to put it where he could keep an eye on it. After a moment the knot in his gut loosened just enough for him to breathe again. He steeled himself and pulled open the shelter door.

Upon entering the building, Jason could hear the quiet murmur of a distant conversation, but the place was otherwise empty. Even most of the shelter's regular visitors were gone. The only people Jason could see were two shabbily dressed homeless men sleeping on chairs in opposite corners of the cafeteria. The lack of activity left him feeling uncertain, and the near silence made his skin crawl.

"Where is everyone?" he wondered aloud. When no answer came, he began to move warily across the cafeteria, his improvised cane tapping against the hard floor with a syncopated beat that was out of time with the rhythm of his feet. The distant conversation grew a little louder, seeming to come from a small activity room at the rear of the building. He followed the voices cautiously, as curious as he was nervous.

As he came closer he was able to pick out the nasal speech of Benito Reyes, with Gabe Batista's gruff, clipped voice forming a low counterpoint. The gang leader sounded calm and in control; his tone was not that of a man whose people had failed him. A moment later he heard Marcus' voice join in, and Jason froze, his rage again threatening to boil over.

He suddenly wasn't sure he could stand seeing the man's face again. The events of yesterday flooded back and in his mind's eye he watched Marcus drive away, leaving Mateo and him to die in the street. He scowled at the memory and felt his teeth begin to grind.

It slowly dawned on him that his hand had begun to ache. He looked down at it and realized that he was clenching it tightly, and the nails were biting into his palm. He took a deep breath and forced his hand open again; he needed to keep his wits about him. He didn't bury the anger though; he wanted it as fuel for what came next.

Grim faced, Jason stepped forward into the open doorway, leaning on his cane. Inside, Benito, Gabe and Marcus formed a loose triad standing in the center of the room, while Angel sat in the room's only chair, looking bored. Marcus wore a white bandage tied around one arm but as he gestured with it, it was clear he wasn't in much pain.

Benito was the first to notice Jason standing in the doorway and directed Gabe's attention to him. Gabe and Marcus stopped talking almost immediately and turned to face him.

"Finally!" Gabe announced loudly, sounding more pleased than annoyed.

Jason stepped into the room, glaring at Marcus. Marcus returned the look sheepishly, as though what had happened between them could be easily forgiven. Leaning conspicuously on his cane, Jason joined their circle. There was a heavy chill in the room and for a few moments no one spoke.

"How's the leg?" Marcus asked, breaking the silence. His tone was inscrutable; it could have been idle concern just as easily as mockery. In the end, Jason found he didn't care which it was. Keeping his left hand planted on his cane for balance, he swung his right fist hard into Marcus' jaw. The big man staggered back, shocked. Careful to keep his feet under him, Jason moved in and swung again, this time bloodying Marcus' nose. A third punch went wild, hitting Marcus in the neck and snapping his head to one side.

"What the fuck?!" Marcus exclaimed indignantly. He ducked away and snaked out with his foot, catching Jason's cane and knocking it away. Without its support, Jason fell hard to the floor. Marcus moved in viciously, ready to kick him in the ribs but paused when Angel spoke up sharply.

"Knock it off!" he commanded, standing up from his seat. Marcus lowered his foot, reluctantly ending his attack but the expression on his face remained ugly. Angel moved in close, staring at him coldly and invading his personal space. "I'd say that was justified, wouldn't you?" Angel growled, a low threat in his voice. Marcus flushed at the rebuke but nodded silently as he backed down. With his warning given, Angel stepped aside and under his watchful eye Marcus bent to help Jason up from the floor.

Jason was loath to take Marcus' hand, but eventually he allowed the big man to pull him up. He got to his feet unsteadily as they continued to watch each other, neither of them sure if the conflict was really over. Benito finally broke the tension by retrieving Jason's cane and handing it back to him.

Gabe exchanged a meaningful look with his brother, then turned to Marcus and said, "Go get cleaned up. After that, meet us in the office. We've got business to discuss." To Jason he said, "I want you there too." Marcus raised a hand to his face to daub at his bloodied nose, then nodded in acknowledgement.

Satisfied, Gabe and Angel left the room, followed closely by Marcus, who turned and headed toward the shelter's washroom. Jason hung back; after that confrontation, he needed time to decompress. Besides, he knew the meeting wouldn't start until Marcus had stopped his nosebleed and joined them in the gang leaders' office.

After a minute it dawned on Jason that Benito hadn't left the room with the others. He shot the diminutive revolutionary a wary glance and saw that the man was smiling ear to ear. In fact, he hardly seemed able to contain himself. Against his better judgement, Jason asked, "So what's with you?"

Benito couldn't restrain himself any longer. "Oh Lucas, it's wonderful! *Maravilloso!*" he breathed ecstatically. "The Resistance is coming back; Gabe and Angel told me so! They said The Resistance contacted them! Gabe told them what I've been saying, what I've been telling everyone! *Venganza!*" Benito's voice rose with excitement, leaving him almost tongue-tied. He smiled and took a breath before continuing. "Gabe said they were impressed, and that they asked me to write a speech for them! They want to use my words to announce their return to the whole planet!"

Jason was dumbstruck. His mouth was suddenly dry, but he managed to ask, "When did this happen?"

"Gabe says they called him *Anoche.* After he told me, I worked on the speech all night. It was tough, but I think it's nearly perfect! I wrote them something strong, something that will force the Anglos to deal with us!" Benito raised his chin and closed his eyes as he began to quote from his speech. As he spoke, he lowered his voice an octave, trying to sound commanding.

"There will be casualties on both sides; we do not deny it. As you have witnessed before, we are willing to die for our freedom. Today's strike should make it clear that we are willing to kill for it too. Bear that in mind as you decide how to respond to our demands. One way or another, we will be free.

Libertad!"

Benito sighed rapturously as he finished, clearly in love with his own words. In the silence that followed, Jason felt the hair on the back of his neck prickle uncomfortably. This was madness! If The Resistance was returning, he needed to find answers fast.

Out in the cafeteria, Marcus returned from the washroom having cleaned his face and stanched his bleeding nose. Seeing that Jason was still with Benito instead of going to the meeting, he stopped and scowled. "Come on!" he demanded irritably.

Jason wasn't inclined to follow Marcus' orders any longer but after what Benito had just told him he definitely wanted some time with Gabe and Angel. Without answering Marcus directly, Jason fell into step behind him, his cane tapping the floor slightly out of time with his steps. They crossed the empty cafeteria in silence and made their way toward the office.

As they walked, Jason surreptitiously reached into his pocket and activated the record function on his micro. He was taking a risk, and the only video he'd get would be of the inside of his pocket, but the audio should prove interesting. If he was lucky, it would be the start of proving his innocence and bringing down The Resistance!

Upon entering the office, Jason squeezed past Marcus while the big man closed the door behind them. Gabe and Angel were already seated on one of the two black leather couches, leaving the other empty for their guests. Marcus grunted as he took a seat on one end of the unoccupied couch. Grudgingly, Jason took the other. After a moment both men shifted uncomfortably, trying to put as much distance between them as possible. Jason didn't like it any more than Marcus did; he hated being this close to him, but he had to admit that it felt good to rest his leg. He laid his cane across his lap and forced himself to relax while they waited for Gabe and Angel to reveal why they had been called here.

The brothers watched Jason and Marcus take their seats, then were momentarily distracted by a micro which lay on the low table in front of them. The device chirped quietly, prompting Angel to hold it up for Gabe to see, his eyebrows raised in a silent question. Gabe examined the screen carefully before nodding and saying, "Go in five." Angel then keyed something into the device before setting it back down, the screen now dark except for a clock display. The brothers then gave the two men in front of them their full attention, studying them as if trying to come to a decision. Their stare was unnerving and Jason couldn't help but think about the disastrous meeting with the Seps. Again he wondered if Marcus had blamed him for it and if so, whether the brothers had believed him.

"You're probably wondering where everyone is." Gabe began, speaking to Jason. A faint smile played at his thin lips.

Jason felt like he was walking on eggshells. "Yeah, I did wonder about that." he answered cautiously, then added, "Actually, I thought you were going to ask about the meeting with the Seps." He didn't want to bring it up, but asking was better than having it continue to hang over him.

Marcus looked at him sharply but stayed silent. The room seemed to hold its breath for a moment, then Angel answered for his brother. "I'll admit that didn't go exactly the way we planned. It's shitty what happened to you and Mateo. Real shitty." He leaned forward, resting his elbows on his knees. "We've already talked to Marcus about it." His eyes flicked over to Marcus for a moment and a scowl crossed his face, almost too quickly to be seen. "We think we have the full story. To be honest, it doesn't make him look too good. We're glad you got Mateo out."

Jason was surprised; he hadn't expected Marcus to own up to his part in how their mission had unravelled. He wondered how long it had taken him to do so, and what threats or intimidation had been needed. He noted with no small satisfaction that Angel was watching Marcus with barely concealed disgust, though as far as he could tell, Gabe hadn't evinced an opinion one way or another.

Gabe put a hand on his brother's shoulder, causing Angel to fall silent. "Actually, your meeting with the Seps is the reason Casa Preciosa is empty right now." he explained to them evenly. "After what happened last night, we had to strike back hard. So we sent every man we have out to kill those fuckers." A hot anger had begun to creep into his voice but when he continued, he again sounded cold and indifferent. "We're going to wipe them out and take over their business." he finished flatly.

Jason felt as if the world had fallen away beneath him. "Jesus! You sent everyone?" he asked, amazed. "The cops would see you coming a mile away!"

Gabe and Angel both smiled at that, unconsciously mirroring each other. "We planned for that, actually." Gabe said. "We'd hoped to wait. We wanted to do this when we were better prepared, but we knew the meeting with the Seps might end like this. We made sure we were ready if it did."

Jason's brow furrowed as he tried to make sense of what Gabe had said. "You were never going to give the Seps a deal, were you? You were just..."

Angel broke in, interrupting him before he could finish his thought. "No, the offer was legitimate. It would have let us focus our resources elsewhere while we got ready. We were going to move on them eventually but the offer was real, as far as it went."

Beside Jason, Marcus was frowning and looked bored. Apparently he'd been told all of this already. Jason however, was speechless and for a moment silence filled the room.

Gabe glanced down at the micro on the table, then leaned back in his seat and put his hands behind his head. Seeming to relax, he said, "You said the cops would see us coming." Jason nodded dumbly, uncertain where this was going. "You're right. That's why we set up a little distraction for them."

At that moment the micro chimed, the sudden sound making the device vibrate against the table's hard surface. Gabe picked it up and with a gesture transferred the image on its screen to a large wall-mounted monitor.

The display came to life, showing one of the city's endless news and discussion feeds. Professionally dressed men and women sat gathered around a circular table while a camera drone floated above their heads, changing focus and moving to follow the discussion as each person spoke.

The program seemed to be centered on a recent renovation to Ross b's capitol building, with some members of the panel defending the expense while others were loudly denouncing it as yet another example of government waste. As the talking heads tried to shout each other down, Jason turned to Gabe with a puzzled look on his face. Seeing his confusion, Gabe merely raised his hand to forestall any questions. His expression said to be patient; whatever it was they were waiting for, it was yet to come.

On the screen an irate woman wearing too much makeup was imploring her counterpart to come to his senses when the microphone caught the sound of distant shouting. Or rather, the shouting only sounded distant; in reality it must have been nearby because the woman stopped talking and a look of confusion replaced her grimace of false outrage. A moment later her jaw dropped and a look of alarm twisted her features. She rose in panic, the camera tracking her face and faithfully transmitting every nuance. Beside her the other panel members were also rising in silent horror and confusion. They milled about fearfully behind the table, clearly wanting to flee but not knowing which way to run.

Rendered mute by their fear, the panel of commentators fell silent, though the studio mics were still active and transmitting. For nearly fifteen seconds the only sound was that of some unseen chaos coming closer. This was followed by a series of staccato 'pops'; the sound of gunfire pressed thin by the microphones, and as one organism those gathered around the table finally began to run, knocking chairs and equipment aside.

The camera drone tried to track them, but they quickly fled beyond its field of view. Defeated, the image returned to a central shot showing only the empty table and overturned chairs. For a long moment there was silence, then, as if it were staged, a thin male figure entered the frame. He pulled a gray mask and sensor net from his head as he entered, revealing a worn, brown-skinned face and long unkempt gray hair. He confidently took up a position near the center of the table and Jason could see the small semi-automatic rifle he held loosely in one hand. Finding the camera, the man stared directly into the lens.

Even before he spoke Jason could see the intensely purposeful mania behind the man's eyes. When he opened his mouth, his words sounded clipped and tight, as if they were being forced from his throat.

"I am here to make a statement and to set an example!" the man announced, his eyes shining unnaturally and his voice strangely high-pitched.

Something about the man's demeanour struck Jason as odd, even a little familiar. For a moment he couldn't quite place the feeling, but then all of a sudden it clicked; the man was on Helium! The look in his eyes and his tight body language said he was on something else too; Rush, and a lot of it!

Now that he'd recognized the signs, the effects of the drugs were unmistakable. Then Jason froze as he realized something else as well; this wasn't the first time he'd seen someone like this. It wasn't even the second! Like a shot, his mind went back to that day at the bazaar; to the small park outside the shoe shop and the moment his life had changed so drastically.

"Hello there! So glad you could make it!" the man had said as they stood in the gazebo, his face hidden behind a mask. Jason heard the words echo again in his head, heard the man's tight, high-pitched voice as he relived the attack.

On the screen, this new man was still speaking. *Was* it a new man? Jason couldn't be sure. "Who is that?" he breathed in awe and horror.

"He's nobody." Gabe said dismissively.

The gunman on screen was now pointing his rifle at a frightened young woman. From her headset, she appeared to be one of the studio's technical directors. "Play this." he demanded of her. "Play it now so everyone can see or someone gets shot!" There was a growing mania in his voice, and he seemed to be on the verge of losing control. With his free hand he held out a micro, ordering the woman to take it from him. Under the gunman's watchful eye, she took the device, then interfaced it with the studio's video systems and selected a file. Given the speed with which she found it, it must have been the only thing on the micro. Never taking her eyes off his gun, she started the playback and stepped away.

A smile played across the gunman's lips before the screen flickered and a static image took his place. The photo that appeared was that of a brown-skinned man with dark black hair, holding a rifle and looking wild. To Jason's horror, he realized that he knew the man in the picture well. His hair was different and he was clean-shaven, but he recognized those features; he saw them every time he looked in the mirror.

Time seemed to stop. It was all over now; it had to be. There was just no way that Gabe, Angel or Marcus wouldn't realize it was his image on the screen. Holding his breath, he watched them for any hint of recognition but incredibly, no one reacted. Their eyes remained focused on the broadcast, watching it with interest, but nothing more. Somehow the resemblance, which was so obvious to him, had escaped them.

Mercifully, the image quickly dimmed and a field of scrolling text was placed on top of the picture, partly obscuring it. A digitally altered voice, strong and inflected, spoke the words as the text began to fill the screen.

"We are The Latino Resistance Front, and we speak for all Hispanics on Ross b. We had hoped the riots of three months ago would lead to profound changes in how Hispanic people are treated by the Anglo dominated government. We now see that we were wrong. The riots have been all but forgotten and our people continue to suffer at the hands of the Anglos. We have remained silent for too long, but today we return to correct that mistake.

Once, this government and its Citizens promised we could earn our place here. That we could stand alongside them as equals. Those promises have gone unfulfilled for well over a hundred years now, and we are done waiting! We are no longer merely asking to be taken seriously; we are demanding it! With today's strike we return to collect on a debt long owed to us! We return to take righteous vengeance on those who would deny us our birthright and unless our people are given the Citizenship we were promised, this attack will not be our last. Rather, it will merely be the herald of our return!

The man who carries out this action today is our instrument, and he is only the first of many. He does not expect to survive and he will gladly become a martyr for his people. Before his life is ended, he will take as many Citizens with him as he can. He does this in our name, and he does so out of necessity. We use violence so that you will not mistake the seriousness of our demands. The Hispanics of Ross b will seize our very humanity back from those who have stolen it!

There will be casualties on both sides; we do not deny it. As you have witnessed before, we are willing to die for our freedom. Today's strike should make it clear that we are willing to kill for it too. Bear that in mind as you decide how to respond to our demands. One way or another, we will be free. Libertad!"

As the voice stopped and the scrolling text faded away, Jason's image mercifully faded with it. The gunman reappeared, now glaring with satisfaction at the camera.

"You have heard our announcement," he said. "and unlike you, we keep our promises! Now it's time to follow through." Aiming the rifle offscreen, he bellowed, "All of you! Over here, now!"

Slowly, the frightened panelists made their way back into frame and at the gunman's order, each took their place around the table. Some of them were crying openly, while others were visibly pale and held deathly still.

With the stage now set, the man with the rifle turned back to face the camera. "We said that we are willing to kill for our freedom. We were not lying; remember that." he said, then spun and raised his weapon. The gathered victims were executed one after another in rapid, violent succession. Jason had to turn away, but he saw with horror that Marcus continued to watch rapturously as the event unfolded. Screams ripped from the speakers and filled the room before Gabe turned off the monitor, ending the gruesome display.

"That ought to get their attention." Gabe said as he settled back in his seat. Jason struggled, but he knew he had to hide his revulsion at what he'd just witnessed. Though it left him cold inside, he managed to keep the rising terror from his face.

Marcus sat up straight and looked over at Gabe and Angel with amazement. "Holy shit!" he exclaimed. In a voice tinged with excitement, he added, "That'll get *everyone's* attention!"

"So long as the police notice, that's all I care about." Gabe answered, accepting the praise with a faint smile.

Marcus' awed expression shifted to one of confusion. "But what about the speech? Don't you want..."

Gabe cut him off with a frown, saying, "Jesus, Benito wrote it for us! I didn't care what garbage he came up with, but I knew it would be something the cops couldn't ignore."

Jason realized that the end of the speech *had* sounded familiar; Benito had quoted it to him just minutes ago! Feeling like he had stepped off a cliff, he asked, "If Benito wrote it, how'd you get it to The Resistance?"

Gabe paused as if considering how much to reveal. In the end he simply shrugged and said, "Just wait. If everything else goes as planned, you'll know soon enough." He smiled and checked the time. "Give it ten minutes or so." he said.

For Jason, the wait was brutal. To keep from saying or doing anything stupid, he closed his eyes and pretended to sleep while his mind raced. Gabe and Angel pulled a bottle of brown liquid from a small cabinet and poured themselves a drink. When they offered some to Jason, he shook his head numbly in silent refusal.

After what felt like an eternity, the micro on the table lit up with an incoming call. Angel responded by setting his drink down carefully on the low table and using one thick finger to open the connection. In the dimly lit room, the light from the small screen illuminated his face with a mottled yellow and blue pattern.

A man's face appeared on the micro's display, taking up the entire frame and blocking the background from view. Jason recognized him as Tomas something-or-other; one of Angel's favored henchmen.

"It's done." Tomas said firmly.

"You got everybody?" Angel asked.

Tomas nodded curtly. "Yes, we just finished mopping up. I saw to Billy myself."

Angel gave a small, satisfied smile. "Good. I think the police will be tied up for a while, but don't hang around there any longer than you have to. Set the charges and get out. We'll talk when you get back." With that he ended the call.

Gabe looked pleased and slapped a large hand down on his brother's leg. "Alright!" he said triumphantly. With a smirk at Marcus and Jason, he said to Angel, "I think we're ready. Let's do this."

Angel nodded in agreement. He sat up and said, "That was Tomas. He just led an attack on the Seps. We told him to go down there and kill every last one of them, and now we're going to blow up their stupid club too. There won't be anything left of those fuckers after this."

Jason felt empty. After everything he'd witnessed in the past hour, the news of the Sep's slaughter barely even registered. "Revenge?" he guessed thickly. "For what they did to Mateo?"

"In a way." Angel said. "We're taking over their business. All of it."

Marcus was leaning forward in his seat. "Why?" he asked stupidly. To Jason, the answer was already clear; it was all about power. Now he understood why Gabe had put Marcus in the role of diplomat with the Seps. He'd hoped that their meeting would fail so that he'd have an excuse to attack!

Angel stopped cold, stunned by Marcus' unthinking question. "What do you mean, 'why'?!" he shouted, incredulous. "They were dealing on our turf! There had to be consequences!" Angel was glaring at Marcus and Jason saw the disgust in his eyes. He was certain now; Angel didn't like Marcus very much at all.

Beside him, Gabe was clearly feeling more forgiving. He gave his younger brother a sharp look, and Angel reluctantly backed down. He then spoke softly to Marcus, taking the sting out of Angel's harsh tone. "There's good money in the slave trade." he explained. He picked up the bottle and poured another drink, then handed it to Marcus. "But taking it from the Seps is going to more than double the size of our operation. So, we're going to split things up; Angel will run the drug business while I focus on our 'new interests'."

Angel's posture indicated he hadn't forgotten his anger, but as he spoke he made an effort to sound calm. "But that leaves us in a tough spot." he said. "We were able to pull off this attack on the Seps because we distracted the cops. It worked great, but this isn't the end. We have some other long-term plans and we're going to want to keep the cops busy for those too."

Jason was lost. "What..." he began, but Gabe silenced him with a look.

"You asked me how we got Benito's speech to The Resistance." Gabe said. "I'll let you guys in on something. It can't leave this room, but you'll need to know as we go forward." He paused and took another sip from his drink. When he spoke again he sounded like a magician revealing an obvious secret. "Look, The Latino Resistance Front is just bullshit. It's a bunch of talk we borrowed from Benito out there, backed up by just enough guns and bombs to get the cops' attention and make it look real."

Jason was suddenly intensely aware of the weight of the micro in his pocket. He hoped to god it was still recording, because holy shit!... He blinked, and for a moment he saw the face of the attacker they'd seen on the screen just minutes before. The room felt like it was spinning out of control. "So you ordered your guys to go shoot up someplace visible just to distract the cops?" he asked, barely able to keep the disgust out of his voice.

"No, no." Gabe said, shaking his head. "The shooters are just assholes from the neighborhood who got strung out on Rush and Helium. They're not much good for anything else, and the drugs make them... controllable." He snorted as if that were funny, then added, "Kind of, anyway. The Rush-Helium combination is weird; it makes them paranoid as fuck, but together the drugs make it so they'll imprint on someone they trust. We just make sure that's us. After that, they'll do anything we tell them to, including shoot people."

Slowly, Jason began to understand. In fact, it was actually genius in a terrible sort of way. Too much Helium left the user suggestible but unfocused. The only way to get someone in that state to do what you want would be to stay with them the entire time. Rush, on the other hand, led to a crippling paranoia. Combine the two however, and you create a victim who forms an unshakable bond with one trusted person but who becomes intensely aggressive toward anyone else. On a word from their handler, a person like this would happily attack anyone they were told is a threat! Jason felt sick as he realized that Gabe and Angel had found a way to manufacture martyrs.

He was still trying to process this revelation when he realized that Gabe was still talking. "...didn't do much with The Resistance after the riots because we weren't ready." Gabe explained. "We were still getting the drug trade up and running after we took out the Nortown Crew."

Jason interrupted him incredulously, saying, "Was a fake revolution really the best you could come up with to distract the cops?" He regretted the words almost immediately, but it was too late to call them back.

Gabe's face clouded over, but Marcus joined in, appearing to take the news of The Resistance's false nature personally. "Yeah!" he said angrily. "I mean, this shit was real to me, and now it turns out it was all just bullshit?"

Angel leaned forward before Gabe could reply, saying defensively, "Hey, we didn't start out playing at revolution. At first it was just snipers and shit to keep the cops busy, like the guy who shot up the bazaar a few months ago."

"You mean that asshole in the picture?" Marcus interjected incredulously, waving a hand at the darkened monitor on the wall.

Angel snorted. "We stole that photo off the police alerts. I don't know who that fucker was; I guess he's pretty screwed now. The picture looked good though, so we used it. The cops have been scared of a Latino uprising for years, so we decided to give it to them. Every time 'The Resistance' showed up they'd go running. It kept them off our backs so we could take care of business."

Gabe interjected, adding, "We hadn't counted on the riots but we took advantage of them when they happened. We took out the entire Nortown Crew in one night and the cops didn't even notice."

Marcus still looked angry and confused but as Jason

watched him, he could see the thug coming to terms with the explanation. "If this is supposed to be a secret, why are you telling it to us?" Marcus asked with an uncertain scowl.

Gabe hesitated, then said, "Because with Angel and me concentrating on the two sides of our business, we want the two of you to take over running The Resistance for us. You'll still answer to us, and you'll only do what we say. That doesn't change, but this is still a huge step up for you. Think of it as a promotion."

Marcus looked wary, like an animal sniffing at a trap. "Why us?" he asked, echoing Jason's own thoughts.

Angel scowled faintly at his brother but sat back to let him answer. It seemed to be something they'd already had a long discussion about. Gabe looked at Angel meaningfully before turning back to Marcus. "Because you've always been loyal." he said. "You're good in a fight, and you do what you're told." Though he addressed Marcus, he seemed to aim the words at Angel, as if to drive home a point. To Jason, he said, "And you're smart. You keep your head in a crisis. Your job now is going to be to make sure Marcus doesn't act before he thinks."

"So we're *both* in charge?" Marcus exclaimed, bristling at the idea.

Angel broke in before Gabe could respond. "Yes." he said firmly, locking eyes with Marcus.

Marcus ground his teeth, not happy to have anyone second guessing him. As Angel continued to stare him down he lowered his eyes and glared impotently at the floor instead. The tension in the room was broken by a soft knock at the door. Gabe rose and opened it to reveal a baby-faced teen that Jason knew the gang often used as a courier. Before letting the boy in, Gabe turned back to his guests and said, "You two take the rest of the day off. It should be quiet around here until tomorrow. We'll call if we need you."

The meeting was clearly at an end. Jason leaned on his cane for support as he stood, and suppressed a brief flash of anger as he watched Marcus rise easily under his own power. Awkwardly, they both made their way out the door as the boy took their place inside the office. Jason was the last one out and the door was locked behind him as soon as he was through.

Out in the cafeteria Marcus was scowling. He paced back and forth and then turned to Jason as if to speak. As he did so, Jason felt his ire begin to rise again. He didn't care what Marcus had to say; not anymore. Ignoring him, Jason turned and began to hobble toward the exit rather than stay to find out what was on the thug's mind.

He'd hoped that walking away would put an end to it, but as Jason reached the door there were heavy footsteps behind him as Marcus hurried to keep up. 'Fuck him.' he thought, and pushed open the door. His heart sank as Marcus finally caught up and together they stepped out into the perpetual sunlight. Unable to avoid him any longer, Jason turned to face his pursuer, expecting the worst. Surprisingly though, Marcus wasn't seeking a confrontation. Instead the man's expression was anguished, catching him off guard.

Now that he had Jason's attention, Marcus' body language changed subtly. After a moment he said dejectedly, "So, I guess now we're in charge of the 'revolution'." His tone was bitter and the muscles in his jaw worked visibly, mirroring some internal struggle. Suddenly looking betrayed, his anger flared as he flung his arm wide and pointed back toward the shelter. "They're a couple of fucking assholes!" he nearly shouted, referring to Gabe and Angel. "They might have done it just to keep the cops busy but the people needed it! They still need it! Somebody's gotta change things!" There was a pleading in his voice now and a look of desperation in his eyes.

Jason nodded stiffly. There might be some truth to what the big man was saying, but he was unwilling to agree with him out loud. Marcus accepted the nod without comment, then stared at the ground thoughtfully. In the silence that followed an unexpected breeze rose up, carrying the scent of the city and gently ruffling their clothes. After a moment Marcus raised his eyes and his expression was unreadable.

"I thought The Resistance was important. It was something real, or at least it was to me." he said broodingly. He sounded defeated but there was something else there too, on the verge of becoming dangerous. Jason nodded again warily, uncertain how to respond. He waited for Marcus to say more but instead the big man simply stood on the curb, lost in thought. After a few minutes he walked over to his car without a word and drove sedately away, leaving Jason to stand alone in front of the shelter.

As Marcus' car disappeared in the distance, Jason waited a moment before pulling out his micro to summon a car for himself. To his relief he saw that the device was still recording, capturing video and, more importantly, audio. He ended the session, making sure it had saved and backed-up the file. He finally had it! This was everything he had started all this for! Compulsively, he checked the backup again just to be sure. Everything was fine, safe and secure. Now, he just needed to figure out how to use it without going to jail himself.

CHAPTER 21

Nine PM found Jason on a tram bound for the El Rey Latino Outreach Center and a meeting with Jonah Rodriguez. He'd let Jonah know he was coming but kept the reason vague, preferring not to say too much before they met in person. He'd asked Anne to be there as well. This would affect her too; she definitely deserved to be involved as they decided what to do next.

While his plan was murky at best, his goal was clear; to exonerate himself and his family, while at the same time bringing down The Brotherhood. The problem was, he couldn't yet see a way to make it happen. The police were unlikely to listen to anything he had to say, and would probably shoot him the moment he showed his face.

He needed help, and the more he thought about it, the more going to see Jonah felt like the right answer. Jonah had helped him get set up in this new life and he had given Anne a place to teach again, if only as a tutor. He was a good man and Jason knew he had a contact within the police department. If anyone could find a way forward for him and his family, it would be Jonah.

As these thoughts ran through his mind, his stomach gurgled unnervingly, a sound that said more about the quality of his dinner than the quantity. The bowl of leftover noodles and rubbery chicken had been filling enough but the taste had left something to be desired. He tried to ignore the residual sour feeling in his gut and instead watched the video screen overhead. No sound accompanied the program; as with so many of the trams, the speaker seemed to be missing, perhaps stolen. A dirty and smudged sheet of acrylic protected the screen and blurred the picture, but without its presence the monitor would probably have been stolen as well.

The images it showed were incomprehensible. Jason saw a well-appointed apartment in which two women and a man stood looking at each other, their mouths hanging open in shock. If any of them were speaking, there was no sign of it. Then the door burst open and a shirtless burly man holding a sword in each hand charged dramatically into the room. Upon seeing the people standing there, he froze, then backed out slowly with a worried look on his face. The whole thing made no sense and the bizarre scenario made Jason's head hurt.

Wearily, he tore his eyes from the screen and looked around the tram. While Jason had a seat to himself, many of the other passengers were doubled or tripled up. Judging by their clothes, most were either heading out for the evening or going home, depending on how lucky they had already been. Some sat with their heads bent close together, sharing private conversations too softly to be heard over the whooshing of the pneumatic tube that surrounded the car. Others were more isolated and stared at the overhead screen, apparently desperate for anything that could be called entertainment. Jason studied one man in particular, his attention focused intently on the program displayed above them, leaving him oblivious and allowing Jason to observe him without being seen.

The man wore the patchy stubble of someone who hadn't shaved in several days, though from his overall fashionable appearance, it seemed that this was by choice. His clothing was stylish, falling somewhere between a business suit and upscale casual. The man's skin was a light brown, provisionally marking him as Hispanic, but there was nothing about his bearing that suggested the poverty Jason had reluctantly come to associate with non-Citizens. With an internal smirk, Jason realized that this man could easily be just as Hispanic as he himself was; meaning none at all. It was eye-opening to realize that despite being an exception himself, he still fell victim to Ross b's unconscious stereotypes. He would need to work on that, he told himself gently.

Abruptly, the man sighed and leaned back in his seat uncomfortably. Jason watched his interest in the screen above them evaporate as the man's eyes finally unlocked from the display. He stretched, then turned his head and instead began to stare absently out the window at the gray cityscape scrolling by. Jason quickly looked away from him, then up at the monitor to see what had caused the change.

On the dirty screen, the previous program had ended and in its place a serious looking newscaster had appeared. The woman's mouth moved silently as she delivered the hourly news update. Jason didn't need to be able to read lips to see that the lead story was all about The Latino Resistance Front's attack on the video production studio earlier that day.

As the presentation went on, a list of bullet points began to appear in the air beside the news anchor's head, the list growing longer as she spoke. Jason felt a sense of second-hand guilt and horror, but was unable to look away. Silently, the brutal details of the attack were laid out:

- Terrorist attack on the Robbins Studio.
- Fourteen reported dead, including the attacker. Six reported injured.
- The Hispanic Representative to the Government has denounced the attack.
- The governor has not re-invoked martial law at this time, but will do so if the situation worsens.

Jason noted the gunman's death numbly and wondered if that too had been part of his programming; a suicide order that was just one last act he had to perform. His stomach clenched again as he thought about it and this time it wasn't because of his dinner.

Abruptly the newscaster disappeared, though the list remained in place on the right-hand side of the screen. Two photos took her place; one of Jason and one of Anne. Jason's photo was the one taken at the bazaar attack, while Anne's appeared to have been pulled from her official ID file. Next to their pictures the list of bullet points continued to lengthen.

- The Latino Resistance Front has claimed responsibility.
- Jason Menounos and Anne Menounos are believed to be working together.
- Police are actively seeking their whereabouts at this time.
- Use of identification checkpoints will be expanded throughout the city.

Jason's face burned hotly. With his picture displayed on the screen above, he felt wildly conspicuous but as far as he could tell no one on the tram was watching the broadcast. Their images remained there for a few seconds before vanishing, to be replaced by the newscaster's face. The bullet points were gone now too, their place taken by a series of shifting text and graphics which served to summarize the rest of the day's news. Most of the items meant nothing to Jason but one card lingered longer than the others. It read, "The abandoned LV nightclub in north-central Cosmopolis exploded this afternoon. Reports indicate it had been used as an illegal drug lab, which led to the explosion. Due to their priority response to today's terrorist attack, police have so far been unable to verify these reports but will send investigators as soon as possible. Citizens and others are advised to avoid the area until further notice."

So, it seemed that Gabe and Angel's plan to distract the cops had paid off, at the cost of fourteen people's lives, Jason thought bitterly. Above him, the news update came to an end and another program quickly took its place.

Jason risked a careful glance around the car. No one was looking in his direction; it seemed he'd escaped detection once again. He felt as if he'd dodged a bullet but he couldn't help wondering how much longer his luck could hold out. Mercifully, he noted that the First Street station was only five or so minutes away. He gripped his cane tightly and stared out the window at the city passing below.

As the city's opulent downtown came into view, Jason watched with foreboding as stacks of folding barricades and other equipment were being unloaded from large trucks. Much of it was still packed in 'storage mode' and would take significant work to set up, but the news report of expanded checkpoints hadn't been wrong. The police seemed to be taking the sudden resurgence of The Resistance very seriously, at least here in the city's center, and life was about to get much harder for Ross b's Hispanic population. Grim faced, Jason sat back and waited as the tram continued past the downtown area toward the much more modest First Street station and began to slow.

****

When the tram doors opened, Jason exited the station and descended to street level, feeling the warm breeze on his skin. His leg ached dully but the cane helped to make the pain manageable and his steps didn't falter. Around him, his fellow travellers quickly dispersed, each tending to their own business. Soon he was alone on the sidewalk. He set out, walking north toward the El Rey Latino Outreach Center.

He'd been worried he may encounter police checkpoints here too, but was relieved to find that wasn't the case. Apparently, they intended to cordon off the downtown area first before expanding outward. That meant that their main focus was still a few blocks away, but Jason knew it wouldn't be long before the checkpoints were erected here as well.

Those fears were confirmed as he reached the El Rey Latino Outreach Center. Jason stood in front of The Center, but just one block to the north a group of men supervised by uniformed police were working to set up a checkpoint. As with the one he'd seen from the tram, it wasn't operational yet, but its presence felt like a cancer. It's placement meant that it would cut off access between The Center and parts further north, including the store where Anne and Brodie worked. Passage would still be possible, either through the checkpoint or by going around, but clearly it was already becoming increasingly difficult to move around the city center.

Jason stopped to watch them work, taking care to stay far enough back that they wouldn't notice him. His eyes were drawn to a large metal crate carried by two men as they unloaded it from a flatbed truck. Obviously not in any hurry to finish the job, the men talked and joked as they worked. They lifted the crate down as a team and then set it alongside the vehicle before turning to grab another one. With their attention elsewhere, Jason casually moved a little closer and saw that the side of the container read 'Biometric Scanner' in plain stenciled letters. The words brought him up short.

Until now, those few checkpoints still in operation had relied on ID readers and the observational skills of those who ran them. The false ID Jonah had given him had seen him safely through several checkpoints over the past three months, but if biometric scanners were now being deployed as well, they might be able to identify him no matter what disguise he used! He consoled himself with the fact that this particular checkpoint wasn't between himself and the tram station. It seemed the scanners weren't operational yet either; he still had some time to figure out how to deal with them before he was trapped.

Swallowing, he turned back to The Center and felt the day's light breeze rise suddenly, blowing specs of grit into his face. During his walk from the tram station, the breeze had been steady but now it began to tug at his clothes as it whipped around his body. It seemed that they were in for a storm, though the high, thin clouds blowing overhead didn't promise any rain. He climbed the steps to The Center's front door, turning his head and using his hand to block the dust. As he neared the entrance he heard the lock click open and Jonah opened the door to greet him.

"Come in, come in!" Jonah said, holding the door against the rising wind.

Jason hurried through, and Jonah quickly pulled the door closed behind him. The sound of the gusting wind died down and the two mens stood together in the entryway. Feeling ragged and dishevelled, Jason shook himself to shift his jacket back into place across his shoulders. Ruefully, he ran a hand over his bald head and said, "It's been breezy all day, but I guess it's really starting to pick up out there!"

Jonah smiled and clapped him on the back, saying, "No doubt about that."

"Is Anne here yet?" Jason asked, looking around hopefully.

"Not yet." Jonah replied, then hesitated. "I assume you saw the checkpoint they're setting up on the next block?"

"I did." Jason sighed.

"It's not operational yet, but I asked Anne to take the long way around just in case." Jonah explained.

"Good idea." Jason said with a nod. "I saw them unloading..."

Before he could finish, the door blew open again and let in a sudden blast of lukewarm air. Anne appeared in the doorway and quickly hurried inside, pulling the door closed once more. The blustery weather had whipped her hair and clothes, leaving her a mess and, to Jason's eyes, beautiful. She brushed the hair back from her face with her hand and then smiled as she saw Jason waiting for her. They embraced tightly before Jason looked her in the eyes and said excitedly, "Honey; I've got it!"

"What?" she asked, her brow furrowing.

"I found the proof; of everything! It's why I called you!" he said breathlessly.

Jason was about to explain but Jonah interrupted, saying, "Let's go up to my office first. I've been on my feet all day and I'd really like to sit down."

Jason agreed and Jonah began to lead the way upstairs. Jason and Anne followed a few steps behind, enjoying the chance to be together. Jason took the stairs slowly, leaning on his cane for support while Anne held his arm and helped him maintain his balance.

She looked down at his cane, then did a double-take. "Is... is that a curtain rod?" she asked, feigning awe to cover her amusement.

"Yeah; I took it off the wall in my apartment."

Carefully keeping a straight face, Anne replied, "Looks pretty good."

Jason saw through her ruse easily and smiled. "So where's Matthew?" he asked, changing the subject.

"Brodie took him and Arabelle to the park. I know it's late, but with Mateo in the hospital she wanted to give the kids something else to think about for a while." Anne answered. Jason couldn't help feeling disappointed; he missed his son but he understood Anne keeping him away from things like this. He still had nightmares that one day Gabe or Angel would find him. In the end, this was probably for the best.

By now Jonah had reached the top of the stairs. As Jason and Anne joined him, he turned and entered his office, sitting down behind the desk. Jason and Anne took the remaining seats; the same seats they'd sat in months ago as Jonah had given them their new identities. Jason fought back a sense of déjà vu as he pulled the micro from his pocket.

"I got called into a meeting today with Gabe and Angel." he told them. "Before I went in, I set my micro to record and left it going the whole time." As Jason spoke Jonah leaned forward in his seat, listening intently. "I should probably just play this for you." Jason said, gesturing with the micro he held in his hand. He set the device down on the desk and cued up the recording. Instinctively, Jonah and Anne craned their heads toward the screen, which remained dark. "I kept it in my pocket, so there's no video." he explained apologetically. "You won't see anything. Just listen."

The recording was long, running for over twenty-five minutes. The audio it contained was muffled and muddy at times, but the words were clear enough. Jason resisted the temptation to skip any silent parts and instead let it play while quietly providing clarification when needed. When Gabe revealed the truth about The Resistance, Anne looked up at her husband with her mouth open. Jonah sat with his eyes closed and his fingers tented in front of his chin. He didn't react visibly, instead letting the words wash over him.

When they'd heard the entire recording, Jason turned the micro off and sat back in his chair. "So," he said lamely, "now we need to decide what to do with this."

Jonah was thoughtful. "They might be fake revolutionaries, but they're still real terrorists." he observed sadly. "At the risk of stating the obvious, I'd say we need to get this to the police. The problem is, they aren't likely to believe an anonymous source and you'd probably be arrested if you brought it in yourself."

In the seat next to Jason, Anne was visibly frustrated. She wanted to help somehow, but knew she faced the same problems as her husband. If she got involved, the authorities wouldn't treat her any better than they would him.

"I still have my contact in the police department." Jonah offered. "I could give it to him. Maybe with his support it would be heard."

Jason didn't like the sound of 'maybe'. "Do we have any other options?" he asked, sounding exhausted.

Jonah sat thinking for a long moment, then said, "Martin Luther King Jr. once said that only light can drive out the darkness. If we deliver this to the police, there's a chance it would be buried or ignored. On the other hand, if the public were to hear it, they would be outraged. They would insist that the police do something about it." He rubbed his chin, considering. "That's it!" he said suddenly, sitting up straighter in his chair. "We'll give it to them both; the police and the public, at the same time. Public pressure will force the police to take this seriously! They'll have to act. The police have the ability to take down The Brotherhood, we just have to make them do it."

Jason was struck by the simplicity of the idea; it made perfect sense! If they gave the recording to everyone, there was no way it could be ignored. "They can't bury it then!" he agreed enthusiastically. He felt giddy! They finally had a real plan; a way to actually make things better! Beside him, Anne was smiling and the sight of it nearly overwhelmed him.

Jonah wore a far away look as he began planning in his head. "I'll call a press conference," he said, "but I'll need some time to put everything together. I want to get as many city leaders to come as possible and it may take a few days to convince enough of them to show up."

"Thank you." Jason told him with heartfelt gratitude. "I couldn't have done this without you."

Jonah smiled modestly. "The violence and hatred in this city, on all of Ross b, won't get any better unless everyone works to stop it. It seems to me you've already done more than your share." He let the compliment linger for a moment then laid his hands flat on his desk, changing the subject. "It's getting rather late. I'll get started making the arrangements in the morning. You two should get some sleep."

Jason sat back, feeling free for the first time in a long, long while. It didn't quite feel real. Beside him, Anne slid her chair back and stood up.

"Yeah, I should be getting back to the apartment." she said. "Brodie will be bringing Matthew home soon and I want to be there when he shows up."

Jason suddenly remembered something. "Did you get a look at the police checkpoint they're setting up on the next block?" he asked Anne.

"No." she said. "Jonah told me about it though, so I came up through the alley instead."

"They had something there; a biometric scanner. They didn't have it set up yet but if they're putting those things all over the city, it's going to be a problem for us." Jason said.

Jonah looked concerned. "I hadn't heard about the scanners. You saw one?"

"I did." Jason confirmed with a nod.

Jonah sighed heavily. "You two could stay here." he offered. "It might not be worth the risk to go out until we clear your names."

Jason considered remaining at The Center but ultimately decided against it. "I can't." he said apologetically. "If I disappear, The Brotherhood is going to know something is wrong. We need them to stay in the dark until your press conference is ready."

Jonah nodded, reluctantly accepting Jason's logic. He then looked to Anne but she too declined the invitation. "I want to get home to Matthew." she said. "If the scanners aren't set up yet, this might be my only chance to make it back."

Jason hated the idea of Anne putting herself in danger by leaving, but he couldn't disagree with her decision to be with their son. "Once the scanners are up and running, what are we going to do?" he mused aloud.

"Well..." Jonah began, stretching the word out. "Maybe they will only scan people who look suspicious?" He shook his head sadly, realizing as he said it that all too often members of law enforcement considered everyone with brown skin suspicious. "I'll talk to my contact in the police department in the morning." he said gravely. "Maybe we can find another option."

****

Leaving Jonah in his office, Jason and Anne made their way down the stairs. Despite the potential problem with the scanners, Jason couldn't help smiling. They were so close to setting things right again! Anne was holding onto his arm to steady him on the steps and he used her grip to pull her closer as they descended.

"This is it!" he said excitedly. "Once everyone has the file, the police will have to look into it! They'll see that I didn't kill anyone; that *we* didn't do any of this!"

"I hope you're right." Anne replied, grinning. She wasn't quite as ebullient as her husband, but she remained hopeful nonetheless. "We could get our lives back. I could teach again! We just have to make it through the next few days."

As they reached the bottom of the stairs, Jason felt his leg begin to shake ever so slightly as he pushed it to its limit. The quiver was barely noticeable though, and his leg didn't actually hurt at all. He took this as a good sign. He might still need the cane but he was getting better even faster than he'd hoped. It was yet another thing that made him smile.

Jason and Anne lingered at the door, neither one wanting to leave. Finally though, they had no choice. Frowning, Anne said, "If I'm going to beat Matthew home, I really do have to go."

"I understand." Jason said. "I wish I could go home with you but if this all works out, we'll all be together soon."

Anne wrapped her arms around him and hugged him so tightly that for one delightful moment he couldn't breathe. She kissed him passionately, her lips soft and moist, and he suddenly felt lightheaded. As he caught his breath, Anne squeezed his hand one last time before disappearing through the door. 'She is amazing...' he whispered to himself, dazed.

Following Anne, Jason exited The Center and descended to the sidewalk. To his relief, the earlier strong wind had dwindled and was now reduced to a light breeze. He looked north, hoping to catch one last glimpse of his wife but found that she'd already vanished into the alley beside the building.

As a sudden wave of fatigue hit him, he realized that the last rest he'd gotten had been while sitting upright in a hospital chair. It would be good to get back to his apartment and sleep in his own bed for a change. Sighing heavily, he turned south and began walking toward the tram station.

CHAPTER 22

"My contact with the police finally got back to me." Jonah said, his image sharing the screen on Jason's micro with that of Anne. Jonah had called them both and then conferenced everyone in together.

The call had arrived while Jason sat in front of a nearly empty plate in a small restaurant near his apartment. Though it was still technically morning, it was after prime breakfast hours and the place was empty except for an elderly woman sitting at the counter near the door. The booth Jason occupied was by the back wall, far enough away to prevent eavesdropping so long as he kept the volume low. As Jonah spoke, Jason balanced his micro against a convenient saltshaker and used his toast to mop up the last bits of egg yolk.

The micro's small display had automatically reconfigured itself to show both Jonah and Anne, but the change had reduced the size of their images by half. Jason had to squint to make out any details, and the reflection from the window near his seat didn't help. He shifted the angle of the device a bit to compensate.

Jonah had called with an update regarding the biometric scanners. In the time since they parted last night, Jonah had spoken to his inside man at the police department to see if he could learn anything useful. Judging from his expression, the results had been mixed.

"First, the good news." Jonah said, checking his notes. "When we set up your new identities, biometric information based on your current appearances was added to those files. Apparently the scanners mostly rely on facial shape and bone structure, but there is always some room for error in how these things work due to differences in lighting or a particular scanner, etc. The good thing for us is that they also take hair and eye color into account, though they aren't weighted as heavily. Since you've both changed your appearance since the last time the police saw you, that means a biometric scanner *might* match you to your new, false identities first, and then stop there. At least, that's the hope."

Jason waited a moment before prompting him to continue. "What's the bad news?" he asked guardedly.

"The bad news is that this is the best we can do, and my contact can't promise it will work. Truthfully, your best bet would be to avoid the checkpoints entirely. Fortunately the citywide rollout of the scanners isn't going as quickly as they would have you believe. There's been some problems and, as of now anyway, the one outside The Center is still offline."

Jonah gave a small, guilty smile. "It turns out I know one of the technicians setting up this particular scanner. I can't ask him to do anything too obvious, but he says he can delay activation until tonight." To Anne, he said, "After your shift at the store, I think you should come to The Center and stay here for the duration. Matthew is already here and you should be with your son."

Anne nodded. "I will," she said, "but I have to stay here until five PM. Will that be soon enough?"

"It should be." Jonah answered. "Jason, I'd ask you to come stay at The Center too but I know you still need to keep up appearances with The Brotherhood."

"I don't plan on taking any unnecessary risks." Jason vowed, seeking to reassure them both.

Anne smiled wanly at her husband. "I'd say you already have" she said, then quickly added, "but I love you anyway." to remove the sting from her words.

"I'll make sure Matthew stays here." Jonah promised them solemnly, then paused to examine his notes again. Looking back up, he said, "I think I'm making progress on the press conference. We need as many people as possible to come, so I'm calling it a 'Unity Rally'." He smiled as he said it. "I know it's a silly name but it makes it sound like a party, and people love a party. I'll send out the public invitation when we're done here. I'm still working to get commitments from civic leaders and others to attend but I don't want to wait too long to make the announcement. I'm going to set the date for Saturday and I want people to have time to get excited about it."

Jason's eyes widened as he realized that Saturday was only two days away. "Sounds great!" he said, grinning broadly as Anne enthusiastically echoed him almost perfectly.

Suddenly an incoming-call alert appeared on Jason's screen, causing his smile to falter. He scowled as he saw that the call was from Marcus. He desperately wanted to ignore it, but remembered that unfortunately, he still had to keep up appearances.

"I have to take this. I'm sorry." Jason told Anne and Jonah apologetically.

"Understood. I'll talk to you both later." Jonah said, then disconnected with a wave. As he vanished, Anne's face expanded to fill the small screen. Now that he could finally make out her beautiful features, Jason couldn't help but smile.

"I'll try to call you tonight. I love you." Anne said before departing. She closed the connection and her image winked out, leaving Marcus' incoming call to take over the screen. Ignoring his distaste for the man, Jason stabbed 'Accept' and Marcus' brutish face suddenly filled the display.

Marcus gave him no preamble at all. "Lucas. Get back to the shelter, now." he said roughly. "I've got something planned but Angel says I need to have you here." Marcus was obviously trying to give him an order, despite Gabe and Angel very clearly putting them *both* in charge of The Resistance. Marcus fixed him with a glare like a pack animal trying to assert dominance.

Jason's jaw tightened but he held his tongue, reminding himself that he would need to play along until Jonah's

Unity Rally happened. Biting back the acidic reply that sprang to his lips, he said, "Tell Angel I'll be there in an hour." and then broke the connection without waiting for a reply.

He hated dealing with Marcus. The exchange had left him feeling tense and he noticed a twinge of pain in his leg for the first time since he sat down. He rubbed the injury lightly and took a deep breath, forcing himself to relax.

In reality, his leg had felt much better after a good night's sleep; so much so that he had decided to leave his cane in the apartment today. The short walk to the restaurant had served as a test of his abilities, and he'd arrived tired but not actually sore. He still limped noticeably, but he was getting better quickly. The ache he felt now was likely due to stress, and even that was beginning to fade as his breathing slowed. The pain was gone entirely a moment later.

Sighing, he looked down at his empty plate. He couldn't put it off any longer; in order to get to Casa Preciosa on time, he would have to leave now. Rising carefully from his seat, Jason paid for his meal before walking, stiffly but steadily, toward the nearest tram station.

****

As the elevated tram carried him over the city toward Casa Preciosa, Jason stared absently at his micro. He had very little else to do, as the tram's overhead screen was broken or at least turned off. Instead of trying to watch the video feeds, he periodically checked the Cosmopolis Public Communications Bulletin Board, looking for Jonah's Unity Rally announcement. Eventually the notice appeared and was placed at the top of the list. The professional looking invitation read:

--UNITY RALLY--

A chance for the city to come together!

As we struggle to answer this most recent attack, it is more important than ever that we respond with

a sense of peace, mutual respect and community.

In that spirit, Citizens and non-Citizens alike are invited to attend a peaceful rally at 12:00 PM this Saturday at the El Rey Latino Outreach Center.

We will use this opportunity to call for honest dialogue and real justice for everyone who lives here.

We, the people, will show that these terrorists do not speak for us all!

Thank you,
Jonah Rodriguez, Director
El Rey Latino Outreach Center

The announcement was so bright and optimistic that Jason couldn't help but smile. He hoped it would be enough to get people to show up. Their whole plan depended on the public hearing what Jonah had to say, and it wouldn't work if no one came.

His weight shifted forward gently as the tram slowed and then came to a stop at the station. The people around him stood as he pocketed his micro and made ready to disembark. The tram station was three blocks from Casa Preciosa and even yesterday he would have balked at walking that far. Today though, he thought that if he paced himself and rested periodically, he would be able to make the trip. If all else failed he could summon a car but he told himself it wouldn't come to that.

He let those in front of him get off first, then carefully exited the tram and descended to the street, eyeing the aging neighborhood around him. Notably, there were no police checkpoints anywhere to be seen. The news had said that checkpoints were to be placed in every part of the city but so far he'd only seen them in the wealthy downtown and around the capital, protecting the establishment and leaving non-Citizens and the poor to fend for themselves. The over-sight was conspicuous; if the police and the politicians truly cared about everyone in their city, wouldn't they be working to protect *all* the people? It wasn't that he actually wanted to see checkpoints here, but the lack of them certainly showed where the city's priorities lay. Depressed, he began putting one foot in front of the other, making his way toward Casa Preciosa.

Twenty minutes later, he was regretting his decision to walk. It was a warm day and he was sweating profusely by the time he arrived outside the shelter. To make matters worse, his leg had begun to ache again. Whether that was due to the walk or the stress of returning to Casa Preciosa, he had to admit he really wasn't looking forward to hearing what Marcus had come up with.

He would have to find out eventually, but as he stood on the sidewalk he couldn't quite make himself go inside. Re-belling, he instead decided to procrastinate for a few minutes more. Limping around to the shady side of the building, he sought some meager respite from the heat and a place to re-cover his strength.

Leaning against a wall, he wiped the sweat from his brow and tried to ease the throbbing in his leg. When his eyes adjusted to the dim light, he found that he was sharing the shade with the shelter's orange cat, which looked alert, if a bit thin. It lay quietly under a nearby trash can, almost hidden by debris and watching him carefully. The base of the can was raised a few inches, which created an opening underneath. It dawned on him that he might have found the animal's home. He knelt down carefully and reached out a hand to pet it but the cat darted away, disappearing into the alley and leaving him disappointed.

With the animal now gone, Jason stood back up, the effort causing his leg to ache again dully. The pain remained distant though and the short rest had done him good overall. It was time to go see what sort of havoc Marcus had planned and whether he could find a way to stop it.

****

Jason walked into chaos. Even before he had the door open he could hear Angel's gruff, commanding voice echoing loudly throughout the building. Inside, he saw the gang leader standing in the middle of the cafeteria, dressing down a shorter, thick-set man. The man was armed, and in any other situation he would have been intimidating, but now he cowered in front of Angel. Members of The Brotherhood stood gawking in a loose group, curious but doing their best to stay out of the way.

"You said it to my face! You said you got them all! You even blew the fucking place up! What the fuck do you mean, you 'must have missed some'?!" Angel roared. His brown face flushed red with rage as the man in front of him tried to formulate an answer. Jason realized that the man was Tomas, whom Angel had sent to kill the Seps and destroy their club.

Jason decided he wanted no part of the scene unfolding in front of him and instead scanned the room for Marcus. After a moment he found him near the back of the crowd, taking obvious pleasure in Tomas' misfortune.

Giving Angel and Tomas a wide berth, Jason circled around to where Marcus stood. Marcus' attention remained focused on the argument in front of him, and so didn't notice Jason move in behind.

"What's going on?" Jason asked him a little too loudly.

"Shit!" Marcus exclaimed, jumping as if hit by an electric shock. Seeing Jason standing behind him, he scowled darkly before nodding toward Tomas and Angel. "Billy Ghoul sent Angel an 'I'm still alive, so fuck you!' message." he explained. "The way Angel's going on about it, I don't think it's just Billy that lived either." Marcus shook his head, an ugly grin spreading across his face. "Tomas is *fucked.*"

Jason looked over at Angel and Tomas. The gang leader

was still berating the shorter man, but a deadly calm had now replaced his earlier rage. Jason dreaded to think what might be coming next.

"Come on." Angel commanded sharply, spinning Tomas around violently and shoving him forward. He kept pushing until both men disappeared into the small office, slamming the door behind them and leaving the gathered gang members to mutter in disappointment now that the show was over.

Moments later a single gunshot echoed loudly from behind the closed office door. The sound hadn't been unexpected, but the irrevocable finality of it still caused Jason to flinch internally.

The office door opened again and Angel emerged alone, a pistol in his hand and a crimson spatter of blood on his shirt. He slid the weapon into his waistband and pulled the shirt back down to cover it. He then gestured distractedly to the man positioned nearest the door. The two spoke quietly for a moment and then the man nodded and left, presumably to deal with the body. With that done, Angel looked up and saw Jason and Marcus standing near the stairs.

"Let's go talk upstairs." Angel said to them, his voice sounding a little hoarse as he broke the funereal silence that filled the room. "I think we're going to need you sooner than we thought."

Angel led the way, leaving Jason and Marcus to exchange looks before quickly following him. At the top of the stairs, they heard Angel shout, "Not fucking now! Get out.", followed by Benito's pleading whine.

Benito sidled past Angel and began to back reluctantly down the stairs. "But this is *importante*!" he insisted, glaring up at Angel and standing sideways to let Marcus and Jason pass. His nasal tone was almost comical, but Jason was taken aback at the righteous anger he saw on the small man's face.

His patience gone, Angel stepped toward Benito threateningly, causing the smaller man to flinch. As Benito stepped backward on the stairs, he tripped and began to windmill his arms wildly. Marcus reacted quickly, grabbing his shirt and pulling him to safety. Then, without a word, Marcus let go and followed Angel and Jason into the now empty room at the top of the stairs.

Once Jason and Marcus joined him, Angel ignored the unsettling confrontation with Benito. "Okay, here's the deal;" he told them seriously. "we're going to need another Resistance attack. Probably soon. Billy Ghoul and some of the other Seps survived, and that asshole sent me a message saying that he's going to come kill us." He then bared his teeth in what probably passed for a smile. "I don't think they're going to be a problem, but we need to make sure we finish those fuckers off this time. We're going to do it right, so we'll definitely need a distraction for the cops. I want you to pull together something big enough to keep their attention for a while."

Marcus leapt at the opportunity. "That's great!" he said eagerly. "What about the idea I told you about earlier?"

Angel frowned. "I want you to run it past Lucas first." he said gruffly. Jason heard the disdain in his voice and remembered the contempt the gang leader had shown for Marcus the day before. "Really, I don't care what you two come up with, just make sure Lucas is on board with it first. You two are doing this *together*." he finished, his voice dripping with scorn.

Marcus ground his teeth visibly before finally swallowing his pride. "I will. We'll do this together." he said, his voice tight.

Jason opened his mouth to ask what the plan was, but was interrupted when Benito stormed back into the room.

"*Lo siento*, but this can't wait! It's too important." Benito said, breathing hard. Conviction had apparently made him brave, and he nodded to Jason and Marcus, saying, "And they should hear this too."

Incensed that the small man had dared to interrupt gang business, Angel stepped forward angrily, his hand moving toward his pistol. Jason felt the temperature in the room drop as Marcus tensed. The moment seemed to last forever, but in the end Angel decided that Benito wasn't worth it. "Fine." he said coldly, letting his hand drop back to his side. "Say what you came to say."

Benito swallowed, aware of the risk he had just taken. Jason had to give the man credit; though clearly afraid, he had come to speak his mind no matter what.

"You can't take over for the Seps!" Benito told them, his voice twisted in anguish. "It's not right!"

Angel eyed him warily. "Why not? You know what we do." he said. "It's all about territory and business. Taking over the Sep's trade is just that; good business."

"But it's slavery! *Esclavismo*!" Benito said, drawing out the words. "And not just of the Anglos. The Seps enslave more Hispanics than they do Whites! It's not right! It's not just! These are our people; *your* people! The Anglos enslave us and now you want to do it too? What would The Resistance say?! *Vergonzoso*!"

Angel clenched his teeth. "It's just business." he said in a voice that was low and harsh. "We let you hang around here, but it looks like you forgot you don't actually belong. You don't get to tell The Brotherhood how to do things. Now get the fuck out of here before I really do shoot you."

Benito's eyes widened as Angel drew his gun for emphasis. He bravely tried to hold his ground but as the weapon rose with a slow menace, he finally broke. "Okay, okay!" he pleaded. "I will go for now. When your brother returns, maybe he will understand; *entender*." With that he backed out of the room and down the stairs, not taking his eyes off Angel until he was gone.

Though Benito was now out of earshot, Angel answered him anyway. "Good fucking luck with that." he said bitterly and returned the pistol to its place against his hip.

Marcus was quiet and tense, visibly shaken by the confrontation between Angel and Benito. For a moment he looked as though he might try to defend his mentor to the gang leader, but abandoned the idea when Angel turned to him with a dark look on his face. "Lucas and I will get to work." Marcus said instead, sounding defeated.

"Good." Angel growled, and strode from the room.

After Angel left, Jason stood looking at Marcus. He hated being forced to work with him and was unsure how to even begin. What he really wanted to do was leave; he certainly didn't want to help Marcus plan a terrorist attack! He had to find a way to stall things until after Jonah's rally.

The strained silence was broken as both Jason's and Marcus' micros suddenly chimed, displaying an updated city-wide invitation to the Unity Rally. Jason saw that the invite read the same as before, but now added:

Speakers confirmed:

Kenneth Wright - Journalist
Julia Arroyo - Poet and Novelist
Sylvia Anzaldúa - Latino Rights Activist
Joseph Clinton - Cosmopolis Police Captain

Jason was impressed; Jonah had clearly been working hard to get luminaries and civic leaders to appear and it looked like his efforts were beginning to pay off. Most of these people were names he'd actually heard of, and getting the police captain to appear was important for more than one reason. The 'Unity Rally' may actually live up to its name!

"Fucking traitor..." Marcus murmured disgustedly, looking down at his own micro.

Jason was stunned. "What?" he asked, dismayed.

"This 'Unity Rally' bullshit. The fucking Anglos spend a hundred years arresting us, beating us and making sure we stay 'in our place', and now this Uncle Juan asshole wants us to make nice with them; *thank* them for doing such a good job running the planet?"

Jason was speechless. "That's not it at all!" he said finally, astonished that anyone could doubt Jonah's intentions. "He's trying to stop the violence! Fake or not, 'The Latino Resistance Front' hasn't helped anyone! All it's done is kill a hell of a lot of people, *including Hispanics*. Your so-called 'revolution' has some pretty shitty aim!"

"So we'll make it real!" Marcus shouted, suddenly enraged. "We have a chance to fight for real change now! Gabe and Angel have handed us a weapon and I say we use it!"

"Fuck you!" Jason snapped. "I'm not going to let you kill people like that." He took a breath, suddenly aware that if he outright refused, Gabe and Angel would likely turn on him. He had to be very careful in what he said next. "At least not Hispanics." he hedged, eyeing Marcus angrily.

Marcus glared back at him, his face hard. "The Resistance is supposed to distract the cops during the attack on the Seps. That's what Angel asked us to do and I've already got a plan figured out. It'll work great and keep the cops busy all fucking day." His voice took on a sarcastic edge. "Do you want to hear the plan?" he asked caustically. "You and I are supposed to be a team now, after all."

Jason felt trapped. He saw no way out; no way to stop this, and suddenly he couldn't stand to be in the same room with Marcus any longer. Not trusting himself to speak, he simply walked away. Marcus followed him down the stairs, shouting, "Hey! Where the fuck are you going?!"

At the front door Marcus grabbed his shoulder and Jason whirled on him, red-faced and shouting. "It's too fucking hot in here!" he snarled. "I'm going out to get some air! I'll be back later; you can tell me all about your fucking plan then!"

Jason saw Marcus' face darken with anger, and he wondered if he'd just signed his own death warrant. No matter; it was too late now. Limping, he left the shelter and slammed the door behind him.

CHAPTER 23

"It's only two more days. If I just vanish they might come looking for me, but I just don't think I can go back there." Jason said, leaning against the counter while Anne checked an electronic invoice against a pallet of various food items, verifying that the shipment was complete. Behind her, Brodie sat on the floor breaking down a second delivery and moving its contents onto the shelves. There were no customers in the store at the moment, giving them a chance to take stock, check their inventory and get ready for the evening rush. As a result, the buzzsaw shriek of Brodie's ever-present music filled the building.

Anne set the pad down on the boxes in front of her and looked up at her husband. "Then don't!" she said emphatically. "The Rally is Saturday. The Brotherhood might wonder where you are tomorrow, but that's all. One day missing shouldn't be too bad."

Jason's beard and shirt were damp with sweat; the day had started out hot and had now become muggy on top of it. His shirt clung to his chest, making him look a little silly and bringing a smile to Anne's lips. With the new checkpoints and police patrols, he'd used a car to get to the store instead of walking from the tram station but even so the heat and humidity were getting to him.

She watched the way he leaned against the counter, and saw the subtle way he was still favoring his left leg. She would offer him a chair, but knew he would refuse it. She loved him, but he could be so stubborn sometimes...

"I..." Anne started to say, then stopped herself. She

knew it would hurt him to hear this, but he needed to know. She began again, saying, "With the new checkpoints they put up, I'm cut off from Brodie's apartment." She saw Jason's brow knit with concern and quickly added, "I've already spoken to Jonah. Matthew and I are going to stay at The Center until this blows over. Matt's already there and since the checkpoint between here and The Center won't come online until sometime tonight, I'll head over there before that happens."

Jason looked like he wanted to say something, offer anything to help, but just couldn't come up with the right words. The muscles in his jaw worked in frustration but after a moment he merely said, "Makes sense. Jonah wanted us to do that anyway." He trailed off and looked thoughtful as he considered the broader situation. "You know, the only new checkpoints I've actually seen have been downtown. There's one by your apartment now?"

"Kind of." Anne explained. "Since we're on one of the main roads into the city center, the police put the checkpoint up just outside our building to control traffic. It cuts the whole neighborhood in half and Brodie's apartment is on the wrong side. I was able to get out this morning before it went online, but Brodie checked a little while ago and they have it up and running now."

From her place on the floor Brodie spoke up angrily, her voice dripping with venom. "I hate all that 'show us your papers' gestapo bullshit." she spat. Suddenly sweetening, she turned to Anne and added, "They aren't looking for *me* though. The fucking cops don't give a shit who I am. After work, I'll bring you your clothes and stuff, and Matthew's too."

"Thanks." Anne said. "Hopefully this will all be over Saturday, but we won't get through it without your help."

"I know." Brodie replied modestly, giving her a smile. "Did you have much trouble avoiding the cops on your way here?" she asked Jason.

"Like I said, I've seen them setting up checkpoints around the city center but, as of this morning at least, most of them weren't online yet." he said. "I had the car avoid the whole area and then stick to alleys and side streets." He smirked ruefully. "I really did feel like a criminal but once you get away from the downtown it's not too bad. I guess the police are either terrible at their job, or they don't actually care about anything other than the rich part of town."

Brodie snorted. "I'll let you guess which one it is." she said darkly.

Anne finished checking the shipment and leaned up against the counter next to her husband. "I heard from Valarie today." she said. "She says Mateo's doing a lot better. He lost a lot of blood but the bullets didn't hit anything vital. I guess that after we left the doctors gave him another treatment and it really helped. Valarie's still pretty upset, but she did sound better. She said Mateo asked about you."

Jason was pensive. "That's good." he said, forcing a smile that didn't quite reach his eyes. "I still feel shitty about what happened."

Anne squeezed his arm sympathetically. "She said that he could be discharged tomorrow."

"Wow!" Jason said, genuinely amazed. "Good doctors, I guess."

"I guess so." she agreed. She was quiet for a moment, then asked, "Did you know that Valarie is pregnant?"

The question seemed to come out of nowhere, but the words jogged Jason's memory. "Actually, yeah I did. Mateo told me a few days ago." he admitted sheepishly.

"You didn't think to tell me?" Anne asked, teasing him a little.

"It must have slipped my mind. I've been kind of busy lately." he replied, smiling for real this time.

Anne pressed against him playfully before picking her pad back up and returning to her job. Jason watched her work, wondering how it was that anyone could look that good in an ill-fitting vest. Her cut and dyed hair had changed her appearance, but it certainly hadn't done anything to spoil it.

From outside an angry electric hum rose in pitch and volume as it came closer, becoming a shriek before spooling down suddenly. A glance through the window revealed that a car had parked outside, the modified motor and garish purple paint job instantly recognizable. Jason's blood ran cold as he saw Marcus exit the car and look around with an ugly look on his face.

A sudden fear gripped him. *'Not here; not now!'* he thought. Had Marcus followed him? It was possible, though it was just as likely Marcus had simply used his 'Contacts' list and accessed Jason's location. By default, the micros would share location data with anyone marked as a 'friend'. In this moment he kicked himself for not turning that feature off, but it was too late now. Outside, Marcus began striding toward the door and a chime sounded as he entered the building.

Without looking up to see who had entered, Brodie shouted over the shelves with her usual style of belligerent customer service. "What?!"

Marcus ignored her and instead focused on Jason. "So this is where you hang out?" he said, sneering as he walked toward the counter. His steps were just a little unsteady, and Jason couldn't tell whether he had come looking for a fight or just to talk. Maybe both, somehow.

Jason stepped forward to meet him and they stopped together in the middle of an aisle. Jason turned slightly, positioning himself so that the racks of food and other items blocked Marcus' view of Anne. As he got closer, Jason could smell the sour scent of beer on his breath.

"What do you want?" Jason demanded sharply, trying to keep Marcus' attention focused on him. Despite his best efforts, his two lives were colliding in front of him and the threat that presented was very real. Under no circumstances whatsoever did he want The Brotherhood anywhere near his family, and this was a near-worst case scenario.

"You weren't just getting some air." Marcus accused him angrily. "You fucking left!"

Jason felt someone come up behind him. "Lucas." Anne said protectively from over his shoulder, forcing herself to use his false name. "Do you need anything?"

Jason tried to swallow the lump in his throat, never taking his eyes off Marcus. "No, I'm fine." he said, his voice tense.

Marcus had seen the flash of fear in Jason's eyes. Now he seized on it. "Who is this?" he asked Jason menacingly.

Jason did the only thing he could think of to get Anne out of danger. "Let's go talk outside." he said to Marcus, purposefully stepping into his personal space and trying to force him toward the door. Marcus seemed confused rather than threatened by the move, but stepped back after a moment. At Jason's urging, he left the store and Jason followed him out. As Jason left, he shot Anne a look that mixed fear and apology with an urgent message of '*stay here!*'.

When the two were outside, Marcus confronted Jason again. "What the fuck is that?!" he demanded, outraged and pointing back toward the store. Jason could tell that he was no longer talking about their encounter at Casa Preciosa. "That's Lena, isn't it?" Marcus exclaimed. "Your girlfriend? She's fucking White!"

Jason intentionally hadn't said much about his personal life to anyone in The Brotherhood, but he had mentioned in passing that he was dating someone named 'Lena'. It was an innocuous comment that had gone unremarked at the time. He'd regretted saying even that much, but until this moment he thought it had been forgotten.

"So what?" Jason asked, his voice as hard as granite.

"Fucking Anglos, that's what!" Marcus retorted with a sneer. "They shit all over us and now you're dating one?" Though Jason could still smell the alcohol on his breath, Marcus seemed frighteningly sober now. Overhead, the hot, muggy weather had given way to a smear of slowly gathering clouds and in the distance thunder rumbled quietly.

"Just say what you came to say." Jason stated harshly.

He wasn't sure he could take Marcus in a fight but if he tried to hurt Anne, he would *find* a way to kill him.

Marcus glared at him, hearing the challenge in his tone. He took a threatening step toward Jason but at that moment Marcus' car door opened and the boy Daniel got out. Daniel looked at them, his gaze moving from one to the other, with a strange look on his face.

"Get back in the car!" Marcus snapped at him.

"It's hot in there." Daniel protested, whining.

"I don't care! I'll be done here in a minute." Marcus answered dismissively. Daniel frowned but reentered the car, slamming the door closed and sealing himself inside. Marcus turned his attention back to Jason but the threat of imminent violence had passed.

"You brought him with you?" Jason asked, shocked. Daniel had been tagging along with Marcus off and on for nearly a week now, and it still wasn't clear what he planned to do with the boy. Still, at least Daniel hadn't mysteriously disappeared. That was more than could be said for the Asian kid they'd rescued alongside him. No one had spoken a word about him since they brought him in, and Jason wasn't sure if the boy was even still alive.

"Kid doesn't have anywhere else to be. I'm looking after him; it's more than anyone else is doing." Marcus answered defensively.

Jason didn't want to get pulled into a debate about what would be best for Daniel, so instead he said, "What did you come here for?", trying to keep his tone even.

"I need you to tell Angel you're okay with my attack plan!" Marcus said exasperatedly. "You fucking left without letting me tell you what it is! I told you I've already got it figured out, but there's prep work to do. Just say you're fine with it and I'll take care of the rest." Marcus said.

There was absolutely no way Jason was going to approve of anything Marcus told him, but right now it was even more important to get him to leave. The fastest way to do that would be to let him talk. "So what's your plan?" he asked warily.

Marcus grinned in evil anticipation and again seemed a little drunk. "We steal a shuttle from the spaceport." he said.

Steal a shuttle? Jason's forehead wrinkled as he tried to make sense of it. "How's that going to distract the cops?" he asked. "The Resistance are supposed to be terrorists, not thieves. What will stealing a shuttle get us?"

"The shuttles use liquid fuel to get into orbit. We'll have a gunman drive a bunch of people into one place, fly the shuttle over them and dump the fuel. Then we ignite it!" Marcus said with hushed enthusiasm. "That should keep the cops busy for days!"

The scale and horror of the monstrous proposal left Jason speechless. His mouth hung open as he pictured it and his blood ran cold as ice. "Jesus christ!" he breathed in dismay. His mouth was suddenly dry and he nearly choked before managing to croak out sarcastically, "Fuck! Why don't you just bomb them?!"

"We're The Latino Resistance Front." Marcus answered with a grim fervor. "I want to send the Anglos a message!"

Time seemed to slow, and Jason suddenly felt as if he were watching himself from a distance. He couldn't even begin to understand how he'd ended up here. How could Marcus think he would ever approve of this atrocity?! He searched Marcus' face for any hint of reason, for some way to pull the situation back from the brink but the cold certainty in his eyes was that of a zealot.

"No way! It's complicated as fuck! There's too much that could go wrong!" Jason protested, hiding his true objections behind the logistical difficulties. "Besides, the spaceport is a government facility. Could you even get to a shuttle to steal it?"

Marcus nodded. "It'd take a little time, but yeah, with enough firepower we could. Plus, I know a guy who can fly it too."

Jason knew that arguing with him was pointless, but the vision of the attack was just too much to take. He couldn't stop now. "You're going to kill a fuck-ton of people," Jason shouted. "and you have no way to make sure they're just Anglos! If you're 'The Resistance' now, shouldn't you avoid killing your own people?!"

For a moment Marcus actually appeared troubled by this. "I know," he admitted, before his temper flared again, "but it'll be worth it to make the point! If there was some way to avoid it I would, but in a revolution sometimes we have to pay the cost!"

Jason looked Marcus squarely in the eye, contempt written all over his face. "Fuck you." he said bluntly. "You know who else has killed our people? The cops. And under Gabe and Angel, The Resistance have killed at least as many Latinos as they did Anglos! You want to make 'the revolution' real, but still play by their rules? Fuck you. You're just as bad as they are."

Marcus stepped back as if he'd been hit and braced himself against the hood of his car. After a moment he asked flatly, "So you're not going to support me on this?"

"No!" Jason replied incredulously.

"You're a fucking *TRAITOR!*" Marcus shouted, and flecks of spittle flew from his mouth as he roared. "You've lived it, the same as I have! The police hassle me for just walking down the street! My aunt's landlord evicted her just to make more room for his White friends! Shit, we can't even keep a job if some Anglo fucker wants to take it away! It's all bullshit and it's past fucking time we hit them back hard!"

The outburst had brought Marcus' bitter anger out into the open, but the exposure did nothing to quench it. He seethed with a venomous rage as words failed him. Suddenly, he seemed to reach a breaking point and in a fury rounded the front of the car like a predator. He threw open the door and the electric motor screamed to life as he took manual control. The car sprang forward violently, forcing Jason to jump back as the car mounted the curb and sped past, only narrowly missing him.

As Jason watched the car swerve into traffic and disappear, he knew with absolute certainty that Marcus was going to carry out his terrifying plan whether it was 'approved' or not. There was only one slim chance to stop it; he had to tell Angel what was going on. He just hoped the gang leader would be willing to help. He pulled out his micro and summoned a car to take him to Casa Preciosa.

****

Jason felt anxious and miserable. His stomach hurt and he shifted uncomfortably in his seat as the car rounded yet another corner at high speed. He'd told himself he wouldn't ever go back to the shelter but the stakes were too high to avoid it now. He had to stop Marcus, no matter what.

The micro in his lap displayed a city map, with a small yellow arrow that tracked Marcus' current location using the same trick Marcus had used to follow him to the store. He was somewhat relieved to see the arrow moving across town, at some distance from Casa Preciosa and in the opposite direction. Even if Marcus were to turn around now, it would still take him some time to reach the shelter. That meant that Jason would get there first; he just hoped it would make a difference.

He felt stupid, unknowingly leading Marcus right to the store. He'd put Anne in danger! He had thought he'd been careful enough, but this mistake had shown how wrong he'd been. It was a lesson he didn't want to learn twice and, for all the good it would do him now, he'd finally disabled location sharing on his micro. It wasn't much, but he intended to disappear after today and, if Jonah's plan worked, he would never see anyone from The Brotherhood again.

Right now however, all that was secondary to stopping Marcus' attack. Jason hoped that the plan was too complicated to pull off in time to attack the Unity Rally on Saturday, but he couldn't be certain. The timing didn't really matter though; whenever and wherever it happened, the number of lives lost would be horrific. Somehow, he had to stop it.

Angel could be the key to that, but would the gang leader help him? He knew Angel despised Marcus. Jason hoped, unlikely as it seemed, that this would be enough to convince him to help stop the attack. It was a vanishingly thin chance, but it was all he had.

As the car deposited Jason at the shelter though, Angel was nowhere to be found. He rushed inside and was brought up short by a mixed group of low-level gang members and the shelter's homeless population that had gathered in the cafeteria. They were huddled closely around Gabe, who stood in the center of the crowd. The churning knot of people weren't looking at Gabe, however. Instead, their eyes were cast downward, staring somberly at something just in front of him.

Puzzled, Jason moved closer, trying to see what it was they were staring at. In the process he bumped into a homeless man he recognized as Hugo Garcia, one of the regular visitors to the shelter. Hugo turned to see who it was that had touched his shoulder and saw Jason trying to peer through the crowd.

"Did you hear?" he asked Jason in a hushed tone.

"No; what happened?" Jason replied, rising up onto the balls of his feet as he tried to see over the heads of those standing in front of him.

"The cops shot Benito! They killed him!" Hugo informed him breathlessly.

"What?!" Jason replied, stunned.

"Gabe came in just a few minutes ago carrying his body! Said he found him outside a police checkpoint and that the cops were laughing about it!"

After sharing this news Hugo turned back to the crowd and pushed forward, trying to find a way to get closer. As the throng shifted around him, Jason caught a brief glimpse of Benito's lifeless body lying on a table in front of Gabe. The gang leader was trying to back away but the press of the crowd made it difficult. He turned one way, then the other, clearly becoming irritated.

"Back the fuck off!" Gabe shouted in frustration. The crowd started as if waking from a dream and quickly cleared a path. Scowling, the gang leader stalked across the room and into his office, angrily closing the door behind him.

Jason stood motionless, watching in shock as the scene unfolded before him. Benito had been a fixture at the shelter; an institution. Except for Marcus, no one in The Brotherhood had bought into his revolution but he had been a powerful influence among the shelter's homeless population and even the gang members had come to respect him, if only a little. He never used his fists or held a gun, but he always stood by his principles and he would be missed.

Benito's death at the hands of the police was a tragedy, but Jason couldn't help feeling that there was something about it that didn't add up. What had Benito been doing at a checkpoint? There were no checkpoints anywhere around here and, come to think of it, Jason had never known him to leave the neighborhood. The man had practically lived at the shelter. Following a grim hunch, he walked over to Gabe's office and knocked.

"What?" came the surly response.

"It's Lucas. Can I talk to you for a minute?" Jason said to the featureless door.

After a moment of silence Gabe answered grudgingly, "Fine. Come in."

Jason entered the dimly lit room and carefully closed the door behind him. He turned to find Gabe sitting in one of the office's two couches. Despite inviting him in, the gang leader ignored his presence and instead studied his micro intently. When Gave didn't acknowledge him, Jason decided to risk being blunt.

"So what really happened to him?" he asked flatly.

Gabe looked up sharply at the unexpected question.

For a moment his eyes were keen and suspicious, then his face changed and he halfheartedly tried out an innocent expression before abandoning it, perhaps realizing it didn't suit him. A smug, self-satisfied smile took its place as he lowered the micro and sat back in his seat.

"Figured it out, huh?" he asked, seemingly untroubled at having been found out. "What gave it away?"

"There aren't any checkpoints around here and I don't think Benito ever left the neighborhood. There's no way he was at a checkpoint." Jason answered.

Gabe nodded ruefully. "Well, it was the best story I could come up with after they saw me carrying his body." he said almost apologetically. He laid the micro down on the low table in front of him before continuing. "He cornered me outside. Kept saying that we shouldn't take over the slave racket because some of the slaves are Latino. He was getting in my face about it and I finally got pissed and shot at him. I didn't really mean to kill him but I hit him dead-center and it was too late after that. I shot him again to end it; no reason to make him suffer."

Gabe actually appeared a little regretful as he finished the story, leaving Jason to wonder what to believe. "So you told everyone the cops did it." he said after a moment, feeling hollow.

"Yeah, well *they* bought it." Gabe answered, pointing through the closed door at the crowd still gathered around Benito's corpse. "The cops probably *would* have shot him if they'd had the chance. Blaming them seemed like some kind of justice, anyway."

Jason frowned as a dark thought occurred to him. "You know, Marcus isn't going to take it too well when he hears what really happened." he said. This was an understatement; the man was a ticking timebomb and the murder of his mentor wasn't going to help.

"You're not going to tell him a fucking thing!" Gabe warned harshly, his eyes flashing. "You two have a distraction to plan and I don't want him moping around or some shit!"

Jason started to protest but Gabe suddenly changed gears on him, saying, "Actually, Angel says Marcus wants to steal a shuttle and dump fuel on a crowd. He doesn't like it; says it's too complicated, but I don't care. It would create one hell of a distraction!"

"Marcus already told me about it." Jason said defensively. "Angel's right; it's a mess! It's way more than we need and it's going to kill a *LOT* of people!" He saw Gabe's face darken and he realized too late that it had been the wrong thing to say.

"I don't give a shit how many people it kills, so long as it keeps the cops busy while we take out the Seps!" Gabe erupted. As the echo died away, he sat back and stared appraisingly at Jason. "You know, I think we made a mistake earlier." he said with a deadly calm. "We're going to go ahead with Marcus' plan. *I'M* approving it, so I don't care whether you sign off on it or not. And when Angel gets back, he and I are going to change this arrangement between you and Marcus. Now get the fuck out of here. I think I've heard enough from you."

The harsh dismissal carried with it an implicit threat. Tasting ashes, Jason turned and left quickly, expecting with every step to be shot in the back. The feeling was so intense his spine tingled and his flesh crawled uncomfortably. Somehow though, the shot didn't come. Keeping his eyes fixed forward, he kept walking and soon found himself miraculously standing outside on the sidewalk in one piece.

He'd taken a huge risk arguing with Gabe, and had failed. He might have been able to persuade Angel to stop Marcus, but a plan to burn people alive clearly suited Gabe. He didn't care about the lives it would take; to him, other people were just pawns to be sacrificed. Despite Jason's best efforts, hundreds, maybe thousands of people were going to die screaming.

He began walking aimlessly away from the shelter, seeking to put as much distance between himself and Casa

Preciosa as he could. The vision of the coming attack still haunted him; he knew he should go to the police with what he knew, but he just couldn't make himself do it. It might not matter anyway; if they didn't simply shoot him on sight, they still wouldn't believe a word he told them. There had to be another way to stop this...

The idea came to him a few blocks later. Maybe Jonah's man inside the police department could do something? He felt an ember of hope reignite as he considered it. He didn't know if it would work, but he had to at least try! With a renewed sense of purpose, he stopped walking and summoned a car to take him to the El Rey Latino Outreach Center. Overhead, the first drops of rain began to fall.

****

Marcus arrived at Casa Preciosa with adrenaline pumping through his veins. Gabe had sent him a message telling him what had happened to Benito and he had rushed madly across town to be there. He wanted to at least say goodbye to the man who had taught him so much. Marcus had loved him like a father; more than that, even. Benito had done more for him than his own absent father ever had.

Those Anglo bastards! The fucking cops would pay for this!

He burst into the cafeteria where Benito's body still lay where Gabe had left it. The room was crowded and the homeless standing vigil now far outnumbered the members of The Brotherhood. Marcus pushed his way through the throng and finally arrived at his mentor's side. Benito's clothes were stained with blood but his face still managed to somehow look peaceful. For reasons he couldn't explain, this just made Marcus angrier. Bile rose in his throat and he bellowed in inarticulate rage. He would kill them for this; he would kill them all!

He held back a sob and in his anguish the Unity Rally

came to his mind, unbidden. The thought made him sick; that contemptible party where everyone would get together and pretend they were friends, holding hands and acting like the fucking Anglos hadn't been standing on the backs of Hispanics for over a century! They were all traitors, he thought angrily, every last one of them. He remembered then that there would be speakers there too, and that a police captain would be among them!

A terrible plan began to form in his mind and unlike stealing the shuttle, this one was brutally simple. It had nothing to do with The Brotherhood or the attack on the Seps. It was simple and direct, and he had no intention of distracting the cops beforehand.

He looked around the room at the Army of indigent acolytes and mourners who had gathered to pay respects to the man who'd worked and preached for their freedom. He raised his voice, loud enough to be heard by them all.

"Hey!" he bellowed. "Those fucking cops killed Benito because they think we're weak! Let's show them how wrong they are!"

His words echoed throughout the crowded space and the dejected grief that hung over the room suddenly crystalized into a furious rage. All around him, the gathered mourners roared for vengeance. Marcus gave a black smile; they were with him.

CHAPTER 24

Jason had been troubled as he drifted off to sleep. His dreams were filled with a suffocating sense of panic and crisis. Adding to this was a growing awareness of the newly resurgent pain in his leg. The ache had returned in the night and was now slowly forcing his consciousness to the surface.

"We have to stop the attack. Right now, that's even more important than the Rally..."

The memory remained as he opened his eyes, an echo from his fevered dreams. As the panic faded though, he remembered there had been good things about the night too. The space beside him was still warm where Anne had slept. She was gone now, presumably to go get breakfast, but sleeping next to her again had been wonderful. It was only a small shred of their old life, but it felt important. He let his hand rest for a moment in the faint depression on her side of the bed, smiling to himself despite the pain and worry.

Jason lay in Jonah's upstairs apartment at the El Rey Latino Outreach Center. He had arrived there late last night, just before the scanner at the nearby police checkpoint went online. Inside, his family had been waiting for him. He, Anne and Matthew had all slept in the same room, with Jonah graciously providing a folding bed for Jason and Anne, and tossing a blanket over a nearby sofa for Matthew. A sideways glance revealed that like his mother, Matthew was already up and gone.

Jason was fully awake now, but not yet ready to move. He lay there, balanced between comfort and the need to take action. He had so much to do, it seemed overwhelming. Between doing what he could to stop Marcus' attack and helping

Jonah prepare for the Unity Rally, the day promised to be a long one.

Eventually he could put it off no longer. Forcing himself to move, he rolled over and swung his legs over the edge of the bed. As his feet touched the floor he tried to stand up, but the ache in his leg suddenly bloomed and he sagged back down onto the mattress, gasping.

After a moment the crippling pain subsided, but it didn't vanish entirely. The bone-deep ache that remained held the promise of suddenly worsening if he tried to exert himself. He waited for his breathing to return to normal and gently massaged his lower leg as he considered what his next move would be.

If he was going to get out of bed, he would need to get dressed. Regretfully, he noted that yesterday's clothes lay crumpled on the floor several feet away. He hadn't given any thought to their placement as he undressed, but now the distances involved seemed enormous.

Gritting his teeth and relying on his left leg as little as possible, he slid along the edge of the bed and reached out with his right foot. At full extension, he was just able to snag his pants with a toe and pull them close. After picking them up and shaking them out straight, he gingerly lay back down on the bed and folded himself until he was able to pull the pants on without getting up. Afterward he lay there motionless, taking a brief respite before getting up the nerve to try for his shirt.

He was startled a moment later as the apartment door opened and Anne backed into the room, holding the door open with her body while carrying two trays of scrambled eggs. Matthew entered a moment later, holding a plate of his own. Once inside they set the food down on the apartment's modest dining table and then turned to look at him.

"You brought me breakfast?" Jason asked Anne, pleasantly surprised by the gesture. Somehow, he'd forgotten the little joys of having a partner in life.

"It's just scrambled eggs." she answered with a smile. "They're cooking them downstairs so I thought I'd bring you some. No bacon today, though. Sorry."

"That's fine!" he answered eagerly as he sat up on the bed. Forgetting about his injury for a moment, he tried to stand, but as he did so the pain in his leg returned sharply. Wincing, he sat back down, sucking air in through his teeth and hissing in repressed agony. Anne saw him cringe and frowned at the strained expression on his face.

"Your leg still hurts?" she asked, concerned.

Jason nodded. "Yeah. It felt better yesterday, so I didn't use my cane much at all. I must have overdone it, though. It hurts pretty bad now if I try to stand up."

Anne came over to his side and rolled up his pant leg to examine the still healing wound. "I don't see anything new," she said, "but I don't really know what to look for. Do you want to go back to the doctor?"

Jason considered this for a moment. "Not yet." he said finally. "Let's get through tomorrow first. If it's still bad after that, I'll go in."

"Mmmhmm." Anne murmured noncommittally, eyeing him critically.

"I will. I promise." Jason said, trying to reassure her. He then looked down sheepishly at his bare chest. Feeling a little helpless, he pointed at the twisted shirt that still lay on the floor near her feet and asked, "Could you hand that to me?" Anne's expression was still worried, but she handed him the shirt and he quickly pulled it down over his head.

Jason then looked toward the table across the room, considering the distance with some skepticism. Anne saw his concern and said, "Here, let me help." She crouched by the bed, positioning herself so that he could throw his arm over her shoulder. They rose together and made their way across the room, with Anne holding him up firmly as they went. Once at the table, she loosened her grip and allowed Jason to sink into the seat beside Matthew before taking the remaining chair for herself.

With everyone seated, the family began to eat. Between bites of egg, Anne said to Jason, "After breakfast Jonah wants you to come over to his office. He said his police contact wants to ask you some questions."

"Do you know what for?" Jason asked, unsettled. He trusted Jonah but the idea of talking to the police made him nervous.

"No," Anne admitted, "but I don't think it will be a problem. Whoever he is, I doubt this 'contact' wants to be exposed any more than you do."

Jason chewed his food slowly. Jonah asking him to talk to his contact had caught him off guard, but it probably shouldn't have. Before he went to bed last night, Jason had told Jonah of Marcus' plan and of Gabe's determination to carry it out. Jonah had agreed that the threat was urgent and had sent a warning to his police contact immediately, keeping the source of his information anonymous. If that contact now wanted to talk to Jason about it himself, that was understandable.

Despite Anne's reassurances though, he remained uneasy. The past few months had made it a reflex for him to keep a low profile and to hide from the police. Those instincts had served him well, but he realized that now maybe the time for hiding was over. Knowing it was a risk, he resolved to do as Jonah asked.

As he chewed, he slowly became aware that the room had fallen silent around him. He looked up to find Anne and Matthew watching him carefully and realized that he'd been ignoring them. Swallowing a bite of egg, he reached out a hand and ruffled Matthew's hair. The gesture felt forced but he knew it was important.

"Looks like you need a haircut." he said, trying to make up for the silence.

Matthew smoothed his hair back down self-consciously. "I'm growing it out." he said. "Valarie says that long hair is cool right now. Plus it means I don't have to hold still while she cuts it."

"Yeah, I never liked that part either." Jason said, running a hand over his own shaved head and smirking. "This was easier."

His son stared at him a moment, considering. "I like it." he said eventually. "It's aerodynamic."

Jason snorted at this, laughing out loud. It was something he might have said himself at Matthew's age. He looked again at his son, noting how Matthew's golden brown skin matched his own. It was something that, though he wasn't actually Hispanic, had set the tone for his life and would most likely do the same for his son. He knew it would be a burden at times but still Jason felt privileged that Matthew would be there to carry on his legacy. It made him feel like a link in a chain and gave his life a sense of context and meaning.

The surreal moment hung in the air, but passed as Anne began to clear the table. "Matt," she said, "I want you to help your dad walk over to Jonah's office, then come back here and help me carry the dishes downstairs."

Matthew nodded and stood as Jason pushed against the table, using his arms to raise himself up. Once standing, he found that his leg didn't hurt quite as much as before, but it still felt weak. He had definitely done too much yesterday and was paying for it now.

As Matthew stepped in close, Jason put a hand on his shoulder, using it as a sort of crutch. Together, father and son left the apartment and made their way down the hall to Jonah's office.

There, they found Jonah engrossed by a tablet sitting on the desk in front of him. Jason knocked on the open door and Jonah looked up. "Jason. Come in." he said, rounding the desk and taking Jason's arm from Matthew. Matthew turned to go but Jonah stopped him. "Could you go down the hall to the storage room?" he asked. "Inside is a large box marked 'Lost and Found'. There should be a black cane there. Would you please bring it back here for your father?"

"Sure." Matthew said lightly, then disappeared out the door.

Jonah helped Jason over to the chair in front of his desk, then returned to his own seat. From out in the hall both men could hear a muted clatter as Matthew rooted through the 'lost and found', looking for the cane. Jonah smiled. "Matthew's been a great help around here." he said. "He never complains; just does what's needed. I wish all our volunteers were that willing!"

"He's a good kid." Jason agreed, genuinely touched. It may only have been smalltalk, but the compliment warmed his heart nonetheless.

A minute later Matthew returned holding a glossy black cane with a tarnished brass top. Jason took it from him, saying, "Wow, this is a lot nicer than my other one." He hefted it in his hand and looked at it appraisingly. "This doesn't belong to anyone?" he asked Jonah dubiously.

"It was here when I took over the building." Jonah explained. "I found it again yesterday as I was getting something out of the storeroom. I don't know who it belonged to, but I'd guess that by now they don't need it anymore. I would have given it to you last time you were here but I'd forgotten about it."

Jason turned back to his son and said, "Thanks Matt, now go help your mom. I need to talk to Jonah for a while."

Matthew gave him a look that said he knew he was being kept away from something interesting but replied, "Okay." and left, softly closing the door behind him. Jason watched him go as if trying to memorize the moment.

"Ready?" Jonah prompted gently.

"Sorry. Yeah. It's just kind of unreal, having my family around again. This has been tough..." he trailed off, swallowing a lump in his throat. After a moment, he looked up and said, "So, your contact wants to ask me something?"

"Yes. I told him everything that you told me but to be

honest, I think he just wants to hear it from you, to make sure I didn't leave anything out." Jonah answered.

Jason nodded. "Okay." he said, giving Jonah permission to proceed.

Jonah picked up the tablet from his desk and poked the screen several times in quick succession. "I'll keep the call on voice-only and if you don't mind, I'll hold on to the tablet." he said. "My contact wants to stay anonymous, and I know that you do too."

"Thank you for that." Jason said, relieved.

"This isn't the first time I've helped him out, and he understands the kind of people I end up dealing with here." Jonah said reassuringly. "As far as he knows you're just someone who gave me a tip to pass along."

A moment later the call connected. Jonah angled the tablet so that Jason could hear the voice without seeing the screen.

"Hi Jonah. Do you have him there with you?" the voice asked. The sound had been pressed thin by the small speaker, but the voice was still identifiably male.

"He's here." Jonah confirmed.

"Great." came the reply. Addressing Jason now, the voice asked, "So, you're the one who told Jonah about the plot to steal a shuttle?"

"I am." Jason answered, reflexively raising his voice to be heard.

"How did you come by this information?"

Jason took a deep breath, knowing that he was taking a huge risk telling anyone about what he'd been doing, let alone the police. "Let's just say I work with The Brotherhood." he said, trying to divulge as little as possible.

"That's the new gang in the southwest quarter?" the voice asked, seeking confirmation.

"Yeah. Like I told Jonah, the plan is to steal a shuttle, fly it over a crowd, then dump the fuel and set it all on fire."

The voice was silent for a moment before asking, "And

why would they do that?"

Jason hesitated, uncertain how much he should reveal. "I'd rather not say right now," he said eventually, "but I can tell you who is involved. If you bring them in, you can stop the attack!"

"It would really be helpful if you could tell me something about why, or at least where, they are planning to do this." the voice said, pushing him. "Names are good, but I want more if you can give it."

Jason began to worry that if he didn't tell him *something,* his warning would be ignored. "They didn't say where they were going to attack; I don't know if they've picked it yet. I assume it will be somewhere with lots of people. As for their names, they are Gabe and Angel Batista, and Marcus Ortiz. Gabe and Angel run the gang, and Marcus works for them."

There was a quiet tapping sound in the background, as if the contact were making notes. When the voice spoke again, Jason couldn't tell if he'd been convinced but he did at least seem willing to investigate. "Okay," he said. "I'll see what we can do. Do you know where we can find them?"

"They operate out of a place called Casa Preciosa." Jason told him. "It's a homeless shelter in the southwest part of the city. Gabe and Angel spend most of their time there. Marcus could be there too, but I don't know for sure."

His uncertainty over Marcus' current whereabouts was frustratingly true. Since leaving Casa Preciosa, Jason had made repeated attempts to reach him and tell him what had really happened to Benito, but the calls had all gone unanswered. On top of that, Marcus had apparently switched off his micro's location data sometime in the night. It was an ominous sign, to say the least.

"Well, it's a start." the voice said, sounding resigned. "I'll make sure we put out a bulletin to have them picked up for questioning. It's not quite an arrest but it should at least slow them down." He paused, then added, "We can also send a patrol up to the spaceport to check on the shuttles. Unfortunately, there's not a lot else we can do until they make their move."

"Thank you." Jonah said, taking back control of the conversation. "Whatever you can do will help."

"I appreciate the tip, Jonah. You've been a big help." the voice said. "I'll let you know if we find anything. Talk to you later."

Jonah ended the call and set the tablet face down on his desk. "If he calls back, I'll be sure to let you know. For now though, I think we've done everything we can." he said.

"I hope so." Jason replied with a heavy heart.

****

Jason left Jonah's office leaning heavily on his new cane and made his way carefully down to the dining room. There, he found people from the neighborhood, smiling and chatting as they shared The Center's charitable community breakfast. Most of those present were Hispanic, but not all were. Some in the churning crowd were dressed better than others, but Black, White and Latino, they were all friendly and shared an obvious sense of camaraderie.

Finding himself awash in the crowd, Jason worked his way over to the wall and tried to stay out of the way as he watched people eat and say hello to friends. The atmosphere was light, and he couldn't help but notice the contrast with Casa Preciosa. While The Brotherhood's shelter was a place where old wounds were left to fester, Jonah's El Rey Latino Outreach Center was instead a place for them to heal. Reflexively he breathed in deep, trying to absorb as much of the hope and optimism around him as he could.

After a while the kitchen door opened and Jason caught sight of Anne standing near a sink, sorting a load of dishes to be washed. He smiled; he should have guessed that after breakfast she would come down here to help. Before the door could close again, Jason waved and drew her attention. Anne waved back and mouthed a greeting, gesturing that he should come join her. Keeping near the wall, he worked his way around the room and entered the kitchen, meeting Anne at the sink.

"Hi beautiful." he said playfully as he rested his cane against the counter.

"Hi yourself." she replied, smirking and handing him a towel. "You're drying."

"Sounds good." he answered and began to wipe the water off the dishes as Anne handed them to him. After a moment he said, "It's busy out there. I guess I've never really seen this place in full swing; is it always like this?"

"Most Fridays it is. It's slower in the middle of the week." Anne said, washing another plate.

"It's a good thing you're here to help out." Jason said.

"Matthew helps too; right now he's carrying a load of trash out to the dumpster. On Friday mornings they can really use the extra hands, so I try to make sure we're both here to help." Anne replied. She was quiet for a while as she scrubbed at a stubborn stain, then lowered her voice to keep from being overheard. "You talked to Jonah's contact?" she asked.

"Yeah." he answered softly. "He wanted more details about the attack. I told him what I could, but I don't know how much help I was."

"At least it's something." Anne replied. "Did you tell him it's The Resistance?"

"No; I told him it's The Brotherhood. It's the truth, and I didn't want to get into the whole 'using terrorism as a distraction' thing before we give them the proof. I was worried that would just give them a reason not to believe me."

"Do you know if they are going to do anything about it?"

"He said he would have the police pick up Gabe, Angel and Marcus for questioning. He also said they'd send someone to go watch the spaceport."

"Then I think you've done all you can." Anne said, trying to comfort him. "Besides, the Rally's tomorrow. If that works, we'll be done with all this. In the meantime you can spend the day with us."

Jason nodded as Anne handed him another dish. She was right; he'd done all he could. Now he just had to wait for the Rally. After that, they would be free. Choosing to put aside his worries and enjoy this time as best he could, he smiled and said, "That's exactly what I'll do."

****

Jason spent the rest of the morning and into the afternoon helping Anne and Matthew as they served meals and cleaned up afterward. It was slow, mindless work, but it kept him busy. The labor felt good and he enjoyed the time spent with his family.

This was the most time he'd been able to spend with them in months, and it left him struck by the subtle ways in which they'd changed. Matthew, who had been introverted and obsessed with video shows, had now opened up and made friends with the people from the neighborhood. Few of them were his own age, but they all appeared to like him. Anne too seemed well respected and he saw her talking quietly with more than one family and their kids. With the children, Anne would get down on one knee and speak with them as if they were the most important person in the world. He knew this was something she'd done as a teacher, but now it was also something more. She'd come to care about these people and in doing so had found a place to belong. He realized that even if the Rally was successful in clearing their names, the life they'd lost would never return the way it was. Inevitably, they would have to become something new.

In a free moment between tasks, Jason and Anne were sitting together in The Center's lobby when her micro chimed with an incoming call. Anne picked it up and Jason saw Valarie's name prominently displayed on the screen. Remembering how upset she'd been with him the last time they'd spoken, he made sure to stay out of view as the call connected.

"Hi Val." Anne said, watching Jason from the corner of her eye.

"Hi. I can't talk long, but I wanted to let you know that the doctors let Mateo come home this morning! I thought you and Jason would want to know." Valarie said, sounding happy but exhausted.

"That's fantastic!" Anne replied enthusiastically. "I'll be sure to let Jason know. So Mateo's starting to feel better?"

"A lot better actually, but he still has a ways to go. The doctor says he'll have to be in a wheelchair for a while but that he can do the rest of his recovery at home."

"I'm so glad to hear it! That will be good for him." Anne said, then hesitated. "You guys know about the Unity Rally tomorrow, right? We'll understand if you can't make it, but it would be great to see you and Mateo, and Arabelle too."

Valarie nodded. "Yeah; we'll try to come. If Mateo isn't feeling up to it, then I'll stay home with him but right now he says he wants to go." A faint noise came over the speaker and she looked away, distracted. "Look, I've got to go." she apologized. "I just wanted to make sure you knew how Mateo is doing."

"That's okay. Thanks for calling! See you tomorrow, maybe." Anne said as the call ended.

When the screen was dark again, Jason slid back over. "Mateo's doing well enough to go home!" Anne told him, smiling.

Jason grinned, then looked pensive. "I hope he can make it to the Rally. I'd really like to tell him how sorry I am." he said.

"I think he knows." Anne replied gently.

****

Jason kept busy the rest of the day, but eventually realized that he hadn't seen much of Jonah. The bespectacled director had made an appearance during lunch but quickly disappeared upstairs again, taking his meal with him. When Jason mentioned this to Anne, she said that Jonah had been working on his speech for the Rally.

"He's been at it all day!" Jason replied incredulously.

"He said he's always been a slow writer. He'll write a line, then have the tablet read it back to him. If he doesn't like the sound of it, he'll change it or start over." Anne said. "I offered to help but he said he has to do it himself or it'll sound wrong."

It was sometime in the late afternoon when Jonah finally emerged again. Jason saw him descending the stairs and met him at the bottom, leaning on his cane.

"Jason." Jonah said upon seeing him. "Good, I was just coming to find you."

Just then the building's front door opened and Courtney entered the lobby, still in her uniform. The sight briefly brought Jason back to the night Mateo had been shot but he shook himself, quickly dismissing the unpleasant memory.

"Hello! Come to help out with dinner?" Jonah asked, greeting her warmly.

"Yes." she answered, inclining her head slightly. "Brodie says she can't make it today but she promises she'll be at the Rally tomorrow. We'll both be there." She looked down at the black cane in Jason's hand. "Nice! Looks good; very stylish!" she said. Jason smiled, unable to tell if she meant it or was just amused.

"I think they're just beginning to get set up in the kitchen." Jonah told her. Courtney nodded in thanks before leaving to go lend a hand.

As she left Jonah spoke quietly, as if to himself. "I know I've said it before, but she has been so helpful. Sometimes I think she could run this place without me."

When he didn't go on, Jason prompted him gently. "So why were you coming to find me?" he asked.

The elder man shook himself visibly as he recovered his train of thought. "Oh, right. My contact sent me an update." he said, getting back to business. "He says that they were able to pick up Gabe and Angel at the shelter but that there was no sign of Marcus. Gabe and Angel are claiming they don't know where he is, and in fact they say that he went 'rogue' and left, whatever that means. I know you've already told us everything you can, but my contact asked me to check with you again to see if you have any idea where he might have gone."

Jason searched his memory for anything that might help but came up frustratingly empty. "I'm sorry, but I don't." he said finally. "I tried locating him earlier, but it looks like he turned off his micro or something." The thought of Marcus disappearing worried him; even without The Brotherhood, he could still be a problem. "Did your contact say anything about the shuttle?" he asked, his brow furrowed with concern.

"The police have placed officers all around the spaceport. So far there haven't been any problems and the shuttles are all accounted for. They're going to maintain the patrols for at least forty-eight hours; that puts it past the time of the Rally." Jonah reassured him.

"Good." Jason said, grateful for some good news. Until Marcus was found, he remained a threat but Jason felt better knowing the shuttles were being watched. Perhaps the Unity Rally would be safe after all.

At that moment a young man holding a tablet emerged hesitantly from the dining room and drew Jonah's attention. After giving Jason a reassuring pat on the shoulder, Jonah followed the man into the dining room, leaving Jason standing at the foot of the stairs.

Alone with his thoughts, Jason sank into a nearby chair. He knew he'd done all he could to stop the attack but he still worried it might not be enough. Futilely, he pulled the micro from his pocket and again activated the locator screen. A map of the city appeared but, as before, Marcus' location stubbornly refused to show itself. The irony was not lost on him as he realized that for once he would have to hope the police could actually find the man they were looking for.

CHAPTER 25

Pablo made sure to keep hold of Isaiah's hand as they made their way into the crowded street in front of the El Rey Latino Outreach Center. The buildings surrounding it were shabby and run-down, but The Center itself stood out. It had been brightly decorated for the Rally and seemed out of place in this tired neighborhood. A temporary stage, empty for now, protruded from its steps and out onto the sidewalk.

Since getting off the bus from Aberdeen, Pablo had heard people talking about the Unity Rally. Now, standing with his boyfriend among these people, in a street which had been closed to make a space for everyone, he could see why. The smiling faces told him that this was a place of refuge and community. Their optimism was infectious and he was glad he had accepted the invitation when Valarie asked him to attend.

The Rally also gave Pablo a chance to introduce Isaiah to his friends. He and Isaiah hadn't been dating long before Valarie and Mateo left Aberdeen for Cosmopolis, and so when Valarie had asked him to come to the Rally, it had seemed like the perfect opportunity.

Cosmopolis occupied a sort of dual place in Pablo's mind. He had always viewed the big city with a dose of suspicion, but ever since he helped Jason and his family escape the violence in Aberdeen, it had called out to him. That night had been something of a turning point for them all, though what it meant still seemed a bit uncertain. It worried him that he hadn't heard anything from Jason or Anne since he'd dropped them off outside the city. He tried to view the silence as a good thing though, since it meant they hadn't been caught yet. So long as they remained free, there was hope.

Jason's family hadn't been the only one he'd helped escape that night, though. Valarie and her daughter had been in the truck with him as well. He'd seen all of them safely to Cosmopolis and then, when Mateo got out of jail, he too had left Aberdeen to join his family in the big city. Although Pablo still spoke to both of them by micro occasionally, he hadn't seen either of them in months and was looking forward to a reunion.

He paused and checked his micro one last time; the screen showed Valarie's marker nearby. With Isaiah's hand firmly grasped in his own, they pushed through the throngs of people and soon found her standing near the stage. Mateo was with her, sitting in a low silver wheelchair. He looked a little pale and was obviously recovering from an injury, but he smiled broadly upon seeing them.

"There you are!" Mateo called out happily. Despite his obvious injuries, his voice was strong. "Val said you were coming!"

Pablo grinned. "Wouldn't miss it!" he said, raising a hand to shade his eyes from the bright red-orange sun. "Besides, I wanted you both to meet Isaiah."

Isaiah offered his hand and Mateo shook it, saying, "We've heard a lot about you. Pablo says you're a pretty good guy."

Isaiah didn't quite blush. "Glad to hear it; nice to meet you too." he replied awkwardly.

Mateo nodded. "It's great that you both could come." he said. "This is supposed to be one hell of a party!"

Pablo stepped back and eyed Mateo's wheelchair critically. After a moment he made a face and said, "Okay, I guess I've got to ask; what happened?"

"A little accident at work." Mateo answered with a small, cryptic smile. Pablo could tell that he wasn't getting the whole story, but decided to let it pass. Behind Mateo, Valarie frowned.

Isaiah looked around at the large crowd, seeking to change the subject. "With The Resistance back, is this really a good time to hold a rally like this?" he asked.

"It should be fine." Mateo answered with some reservation. "There's some cops walking around looking for troublemakers, and then there's the checkpoints they set up everywhere downtown." He scowled faintly. "Hell, there was even a checkpoint *here* until a few hours ago. They had to move it up the street a block to make room. It looks like they're keeping a bunch of cops there too in case there's a problem."

While Mateo spoke, Pablo became distracted as a solidly built man with golden brown skin, a neatly trimmed beard and shaved head approached Mateo from behind, limping as he walked and leaning on a cane. There was something familiar about him... Pablo experienced a moment of disorientation before he realized; this was Jason! In a daze, he held out his hand and Jason shook it warmly.

"Pablo!" Jason exclaimed.

"Shit, man!" Pablo swore. "I almost didn't recognize you! I knew you shaved your head but still, you snuck up on me! What's with the cane?"

Jason forced a smile. "It's just until my leg gets better. An accident at work."

Mateo stifled a laugh and Pablo shot him a curious look. "What kind of work have you guys been doing?" he asked guardedly.

"It's a long story." Jason answered with a sigh. "I'll fill you in later. So, did you come in just for the Rally?"

Pablo nodded, letting the issue drop once more. "Yeah, Valarie invited us. Actually, I want you to meet Isaiah. Isaiah, this is Jason."

Jason shook Isaiah's hand firmly before turning back to Pablo. "I'm glad you guys came." he said. To Mateo, he asked, "Have you seen Matthew and Arabelle? They were here a minute ago."

Mateo shook his head no, but Valarie nodded affirmatively. Jason thought she still seemed a little reserved, but her anger had cooled now that her husband was out of the hospital.

"Courtney and Brodie took them up to go see the stage." she said. She pointed over the heads of the crowd and Jason finally spotted the four of them standing on the elevated platform. The adults were keeping watch as the children looked out over the crowd and Jason smirked as Matthew windmilled his arm, pretending to play a guitar.

"Can't say I blame them." Pablo commented. "I wanted to be on stage when I was their age too."

The stage had been built directly onto the steps of The Center, allowing the use of the building's interior as a sort of back-stage area. The day's guest speakers, as well as Jonah and Anne, were all waiting inside, taking a break from the crowd out front. As Jason watched, a technician mounted the stage and began to test the equipment. The PA system crackled to life, and Courtney wisely hurried the children inside, keeping them safely away from the temptations of electronic amplification.

"It looks like they'll be starting in a few minutes, so I need to go get ready. I'll meet back up with you guys afterward." Jason promised before heading for the stairs on the far side of the stage. Pablo shot Mateo a confused look.

"Is he helping out with the Rally?" he asked, his brow furrowed.

Mateo chuckled. "Yeah, but strictly behind the scenes."

****

This was going to be a good day, Jason decided as he mounted the stairs and walked toward the Outreach Center's doors. Though his cane produced a dull thud with each step, it did nothing to ruin his mood; his leg hardly hurt at all and his limp was almost gone.

It had been great to see Pablo again! Pablo was one of his few remaining ties to Aberdeen, and seeing him had filled Jason with the hope that he might actually be able to recover something of his old life. Even just a few days ago that had seemed nearly impossible, but now it felt like it might really happen.

Before entering The Center, Jason paused and looked out over the crowd. Though the street was packed, there were gaps here and there as people kept their distance from those police officers that Jonah had allowed to patrol the event. Their presence was a delicate subject, but Jonah had been very careful when choosing which officers to allow in.

Privately, Jason was amazed that Jonah had been given any say at all in that, but the department had been unusually cooperative on this occasion. Was this the influence of Jonah's mysterious contact? For their part, the crowd were understandably wary. Still, nothing had gone wrong so far and the atmosphere remained non-confrontational.

The makeup of the crowd before him was diverse. While many were Hispanic, others, perhaps most, were a mix of the Caucasians, Blacks and more that made up the Citizens of Ross b. They had come to show support for their Latino neighbors, and the sight of so many different faces coming together made him smile.

A minor commotion near the back of the crowd drew Jason's attention to a small group of poorly dressed Hispanic men as they joined the sea of people already standing in the street. The men appeared to be part of the city's homeless population. As they entered, they dispersed among the crowd, keeping as far from the eyes of the police as they could. Jason didn't blame them for that; he'd have done the same thing in their place. He saw a few people grimace but he reminded himself that these men were welcome here, just like everyone else.

Before he went inside, Jason noticed a reporter speaking to a floating camera drone near the side of the stage. The sight surprised him, but he quickly realized that it shouldn't have. The Unity Rally was turning out to be one of the biggest events in the city and it made sense that the media would be here to cover it. In fact, this might be a good thing; their message would now be broadcast to the entire planet! It was an opportunity to open people's eyes and he hoped that Jonah would be able to take advantage of it.

As Jason opened the door, he nearly crashed into Jonah, who came hurrying the other way. Jason tried to apologize but Jonah brushed it off, saying in a rush, "It's time to start! We've got to get on stage!" He seemed a little flustered and in his hand he held an electronic pad with the notes for his speech clearly visible.

Jason quickly stepped aside and Jonah nodded gratefully, then pasted on a smile as he stepped out onto the stage, accompanied by the day's guest speakers. Courtney, Brodie, and Anne emerged next, followed by the children. Jason brought up the rear, staying close to Anne as everyone seated themselves in a row of folding chairs which had been placed behind the podium. Only the guest speakers would be part of the planned presentation, but Jonah had given the rest of them the honor of watching the event from the stage itself.

Once everyone was seated, Jonah approached the podium, set his tablet down and placed his hands firmly on either side of the lectern. The nervousness of a moment ago was now gone. "Welcome, people of Cosmopolis!" he announced loudly, his voice amplified by the PA system. A cheer rose from the crowd and Jonah let the sound rise and fall naturally, using the moment to set the mood.

"We are here today for a Unity Rally." he continued once the crowd had quieted. "And it is *our* Unity Rally. Yours and mine, Hispanic and Black, Asian and Caucasion, Citizen or not. It belongs to each one of us, regardless of race or legal status. It belongs to *all* of us who want it, and as one people we come together today to loudly reject the violence that has been committed in our name!

This planet is far from perfect; we all know there are problems. The law of this land pits Citizen against non-Citizen but we are, *each one of us*, humans first! No matter what the law says, our shared humanity is what defines us. It guides us in how we should treat each other, and it tells us the worth and value of each person we meet. We are all *one* people, even if the law says we are not.

In that spirit, the four guests I've invited to speak with us today will share with us their knowledge, insights, and struggles as they have worked to remind us all who we are. They are not here as Citizens, or as representatives of their races. They are here to speak to us as *people*, and to help us connect with the shared humanity inside us all."

Jonah paused to consult his notes and smiled as another cheer rose from the crowd, appearing to catch him off guard. He held up a palm and after a moment it subsided.

"Our first speaker today is Kenneth Wright. You may know him as a journalist and frequent panelist on the 'Allison Graves Report'. He received the Nagal Journalistic Diligence Award last year for his three-part report on abusive labor practices in the frontier areas. Mr. Wright?"

Jonah stepped away from the lectern as a dark-haired Caucasian man in a pale blue shirt rose from his chair and approached. He shook hands with Jonah before moving to the front of the stage and beginning to address the crowd.

Relieved to no longer be the center of attention, Jonah retreated to the row of chairs and sat down next to Jason. Leaning over, he asked, "Good so far?"

"I'd say great!" Jason answered, grinning. A sudden cheer rose as Mr. Wright worked the crowd, seeming to speak from the heart while at the same time keeping the mood light. Jason leaned closer to be heard over the noise. "I can't believe you put this all together so quickly!" he said.

Jonah was modest. "I had to call in a few favors, but really most people genuinely wanted to help. Even setting aside the problem of The Resistance, the city needed this. We're just giving them an excuse to do it."

Twenty minutes later Kenneth Wright's speech came to an energetic close. As he returned to his seat, Jonah rose to introduce the next guest; Julia Arroyo, a woman widely known for her volumes of florid poetry and idiosyncratic novels. Her speech was more subdued than Ken Wright's had been but it didn't matter to the audience. She held their attention raptly as she read from a haunting and poignant free-verse poem which she had written only the night before.

The next speaker to appear was Sylvia Anzaldúa. As a Latino Rights Activist, her speech was more politically charged than Julia Arroyo's had been. Unlike Arroyo, Anzaldúa paced back and forth across the full width of the stage, eschewing the light touch of poetry in favor of hard facts and blunt calls to action. The people responded enthusiastically and their energy was reflected in the intensity of her presentation. From his place on the stage, Jason watched the police officers embedded in the crowd keeping a careful eye out, knowing they must show restraint but ready to act if needed. It wasn't an easy task and Jason was again glad Jonah had been able to allow in only those officers who could be trusted not to overreact.

Ms. Anzaldúa's speech reached an impassioned climax after which she raised her fist defiantly before relinquishing the stage. As she returned to her seat, Jason noticed a shuffling among the audience as a young boy of perhaps twelve pushed his way to the front. Unlike those around him, the boy's expression was blank, sharing none of the enthusiasm of the crowd. His features were vaguely Asian, with dark eyes that stood out against a pale face. Jason found his sudden appearance in the front row troubling, though he couldn't say precisely why. He continued to watch the boy uneasily as Jonah began to set the stage for the next speaker.

"Up until now, our guests have been cultural commentators or activists of one sort or another. Our last speaker, however, is different." Jonah told the crowd. Those listening quieted somewhat but a murmur of discontent began to grow as he went on. He raised his hands in acknowledgment, trying to allay their concerns. "Cosmopolis Police Captain Joseph Clinton has agreed to appear with us today as a favor to me personally, and I ask that you listen to what he has to say. Just like yours, his perspective is one we all need to hear and understand, and with the resurgent threat of The Resistance, that is now more true than ever."

He then paused and carefully set aside his tablet, as if to signal that he was now going off-script. "And there is something else as well; something that affects us all. After we hear what Captain Clinton has to say, I ask that he and all of you in the audience as well, please stay for one final announcement."

The police captain, a middle-aged Black man wearing a dark blue uniform, had risen from his seat and was now standing next to Jonah. Jonah now turned to face him, saying into the microphone, "Captain, I must apologize. I know that this was not included as part of the official agenda, but there is something that both you and the people in front of us need to hear together. With all of us here to bear public witness, we can all be certain it will be acted on in good faith."

Captain Clinton had been studying his speech but at Jonah's surprise announcement he raised his head, looking startled and concerned. He obviously hadn't known this was coming and now felt ambushed. As Jonah stepped aside and offered him the microphone, the two men exchanged looks; Captain Clinton's dark face uncertain, while Jonah's plaintive expression offered him a wordless apology.

The captain was caught; with no way to back out gracefully, he reluctantly stepped up to the microphone and cleared his throat, taking a moment to check his notes and try to get back on track. In the front row, Jason saw the Asian boy tense and step even closer to the stage. His pulse quickened as his sense of unease about the boy only intensified.

Captain Clinton began to give his speech, reading a

little stiffly from the tablet in front of him. "I'd like to first speak to you on my own behalf, and not as a police officer." he said. "It is a sad truth that humanity's history of progress and potential is also a history that is filled with unjust laws and broken promises. My own family's presence in the United States is a visible testament to that fact. The history of Ross b is no different. It is a story rife with examples of those sins, perpetrated by those who were willing to sacrifice others to raise themselves up. This time, many of you, the non-Citizens of Ross b, have been forced to bear the brunt of those injustices. I won't defend the breaking of the promises that were made to you; indeed, I cannot."

The previously restive crowd began to settle down as his words sank in. Though the captain wore a uniform that many of them distrusted, what he said offered at least the seeds of reconciliation. Jason however, was not listening to the carefully chosen words. He had suddenly recognized the Asian boy in the front row, and in a series of intuitive leaps that came too late, he realized the danger.

Showing the intense hyper-focus that marked an overdose of Helium and Rush, the boy produced a small pistol that had until that moment been hidden under his shirt. As if in slow-motion, Jason watched him lift the gun and aim it at the police captain's chest.

Jonah was seated nearest to the podium and saw the boy raise the weapon. Without a second thought, he leaped toward Captain Clinton, shielding him with his body as the gun in the boy's hand fired twice. Jonah fell heavily on top of the captain and both men crumpled to the floor as people standing near the boy screamed and tried to flee.

The shots turned out to have been a signal. Seemingly everywhere at once, the Rally erupted into chaos. From his place on the stage, Jason watched in dismay as the audience tried to run, only to be shoved back violently. There was sporadic gunfire and panic, and his mouth went dry as he realized that the homeless men among the crowd were suddenly armed. Toward the back, one of them cleared a space around himself then held his gun high and fired a long burst, drawing the crowd's attention.

"We are The Resistance!" the man shouted loudly. Jason felt a chill as he recognized the voice. Unmistakably, it was Marcus, making real the counterfeit terrorist group he had been gifted! Jason looked over at his family and saw their faces drawn in alarm.

"Everyone get inside, now!" Jason yelled as he sprang from his seat, leaving his cane behind as he rushed forward to help Jonah and the police captain. Behind him, the guests and Jason's family scrambled for the safety of the Outreach Center's door.

Standing tall in the center of the panicked crowd, Marcus' face began to turn red as he continued to shout. "This is about justice!" he bellowed hoarsely. "Two days ago the police killed Benito Reyes at one of their so-called checkpoints! They fucking murdered him! Benito was a great man! He just wanted you to treat us like people and the cops fucking killed him for it!" Throughout the crowded street, Marcus' horde of revolutionaries howled. He went on, glowering menacingly and feeding on the fear of the masses. "Well, now that he's gone we want something else too. We want revenge!"

On the stage, Jason reached the podium just as Captain Clinton pulled himself free of Jonah. He hesitated, unsure of what to do, but crouched down as the captain frantically waved for him to come closer. With a sense of dread, Jason saw that Jonah wasn't moving and noted the dark spots of blood that had appeared on the back of his shirt, spreading until they touched.

"We need to get him inside!" Clinton said urgently, trying to throw one of Jonah's arms over his shoulder. As Jason moved to help, a burst of gunfire ripped into the top of the podium, forcing them both to take cover. The captain dropped to his knees and crouched low, out of the line of fire. Jason did the same, covering his face as small pieces of debris fell in front of him. “Christ! Who are these people?!” Clinton exclaimed.

“It’s Marcus.” Jason answered, though in the chaos he didn't expect the police captain to understand. He reached out to lift Jonah again and paused, realizing with a growing sense of alarm that his friend wasn’t breathing. Frantically, he felt for a pulse. After a long, hopeless moment he pulled his hand back and looked imploringly at the captain.

Gently, Clinton checked Jonah himself but could find no heartbeat. “Shit.” he swore quietly. Jason’s mind raced as he tried to think of something, anything, that would help, but in the end there was nothing that they could do. Pinned down by gunfire, they were forced to watch helplessly as Jonah’s life came to an end.

Overwhelmed, Jason turned away in despair and looked out into the crowd. There, beyond the edge of the stage, he saw two policemen as they converged on the Asian boy in the front row. The boy’s face remained impassive as he leveled his gun at them and fired, making no attempt to escape. One of the officers was hit in the chest and fell heavily, but the boy was brutally cut down as the second man returned fire. The boy’s drug-hardened features turned to shock as he dropped out of sight, a vision that would haunt Jason for the rest of his life. Jason stayed there, transfixed by that moment until Captain Clinton grabbed his arm and broke the spell. Reluctantly, they began crawling toward the relative safety of the building’s interior, leaving Jonah’s body behind.

****

Mindful of her husband’s wheelchair, Valarie had staked out a place for them both near the stage early on. At first they’d been in the front row but as the street became more crowded, oblivious spectators began to fill in the space around them and quickly blocked Mateo’s view. Valarie was frustrated but Mateo eventually convinced her that he didn’t mind, as simply being out among the people felt good. Truthfully, he hadn't come for the speeches anyway. The sense of community had been the real attraction, and for him the scheduled speakers were merely an afterthought.

He breathed in deep and looked around at the crowd, enjoying the day despite the lingering pain in his chest and stomach. His wounds had healed enough to allow him to leave the hospital but they still ached and he had to be careful in how he moved. None of that mattered now, though. He was happy, spending time outside surrounded by friends and family. Jason had made an appearance and Pablo had even come in from Aberdeen! Hell, Pablo had even brought his boyfriend Isaiah along to meet them! Then, to make the day even better, Jonah had arranged for Arabelle to watch the Rally from the stage, an offer she had accepted eagerly!

The positive atmosphere all around him kept Mateo's spirits riding high, but as the Rally got underway he began to get the sense that something was off. He'd see something out of the corner of his eye but when he turned to look, he couldn't say what had drawn his attention. Eventually, he faced his wheelchair away from the stage so that he could watch the crowd.

Fleetingly at first, and even then only in fragments, he began to understand what it was that had caught his eye. Perhaps a dozen shabbily dressed men crept through the crowd around them, standing in small groups or dispersed among the people. Their clothing wasn't what bothered him though. Somehow, these men seemed different; separate. They kept to themselves as they walked, moving through the audience without becoming a part of it.

Valarie caught him staring. "What's wrong?" she asked, but he shook his head uncertainly.

"I don't know. Maybe nothing." he answered hesitantly. One of the strange men, shorter than the others by at least a foot, now stood only a few yards away. Mateo watched him unnoticed as the man rose up onto the balls of his feet and peered toward the stage. When he turned his head, Mateo realized with a start that he wasn't a man at all, but a young Hispanic boy.

"Val, grab Pablo and Isaiah. Let's all start moving closer to the stage." Mateo said urgently, putting his hands on his wheels. "I know that kid from Casa Preciosa; his name is Daniel and he hangs out with Marcus. I'm not sure what's going on but I want to be close to Arabelle just in case."

He pushed forward and started the chair rolling but moments later they heard the sharp, unmistakable crack of gunfire. All at once the crowd around them began to churn violently, forcing them away from the stage and threatening to trample them all. Valarie braced herself behind Mateo's wheelchair, holding it in place while a torrent of panicked people flowed around them. Pablo and Isaiah were nearly swept away but managed to rejoin them a moment later.

In flashes between the pressing bodies, Mateo saw an elderly Caucasian man trying desperately to keep his footing. Daniel suddenly appeared near him and as Mateo watched, the boy produced a small, menacing looking gun from beneath his overcoat and pointed it at the old man. The man froze, his face twisting into a mask of fear and confusion. Mateo wanted to help but the crowd between them surged suddenly, blocking his way. When he could see again, both Daniel and the old man were gone.

The sound of the panicked crowd was endless, a continuous wail of piercing shrieks punctuated by bursts of staccato gunfire, but soon Mateo realized that he was hearing something else as well. Incredibly, it was Marcus' voice, raised angrily and demanding that people listen to him. Mateo could barely make out the words, but those fragments he caught sounded like a twisted parody of what had been said on stage, fervent and unyielding.

All around them, the chaos was only getting worse and the stage was still too far away. Mateo realized with a sinking feeling that they would never be able to get to their daughter this way; they needed another plan.

"Never mind the stage!" he said, pointing back toward the edge of the crowd. "Head that way, toward the police!"

"What about Arabelle?!" Valarie asked, her voice tight with concern. Behind her Pablo and Isaiah were trying to hold back the crowd.

"We'll try to go around back and get to her that way! Right now I'm just glad she's not down here with us! Now, come on!"

The four of them began struggling toward the edge of the crowd, pushed and pulled by currents that hindered as often as they helped. Things seemed to be getting worse all around them but suddenly there was a loud 'BANG!' and the tide began to turn. A cloud of dense smoke rolled through the street as people started to cough; someone had deployed tear gas! Moments later Mateo saw officers in masks and heavy armor pushing through the crowd, trying to isolate the attackers, but oblivious to the panic they were causing themselves.

Only a few feet away from Mateo a terrified Caucasian woman tripped and fell. Despite his injuries, he instinctively launched himself from his chair and grabbed her arm to keep her from being trampled. She kept shrieking hysterically as he tried to steady her and in the chaos, he didn't see that her screams had drawn the attention of the police.

"Let her go!" the officer bellowed as he appeared behind Mateo, brandishing a baton. The man's voice was muffled by his gasmask but the threat of violence was clear.

Now that the woman was back on her feet and the danger had passed, Mateo's injuries began to reassert themselves. Sagging, he was forced to lean on her for support. He panicked but knew that if he let go of her arm, he would fall. Without waiting for him to explain, the officer swung his truncheon, hitting Mateo across his forearm and breaking his grip. He cried out in pain as he fell to the ground, collapsing just as a second officer appeared. The first one handcuffed Mateo without helping him up, while the second officer verified that the woman was uninjured.

All of this happened in mere seconds. Valarie screamed Mateo's name but the mass of bodies between them prevented her from reaching him. As she pressed forward, additional officers appeared and began to force her back, along with Pablo and Isaiah. The last thing she saw of her husband was him being pulled roughly to his feet and dragged bodily away.

****

"Are we ready?" the reporter asked, checking her reflection in a nearby window.

The technician glanced at the floating camera drone, then down at the monitor on his pad which displayed the reporter's carefully manicured image, overlaid with a small graphic in the lower right-hand corner which identified her as 'Rachael Stannis - Foreault News Service'.

"Yeah, we're ready." he said, transferring control of the drone to Stannis' micro.

Rachael sighed, resigning herself to the task at hand; cover the Unity Rally and collect a few 'person-on-the-street' interviews. "Okay, thanks. I'll meet you back here when I'm done." she said. The tech nodded and climbed back into the mobile studio to monitor the signal while she waded into the crowd.

The sea of people in front of her was dense, but with some effort she made her way to what she estimated was the middle of the crowd. There she staked out a position from which she could see the stage, as well as keep an eye out for anything else she may want to use. She checked the camera's POV display on her micro, making adjustments as needed while she tried to decide where to begin.

There had already been three or four presenters on stage so far but she hadn't really been paying close attention. It was all being recorded anyway; she would review the footage later to decide what to include in her report.

Looking around at the crowd, she had to admit that they appeared enthusiastic. She angled the drone, making sure to get some shots of the cheering audience before turning the lens back toward the stage. As a police captain took the podium, she placed the drone on automatic and rose onto her tiptoes to search the nearby faces for anyone who looked like they might be able to string a sentence together on camera.

A pair of sudden, sharp popping sounds from somewhere in front of her made her jump, and at first she didn't realize what had happened. Near the stage all she could see was the backs of people's heads as they ran, frantically seeking shelter. Holding her breath, she quickly checked the drone's video feed. Incredibly, it showed Jonah Rodriguez, the Rally organizer, lying collapsed on top of the police captain! Her heart pounded; had he been shot? Even hindered by the micro's small screen, she could see a blood-soaked spot beginning to form on his back. She spun the camera around rapidly, trying without success to find the gunman.

Engrossed by the camera's video feed, she was startled when only a few yards away a large Hispanic man drew back his coat to reveal a menacing black rifle. She stood there frozen, transfixed as he raised the gun to the sky and began to shout.

"We are The Resistance!" he bellowed.

His hard face was twisted in anger and his voice was loud and rough. Knowing the risk, Rachael quietly focused the floating camera on him and set it to follow his movements. The drone slowly drew closer as the man delivered his demented sermon, but he didn't seem to notice. When he loudly called for revenge, an answering echo came from all around her. It was only then that she realized he was not the only gunman in the crowd.

All around her, frightened people began to push and shove desperately as men with guns appeared throughout the rally. The Hispanic man who had announced the attack disappeared into the crowd, but Rachael's micro reassured her that the camera was still following him. The image showed the man forcing his way toward the stage, firing his gun seemingly at random as he went. Without thinking, she began to move toward the stage herself.

She kept an eye on the video feed as she pushed through the churning crowd. Using the drone's internal logic to help frame the shot, she managed to get an image which showed both the man she was following and the stage. His dark eyes remained fixed on his goal, so when he suddenly stopped in his tracks, it caught her off guard. Adjusting the camera again, she saw movement near the podium as someone tried to help the police captain lift Jonah Rodriguez and carry him to safety.

Suddenly the man she had been following became enraged. "What the fuck! Lucas?!!" he roared. His voice crackled over the micro's small speakers and the drone adjusted to focus on him while keeping the stage in view. His lips parted, baring his teeth in anger as he raised his rifle and fired, hitting the podium and forcing the two men there to abandon Jonah and drop out of sight.

Seeking a better shot, Rachael commanded the drone to float higher, letting her see behind the stage's modest cover. She watched as the men there reluctantly left the injured Jonah behind and crawled for the safety of the El Rey Latino Outreach Center's doors. When they were gone, she refocused the camera on the man she'd come to think of as the terrorist leader as he again pressed toward the stage with a renewed vigor, radiating a violent, murderous fury.

Keeping to what she believed was a safe distance, Rachael saw with relief that the police were beginning to arrive. After launching tear gas, they began a sort of pincer maneuver, methodically working to find and subdue the armed men in the crowd. The terrorist leader near the stage, however, remained unfazed. As Rachael watched, he vaulted past the podium and ran to the door, disappearing inside.

Ignoring the chaos behind her, she quickly made a decision. Setting the camera drone to follow her, Rachael crept forward and began looking for an opportunity to slip inside the building.

CHAPTER 26

Matthew was terrified. He ran forward, keeping his eyes focused on his mother's back as they sprinted for The Center's door. For a single agonizing moment they were stuck as Arabelle, Brodie, Courtney and the others all tried to squeeze through at once. Everything around him was too loud; people were screaming and there were a bunch of popping sounds that even he knew were gunfire. Once the dam broke and they all made it inside, his mother turned and peered worriedly through the glass door. Jonah lay face-down near the podium and Matthew watched anxiously as his father and Captain Clinton tried to lift him up. Numbly, Matthew realized that Jonah wasn't moving and in a way that he couldn't explain, he knew that Jonah was gone.

Another round of gunshots startled him and Matthew saw his father and Captain Clinton suddenly drop Jonah and crouch down low. Anne gasped and pulled her son close as they heard bullets impacting against the stone walls outside. Frightened, they retreated from the window and backed up against the stairs with the others; safe for the moment but unsure of what to do now.

Moments later the door was opened again and Captain Clinton crawled through, followed closely by Jason. Jason rose and forced the door shut behind them as soon as they were through, leaning hard against it for the space of a long heartbeat. Overwhelmed with relief to see her husband safe, Anne rushed forward and hugged him tightly while Captain Clinton stared through the glass door and watched the panicked crowd outside.

“Dad!” Matthew shouted, running to his father and locking his arms around his waist.

Anne looked at Jason, her eyes filled with concern. “That man; it’s Marcus, isn’t it? Did he say this is The Resistance?” she asked. She was pale with fear, but her voice was steady as she asked the question. Jason nodded his head in grim acknowledgement.

Matthew’s eyes were squeezed shut as he held onto his father but his face was turned toward the door. When he opened his eyes again, they settled on Jonah’s body lying face-down near the podium, unmoving. “We need to help him!” Matthew cried suddenly and bolted toward the door, but his father’s hand came down firmly on his shoulder, stopping him.

“Right now we need to stay here. It’s too dangerous out there.” Jason admonished him. Looking out at Jonah’s body he added, “I’m sorry.”, speaking as much to Jonah as to Matthew.

The sound of more gunfire broke the silence and somewhere nearby they heard a window shatter. Startled, Anne and Matthew let go of Jason and looked around in fear. Captain Clinton suddenly pulled back from the door as more shots were fired. “We need to get away from the windows.” he told everyone urgently.

Courtney spoke up from her position near the stairs. “There aren’t any windows in the dining room.” she suggested.

“All right, let’s get everyone in there.” Clinton said decisively. Pulling out his micro, he added, “I’m going to call my lieutenant at the checkpoint and tell him to move in the reserves.”

Everyone began to move into the dining room while Captain Clinton placed his call. Courtney and Brodie led the way, staying close to Arabelle while the guest speakers meekly followed. Of the speakers, only Sylvia Anzaldúa appeared to have retained any sense of initiative. She looked as though she wanted to go outside and fight The Resistance herself. The rest of them appeared terrified and were more than willing to defer to a police captain’s authority in an emergency. Arabelle began to cry softly, and Brodie pulled her close, trying to comfort her as they entered the dining room.

Jason and Anne hung back, walking a few feet behind the rest of the group. Anne stopped suddenly and looked at her husband.

"You're limping! Where's your cane?" she asked, concerned.

Only now did Jason realize that he'd lost it. "I must have left it out there." he said vaguely, gesturing with his head. "I'll be okay. It's just a little weak, that's all." he reassured her.

It was only partly true; his leg *was* weak but as he began to pay attention to it, he could feel the ache threatening to return with a vengeance. He could walk for now, but didn't know how long that would last.

With no other choice than to try and carry on, Jason again began to limp toward the dining room and Anne matched his pace, staying by his side. He put his arm around her and she let him lean on her just a little; a silent acknowledgement that she knew he hurt more than he let on. Together, they entered the dining room just as Captain Clinton reached his lieutenant.

"Take everyone you have and move in, now!" he was saying. "Use tear gas and the riot armor. There are a lot of civilians out there, so we need to stay non-lethal but do what you have to do! We need to stop them now!"

"Yes sir." came the reply. "You're safe in the building?"

"For now. Get things under control out there before you worry about us."

"Does anyone with you need medical attention?"

Captain Clinton gave everyone around him a quick glance. "I don't think so." he said. "Check on us after you're done out there."

"Will do; I'm sending the order to move in now. I'll let you know when it's safe outside." the lieutenant confirmed before breaking the connection.

Satisfied, Clinton returned the micro to his pocket before facing the group gathered in front of him. "The police are moving in now. We'll wait here until it's safe." he told them calmly.

His delivery was firm and calculated to inspire confidence. Still, the answering silence made it clear very few of them were convinced. Trying to offer what little reassurance he could, he added, "I'll keep you updated as best I can. As soon as I learn anything new, I'll let you know."

He received a series of tepid nods in return, the best any of them could offer under the circumstances. Captain Clinton then approached Jason. "Can I talk to you for a minute?" he asked quietly. Jason agreed and the two of them moved to the other side of the room. When they could no longer be overheard, Clinton leaned in close. "They said they were The Resistance, and you said it was 'Marcus'. What do you know about them?" he asked bluntly.

The captain's voice was steady but there was a hint of warning in his eyes. After everything that had happened, Jason knew he couldn't lie or evade the truth any longer.

"You remember the surprise announcement that Jonah was going to make after your speech?" Jason asked. Clinton nodded imperceptibly and waited for him to continue. "It was about me. I've been working inside The Brotherhood for months. I guess you'd call it undercover."

"The gang run by Gabe and Angel Batista? We got a tip about them yesterday and picked them up for questioning. We've still got them downtown." Clinton told him. As he trailed off, Jason saw the wheels begin to turn in his head.

"That's them." Jason confirmed. "Jonah realized that most of The Resistance attacks were carried out by people who had gone to a homeless shelter called Casa Preciosa for help, so I went there too, trying to find the connection. I found out that The Brotherhood operates out of the shelter. To make a long story short, I got a recording of Gabe and Angel saying that they made up The Resistance, and were using the attacks to distract the police while they took out their rivals. One of those attacks was the shooting and bombing at the bazaar three months ago." Jason paused and looked Captain Clinton in the eyes. "That's where they framed me." he said.

The captain stared at him as if seeing him for the first time, and a spark of recognition flashed. "You're Jason Menounos." he said, and began nodding thoughtfully as he pieced together the truth. "And you were the one who warned us about the shuttle attack..." It wasn't a question. "Jonah always did try to protect his people." Clinton said ruefully. Seeing Jason's bewildered expression, he added, "He tried to protect me too but I guess the time for that is past."

Jason understood the truth before Captain Clinton could finish. "You were his contact with the police!" he realized. "You helped him; you helped him hide us!"

The captain's dark face was solemn. "And a few other things too over the years. Jonah helped out my family when I was young." He smiled sadly at the memory. "I probably wouldn't be here if it weren't for him. We had no one else to turn to and he gave us a place to stay. He trusted us and when I could, I tried to return the favor."

Jason was amazed. It was a story that in some ways mirrored his own. Jonah had trusted them both, and the realization suddenly removed all doubt from his mind. Although it left him vulnerable, he decided to take a risk.

"If I give you the recording, would you promise to look into it?" he asked earnestly. "*Really* look into it, and not let it get buried? It's the only chance I have to show what really happened, and I don't want my family to have to hide any more."

The mention of Jason's family seemed to touch something deep in Captain Clinton. He looked across the room to where Anne and Matthew sat huddled together with the rest of the group. "Is that them?" he asked gently.

"Yes. They're all I have." Jason answered quietly. He felt raw and exposed, but he had no other cards left to play.

The captain's expression softened. "Send me the file." he said. "You have my word we will act on it, and I will see to it your name is cleared... Jason."

Captain Clinton spoke his name, his real name, as if it were an introduction; which, in a way, it was. It was also a gift. With a single word he had been given back his identity. He breathed out and felt 'Lucas' fade away, false and unneeded. He was whole again. Grateful beyond words, he pulled out his micro and transferred the file. "Thank you." he said. "Now, we just have to get through this."

There was a sudden noise from the lobby. Captain Clinton raised a finger to his lips, making sure everyone was quiet before creeping along the wall to the open door. He peered cautiously around the corner but quickly pulled back in alarm. He mouthed to them, "There's someone there." and raised his micro to call for help. The device beeped softly as it came to life and he wrapped his hand tightly around it, trying to deaden the sound as he began to work the screen.

In a blur, an arm flashed past the doorframe and violently struck the micro from the captain's hand. It hit the floor and skidded away as a large male figure burst into the room. The intruder kicked at the fallen micro, sending it out of reach beneath a stack of folding tables. Then, still moving quickly, the figure hit Captain Clinton in the face with the butt of a rifle, dazing him and knocking him off balance.

As he turned, Jason could finally see the man's face. "Marcus!" he shouted, loud enough to draw the man's attention.

"You fucking son of a bitch!" Marcus growled at him angrily.

Jason took half a step forward and winced as the growing pain in his leg flared. He planted his foot and kept his balance, watching intently as he assessed the situation. By now Marcus had whirled to face him and Jason could clearly see the rifle he held clenched in his hands. Enraged, Marcus began to raise the barrel toward Jason's chest.

Captain Clinton had recovered and now suddenly charged at Marcus, drawing his attention away from Jason. As

Marcus spun to face him, Jason ran forward too, pain shooting through his leg with every step. He and Clinton collided with Marcus nearly simultaneously and knocked him to the floor. As they hit the ground Marcus lost his grip on the rifle and Captain Clinton batted it out of reach.

"Get them out of here!" Jason shouted frantically to the captain, gesturing desperately toward his family with his head while holding Marcus' hands down as best he could. Clinton didn't waste any time and immediately sprang up to rush Anne, Courtney, Brodie, the children and the guest speakers out through the door and up the stairs.

While Jason's family were fleeing, Marcus managed to get an arm loose and swung hard, hitting him squarely in the eye. Jason gasped and drew back in pain as Marcus shoved him off and scrambled for the rifle. He recovered the weapon and rose just as Captain Clinton ran back into the room. Clinton saw him and stopped abruptly as Marcus pointed the gun at him and fired a single shot, hitting him in the chest. The captain cried out and staggered against the wall before sagging to the floor. Jason looked on in horror as his breathing became rapid and blood began to soak his shirt.

Marcus gave a brief snarl of satisfaction and then glared at Jason, still kneeling on the floor. The big man held the rifle across his chest, not yet taking aim but ready to do so at a moment's notice. Anger fairly radiated from him as he slowly stalked across the room.

"What in the fuck are you doing here Lucas? With him?!" Marcus demanded, pointing a finger at Captain Clinton. "The cops killed Benito! You know that, right? So I'm going to kill him. And then I'm going to shoot every other cop I can find. They don't give a *shit* about us and it's about fucking time we did something about it!"

"Marcus, the cops didn't kill Benito!" Jason exclaimed. "It was Gabe!"

If Marcus heard him, he didn't give any indication. He raised the rifle slowly and stared down the sights at Jason.

"You fucking traitor." he said, his voice dripping with scorn.

Jason's back was to the door, with the kitchen to his right. A second door behind Marcus led to the storeroom and then to the alley beyond it. As Marcus took aim, Jason saw the storeroom door open a fraction and a short, thin Caucasian woman he didn't recognize peeked out. Marcus saw his attention shift and spun around suddenly, throwing the door open wide before the woman could pull it closed again. He grabbed her roughly by the neck and threw her into the room. A hovering camera followed her, positioning itself a few feet away. Marcus was confused and angry as he stared at the drone.

"Who the fuck are you?" he demanded, pointing the rifle at her.

The woman scrambled back in fear and her jacket fell open, revealing the press identification clipped to her shirt. Marcus read the name with a sneer. "Rachael Stannis?"

"I'm- I'm a reporter!" she stammered, her fear refusing to let her speak clearly. She swallowed, then added, "You're The Resistance!"

Marcus hesitated. As a criminal, his first instinct was to eliminate witnesses but a terrorist craved an audience. "Set up the camera." he ordered her finally. "I have something I want to say."

Hyper-aware of the gun in his hands, Rachael did as she was told. Moments later the shot was ready, angled to include Marcus, Jason and herself in the frame.

"It's on?" he asked. She nodded silently.

Marcus puffed up his chest and addressed the camera. With his rifle still trained on Jason and Rachael, he confidently declared, "We are the Resistance!" and then paused as if he didn't know what to say next. Jason suddenly had the distinct impression that Marcus had only gotten this far by mimicking the other videos he'd seen. After a moment though, the dam broke and an agitated stream-of-consciousness began to spill out.

"This is all bullshit!" he exclaimed. "We get treated

like shit, like we're fucking disposable! You Anglos promised that if we came to Ross b and made it a place to live, you'd make us Citizens but you fucking lied! All you do is use us! We do your shitty jobs; we clean up after your kids and cook your food, and you fucking pretend like we're not even there! The only way a Latino man can make any real money is to steal shit or sell drugs and when we try to do that, the cops harass us! Hell, they fucking kill us for it!"

As Marcus ranted, his temper was rising fast. He was working himself up into a murderous rage, but he was also becoming distracted. Jason watched him carefully for an opportunity to act.

"...and they killed Benito Reyes!" Marcus went on, shouting louder now. "He was a good man and the cops shot him just because they didn't like what he said! It's not fair! If you're watching this and you're Hispanic, join us! Don't let these fuckers keep treating us like shit!"

He trailed off, flushed and breathing heavily. In the oppressive silence that followed, Rachael quietly asked him a question, somehow sounding both brave and afraid at the same time. "If you're doing this for all Hispanics, then why did you kill Jonah Rodriguez?" she asked. Her voice was soft, but still managed to carry in the otherwise still air.

Marcus snorted. "That Uncle Juan fuck? We were trying to shoot the cop and he got in the way! It's no loss though; I'm glad that traitor's dead. He thinks we just need to ask nicely and then the Anglos will treat us better! Well, it doesn't fucking work that way! I won't go to them asking for a fucking hand-out! The Anglos had their chance and now we're taking what we're owed!"

While Marcus' attention was focused on the reporter, Jason made his move. As quickly as he could, he rose and charged, his leg numb and yet screaming in agony at the same time. He crashed into Marcus heavily, knocking the wind out of him and sending the rifle flying. It clattered to the floor and Rachael kicked it, sending it out of reach behind the tables.

Marcus recovered his balance as he shoved Jason back violently. "You fuck!" he howled, and struck out viciously with his foot. The toe of his boot hit Jason's injured leg with a crunch and Jason cried out as bolts of electric pain ripped through his body. The world rapidly turned white, then red as he collapsed onto the floor. Relentless, Marcus stomped again on his wounded leg, nearly causing him to pass out.

Rachael coiled herself and jumped at Marcus, leaping onto his back and reaching for his face to claw at his eyes. Marcus shook her off and whirled, striking her a glancing blow. Rachael charged forward again, ducking under his arm and then bringing her knee up into his groin, causing Marcus to crouch awkwardly before he hit her again, this time in the face. Bleeding from her nose and lip, she fell to the floor, still conscious but unable to continue.

While Rachael fought Marcus, Jason had managed to pull himself along the floor and into the nearby kitchen. He lay there on his back, panting with pain as his leg alternated between a sense of horrible numbness and feeling as if it were on fire. Above him towered cabinets, a sink, a stove, and a solid looking industrial-style mixer that sat balanced on a thin stand. The only way out was the way he came in; he was trapped. He was still trying to catch his breath when Marcus appeared suddenly at his feet, holding the rifle. Marcus roared in incoherent rage as he raised the weapon.

Reflexively, Jason struck out with his good leg and kicked hard at Marcus' knee. There was a jarring crack as the joint gave way and Marcus howled, collapsing onto the tile with his head near the base of the mixer. Jason scrambled backward in panic and his foot caught the edge of the mixer stand, knocking the heavy appliance down from its perch. The mixer landed on Marcus' head with a sickening crunch, twisting it at an odd angle as it drove his skull into the hard floor, leaving a dark smear of blood on the tile. Jason pulled away in horror but Marcus made no move to follow him. He lay still, eyes open as he drew a ragged breath. Jason waited for him to draw another, but it never came. A moment later Marcus was dead.

Afterward, a deafening silence seemed to settle over everything. It seemed as if it would go on forever, but slowly Jason became aware of new sounds coming from the dining room. He heard Anne's voice exclaim in horror, "Shit!"

"The cops are just outside; they'll be here any min-*Fuck*!" came Brodie's voice, which grew louder as she entered the room. "Mom! Get in here, quick!"

Jason swallowed, then called out from the kitchen. "Anne! I'm in here!" he shouted. A moment later she appeared at the door, her face a deathly white.

"Jason!" she cried. Upon seeing Marcus' unmoving body lying on the floor at his feet, she asked, "Are you alright?!"

"I'm fine." Jason answered, though it wasn't really true. Shaking his head, he admitted, "Actually, I think I might throw up."

Anne helped him get to his feet. Still in pain, Jason leaned on her heavily as he limped out of the kitchen and over to a table. She pulled out a chair and carefully lowered him into it before sitting down in the seat next to him. Brodie sat nearby, treating the reporter's injuries as the camera drone floated at her side, all but forgotten.

By the door, Courtney knelt over Captain Clinton, firmly pressing a wad of cloth against his bullet wound while she shouted at someone on her micro to send an ambulance right away. She ended the call viciously and looked up to find Jason watching her.

"Brodie called the police as soon as we got upstairs. I'm trying to get an ambulance here, but it's still nuts outside." she explained frustratedly. Worried, she looked down at her patient. "I think he'll be fine but I'll feel a lot better once we get him into a hospital." she said. The captain's dark face was covered in sweat, but he was awake and as Jason watched he forced a weak smile. Courtney lifted the cloth and checked it briefly before again placing it against his chest. The damp spot of dark red it held was alarming but didn't seem to be growing very fast, and Jason took this as a hopeful sign.

He caught a glimpse of Matthew and Arabelle as they peered cautiously into the room from the open doorway. Jason's relief at seeing his son unharmed nearly brought him to tears. Eyes shining, he waved for them to come in. Arabelle moved hesitantly to Brodie's side while Matthew joined his parents at the table.

Jason's blood ran cold as he heard a sudden clatter coming from The Center's front door. Moments later a loud male voice shouted, "Police! We're coming in!". There was an enormous crashing sound and then a group of six officers in riot gear swarmed into the building. Upon entering the dining room, one of them knelt by Captain Clinton while the others fanned out and quickly checked for any remaining threats.

Jason was tired. At the next table over, Rachael Stannis was speaking to one of the police officers, explaining that her camera had recorded everything. The officer nodded, making notes on his micro as she spoke. As more uniformed men entered the building, Jason suddenly knew what had to happen next.

Knowing this would be hardest on his son, Jason turned to face him. "Matt," he said. "they're going to arrest me, but it's okay. We don't have to hide anymore. Captain Clinton will explain everything to them as soon as he can and then they'll let me go. Stay with your mom, and do what the police say. I'll be okay, I promise. It will all be over soon."

As one officer came over to check on them, Jason looked up into his young face. It was time; no going back now. "Officer," he said. "My name is Jason Menounos. I'd like to turn myself in."

CHAPTER 27

"The Latino Resistance Front is just bullshit. It's a bunch of talk we ripped off of Benito out there, backed up by just enough guns and bombs to get the cops' attention and make it look real."

Jason sat in Captain Clinton's office while Gabe Batista's recorded voice echoed from the tablet laying on the desk in front of him. Though the audio was occasionally muffled and indistinct, the unwitting confession it contained was undeniable. City prosecutor Harlan Fossa stood nearby, listening intently.

"At first it was just snipers and shit to keep the cops busy, like the guy who shot up the bazaar a few months ago." came Angel's voice.

"You mean that asshole in the picture?" Marcus's gruff voice asked. Jason shuddered involuntarily as a brief stab of pain ran up his leg.

On the recording, Angel replied dismissively, *"We stole that photo off the police alerts. I don't know who that fucker was; I guess he's pretty screwed now."*

Jason waited patiently as Captain Clinton and Fossa listened to the recording all the way through. When it was finally done Clinton leaned back stiffly in his chair, careful not to move his chest too much. In addition to the gunshot wound, he wore a pair of black eyes, slightly swollen and obviously painful. He looked expectantly at Fossa. "What do you think?" he inquired.

Fossa's brow furrowed as if he were still making up his mind, but he began to nod. "I think we can use it." he said eventually. "We'll need to explain how we got it, but I think we could get the judge to allow it." He ran a hand through his short red hair and looked at Jason. "You'll need to be a witness obviously, but I think we can build a case here."

Clinton smiled and tapped at a gloss-black panel embedded in his desk. A moment later a rumpled looking sergeant appeared, wearing a question on his face. "Yes sir?" he asked.

"Send a couple guys down to the holding cells. We're going to formally arrest Gabe and Angel Batista on charges of terrorism." Clinton told him.

If the sergeant was surprised by the order, he didn't show it. "Will do." he answered firmly.

"Then I want you to take a squad down to Casa Preciosa." Clinton continued. "It's a homeless shelter, but the Batista's have been running their gang out of there. We need to shut it down and secure any evidence."

The sergeant then nodded and left, leaving Jason alone again with Clinton and Fossa. Technically, Jason was still in police custody and was unsure of what to do now. "So what about me?" he asked hesitantly. "Am I still under arrest?"

Captain Clinton consulted silently with Fossa, who shook his head. Turning back to Jason, he said, "I've already spoken to Chief Edgars. He said that if your recording checked out, and if Mr. Fossa here agreed, we wouldn't press charges." He smiled. "You're free to go. We can take it from here."

'Free to go...' The words echoed in Jason's head. He'd done it! The nightmare was finally over! As the reality of it sank in, he suddenly felt untethered, like a child's balloon set free outside. He smiled and reflexively gripped the arms of his chair to keep from floating away.

As Fossa gave him a polite smile and excused himself from the room, Jason asked Captain Clinton nervously, "So what do I do now?"

"Go see your family!" Clinton admonished him with a grin. "I've got a lot of work to do, you know. We arrested twenty-one people in the attack yesterday and I need to review each of their files to make sure nothing slips through the cracks." He tapped the tablet in front of him, where a flashing icon read 'New Arrest Records'.

His family... Suddenly nothing in the world was more important to him. He rose, leaning on his cane, which had been found in the aftermath of the attack and returned to him. As he turned to go, his leg caught for a moment between the desk and chair, sending a bolt of pain through him. He hissed through clenched teeth and Captain Clinton looked up with concern.

"Your leg?" he asked sympathetically.

"Yeah." Jason admitted as the pain subsided. Looking back at the captain, he added, "You know, maybe I should be worried about you instead. I'm not the one who was shot in the chest!"

"It was just a scratch." Clinton replied with mock bravado. "Actually, the bullet missed anything important and your friend Courtney did a good job making sure I was okay until the medics arrived. I've already thanked her myself, but when you see her again, remind her how grateful I am. I owe her my life."

"I'll tell her." Jason promised.

"And after you see your family, promise me you'll go to a doctor about your leg. It won't get better if you ignore it." Clinton said. His tone was friendly but there was a paternal sternness lurking underneath.

"I will." Jason said, sounding playfully exasperated. "Now, let me go so you can get caught up on your work."

"Just take care of yourself." Clinton said, and as Jason quietly closed the door, the captain opened the 'New Arrests' file and began reading.

****

As Jason left the captain's office, he limped down a short hallway and emerged out into the large desk-filled workspace that dominated the center of the old, ornate building. The decor and color palate laid out before him was an anachronistic homage to an even earlier time, but somehow it seemed right. He rested there a moment and took a deep breath, surrounded by police officers on all sides, but no longer afraid of them.

The visitor's lobby was an austere collection of chairs that sat near the front door. As Jason turned, he saw Valarie sitting there with her daughter. Arabelle appeared as if she had been crying, but her mother was seething with a barely contained fury. Her eyes met Jason's and she immediately bolted from her seat to confront him.

"They arrested Mateo!" Valarie blurted hotly, nearly yelling in frustration.

"What?" Jason responded, caught off-guard by her ferocity.

"During the attack! He was trying to help someone when one of these *assholes* hit him and took him away!" Her voice carried, and Jason saw several uniformed men doing their best not to look at her.

"Have you asked them about it?" he asked, nodding toward the scattered officers who sat working at their desks.

"I did, but no one will listen to me because we're not Citizens!" she exclaimed. She truly was shouting now, and didn't seem to care who heard her.

Jason felt a familiar pang of guilt. Once again, he was benefiting from a two-tiered system of justice while his friend sat in a cell. It wasn't fair, but maybe just this once he was in a position to do something about it.

"Come on." he told her. "Bring Arabelle and follow me."

Together, the three of them went back down the hallway and into Captain Clinton's office. As they lined up in front of the captain's desk, Jason tried to appear reasonable while Valarie stood next to him, radiating a silent fury.

The captain had been frowning at his tablet as they entered. Now he set it down and looked up questioningly at

Jason.

"I need you to check something for me." Jason told him.

"Okay, what is it?" Clinton asked cautiously as Valarie continued to glower at him, her lips pressed into a thin line.

"Yesterday your officers arrested a man named Mateo Martinez. This is his wife, Valarie and their daughter Arabelle." Jason told him with a sense of forced calm. "To put it simply, there must be a mistake. He's in a wheelchair and there's no way he was causing trouble. I'll vouch for him; I promise he didn't do anything wrong."

"Mateo Martinez?" Clinton asked, confirming the name. He picked up the tablet again and studied it. "Actually, I already have him flagged for a second look. Something about it didn't seem right."

Valarie's scowl eased fractionally and she took half a step forward. "Will you let him go?" she asked, hope holding her anger at bay for the moment.

The captain stabbed at the tablet with one large finger. "It looks like the arresting officer was part of the reserves that were brought in after the attack began, meaning he was not one of the ones Jonah had approved." He paused, considering his words carefully. "Let's just say I know this man's reputation and I can't say I'm surprised at what happened."

He poked at the screen again and a photo of Mateo appeared, taken as he was being booked into the holding cells. He was heavily bandaged around the abdomen and looked as though he were going to be ill. A department-issue wheelchair was just visible at the bottom of the frame and two bored looking junior officers held onto his arms, hoisting him into a standing position for the photo. Clinton grimaced. "You said he was in a wheelchair..." he began, staring at Mateo's bandages. "Did my officers do this to him?" he asked quietly.

Valarie had seen the photo and shuddered, covering her face with her hands. When she didn't answer, Jason leaned forward and reluctantly studied the image, afraid of what he might find. To his great relief, there were no new injuries.

"No." Jason said. "That all happened a few days ago. I don't think getting arrested helped, but he doesn't look any worse."

"Alright; good." Clinton said, clearly relieved. He gave the remainder of Mateo's file a cursory review and tapped the screen a few more times in quick succession before placing the tablet back down in front of him. He then used the panel on his desk to summon the sergeant. The disheveled man appeared a few moments later, holding a mug of something hot.

"Please take this woman and her daughter down to the holding cells to meet her husband." Clinton told him. "He is to be released; we will not be pressing charges."

Valarie's face lit up. "Oh, thank you!" she whispered, nearly in tears. She spun and hugged Jason impulsively, squeezing him tightly.

"Go get Mateo." he told her softly.

As Valarie let him go she flashed Captain Clinton a quick smile of gratitude, which he accepted gracefully. She and Arabelle then followed the sergeant back down the hallway, each step bringing them closer to reuniting their family.

With the impromptu meeting now over, Jason bid the captain goodbye for a second time. He couldn't stop smiling as he stepped through the building's front door and walked out into the red-orange sunlight, a free man once more.

****

Jason felt ebullient as he exited the car in front of The El Rey Latino Outreach Center. His leg still felt weak as he stood, but the cane in his hand helped immensely and with its support he was able to stand up straight and tall. He breathed in deeply, feeling that a weight had been lifted.

The car pulled away behind him and he stood there for a moment, taking in his surroundings. The attack had only been yesterday but The Center already looked different somehow; smaller, maybe. The temporary stage still stood out front but most of the decorations had been taken down, leaving it naked. As he watched, a pair of men emerged from the building carrying a large box filled with cables and equipment that Jonah had rented for the Rally.

Jonah was gone... maybe that's why The Center seemed changed. It was a melancholy thought but as Jason entered the building, his hope was rekindled by the volunteers he saw working to clean it up. Jonah may have been the heart of this place, but these people were its soul. One way or another, they would help each other to carry on.

He found Anne in the upstairs storeroom, refilling empty bottles of cleaning supplies and tidying up. As he reached the top of the stairs, she saw him and rushed over to hug him tightly.

"So they heard the recording? They let you go?" she asked breathlessly.

"They heard it." he said, holding her close. "It's over. You, me and Matthew; we're all free. It's done."

EPILOGUE

"Thanks for seeing us." Jason said as he pulled out a chair and sat down.

He and Anne were in the upstairs office at the El Rey Latino Outreach Center. They had been here before, just like this, back when this had been Jonah's office. On that occasion, Jonah had agreed to help hide them from the police. Today though, they needed something else.

"It's been over a month! You're still using a cane?" Courtney asked as she sat down behind Jonah's desk. "Didn't you go back to the doctor?"

"Yeah, I did." Jason answered tiredly. "They were able to help some, but part of the nerve has actually died, so they can't just regenerate it. It will take surgery to replace it and they say the recovery can be tough. I haven't decided whether or not to go through with it."

"Hmm." Courtney murmured noncommittally. "Well, it's still good to see you. Did you bring Matthew? Brodie and I miss him."

Anne nodded. "We brought him, but right now he's with Valarie and Mateo. Since we got back to Aberdeen his friends don't come around much, so we thought it might be good for him to play with Arabelle." she said.

Courtney looked sympathetic. "I understand." she said. "You both spent a long time in the news for all the wrong reasons and now people are keeping their distance. It must be hard for him."

"Yeah, well..." Jason replied, looking uncomfortable as he trailed off. After a moment he took a breath and tried to get the conversation back on track. "It looks like you're doing well, though." he said, looking around the room which was still decorated just as Jonah had left it. "They made you the Director, right? Jonah left some pretty big shoes to fill."

Courtney sighed. "Yes he did. Jonah never told me about it, but apparently he left instructions that I should be put in charge if anything ever happened to him." She stopped suddenly as a lump formed in her throat. When she could go on, she said, "After I found out, I gave my notice with Emergency Services and I start here full time next week." She absently played with a tablet on the desk in front of her. "I'm still not sure how I'll manage it." she confided.

Jason was supportive. "You'll do fine." he said encouragingly. "Things change; you can't be Jonah but you can still be great. He told me how much he relied on you, so it's no accident that he picked you to run things now that he's gone."

Courtney took a deep breath and smiled at him, acknowledging that he meant well. "Things do change." she agreed. "A lot has happened here since you went back to Aberdeen. The Resistance is gone, The Brotherhood is broken and Casa Preciosa has been shut down."

Jason felt a twinge of regret at learning that the shelter was gone. "That's the one thing I feel bad about." he said. "It wasn't just The Brotherhood who used it; a lot of the people who went there really needed the help."

"Actually, some of them have already started coming here." Courtney said. "Casa Preciosa gave them a meal, but I think we can give them more than that. Maybe we can help some of them find a way off the streets. And the building won't stay closed forever; The Center has decided to buy it." Her eyes took on a mischievous glint. "We plan to fix it up and reopen it, but this time as a school. Hispanic kids who can't afford the non-Citizen public school tuition will be able to attend our school for free."

"That's great!" Anne exclaimed.

Courtney smiled. "But enough about The Center. How

have you guys been doing?" she asked, leaning forward in her seat.

Jason suddenly seemed uneasy. "That's actually why we're here." he told her. "Going back to Aberdeen hasn't been great for us." He hesitated as he struggled to find the words. "I don't really have a lot of marketable skills, so there's only so much I can do. I'd hoped the lumber yard would hire me back but they say they don't have any openings. I checked; it's not true. They just don't want *me*. After everything that happened with The Resistance, the owners don't want a 'revolutionary' stirring up trouble in the yard."

He trailed off, leaving Anne to take over. "It's the same with me." she said. "Like Jason, I spoke to the school about getting my position back. The principal said she would talk to the school board about it but honestly, I don't think she's going to do anything to help." She chuckled sadly. "She never liked me much anyway."

Courtney listened to them quietly, with her hands tented in front of her face. "I think they're scared of you." she said when Anne had finished. "Jason was the face of The Resistance and you were guilty by association. It doesn't matter that none of it was true; it's about what you represent, to Citizens and non-Citizens alike. That's what has them frightened." She put her hands down and breathed out heavily. "I think it will pass, but it might be a long while before it does."

Jason looked up unhappily. "To be honest, I think we're done in Aberdeen." he said. "We're here now because we're hoping you can help us to start over in Cosmopolis. We know things are rough here too, but at least there are people here who will help. Would you let us stay at The Center, at least until we can find work?"

Courtney gave him a sort of half-smile. "I think I can do better than that." she said. "We're not quite ready, but I guess now is as good a time as any to ask." Jason wasn't sure what she meant but his hopes rose as he saw the impish expression on her face. She leaned toward them as if about to divulge a secret. "Anne, I told you about our plans for Casa Preciosa for a reason!" she said. "Once we turn it into a school, we're going to need someone to run it. I want that person to be you."

Anne was speechless. "What?" she breathed, sounding dazed.

"The place will need a lot of work before it's ready, but if you start now you can make sure it's set up exactly the way it needs to be." Courtney told her, almost pleading. "You're the only one I thought of for the job. It's yours if you want it."

Anne almost didn't let her finish. "Of course!" she exclaimed.

Jason was grinning broadly. "Thank you!" he told Courtney gratefully and turned to hug his wife.

"I've got something for you too." Courtney said to him, suddenly serious. "The job will be a little harder than Anne's but I think you'll be a good fit for it."

"Okay?" Jason answered with an uncertain smile.

"Jonah truly believed that this place would change the world. He knew it wouldn't happen overnight, but he thought that it was inevitable." Courtney's face was solemn as she spoke of Jonah. "He was absolutely right of course, but I think the time has come to help push things along."

Jason listened with rapt attention.

"The Center is going to establish an official, paid position of 'Civil Rights Liaison'." Courtney elaborated. "The job would be to facilitate a dialogue between Citizens and non-Citizens, Hispanics and Caucasians, and everyone else too. As a Citizen who looks Latino, you are in a unique position to speak to all of them on their own terms. If things are going to change, we'll need people of every stripe with us and I want you to be the bridge between them. You can help change things for the better, just by getting people to listen to one another!"

Jason was overwhelmed as the scope of her offer sank in. "That would be great, but it's a huge job! Do you really think I can do all that?" he asked, trying not to sound ungrateful.

Courtney looked at him kindly. "Not alone, no. But Jonah didn't do all of this by himself either; he had help."

Realization dawned and Jason finally understood. "He had you." he said.

"Among others." Courtney replied modestly. "And if you say yes, you'll have my help too."

He didn't have to think about it; the answer was easy. "Yes." he said.

****

Afterward, Jason and Anne stood downstairs in The Center's common room, watching a news report on the wall-mounted video screen. The room was sparsely furnished except for a large reclining chair where a homeless Hispanic man lay snoring softly. Jason studied his face as he slept but couldn't tell whether he knew him from Casa Preciosa.

On the screen, a news anchor was speaking directly into the camera as she introduced the day's top story. "The trial of Gabriel and Angel Batista is set for next month." she said in authoritative tones. "Alleged to be the true masterminds behind the Latino Resistance Front, their plot was revealed when fellow Hispanic gang member Jason Menounos undertook a daring and self-imposed undercover mission to learn the truth." Jason cringed inwardly as the familiar picture of him appeared on screen, holding a rifle and looking wild. Anne squeezed his hand in sympathy as the image lingered.

Behind them, Jason realized that the snoring had stopped. As he turned, he saw that the man in the chair was now awake and staring at the screen. His eyes slowly travelled from the face on the display to the man in front of him, and in a voice filled with awe, he said, "Hey, you're Jason Menounos!"

Jason glanced back at the screen, which had now labeled his picture with the words 'Hispanic Man Who Single-Handedly Brought Down The Resistance'. Inwardly, he sighed.

None of that was true, but he also knew it didn't matter anymore. Rightly or wrongly, he was now all those things and none of them. The only option left to him was to simply accept it all.

Jason looked into the man's hopeful eyes and answered him without reservation. Yes I am."

ABOUT THE AUTHOR

Jeffery K Strumski

A skeptic and science enthusiast, Jeffery K Strumski grew up in Washington State and has lived on both sides of the Cascade Mountains. After many years of working in an office and fighting a never-ending battle against spreadsheets, he has now finally escaped to embark on a career in writing.

Made in the USA
Monee, IL
31 January 2021